Ane radhas a'leguim oicheamna;
ainsagimn deo teuiccimn.

THE LANGUAGE OF STONES

Robert Carter was born exactly five hundred years after the first battle of the Wars of the Roses. He was brought up in the Midlands and later on the shores of the Irish Sea where his forebears hail from. He was variously educated in Britain, Australia and the United States, then worked for some years in the Middle East and remote parts of Africa. He travelled widely in the East before joining the BBC in London in 1982. His interests have included astronomy, pole-arm fighting, canals, collecting armour, steam engines, composing music and enjoying the English countryside, and he has always maintained a keen interest in history. Today he lives in a 'village' that only sounds rural – Shepherd's Bush.

Visit Robert Carter's website at:
www.languageofstones.com

THE
LANGUAGE
OF
STONES

ROBERT CARTER

HarperCollins*Publishers*

HarperCollins*Publishers*
77–85 Fulham Palace Road,
Hammersmith, London W6 8JB

www.harpercollins.co.uk

This paperback edition 2005
1 3 5 7 9 8 6 4 2

First published in Great Britain by
HarperCollins*Publishers* 2004

ISBN 0 00 716504 8

Typeset in Plantin Light by Palimpsest Book Production Limited,
Polmont, Stirlingshire

Printed and bound in Great Britain by
Clays Limited, St Ives plc

This book is dedicated to Britain's greatest living Welshman – Terry Jones.

Acknowledgements

I would like to thank everyone who helped in the preparation of this book, especially Jane Johnson, Sarah Hodgson, Chris Best, Jessica Woollard, Toby Eady, Mary Judah, Tom Robinson, David Wingrove and Ian O'Donnell – Sláinte

The Realm

CONTENTS

(N.B. In the novels of the 'Stones' cycle there is never a chapter thirteen.)

'First there were nine,
Then nine became seven,
And seven became five.
Now, as sure as the Ages decline,
Three are no more,
But one is alive.'

The Black Book of Tara

PART ONE

A BOY, A MAN

◘ ◘ ◘

□ □ □

CHAPTER ONE

OUT OF THE VALE

Willand son of Eldmar turned his gaze away from the Tops and ran down towards the village. The sun was warm today, the sky cloudless and the grass soft and thriving underfoot. His long hair streamed freely in the sun like golden wheat as he ran past a cluster of thatched cottages and came at last to the Green Man.

'Is Tilwin here yet?' he asked, hoping the knife-grinder was already slaking his thirst. But Baldgood the alehouse keeper shook his head. There was no sign of Tilwin, nor of his grinding wheel, so Will went out and sat on the grass.

Sunshine blazed on the white linen of his shirt. It was a fine spot just here. Daisies and dandelions had come out all over the green, as if it had known to put on its summer best. Every year it was fine and sunny at Cuckootide. There was racing to the Tarry Stone, kicking at the campball, and all the other sports. And afterwards there would be the bonfire. Songs would be sung and there would be dances and games and contests with the quarterstaff before the drinking of dragon soup. It would be the same this year as it had always been, and next year it would be the same again and on and on forever.

In the Vale they called today Cuckootide, the day the

May Pole was put up and all the world came out onto the green to have a good time. But Will knew he could not have a good time – not until he had talked with Tilwin. He looked up at the round-shouldered hills they called the Tops and felt the longing again. It had been getting stronger, and today it felt like an invisible cord trying to pull his heart right out of his chest. That was why he had to speak with Tilwin. It had to be Tilwin, because only he would understand.

'Hey-ho, Will!'

He knew that voice at once – whiskery Leoftan, the smith. His two thick braids hung like tarred rope side by side at his left cheek. He wore a belted shirt of white linen like Will's own and a cap of red wool.

'Your dad'll be putting in your braids soon enough now, eh?'

Will shrugged. 'It's a hard week to turn thirteen, the week after May Day.'

Leoftan put down his armful of wooden tent-pegs. 'Aye, you'll have to wait near another year before you can run in the men's race.'

Will scrubbed his fingers through his fair hair and stole another glance at the Tops. 'Have you ever wondered what it's like up there, Luffy?'

The smith stood up, gave him a distracted look. 'What's that you say?'

'I was just thinking.' He nodded towards the Tops. 'One day I'd like to go up and see what's there. Haven't you ever thought what Nether Norton would look like with the whole Vale laid out down below?'

'Huh?'

The moment stretched out awkwardly, but Will could not let it go. Once he had seen a small figure riding on a white horse far away where the earth met the sky. In the spring there were sheep – thousands of them – driven along by black dogs, and sometimes by men too. He had seen them many times, but whenever he had spoken of it to the others they had fallen quiet, and Gunwold the Swineherd had smirked, as if he had said something that ought not to have been said.

'Well, Luffy? Haven't you ever wanted to go up onto the Tops?'

Leoftan's face lost its good humour. 'What do you want to go talking like that for? They say there's an ill wind up there.'

'Is that what they say? An ill wind? And who are they who say that, Luffy? And how do they know? I wish – I wish—'

Just then Baldulf came up. He was fourteen, a fleshy, self-assured youth, and there was Wybda the Gossip and two or three others with him. 'You want to be careful what you go a-wishing for, Willand,' Wybda said. 'They say that what fools and kings wishes for most often comes true.'

Will gazed back, undaunted. 'I'm not a king or a fool. I just want to go up there and see for myself. What's wrong with that?'

Wybda carried her embroidery with her. She plied her needle all the time, but still her pigs turned out too round and her flowers too squat. 'Don't you know the fae folk'll eat you up?'

'What do you know about the fae folk?'

Baldulf swished a willow wand at the grass near him. 'She's right. Nobody's got any business up on the Tops.'

Gunwold grinned his lop-sided grin. 'Yah, everybody knows that, Willand.'

They all began to move off and Leoftan said, 'Aren't you going over to watch the men's race?'

'Maybe later.'

He let them go. He did not know why, but just lately their company made him feel uncomfortable. He wondered if it was something to do with becoming a man. Maybe that was what made him feel so strange.

'There's a trackway up over the Tops,' a gritty voice said in his ear.

He started, and when he looked round he saw Tilwin. 'You made me jump.'

Tilwin gave a knowing grin. 'I've made a lot of people jump in my time, Willand, but what I say is the truth. They've sent flocks along that trackway every summer for five thousand years and more. Now what do you think about that?'

Tilwin never said too much, but he knew plenty. He was not yet of middling age, and for some reason he wore his dark hair unbraided. He came once in a blue moon to fetch necessaries up from Middle Norton and beyond. Twice yearly he took the carts down to hand over the tithe, the village tax, to the Sightless Ones. Tilwin could put a sharper edge on a blade than anyone, and he was the only person Will knew who had ever been out of the Vale.

'Who are the men who send the flocks through?'

'Shepherds. They come this way because of the ring.'

'What ring?' Will's eyes moved to the smooth emerald on Tilwin's finger, but the knife-grinder laughed.

'Ah, not that sort of a ring. Don't you know there were giants in the land in the days of yore? There's a Giant's Ring away up on those Tops. A circle of standing stones. It's a place of great magic.'

A shiver passed down Will's spine. He could feel the tightness forming inside him again. Maybe it was the Giant's Ring that was calling to him.

'Magic . . . you say?'

'Earth magic. Close by the Giant's Ring stands Liarix Finglas, called the King's Stone. Every shepherd who's passed this way for fifty generations has chipped a piece off that King's Stone until it's now crooked as a giant's thumb.'

'Truly?'

'Oh, you may believe it is so.'

'Why do the shepherds do it?'

'For a lucky keepsake, what do you think?'

Will did not know what he thought. The talk had set his mind on fire. 'Fetch me a piece of it, will you, when next you go up there?'

'Oh, and it's a piece of the King's Stone you want now, is it?' Tilwin had a strange way of speaking, and a strange, deep way of looking at a person at times. 'Ah, but you're lucky enough in yourself, I think, Willand. Lucky enough for the meanwhile, let's say that.'

The strange feeling welled up and squeezed his heart again. His eyes ran along the Tops, looking for a sign, but there was none. And when he looked around again Tilwin had vanished. For a moment it seemed that the knife-grinder had never been there at all.

Will wandered down and stood under the painted sign of the Green Man. It was a merry face – one of the fae folk – green as a leaf and all overgrown with ivy. The sign was bedecked now with white Cuckootide hawthorn blossom.

Cuthwal was inside, playing his fiddle, but there was no sign of Eldmar, his father, so Will wandered away, sat down on the grass for a while and watched folk coming up from way down the Vale. Then it was time for the boys' race and there was cheering as half a dozen lads sprinted across the green and tried to be first to lay a hand on the Tarry Stone.

But Will did not feel like cheering anybody on. Leoftan had mentioned an ill wind, and an ill wind had sprung up – or at least a cold one – and not just over the Tops either. Iron-grey clouds had begun to boil up and gather darkly in the west. At first no one among the villagers seemed to notice, but then as the sun went in, one or two of them started to look skyward, and soon the bunting began to flap and the crowns of the tall beeches in Pannage Woods started to sway and roar. Folk began to feel a sudden chill touch them. It looked suddenly as if it would rain.

The music stopped and folk set to helping one another clear the stalls and tables away. They muttered that this was unheard of, because the last time the May Pole dance had been washed out was beyond living memory. Will had just finished lending a hand when a cry went up. He turned and saw old Frithwold coming up the track, shaking his fists as he ran.

'Jack o' Lantern!' he wheezed as he reached the Green Man. 'May Death cut me down if I tell a lie! Jack o' Lantern's down in the lanes!'

'Now, sit down and catch your thoughts, Frith,' Bregowina, the brewster's wife, said coolly. 'There ain't no warlocks round here.'

'Sit down be blowed! It be Jack o' Lantern in the lanes over by Bloody Meadow, I tell you!'

Baldgood peered past his barrels. 'You've had too much of them cider dregs, Frith.'

'Noooo! It was Jack o' Lantern, as I live and breathe!'

They settled him down, and the clearing away carried on until all the doors were put back on their hinges and everything was closed up tight. There was no doubting Frithwold believed what he was saying – he was grey in the face and more upset than Will had ever seen him. Groups of Valesmen were muttering to one another, scythes in hand, glancing fearfully down the track. He turned to Baldgood and asked, 'Who's Jack o' Lantern?'

'You won't recall him,' Baldgood said, troubled.

'Tell me.'

'He's a visitor who comes to these parts from time to time. And not such a welcome one neither. You'd've been just a babe in arms when last he came this way, or not even born maybe.'

Cuthwal leaned across. 'We don't none of us like the looks of him. And we never did.'

Will looked down the lane and saw nothing unusual. 'Why not?'

'Because he's a *crow*, and up to no good.'

'Don't you fear now, Will,' Baldgood said. 'There's a hue and cry gone up after him. Our stout lads'll drive him off! Now you best get back home.'

Will looked out across the green. Inky clouds filled the sky now. It was almost as dark as night. Then it began to pelt with rain. The May Pole looked forlorn as it swayed with its ribbons streaming out. The wind had got up fiercely and was trying to tear down what was left of the bunting. Bregowina, unruffled as ever, lit candles, and her sons barred the doors. They had just finished when Gifold One-Tooth and both his sons started banging, wanting to be let in. The way they held their pitchforks showed they expected trouble, but nobody had told them what sort.

'What does Jack o' Lantern look like?' Will asked, but nobody answered him.

He folded his arms. No fire burned in the hearth and the only light in the parlour now was from two candles that burned with a quavering, smoky flame. It was a light that did not penetrate far. 'I've never seen a crow. Is that the same as a warlock?'

'None of them knows much about what Jack o' Lantern looks like, Will.'

He turned at the voice that came from the back of the room. At the table in the corner shadows sat Tilwin. He had found a place where nobody had noticed him. His hat was in front of him on the table, and he was thumbing the edge of a long, thin knife. He said, 'The only man in Nether Norton who ever challenged Jack o' Lantern face to face was Evergern the Potter, and he's been dead these ten years.'

'What are you doing, skulking back there?' Gifold demanded, as if he was speaking to a ghost.

'Minding my own business, Gif. Like you should be doing.' Tilwin leaned forward and turned his gaze on the rest of them. 'I slipped in quiet, so I did, while you were all running about down the way like fowls with their heads stricken off. I could have marched an army in here for all you'd have known about it.'

'You're a strange customer, and no mistake,' Baldgood said.

'That I may be, but let me tell you something about your Jack o' Lantern – in this part of the Vale you call him by that name and say he's a crow. Others further down call him "Merlyn", or "Master Merlyn" to be correct about it, though that isn't his true name. Down by Great Norton they say he's "Erilar" and claim he's a warlock. While over at Bruern they put the name "Finnygus" on him and fetch their horses to him to benefit from his leechcraft. But none of them knows who he is, for Jack casts a weirder light than any lantern ever I saw.' Tilwin leaned further forward until the candlelight caught in his blue eyes. 'He runs deep does our friend Jack. Deep as the Kyle of Stratha. Nor does he suffer fools easily. So if he's got business in this place, I'd let him finish it without hindrance – if I were you.'

There was silence. Like everyone else, Will listened and held his peace. He didn't understand much of what had been said, but the thrill of excitement at Tilwin's words made the hairs rise up on the back of his neck.

'Now that's enough of that kind of talk,' Baldgood muttered, bustling out from behind his counter. 'Willand! Now, I thought I told you to get on home?'

Will went to the door but after what Tilwin had said home seemed a long way to go in the pitch dark. In truth it was no more than a furlong – a couple of hundred paces – but it was still raining hard. He poked his head outside.

Water was trickling down the track. Where only a short while before there had been dry dust, now there was a stream. He jumped out into the night and set off at a run until the light from the alehouse gave out. Then he stubbed his toe painfully on a flint and almost fell. After that he groped his way along by the side of the green. His shirt was soaked. Every village door was closed and every shutter barred tight.

So much for welcoming the summer in, he thought as he felt twigs snapping in the grass under his feet. His outstretched hands met the deeply grooved bark of the Old Oak. He paused, listening. Overhead, leaves were rattling in the downpour, and there was something eerie about the sound, as if the tree was talking to itself.

He shook the water out of his eyes and peered into the dark to where a faint bar of yellow light escaped under a door. Home. He stumbled towards it, and soon his fingers felt a familiar latch.

The light guttered in the draught as he came in, then steadied. He saw Breona and Eldmar, his mother and father, standing together by the unlit hearth, and there, seated before them, was a stranger.

The figure was wrapped in a mouse-brown cloak with a hood that shadowed his face. Will's heart beat against his ribs. He was about to speak when his father told him sternly: 'Go up to bed, Willand.'

'But Father—'

'Will! Do as I tell you!'

Eldmar had never barked at him like that before. He looked from face to face, scared now. He wanted to go to his mother's side, but his father was not to be argued with, and Will obeyed. He felt his knees give slightly as he climbed the ladder into the rafters, and dived straight to his nest in the loft. There he lay on the bag of straw that served as his bed. It was warm and smoky up here under the eaves. His wet hair stuck to his forehead and his shirt was clammy on his back as his hand sought out the comfort of a stout wooden threshing flail. He moved as quietly as he could to the edge of the loft where he could watch and listen, telling himself that if anything happened he would pull back the hurdles, jump down and set about the stranger.

But if this was Jack o' Lantern, he was nothing like the warlock the men had spoken about. By his knee there rested a staff a full fathom in length, fashioned from a kind of wood that had a marvellous sheen to it. The stranger himself had a pale, careworn face, with a long nose and longer beard. The hair of his beard might once have been the colour of corn or copper, but it had faded to badger shades of grey. He was swathed in a wayfarer's cloak that was made of shreds, and at times seemed almost colourless in the flickering tallow light. Beneath his hood he wore a skullcap, but under the hem of his belted gown his long legs were without hose and his feet unshod. There were many cords about his neck, and among the amulets and charms that rattled at his chest, a bird's skull.

'It is said that eavesdroppers will often pick up things they do not like to hear,' the stranger said. His voice was quiet, yet it carried. It was touched with a strangeness that made Will think of faraway places.

'Why can't you leave us alone?' Will's mother whispered.

'Because promises were made. You know why I am here. I must have him.'

At that, Will felt an icy fist clutch him. His world suddenly lurched and refused to right itself. He heard his father say, 'But those promises were made thirteen years ago!'

'What does the passage of time signify when a promise is made?'

'We've grown to love him as you said we should!'

'A promise is eternal. Have you forgotten how matters stood when you made it? You and your good wife were childless, denied the joys that parents know. How dearly you wished for a baby boy of your own. And then one night, on the third day past Cuckootide, I came to you with a three-day-old babe and your misery was at an end.'

'You can't take him back!' Will's mother shrieked.

The stranger made suddenly as if to rise. Will's parents took a step back as his grip tightened on the flail. 'He is no longer a boy. A child you wanted, and a child I brought. But now the child is become a man – a man – and I must have this son of Beltane as we agreed. I said there would be an errand for him, and so there is.'

A dark gulf of silence stood between them for a moment, then the stranger spoke subtle words and Eldmar and Breona hung their heads and made no further argument.

Up in his loft Will found himself numbed to the marrow of his bones. He began to tremble. Whether it was from shock or fear or the working of evil magic he could not tell. As the stranger rose, Will's grip tightened on the threshing flail, but when he looked again there was nothing in his hand but a wooden spoon, and the flail was nowhere to be seen.

'Call the lad down,' the stranger suggested. 'Tell him he has no need to fear me.'

Eldmar called, and Will came down the ladder as if his arms and legs had minds of their own. He felt his father's hands on his shoulders, but his father's face betrayed only heartsickness. 'Forgive me if you can, Willand,' he said simply. 'I should have had the courage to tell you sooner.'

'Tell me what?' Will asked, blinking. 'I won't go with him. He's a warlock, and I won't go with him!'

'You must, son.' Eldmar's face remained grim. 'Thirteen years ago we gave our word. We swore to keep the manner of your coming to us a secret. We swore because we so wanted a boy of our own. Each year that passed sons came to others, but never to us. You seemed like our blessing.'

Will drew a hollow breath. 'You . . . should have told me.'

'We were sworn to tell no one,' Breona wailed. 'Even so we meant to tell you, Will. But first you were too young. Then, you were such a well-liked boy that we couldn't find the proper time to upset our happy home. It would have broken our hearts, do you see?'

Eldmar hung his head and Breona held out her hand. There were tears in her eyes. 'Say you forgive us for what we did, Willand.'

Will wiped away his own tears. 'There's nothing to forgive. You're the best father and mother any boy could have.'

'Please,' Breona said, turning back to the stranger. 'Can't you give us just a little more time? Let him stay for one more day, as a mercy to us!'

'It would be no mercy,' the stranger said. 'Of that I am quite sure, for he may be the Child of Destiny, the one whose name appears in the Black Book.'

At that, Breona's eyes flared. She would have thrown herself on the stranger had Eldmar not caught her in his arms. 'He's my Willand, and nobody else!'

Will found himself unable to move. The stranger reached out to touch man and wife, speaking words and making a sign above both their foreheads. 'Do not punish yourselves,' he commanded. 'You are blameless. You have done all that was asked of you.'

Eldmar's eyes drooped, and his wife's hands hung loose at her sides. Then Breona shook her head as if she had just come awake. She hugged Will, her eyes full of tenderness now. 'You must put on a dry shirt, son. I'll fetch out your best jerkin and give you a bundle of sweetcakes for your journey.'

But Will drew back in fear. 'What have you done to them?' he cried.

'Be calm, Willand. They remember nothing of their former fears. They have been comforted.'

'You've bewitched them!'

'I have applied an incantation. There is no harm in it.'

Will tried to launch himself at the visitor, but Eldmar caught him in strong arms and said, 'Willand, be easy! I made a promise, but it's you who must redeem it. That's often the way with sons and fathers.'

Breona kissed him again and went to the linen chest. From it she took a parting gift, an ornament the size of his thumb made of smooth, greenish stone. It was carved in the form of a leaping salmon, and engraved with a figure and some words. Words were beyond Will's plain learning to read, though the figure was three triangles placed one within another. Its meaning – if it had one – was not clear.

'It was inside your blanket when you were brought to us,' Breona said. 'It's only right that it should go with you now. Wear it as a charm, for a mother's love goes with it. And, like the salmon, may you return to us again some day.'

Her eyes sparkled when she smiled at him, and he threw his arms around her neck. 'You'll always be my mother. Always!'

Eldmar said, 'I have nothing to give you, but I will do one thing before you go. Sit down.'

When Will sat down on the three-legged stool, Eldmar caught up a handful of his hair. His big, blunt fingers carefully teased out the strands. They twisted and pulled and twisted again, working expertly until two braids were done.

'There,' his father said as he stood up. 'Now you're a man.'

CHAPTER TWO

INTO THE REALM

They climbed up towards the Tops through the pouring rain, and Will told himself that he had made a fool's wish come true after all. He did not know how or why his feet followed one another, but after a while they felt the tread-worn track peter out and long grass begin. The stranger was leading him onward through Nethershaw Woods. There were thousands of bluebells clothing the ground hereabouts, but blind darkness pressed in all around, and he saw nothing. The air was alive with deep green smells, but apart from the sound of rain, the night was quiet. Creatures of fur and feather had drawn deep inside their holes and hollows, and nothing stirred.

It was as if the journey was happening to someone else. His new, manly braids felt strange as they swung against his wet cheek. He put a hand to them and began to think of his parents again, and that filled his eyes with tears. He stumbled in the darkness and the stranger said, 'Tread softly, Willand, for we have far to go tonight.'

The steady climb brought them out onto open land. It was curious how slow the raindrops seemed to fall here, and how filled with echoes was their noise. Underfoot the going was as gentle as a sheep-cropped meadow. Will had never climbed so high before, nor walked so far or so fast in the dark. The stranger did not lean on his staff as an old man should, he wielded it. His long legs strode out as if he could see the night world around him as clearly as any cat.

A hundred questions about the stranger whirled in Will's head. Perhaps he's a sorcerer, he thought, dread welling up. It's plain he's got the power about him, and he spoke an incantation onto my . . .

His thoughts turned away from Breona and Eldmar. The pang in his belly felt like fear, and underneath it there lurked a dark and dreadful question – if Eldmar and Breona are not my real parents, then who are?

There must be a spell on me now, he told himself, or why else are my legs being forced to follow him?

Will tried to resist, but he could not. In the back of his mind, shapeless fears writhed.

'What's the matter now?' the stranger said, turning.

He wanted to ask the dreadful question, but instead he stammered, 'Are . . . are we going to the Giant's Ring?'

The stranger loomed in the darkness. 'What do you know about the Giant's Ring?'

'N . . . Nothing.'

'Then why do you fear it? Are you drawn by its power? Tell me!' The stranger gripped his arm. 'What do you know about the Ring?'

'Only that there's a stone near it that shepherds say is lucky.'

The stranger's tone softened, and he laughed unexpectedly. 'Forgive me if I frightened you, Willand. We are not going to the Giant's Ring. Nor was that ever a place where folk were ritually slain, or beheaded, or buried alive – as no doubt you have been led to believe.'

Will's heart hammered at the strange answer, but already some of his fear had begun to turn to obstinacy. They went on, crested a shallow rise, and headed over the brow into lands that drained westward. Moments later they skirted the sleeping hamlet of what could only be Over Norton, a fabled place spoken of rarely by Valesmen. A hound barked in the distance, a deep-throated, echoing sound that was full of longing.

At last, Will staggered to a halt. He shielded his eyes from the rain, peering back the way they had come. They had reached another track, this time on level ground, that ran right across the Tops.

The stranger turned. 'What now?'

'I'm . . . scared.'

He flinched away as the stranger reached out and touched his shoulder, but the words that came this time were plain enough. 'I will not say there is no reason for you to be scared. This is the most dangerous night of your short life. But I will do everything in my power to protect you.'

Something seemed to burst in Will's chest and he blurted out, 'Well, if you're so wise, why don't you just magic us to wherever it is we're supposed to be going?'

The stranger paused and regarded him for a long moment before saying, 'Because magic must always be used sparingly, and never without considering gains against losses. Magic must be requested, never summoned, respected, never treated with disdain. It must be asked for openly and honestly. Listen to me, Willand! I am trying very hard to deliver you to a place of safety. But we may not reach it if you decide to defy me. And the danger will be the more, the more you resist.'

The stranger seemed suddenly older than old, a man used to talking high talk, giving important words to important people, not a man who was used to coaxing frightened lads into following him through the night. Will stared at the ground sullenly. 'Aren't there . . . aren't there giants up here?'

The other laughed softly. 'Giants? Now who could have

put that notion into your head? Ah, let me guess. That would have been Tilwin, the well-travelled man.'

Will's mouth fell open. 'Then – you do know Tilwin!'

'I know a great many folk. Did Tilwin say he knew me?'

It was more than a question and Will gave no answer. He gritted his teeth, still fighting the urge that moved his legs forward. 'You still haven't told me where we're going.'

'The less you know about that the better, until we are a good deal closer to it.'

'Is it far?'

'Four more leagues tonight, three as the rook flies, then we shall come to a place of sanctuary.' The voice mellowed. 'Try to be easy in your mind, Willand. There will come a day when you are no longer afraid of giants – but we shall have to work hard to make sure you live that long.'

The stranger's voice was as vivid as lightning – at once exciting, comforting and terrifying. Oh, yes, he must be a great sorcerer, Will thought. For who but a great sorcerer could use words like that? But four leagues! Four leagues was a very long way. In the Vale a single league was a trip from Nether Norton to Pannage then away to Overmast and back again. To go four leagues in one journey seemed unimaginable.

But I'm not going. I'll test his magic long before that, he told himself stubbornly. I'll bide my time. I'll wait until he's wrapped up in his big thoughts, and then I'll fall behind little by little and make a run for it. He won't be able to find me, because I won't go straight home. No! I'll wait till first light, then run down to Overmast and hide in Ingulph's Oak. He'll never find me there.

But a firm grip took him by the collar and hauled him onward. 'Please try to keep up. Have I not already made clear to you the dangers?'

Will tried to pull away from the grip. 'You're trying to enchant me with your sorcerer's whisper-words.'

'Oh, a sorcerer, am I?'

'It's magic you've put on me. I can feel it working in my legs!'

'And what do you know about magic? Your village has not even the benefit of a wise woman.'

'I know sorcerers are evil!'

The stranger made no immediate reply, but then he sighed and his breath steamed in the moist air. 'Do not speak to me of evil, for you do not know what that is. Be assured, your life and the lives of ten thousand others may depend on your obedience to me tonight. Now come along willingly or I shall have to take measures.'

Will refused to believe a word of it, but he could do nothing except pace onward through the gloom and wait for his chance. At length he said, 'In the village they say you're a crow called Jack o' Lantern.'

'Jack is as good a name as any. Noblemen have long used the word "crow" to mean wanderers such as I, but the folk of Nether Norton do not know the difference between a crow and a craft-saw.'

That was no help. 'But it's not your real name.'

'I have a true name, but that may not be learned by others.'

'Why not?'

The stranger's eyebrow arched impressively. 'Because if it became known to my enemy, it would put me in his power.'

'Do you have many enemies?'

'Only one.'

Will thought that was a very guarded answer. 'What's he called?'

'At times he uses the name "Clinsor" at others "Maskull". But those are not his true names any more than Gwydion is mine.'

Will seized on the slip. 'Is that what I should call you?'

The sorcerer laughed. 'Sharp! Let me put your mind at rest. I have been known by many names – Erilar, Finegas, Tanabure, Merlyn, Laeloken, Bresil, Tiernnadrui – but you should call me by the name the present lords of this realm use when they speak of me. Call me Master Gwydion.'

'Master Gwydion,' Will repeated, satisfied. He said portentously, 'Gwydion the Sorcerer!'

'Do not make such jests.' The plea was made quietly, but Will heard in it a solemn warning.

'Why not? You perform magic. You don't deny that. So you're a sorcerer.'

Gwydion put his face close to Will's own. 'Try to remember that words are important. They have precise meanings. I do not *perform* magic, Willand. Magic is never performed. It is not the stuff of conjuring shows, it is what links the world together. And you must never call me "enchanter", "warlock" or "magician" – those words are easily misunderstood by folk of little learning. They cause trouble.'

Will stumbled over a coney burrow and almost fell. 'I wish this rain would stop! I can't see a thing!'

Gwydion grunted. 'Wishes! Every spell of magic I expend tonight must be heavily veiled, but perhaps we might go by faelight for a while without any greater risk of being noticed.'

The sorcerer muttered hard-to-hear words, then he took hold of Willand's head and used his thumbs to wipe the water from his face. All at once Will became lightheaded, and it seemed as if there was a glow in the wet grass around him, a glow like mist caught in a spider's web, like a dusting of green moonlight over a soft land. Then he realized he had not opened his eyes. He gasped in wonder, still more than a little fearful of what was happening to him.

'Am I dreaming?' he asked as the rain began to slacken. A few moments more and it had stopped altogether. But not in the usual way. Each drop was now hanging in the air as if it had forgotten how to fall. He felt the drops collide with his face as he moved through them, like magic dew. Then, quite suddenly the drops began to fall again, but very slowly.

Up above, the clouds began to clear away. They revealed a host of bright, green stars. He heard the comforting call of a barn owl, and through the air it came, silent and huge and white and incredibly slow, as if swimming through the rain-washed air. It shattered the drops in its path and passed so close to him that he could have reached out to touch it. He saw every detail of each wonderful feather on its wings before it vanished. The sight of it astonished him, then all at once they were going along again, and it was as if they had walked out from the region of bewitched rain in a dream, because now the ground was stony and broken and dry as dust. The foot of the sorcerer's staff was beating a rhythmic *toc-toc-toc* on what seemed to be a trackway. Will wandered towards it through the still faintly glowing land, while his mind bubbled and fizzed. Another enchantment had been laid on him, he knew that much. And was that not another very good reason to mistrust this dangerous man?

And yet – what if he was telling the truth about that greater danger?

'Who's Beltane?' he asked at last. 'What did you mean when you said "this son of Beltane"? Is Beltane my real father?'

Gwydion grunted, seemingly amused by the question. A crescent moon had begun to rise, low and large and ruddy in the east. 'How much you have to learn. Beltane is not a person, it is a day. It lies between the equinox of spring and the solstice of summer. Beltane is what you in the Vale call Cuckootide, and what others call "May Day". It's a special day, the day that gave you birth.'

'Who are my real parents?' He said it almost without thinking, and like a painful thorn it was suddenly out. 'Please tell me.'

'Willand, I cannot tell you.'

'But you must!'

'I cannot because I do not know.'

'I don't believe you!'

'I would not lie about it.'

But Will could not let it go. 'Where did you find me, then? Tell me that.'

It seemed Gwydion would give no answer, but then he said, 'When I found you, you were only a day or two old.'

'But *where* did you find me? Who was there?'

The stranger halted. 'No one was there. Willand – you had been left to die.'

The shock of that answer flowed through his heart like icy water. He let the sorcerer turn away and walk on, while his mind wandered numbly. Who would leave a little baby to die? What reason could there possibly have been? What was wrong with me?

The stranger came back, made a sign over Will's forehead and muttered powerful words until the numbness dissolved and he was hardly able to recall the questions that had so troubled him. After that, the journey was like floating through the silent night. He watched the moon rise ever higher in the south-east. Gradually it lost its rosy glow and began to shine chalk white in a clear and star-spangled sky. For some time now a grey light had been seeping in from the east, and when Will next closed his eyes he found that the faelight had left him.

He marvelled at the low, flat skyline: there was so much more sky on the Tops than ever there had been in the Vale. Land stretched as far as the eye could see. It made a man feel like standing straighter and breathing deeper. He looked ahead. Far away the rich brown soil had been tilled and planted. Nearer by there was a shallow ridge and a slope. To the south the land dropped down into a broad valley, and on the far side it rose again in forest. The dawn was coming faster now, a power that would soon send unstoppable rays searching over the land. Already the glimmers revealed tussocky chases beside the trackway, pale stone clothed in a thin flesh of loam and cloaked in green. There were patches of woodland here too, and plenty of folds hereabouts where someone who wanted to make a run for it might choose to hide . . .

That idea brought his scattered thoughts up sharply. He had almost forgotten about escaping. He had walked all night, yet he was neither hungry nor tired. But things were changing. The faelight was gone and now the sensation in his legs had almost drained away too. His braids swung encouragingly at his cheek, and he put a hand to them. The Realm was indeed a bigger and stranger place than ever he had thought.

I won't be able to find my way back if we go much further, he thought. I'll have to make my break now, before it's too late! But carefully, he warned himself. This Master Gwydion may have done me no harm as yet, but he's a lot more dangerous than he tries to seem. Still, I'll bet he can't run as fast as me, nor aim his night-magic so well in full daylight. I'll bide my time then – off! With a bit of luck his hood will stay up and he won't even see me go.

He glanced to left and right. The old, straight track as it ran over the Tops was broken. It rose and fell no more than the height of a man in a thousand paces now, and it kept to high ground where the skin of the land was pulled tightest over its bones. There were sheep droppings among the grass, and coney burrows too. Grey stones outcropped here and there along the trackway, and Will hung back as far as he dared, wondering if these old stones might not be the remains of giants' houses set beside the ancient road.

Tilwin had once said that beyond the Vale there were houses and castles built of stone, wondrous ruins that had lasted since the days of the First Men . . .

Thinking no more about it, Will tore suddenly away and ran down the slope. Once out of sight he went as fast as he could, jinking over the tussocks like a hare, looking once, twice, over his shoulder to check that the sorcerer had not missed him. Only when he was sure did he dive down behind a hillock and lie pressed hard against the ground.

From here he could see where the track wound onward, and soon he spied a tiny, dark figure continuing along the track in the distance, wrapped up in his cloak and seemingly deep in thought. Will exulted. He'll never find me now, he told himself, lying on his back among the moss until he had got his breath back. His clothes were still damp from the rain and he began to feel a certain weariness seeping into his joints, but none of that mattered. He was free. He would lie low until the sorcerer had gone. Then he would find a way home.

He thought of opening the bundle of sweetcakes that was lodged inside his jerkin, but decided against it. He might have greater need of them before the day was done. But thinking about the sweetcakes made him remember his mother and a lonely feeling crept over him. She's not my mother, he thought. Though I don't know how a real mother could have loved me any better.

He took out the fish-shaped talisman and turned it over in his fingers. He could not read what was written on it, yet still its touch comforted him. His feelings towards Breona and Eldmar had not changed, but now there were gaping questions where once there had been certainties.

A male blackbird looking for breakfast turned one wary yellow-rimmed eye on him and began clucking at him as if he was a cat. Will told it to hush, but the bird fled in noisy distress, and he wondered if the sorcerer was alert enough to have noticed it. Then the ground began to tremble and tear. He turned to look behind him and saw a huge grey-green shape that had begun to rise up from what he had thought was a small hill. The hill looked like a man's back, but the shoulders were as broad as a barn door and the skin filthy and warty like a toad's. Dread seized him and held him in its grip. He tried to yell, but the air was already filled with groans.

The creature was getting to its feet. It rose up from its hollow in the ground like a boulder being forced from its bed, and it carried on rising until it was as tall as the May Pole. Two immense legs were each as far around as an oak. And the body was built in proportion, with two heavily muscled arms. But it was the hairless head that was most terrifying – ugly and gross-featured, with a wide mouth filled with uneven, soil-brown teeth, a bone-hooded brow and bulbous, penetrating eyes.

Terror swarmed through Will. He could neither stand nor run, only stare until every self-preserving thought was blotted from his mind. But as the monster turned on him, he yelped and scrambled to get away. His arms and legs would not work fast enough, but then the monster's eyes fixed hard on him. It let out a deep-roaring bellow and began to step forward. Each of its footfalls shook the land. It came so close that he could smell the earthy stink of its breath and feel the closeness of its hands.

Somehow Will ran clear of those flailing arms. He bolted along the trackway, never pausing to look back, certain that if the monster caught him it would eat him alive. His braids banged against his ear as he ran. When at last he did look over his shoulder, he saw that a great stone had been wrenched up from the ground. It was hurled through the air, bounced and blundered past him like a great wooden ball pitched at a skittle. Finally, it came to rest at the very place where a little while ago he had schemed to make his escape.

When Will saw the distant figure of the sorcerer by the brow of the next hill, he flew to him. The old man was continuing in the same way, his staff beating a steady *toc-toc-toc* over the stones. Will's heart was bursting, his lungs gasping for air as he shouted his warning.

'Master Gwydion! Master Gwydion!' His hands grasped at the sorcerer's much-patched cloak as he tried to get his words out. 'A gi – a gi—! A giant coming!'

The sorcerer stopped, put a hand on Will's head and smiled. 'Alba will not harm you so long as you do nothing to harm that which he holds dear.'

'He – he's trying to kill me!'

'Then stay close to me, for I am his friend. One day you will be glad that the flesh of this land is his flesh. But come now. The new day is brightening and we have yet to reach the Evenlode Bridge.'

Gwydion walked on, unconcerned. But the terror was still fresh in Will. He felt it rattling inside him as he plucked up the courage to look back again. There was nothing to see now, nothing except what might be the long shadow of an outcrop thrown across the track by the golden light of the newly-risen sun. As for the great boulder that had been hurled after him, it was there – a lone standing stone that looked as if it had been sitting by the side of the track for fifty generations.

It was a trick! Will told himself with sudden outrage. Just an evil sorcerer's trick! And I believed it!

But a bigger part of him was not so easily persuaded that it had been a trick, and so he hurried to catch up.

CHAPTER THREE

TO THE TOWER
OF LORD STRANGE

By now it was late morning, yet they had seen no other person along their path. Folk must be dwelling close by, Will thought, for someone must work these fields, and once or twice I've seen the thatch of houses in the distance. Maybe we're going the quiet way on purpose.

After walking down off the Tops and some way into the broad valley that lay ahead, Will halted. 'I can't take another step,' he croaked.

The sorcerer seemed uncomfortable that they should stop here. He gave Will a hard look. 'We will rest. But not in this place.' Then he did a strange thing: he drew a little stick from his sleeve and twisted it over the ground, walking back and forth as if testing for something until they had gone a few hundred paces further on.

When he saw Will watching him, he said, 'Do not be afraid, it is only scrying. Do you see how the hazel wand moves? It helps me feel out the power that flows in the land.'

Will stared back mutely, and the sorcerer carried on. The place he eventually chose for them to rest was an

28

oblong enclosure of cropped grass about as big as Nether Norton's green. It was surrounded by a grassy earth bank a little higher than a man's head. Weathered standing stones guarded its four corners, sticking up like four grey teeth. Will had no idea who might have laboured to build such a place, or why, for as a sheep pen it would have been very poor. But as he let the feel of it seep into his bones he had the idea that this was ancient ground and very much to be respected. It did feel good to sit here as the swallows looped and swooped high overhead, but he also sensed an echo of distant doings – dark events – that seemed to run through the land.

Gwydion watched him closely. 'Long ago, Willand, this was a famous stronghold. Here it was that, eighty generations ago, Memprax the Tyrant conspired with his brother, Malin, to gain the Realm. And when the Realm was won Memprax murdered Malin in his bed, and thereafter ruled as a despot. I remember it all as if it was yesteryear.'

Will looked at the sorcerer with astonishment, for who but an immortal could remember events that had taken place eighty generations ago? The thought made him uneasy. He took out and opened his bundle of sweetcakes, chose the smaller one for himself and offered the other.

'That was kindly done,' Gwydion said. 'And in return you shall have this.' He picked up a pebble, and offered it.

'What is it?'

'As you see, a pebble. But a very fine pebble. Or do you think otherwise?'

'Are you laughing at me?'

'Laughing? Why should you say that? This is your reward. You will find that you are able to spend it like a silver shilling, for those who value coins will see it as such.'

'You *are* laughing at me. Or you're mad.'

The sorcerer shrugged. 'If you think so, then throw it away.'

But Will decided to put the pebble in his pouch.

The sun had begun to warm the day and Gwydion pulled back his hood, revealing a high-browed head set with a close-fitting cap of grey linen that covered long, unbraided hair. His face was also long and his dark eyes deeply set under thick brows. It was a kindly face. He wore the beard of an old man, but it still seemed impossible to place a certain age upon him.

After finishing his sweetcake, the sorcerer took out his hazel wand and went back to scrying the ground around the stones. Despite all that had happened, Will could not now think too badly of him. In the sunshine, he seemed to be no more than a pitiful old man – one weighed down with too many cares. Perhaps he had been telling the truth all along. And perhaps it might not be such a bad life to be apprenticed to a sorcerer for a while.

When Gwydion noticed he was being watched, he beckoned Will to him. 'I'm reading the stone.'

'You really are mad.'

'And you really must be careful.'

'Reading it how?'

'With my fingers. I want to see if it is a battlestone.' He walked carefully around the stone, touching its surface with his fingertips. 'Are you any the wiser?'

'What's a battlestone?'

Gwydion straightened, then a wry smile broke out across his face. 'Perhaps there is no harm in telling you. I want to know if this is one of the stones that are bringing war to the Realm.'

Will screwed up his face, but said nothing.

'Oh, you are not alone in your disbelief! All standing stones are powerful and precious things. They were put in place long ago by the fae or else by wise men who knew something of the fae's skills. Only fools have ever tried to move them since.'

Will looked at the stone critically. It was a large, weathered grey rock, much taller than it was broad, and quite unremarkable. He put his hands on it and found the surface nicely sun-warmed.

Gwydion smiled. 'Most stones bring benefits to the land – like the Tarry Stone which keeps your village green so lush and makes the sheep who graze there very glad, but some stones are not so helpful. The worst of them were made long ago with the aim of inciting men to war. That is why they are called battlestones.'

'Is this one?'

Gwydion sighed. 'In truth, I cannot easily tell what is a battlestone and what is not. It has become my wearisome task to try to find them, but so far I have failed.'

'Failed?'

'I lack the particular skill for it. The fae knew well how to protect the lorc from prying.' He patted the stone he had been examining. 'But at least this one may be discounted, for it carries the sign that tells me its purpose is harmless.'

'A sign? Where? Let me see.'

The sorcerer cast him an amused glance. 'Do you think you would be able to see it?'

Will digested Gwydion's words in silence, then he said, 'What's a lorc?'

'The lorc? It is a web of earth power that runs through the land. The battlestones are fed by it, and—'

He stopped abruptly, and Will became aware that the skylarks high above had ceased their warbling song. A powerful sense of danger settled over him as Gwydion looked sharply around him.

'Did you feel that?'

'What?'

But the sorcerer only shook his head and listened again. 'Come!' he said, heading swiftly away. 'We must take our leave of this place. By my shadow, look at the time! We should have crossed the Evenlode Bridge and passed into the Wychwoode by now!'

As he hurried on, Will's sense of danger mounted. The sorcerer behaved as if something truly dreadful was following hard on their heels, but he could neither see nor hear any sign of pursuit. At last, they entered the shade of a wooded valley bottom, and Will's fears began to fall away again. The waters of the Evenlode flowed over stones and glimmered under fronds of beech and oak and elm. A stone wall snaked out of sight across the river and led down to a well-used stone bridge. A woman seemed to be standing some way along the far bank next to a willow tree. She was beautiful, tall and veiled in white, yet sad. It seemed she had been crying. She watched him approach then stretched out a hand to him longingly, but the sorcerer called gruffly to him not to dawdle, and when he looked again the woman was gone.

As they followed the path up into the woodland green, he asked who she was and why she had been weeping. But Gwydion looked askance at him and said only, 'By that willow tree? I saw no one there.'

Will stopped and looked back again, but even the shaft of sunlight in which the woman had seemed to stand had faded. He knew he had seen her, though now he could not say how real she had been.

Gwydion had raised his staff and was exclaiming, 'Behold the great Forest of Wychwoode! Rejoice, Willand, for now you will be safe for a little while at least.'

They travelled deeper into the forest along whispering runnels, among towering trees where sunshine flecked the green gloom with gold. Will heard the clatter of a wood-pecker far away in the distance. Cuckoos and cowschotts and other woodland birds flittered among the trees. After a while, he said, 'Master Gwydion, how is it you've got memories that go back eighty generations? Are you immortal?'

'I have lived long and seen much, but that does not make me immortal. No one is that. I was born as other men were born. My first home was Druidale, on the Ellan Vannin, which some now call the Island of Manx – though that was long ago. I can be hurt as other men are hurt – by accident or by malice – though it is quite hard to catch unawares one who has lived so long in the world. I do not grow old as other men grow old, and many magical defences protect me from different kinds of murderous harm, but one day I will cease to be just as all men cease to be. As for what I am, there is no proper word for that in these latter days. I am both guardian and pathfinder. Once I might have been called "phantarch", but you may call me a wizard.'

'Aren't wizards the same as sorcerers, then? Or is one good and the other evil?'

'There are many fools who would have you believe it. But be careful of such words, for believers in good and evil cannot understand true magic.'

'Believers?' Will said, frowning. 'Do you mean there might be no such thing as good or evil? But how could that be?'

But Gwydion said only, 'For the present you would do well to forget all you have ever learned of light and dark, for the true nature of the world is not as you suppose.'

Will looked about. 'So am I to live with you here in this wood, and learn magic?'

Gwydion seemed puzzled by his question, but then he laughed and clapped Will on the shoulder. 'See there, we are nearing the tower of Lord Strange. He will settle some of your endless questions.'

As Will followed, he wondered who Lord Strange might be. He had never seen a lord, for no lord had ever bothered to tramp through Quaggy Marsh down by Middle Norton. No one except Tilwin ever visited the upper reaches of the Vale. Even so, Will had heard tell of lordly ways, about their finery, about how they feasted in stone-built castles and rode snow-white horses, and most of all about how they wore shining armour and wielded swords in battle. Lords had sounded at once a fine and a fearsome lot.

As for Gwydion, he did not look as though he did any of those things. He dressed simply, like a wayfarer, not in robes of velvet or cloth-of-gold, but in plain wool and linen. And he went barefoot like a man who could not afford himself a pair of shoes. There was no metal about him, nor anything that came from the killing of an animal – no fur, no leather and no bone – except for the bird's skull charm that he wore around his neck.

'Why do you wear that?' he asked, pointing to it as they came over a mossy bank and headed down towards a forest glade.

The wizard looked sidelong at him. 'This? It is an ornament . . . and a safeguard.'

'Against what?'

'The unexpected.' He intercepted Will's finger as he tried to touch it. 'Be careful! It is a trigger that sets off a very powerful piece of magic. It works much as a crossbow works upon a bolt. If the spell were invoked, I would become the bolt.'

Will did not understand. It was only a bird's skull. But there was no time to dwell on the matter, for just then Will saw a fallow deer hind. He touched the wizard's sleeve and pointed her out. She was watching them nervously from beyond a stand of birch trees, but as soon as she knew she had been discovered she leapt away.

Will saw the marks of her cloven hooves in the damp earth, but there were others that were bigger and uncloven. Gwydion examined some droppings then a half-smile appeared on his face. 'These are rare fumets indeed,' he said. 'Unicorn dung! It is most odd. They are not often to be found so far south. Something is amiss here.'

The forest deepened around them and the undergrowth thickened, but just as it seemed their path would be blocked the ground began to fall away into a clearing. There stood a double tower of dressed stone which rose to many times the height of a man. Will marvelled at it, though it seemed a dismal place. It was old and round and green with moss. Its top was battlemented and set with pointed roofs and several small, high windows. Below the tower there was a square moat.

Will's fears returned as they approached the gate. When they reached the bridge a frightening figure came out to bar their way. He was a man, but he was wearing a bonnet of iron and a coat that jangled with countless interlinked iron rings. His body was covered with a red surcoat that displayed the likeness of two silvery hounds. Will had never seen cloth so bright. It was as red as blood.

'Who comes to the dwelling of Lord Strange?'

Gwydion spread his hands. 'Tell your master there is a friend at his gate. One who brings tidings of wind and water and of war to come.'

'Wait here for your answer.'

When the man had disappeared, Gwydion said, 'The warden of the forest is named John le Strange. This is his lodge. His own domains are in the North where many men follow him, but King Hal has made him warden here. The king hunts rarely and has never come to this place, but Wychwoode is a royal forest and must be kept as such. You will soon see why Lord Strange has been appointed to a place where few eyes can linger upon him.'

'Is he . . . ugly?'

Gwydion looked up to the top of the tower. 'He was once the handsomest of men, but his appearance has been *changed.* He wears a ring of gold in his nose. That is his wedding ring which he is loath to cut and cannot otherwise remove. Take care not to stare at him.'

Will's fears surged. 'Why not?'

'Because first impressions count for a lot. You do not want to be thought rude.'

Will swallowed hard. 'Master Gwydion, why have you brought me here?'

'To learn, Willand. To learn.'

The man returned. This time he lifted up the front part of his iron hat and bade them enter. Will followed as Gwydion crossed the threshold and entered the hall. There, attended by his people, Lord Strange came out to greet them both. He was a big man with a chest like a barrel, but what was terrifying about him, and what made Will reel back in horror, was the fact that his head was more than a little like that of a wild boar.

Will managed to steady himself. He rubbed at his eyes, but the sight persisted. The lord's face sprouted grey bristles and his lower jaw foamed where two yellow teeth jutted. His nose was snout-like and did indeed carry a golden ring. Below the neck, though, he had the normal figure of a man and was attired in fine red robes.

To stop himself staring at the hog-headed lord, Will looked instead at the lady who came to stand by his side. She was a long-faced woman, tall and thin, and her hair was swept back inside a veiled hat which was the same grey as her long belted gown of embroidered velvet. The gown was tight to her form at bodice and sleeve, and at her neck was an ornament of silver set with pale stones. She seemed not to care that her husband was a monster.

'You are welcome to Wychwoode, Crowmaster,' Lord Strange said. 'Have you succeeded in your quest?'

'I thank you for your welcome,' Gwydion replied. 'And as for my quest, we must talk urgently, you and I. But first,

I shall beg a favour on behalf of my young companion. He has walked throughout the night and is both weary and footsore. He may fall down soon where he stands if he is not afforded a corner in which to lay his poor head.'

Will felt the shock of the lord's appearance still tingling through him as he entered the tower. After a little while a man and a woman appeared and asked him to follow them up a curving stair of finely mortared stone that was lit by bright rays of dappled sunlight. After a turn or two, the stair opened onto a broad gallery, supported by many carved pillars. Will had never been in such a place, and it filled him with awe. 'I suppose you must be Lord Strange's kin,' he said, offering his hand to the man as soon as he turned. 'My name's Willand.'

The attendants looked blankly at him. 'Sir, we are my lord's servants. We do his lordship's bidding.'

Neither the man nor the woman would smile or speak further to him, and their coldness set him on edge. He could see no reason for their unfriendliness. They were dressed in costly stuff, though the style and cut were lacking in dignity. The man's hair was cut to shoulder length, but he wore no braids. The woman's hair was hidden inside a plain headcloth. They showed him into a gorgeously painted chamber that looked as if it belonged to the lord himself.

He looked around in wonderment. 'Are we to go in there? What a place it is, hey!'

But the woman only looked away and lowered her gaze. 'My lord bids you to take refreshment, and sleep if you will.'

'And food and drink too!' He could hardly believe it. 'I thank you, but tell me—' he lowered his voice and said with a grin '—how did Old Nittywhiskers come by that hog's head of his?'

At once a look of horror came over both the servants' faces, and instead of answering him they made as if to leave.

'Wait,' Will said, as an idea came to him. 'Here. I have something for you.'

He fished the pebble that Gwydion had given him out of his pouch, and gave it to the maidservant. She stared at it in amazement, so that Will could not tell if she was happy at getting a shilling or bewildered at having been offered a pebble. But then the serving man said, 'Thank you, sir!' And the way he said it removed all doubt.

The servants backed away, thanking him again and closing the door after themselves. Will laughed out loud. He saw a plate of food and a goblet of small beer. He fell on it with good appetite, then he climbed up onto the great bed, wiped his mouth on his sleeve and stared up at the ceiling.

It seemed for a moment that a thousand new sights and sounds whirled inside his head, dizzying him, then sleep whispered in his ear and he knew no more.

He awoke in darkness. For a moment he wondered where he could be, but then a dozen memories came flooding back and his belly turned over. He got up and went to the tall, narrow window of lead and horn that opened onto the tree tops of the forest. The night was balmy and dry. No moon lit the whispering trees, but there was glow enough from the castle to show ghostly beech trunks standing motionless in the still air. He could smell the stagnant water of the moat down below, and from somewhere far away there came a strange heartbeat, a low but insistent sound that echoed with a regular *thump-thump-thump* through the forest.

Wychwoode seemed to be a solemn place, not at all what Will had imagined when the wizard had spoken of a place of safety. He ducked back inside the window and went to try the door. It was of thick oak and set with clever crafts-manship into stonework that was as solid as any outcrop of the earth. At first, the door would not open, and he wondered if he had been made a prisoner, but then he found the heavy iron latch ring, lifted it, and the door swung easily and noiselessly.

Outside, a pillared gallery gave onto the great hall below. It was decorated with woven hangings that showed hunting scenes and a painted frieze of hounds and woodcutters. A huge stone-hooded fireplace was set in the far wall, its grate empty. The remains of a meal were scattered across a large table, set with many wooden trenchers and bowls which had yet to be cleared away. Two dozen candles, each as thick as a man's arm, burned brightly on a pair of iron stands and threw back the shadows. Gwydion sat in the lord's own high-backed chair at the top of the table, while Lord Strange and his lady sat on each side and listened to him.

'I have read the portents,' Gwydion was saying. 'And if I had in my pouch a thousand silver crowns and if there was at my command a company of nine dozen men, still that would not be enough to avert the disaster that is surely coming.'

Lord Strange leaned forward in his chair, his moist snout twitching at the mention of silver. 'If war is coming as you say then all our hopes walk alongside you, Crowmaster.'

Gwydion put out his hand and said, 'That is why I urge you to come with me to the court at Trinovant. So far, I have worked in secret, but the time of uncertainties is at an end, and the day is fast approaching when I must bring unwelcome tidings to those who surround the king.'

'Alas for my affliction!' Lord Strange looked away, so that the ring in his nose glittered and the candlelight danced on his blond eyelashes. 'For who will be persuaded by one who carries on him the head of a hog? The queen cannot stomach to stay in the same room as me. She calls me "King Bladud of the Swine" and mocks me. Therefore you would do better to seek the favour of the court without me.'

Gwydion let a long silence stretch out before he spoke again. 'I feared you would answer me thus, Friend John. Listen to me: I tell you there is nothing left to a man in your position save to attend to your duties as honestly and as generously as you may. I say to you that you must not look to others to find the remedy to your ailment, you must seek for it in diligence and prudent action. Give rather than take.'

'You make much of your advice, Crowmaster, and yet you seem to me to speak in riddles.'

'If I do, then perhaps it is because there is no straighter way to speak to you at present.' Gwydion spread his hands. 'Nor do I wish to trouble you with the detail of my own task, but I must make some explanation so you understand something of the import of this news that I bear. Just as water flows upon the earth in streams and in rivers, so there are also flows of power within the earth.'

Lord Strange grunted. 'Power, you say?'

'Just as some places are wetter and drier, so accordingly there are places where there is an abundance of earth power, and other places that suffer from a lack of it.'

The lord's wife looked bored by this. 'Crowmaster, we know this much for we have seen you scry the ground with your hazel wand.'

'Oh, those patterns are wholly natural, and long have I studied them. The Realm is tattooed from end to end with subtle flows that any willing person may learn to feel. They spiral and coil underfoot, always rising and falling as the moon and sun run their several ways. Farmers read the land by them, and use such knowledge to ensure their crops will thrive. A fast flow of power makes for a place of good aspect, whereas a sluggish flow diminishes the life force of all that grows in the ground or goes upon it. This is well known.'

The Hogshead gave a great yawn. 'We will take your word for it, Crowmaster. For we know nothing of such matters and care for them less.'

The wizard leaned forward and his manner became as wily as a conspirator's. 'But, Friend John, this is not the power of which I now speak. Consider this: just as there are natural rivers upon which men ride to trade their goods, yet also men will oftentimes cut artificial canals so they may reach places where no natural river runs. And so it once was with the great flows of earth power, for long ago, during the days of the First Men and before the fae retired into the Realm Below, a thing called the lorc was made.'

'Lorc? We have never heard this word before,' Lord Strange scratched at his chin. 'What does it signify?'

The wizard shook his head. 'No one in these latter days has any knowledge of it. Even we wizards of the Ogdoad supposed it to have been broken by the Slavers some fifty generations ago. Yet according to fragments of the Black Book of Tara which I have lately found in the Blessed Isle, there is reason to believe otherwise. Think of the lorc as channels, built by the fae and set deep in the earth. These channels – or "ligns" to give them their proper name – are nine in number and cross the Realm in different directions. They were made to draw and direct flows of earth power from one end of the Isle to the other.'

'And their purpose?' the lord's wife asked.

'Lady, your shrewdness brings me neatly to my point – their purpose was – and is – to feed certain standing stones which are known as "battlestones". Once primed they are able to incite men to war.'

Lord Strange frowned at this. 'And you now wish to find these battlestones?'

'Quite so. But whereas I can easily scry the natural flows that lie in the ground, I cannot feel the ligns that were made by the fae, for their artifice was ever beyond that of men to comprehend, and in this case has been well hidden from us. I do not know how many battlestones there may be, but since I have become aware of their purpose my hope is to find at least some of them, if I can, by indirect means.'

The lord and his lady exchanged a wordless glance, then Lord Strange said, 'It is your wish to render these battle-stones harmless?'

'It may yet be possible to lessen the slaughter that approaches. But time is already short, and I cannot accomplish my task alone. Men and horses and silver have I none – in short, I must beg for the king's permission and hope for the aid of his court.'

The silence grew heavy. Then Lord Strange said bluntly, 'As I have already explained, I cannot help you at court. I hope you have not come here to ask me for silver, Crowmaster, for I have little enough—'

The wizard held up his hand. 'Have no fear, I will not ask you for silver, Friend John. But it will help me immeasurably if you would agree to look after the young apprentice lad.'

Will almost fell off his perch.

The wizard went on. 'You see, I was obliged to save his life. It is a tiresome tale with which I will not burden you, save to say that for a while I had hopes of using him as my bag-carrier, but so far he has proven himself to be more of an encumbrance. I dare not allow myself to be weighed down by him any longer.'

'You would have us keep the boy for you?' the lord's wife said.

'He is a teasel-headed young churl, yet he may be turned to some use if he were to have some book learning knocked into him. Would you be so kind as to do that, my lady?'

She returned Gwydion's gaze frostily. The lord growled, and it seemed to Will who watched in speechless horror that he would refuse, but then the wizard inclined his head persuasively and it seemed that an atmosphere of compliance came over the hall.

'I would remind you that all such favours come around full circle in time.'

'So you never tire of repeating, Crowmaster.' The great, piggy head tossed. 'However, I shall again do as you ask in the hope that one day—'

'No!' Will shouted. 'I won't stay here! Not in this dismal place! I'm coming with you, Master Gwydion, or else I'll go home! I'm not a teasel-head and you're not giving me away!'

He bolted for the stair, but at a sign from the lord one of the guards stepped forward and grabbed him so that he was carried struggling into the hall.

'You will be quiet!' Gwydion commanded, and momentarily Will was robbed of his power of speech. Then the wizard bent close and whispered, 'Wychwoode is a place of good aspect, Willand. You must stay here at least until Lammastide. A time of great danger follows your thirteenth birthday. It will last for six months—'

'Six months?' Will squealed. 'Oh, take me with you, I beg you, Master Gwydion! Please!'

Gwydion leaned forward patiently once again and took his hands. 'Listen to me, Willand. You were eavesdropping long enough to know that powerful forces are growing in the Realm, forces that will bring down a welter of blood upon the people unless they can be confounded. It is my duty to do what I can to prevent suffering. And it is your duty to do as I say.'

'But I can't live here! Please, don't leave me!'

'How soon your mind changes. Yesterday you were begging me not to take you away from home. Now, you are begging to come with me. What will you want tomorrow, I wonder? I will come for you at Lammastide.'

Some of the fire went out of him. 'But that's still all summer long, Master Gwydion. I can't—'

But the wizard turned about in a whirl of steps and called out subtle words so that all other motion in the hall ceased. He drew a deep breath and spoke very privately to Will. 'For thirteen years you lived as a happy child. You had a loving home and not a care to trouble you. You must thank me for that, for your peace was of my devising. But now there is a threat against your life, a threat that mere keeping spells cannot hold at bay.' He raised a finger to Will's lips. 'Be mindful of your situation. I know you are not a teasel-head – that was said for Lord Strange's benefit. The Wychwoode is the only safe place to spend this most critical season of your life. Do not go beyond its bounds. I will return for you before Lammastide – you have had my word on that. Now, will you promise to obey me in this matter or am I to wash my hands of you?'

And the look on the wizard's face was so grave that Will found himself nodding and making a promise that he hated even before the spell had begun to pall.

CHAPTER FOUR

A LITTLE LEARNING

And so it was that Will was lodged in the tower of John, Lord Strange for the season of the year that ran from Beltane to Lammastide. It was not long before he got used to the long days he had to spend at the tower, and began to forget some of the horror he had felt on first seeing the Hogshead.

The lord's wife had agreed to set about Will's schooling, but it soon grew into a torture for him. First they made him wear a suit of lordly stuff, all stiff and not to be soiled, and a rule was laid on him never to go beyond clarion call of the tower.

At first he obeyed. During the warmth of May and the heat of June he explored the nearer parts of the forest as far as the river, always looking out for unicorns, always mindful of Gwydion's pledge to return for him, and his own not to stray. But no clarion was ever blown to summon him back to the tower, and little by little the lord's strict rule was relaxed.

In the mornings he suffered terrible, spirit-crushing labours, while not a word was mentioned about magic as he had hoped. Instead he was put to reading and writing and speaking out from his slate, and near half of every day was spent chalking marks over and over, and when the slate was full, rubbing them all out again. But at least there were always the afternoons when he could roam as he wished.

Nor was he as lonely as he had feared he would be. On most nights a beautiful white cat came to visit him, and on some days a bent-backed old woman was accustomed to arrive at the tower to deliver firewood. Will felt sorry for her, for she would bring heavy loads on her back – fuel to cook the lord's mountainous dinners. She said that when her summer's toil was done there would be a further stock of wood laid in to keep Lord Strange and his wife warm throughout the winter, and she would have coin enough to pay her keep. So Will began helping her, and that was when he began to get back more than he gave, for without his knowing it the old woman had already begun to teach him the rudiments of magic.

She was known about the Wychwoode as the Wise Woman of Wenn, for she knew much about herbs and field remedies, and even something of the higher arts. She told Will many things as they walked the dusty path beside the river. First she told him about the 'Great Rede', then she spoke of the 'Three-fold Way', and then, as they came close to the hamlet of Assart Finstocke she taught him about the language of birds.

'Fools think that birds and animals are of lesser rank and wisdom than men, but it is not so. Do you know that all crows are left-handed?'

He grinned. 'Crows don't have hands, Wise Woman.'

'Left-handedness has nothing to do with these.' She held up her own hands, then pointed at her head. 'Like most other things it has to do with what's in here. Do you know that all birds dream?'

'Truly? What do they dream about?'

'Songs. Birds are most wise in their way.' She crooked a finger at a green froglet hiding among the reeds. 'And see this little fellow here? A frog is wise in his own special way, for he is much better at being a frog than any man could ever be. What man could live without a stitch of clothing in a frozen pond all winter through? But he can. Likewise, a mole, a squirrel and a seagull can go where no man can go. Each creature of the wild has its own special knowledge of the world. If we scorn the wisdom of beasts we make fools of ourselves.'

The Wise Woman was a marvel. She said that folk who had patience could learn extraordinary tidings from birds and mice and not only from watching their habits or having knowledge of their ways, but from listening directly to their little hearts' concerns and heeding their warnings about the future.

'Don't you know that all animals have foreknowledge?' she asked. 'Bees will swarm when they smell fire, ants know when thunderstorms are coming and hornets can tell which tree lightning will strike. And when it comes to greatness of character, you will never find loyalty in any lord's man greater than that given by his hounds. Nor will you find elegance in any lady greater than that to be found in the cat who comes to sleep on your bed at night.'

'You know him?' said Will, startled.

'Surely I do. His name is Pangur Ban. All the Sisters of the Wise have "familiars", favoured animals who attend us. I am told by my toad, Treacle, that Pangur Ban is the true lord of Wychwoode and a great friend of Gwydion. Has the cat not told you this himself yet?'

Will grinned. 'But surely, Wise Woman, no creature can speak?'

'They all speak. Though no man or woman, no matter how wise, can hear what words are spoken. A hedgehog or a vole or a wasp will not spy for a wizard on the counsels of the great as some say they do, but woodpeckers may always be relied upon to tell if outlaws are concealed in a

47

wood, and starlings can tell you if a village tithe has been paid or not – and, if it has, how much grain still lies in the barns.' She produced a piece of dry bread. 'Here! Take this and feed the ducks. Then perhaps you will learn how it is with ducks, and you will see how they thank you.'

No sooner had Will taken the bread than he turned to see a dozen mallards gliding over the water towards him. They had appeared out of nowhere and with such swiftness that he thought the Wise Woman must have summoned them by magic. Earlier he had seen her receive the bread from a tower guard whose injured hand she had healed the day before. He broke off small pieces and threw them out to the mallards, eager that each of the colourful drakes and each of the brown-speckled ducks should have its proper share. The birds dabbled their beaks and paddled back and forth and sported like children at play until all the bread was gone, then, seeing there was no more, they swam away again, almost as fast as they had appeared – but never a one turned to thank Will for lunch as he now half-expected.

'Do you understand yet?' the Wise Woman asked as Will followed her away from the water's edge.

'But . . . I didn't hear any thanks from them. Should I have? It seems to me that when I had bread they were my friends, but when I had none they were my friends no longer.'

The Wise Woman laughed. 'Oh, not at all! You are not thinking in the way of magic yet.' She patted his belly three times. 'You feel thanks in there – a warm glow just below your heart. Concentrate. Do you feel it now? The spirit of life? It's a power that has come from those ducks – that's their gratitude that burns inside you. A gift as sure and real as any gift of bread that you made to them. Feel it, Will, and learn how to feel it again! Mark it well, for it is a power that can put a smile on a man's face and a spring in his step!'

And Will did smile, and he thought that perhaps he had grasped a little of what the Wise Woman had said after all. There must be in the world chains of good deeds, for had not the Wise Woman healed the hand of the guard who gave the bread that came to Will to give to the ducks who had made him smile? Now, he thought, if only there was someone I could pass this smile on to, then the chain would carry on . . .

'Most folk believe they know nothing of magic, but it is natural for folk to understand it more than they think. No doubt you have heard fragments of great wisdom in old sayings? Many come from magical redes, or laws. One good turn deserveth another – you must have heard that?'

'Why, yes! Many times.'

'That is a rede of magic. So is "All things come full circle". And "A man must be mad to ride a dragon". And "Riches are like horse muck".'

'Riches are like horse muck? That doesn't sound so wise to me.'

'But riches *are* like horse muck, for they stink when in a heap, but spread about they make everything fruitful.'

Will learned how the Great Rede and the Three-fold Way were the taproots of magical law. He discovered how obedience to the Great Rede was the thing that set wizards apart from sorcerers, for it said simply:

Use magic as thou wilt, but harm no other.

He saw how that fitted with what Master Gwydion had said about having to use magic sparingly and never without due forethought as to the balance between gain and loss. A great deal of a wizard's skill, he saw, must come in taking gain in such a way that the loss to others that arrived with it did as little harm as possible. A sorcerer, on the other hand, could ignore the Great Rede, for he abused magic, employing it just as he pleased. A sorcerer took to himself the gains but never cared about the losses. That, in its way, said the Wise Woman, was ever the truest meaning of the word 'evil', and why evil was, in the end, always the cause of its own downfall.

No wonder Gwydion was displeased when I called him a sorcerer, Will thought. Compared to wizardry, sorcery must be a blundering and clumsy thing, full of force and brute magic instead of elegance and skill.

He thought again of the Law of the Three-fold Way, which said:

> *Whatsoever is accomplished by magic,*
> *returneth upon the world three-fold.*

'But doesn't a greedy and uncaring sorcerer soon find himself buried under a heap of evils of his own creating?'

'Magic returns consequences upon the world, not always upon the head of the magic-worker himself. That is why sorcerers can flourish. You will know them by the trail of destruction they leave behind for others to clear up.'

Will was indignant. 'Do they not see what they're doing to others? Don't they feel ashamed to behave that way?'

'Ashamed? Never! A sorcerer has no shame. For, you see, no sorcerer truly believes himself to be a sorcerer.'

Will's head ached at that idea. 'I . . . I don't think I understand.'

'Willand, there is no "good" and there is no "evil". These are false ideas that greedy men have sought to misguide fools with. A sorcerer always believes himself to be special. He falls in love with himself. To him, means can always be justified by ends, and he has excuses for everything. This is because he always breaks the Third Law of Magic, which says:

He whom magic encompasseth
must be true unto his own heart.

'Sorcerers use dirty magic, Willand. They lie to themselves. They always claim the crimes they commit should be discounted for they are done in the service of a greater good. But that is never so, for real advantage is never brought forth from malice. You must be strong to work untainted magic. And strength is, in the end, much the same as selflessness. Now do you begin to see?'

Will's head was spinning. 'I don't know if I do.'

She sighed and pointed to where a pretty flower grew. Its stem was delicate and its head like that of a purple dragon. 'Greater butterwort. The biggest and handsomest one I've seen this summer. Pick it for me.'

He looked at her, surprised. 'But you said it was the work of knaves and fools to go around plucking up wild flowers for themselves when they can be so much better enjoyed alive.'

'Do it. It will teach you a hard lesson. Or do you lack the strength to break such a slender neck without good reason?'

He picked the flower, half expecting some power to prevent him, but the stem snapped easily and he felt a small pang of protest in his heart.

'There,' the Wise Woman said. 'By that action you've lost a day out of your life. Did you feel it go?'

'Why . . . yes.'

'Now crush that flower to pieces! Rub it angrily between your hands until it is all broken!'

A sudden fear bit at him. 'I don't want to.'

'You might as well now.' She took the flower from him and threw it away into the long grass. Then she said with great firmness, '"Real strength never impairs harmony." That's a very clever old rede, Willand. So clever I'll say it for you again in its full form: "Real strength never impairs beauty or harmony, it bestows it." Real strength has much to do with magic. Do you see now?'

He looked at the flowerless plant. It looked bereft. 'No. But I can begin to see why the folk of Wychwoode call you the "Wise Woman".'

She took his hand, 'Cheer up, Willand. It's only one day you've dropped, and that'll be lost from the far end of your life where it'll do you far less good than a day like today.'

He thought about that for a while and decided she was right – he had better cheer himself up. 'Wise Woman, perhaps you can tell me the answer to a question that's been troubling me.'

'I will try.'

'What's a Child of Destiny?'

'That's a curious phrase. Where did you hear it?'

'Master Gwydion used it once about me. He said something about a Black Book too. What does it mean?'

The Wise Woman smiled. Her leathery face wrinkled, but her bright eyes remained fast on his. 'That, Willand, I cannot tell you.'

The answer disappointed him for it was no answer at all, and the Wise Woman's secret smile seemed to raise still more troublesome questions. At last he said, 'Was it a sorcerer who made Lord Strange hog-headed?'

But the Wise Woman only cackled, as if she thought that was a very good joke.

High summer came with the solstice, the day when the sun climbed to its loftiest place in the sky. It was the longest day of the year, but Will wished all of it away. Despite having spent so short a time in the wizard's company, and most of that reluctantly, he ached for Lammastide.

Lammas was no more than what was called in the Vale 'Loaf Day', a day of ritual breadmaking. And Gwydion had told him it was so with the other festivals – solstices were just Midsummer, the longest day, and Ewletide, the shortest. Equinoxes were likewise marked in the Vale as important days in spring and autumn when days and nights were the same length. Lammas was the first day of Harvest-tide, the day that signified the first ripened corn, or the first day of the month of August. But June was not yet past, and the corn was still as green as grass.

Lord Strange and his people counted time only in Slaver months. Nor was any ceremony kept by them at Midsummer. When he asked the lord's wife she told him in her stiff way, 'The churls, the simple folk, have many foolish beliefs. They will go out on Midsummer's Eve to stand beneath an elder tree, or sit within a ring of mushrooms. Perhaps they are hoping to dance with the fae.'

'May I go too?' he asked, delighted at the idea.

But she only drew herself up and said, 'You were sent to us to learn proper ways. We do not observe low customs here.'

Then Lord Strange came in and sat down at his great oak table, which was as usual spread with pies and pastries. He was looking more pig-like than ever, and as he ate he began to count the cost of Will's lodging at the tower, and to complain again that the wizard had laid an unlooked for burden upon him. And in that moment Will pitied the greedy, miserly lord and his desolate lady, for she had a heart of ice, and dared not walk in the sun for fear that it would melt.

'It's time you had your hair cut,' Lord Strange growled as he lifted up the nearest pie.

'What's wrong with my hair?'

'Those pigtails you wear befit a girlchild! We shall cut them off!' He banged the table with his fist.

'They're braids, not pigtails, and they're the sign of a man!'

'A man? A man, he says! Not here. Here the sign of a man is a shaven head. Churls wear lousy locks, warriors have short hair. Like mine. See?'

Will looked at the ridge of grey bristles of which Lord Strange seemed so proud. He set himself defiantly. 'Your soldiers may do your bidding, but I'll not!'

'*Whaaat*?'

'Try and cut my hair if you dare. If you do that, Master Gwydion will never take the pig spell off you! Remember what he said – all things come full circle!'

Sudden rage burst from the Hogshead and he threw down his pie. 'Is that what he told you? That it's his spell! I knew as much!'

'I didn't say that! You only think that because you're stupid! Stupid as a pig!'

'Come here!'

Will leapt out of the lord's reach.

'Come back, you young louse! You shall be made a scullion for your insolence! A scullion, do you hear me? You shall wash pans and pie dishes until you've paid for your keep! Come here, I say!'

But Will escaped the bellowing voice. He dashed from the tower and dived into the forest. And there he ran and ran, and after he had run all the breath and all the bile out of him he lay down in a glade and stared up at the sky. 'Whatever came over me?' he asked himself, unable to remember when he had endured such violent feelings of disobedience before. To calm himself he began to listen to the birdsong. He wondered what songs blackbirds dreamed about, and what was the true name of a wren he saw hiding in a holly bush. Perhaps the birds used true names when they sang to one another. He listened hard, trying to fathom their language, but he could not.

At last he adjusted his ear to the other sound, the one he had once thought of as the malign heartbeat of the forest.

It had become so familiar that he usually blanked it out, but now he became aware of it again. This time it sounded deeper and more sinister, and there seemed to be something insistent to it. He followed it, feeling out the direction as best he could, and came to a place where the forest began to thin. This was its margin, where dusty fields stretched out in hot, shimmering brightness to envelop the land beyond Wychwoode. The insistent rhythm was strong here. He felt it in his feet, a low *thump-thump-thump* that was not a wholesome sound at all, but morbid and relentless. There was something else too, for the air here was no longer green and clean, but tainted by the smell of smoke.

Then, quite suddenly, the sound stopped.

The slope ahead of him fell steeply down to a sluggish stream. He followed it and saw it widen and slow into a broad, scum-covered reach. And there his eye halted. For a moment he thought he had glimpsed a figure, that of a woman floating just under the water. From the corner of his eye it seemed that white veils were rippling in a slow current, but when he looked again he saw that it had been no more than a trick of the light.

At the other end of the reach a great dam of earth and timber blocked the stream's flow. The water was held back in a long, stagnant pool that had crept up the sides of the valley and drowned many fine trees on the lower slopes. But the level had once been much higher, as if the feeder stream had not been strong enough to keep the pool up through the dry summer months. Then he discovered the reason the dam had been built – there was a mill.

It had a big undershot wheel, twice the height of a man, that sat in a race to the side of the dam, and there were men standing by the sluices. More were in the clearing beyond, tending smouldering mounds of earth or walking to and fro.

He watched them for a while, fingering his fish talisman

and lying low. He wondered who the men were, but decided not to make himself known to them just in case word got back to Lord Strange. Then three men started to walk towards him – one wore a blue robe cinched with a broad belt, a shorter man was dressed in grey, and a tall, silent man in a belted shirt brought up the rear. Caution made Will hide himself behind a tree as they came along the path that ran below him. He crouched down as they stopped.

'A thousand,' the first man said. 'That's the order. We're to begin cutting tomorrow. And this time I'll choose them myself.'

The smaller man simpered. 'How many oaks in all, master?'

'All the big trunks. Them's to be saved. Ones so wide two men can't hold hands around. I want them all, and the rest you can cut up as you like.'

The smaller man seemed satisfied with that, but the tall man looked sadly around at the greenery. 'There's to be a lot of changes round here, then?'

'It's the times that are changing! Warships! That's what the Realm needs now. Warships, not deer haunts and forgotten bramble patches. I want this lot cleared.'

'What about the king's hunting?' the tall man said.

The other turned to him. 'Hunting? If we're to be rich it's trade we wants, not bloody deer-chasing. And to have trade we must have ships, see?'

'You said warships.'

'Aye!' The man in blue gave him an impatient glance and turned away. 'Trade, war – what does it matter? We'll grow rich on either one, or both together if you like!'

The man in blue continued to gesture broadly, showing off his plans for the Wychwoode, while the others trotted after him. Will looked up at the threadbare leaf canopy. The forest already looked sad and shabby where it had been drowned and cut back. Still, it seemed an enormous crime to chop down the biggest oaks, he thought, trees that had taken many human lifetimes to grow and made any place what it was. The Wise Woman had said that more creeping things took food and shelter from oaks than from any other kind of tree. 'Beetles and butterflies make the oak their trysting place. Squirrels, jays and pigeons take his acorns, even badgers dig their sets among his roots. And after the rutting season, when stags eat little, the oak's autumn bounty of acorns arrives at just the right time for deer to fatten themselves against the coming cold.' If there are to be no oaks here, he thought desolately, what will the deer have to eat? And what about the unicorns?

'Here! What's your game?' said a voice behind him.

Will jumped up and almost knocked himself cold on an overhanging bough.

'Listening in on other people's business, I suppose?'

When he looked round he saw a girl was watching him. She was lithe and trim in a boyish garb of dark green but she had a pretty, heart-shaped face framed by wisps of yellow hair. She seemed to be about his own age.

'Oh, poor thing! Did I startle you?'

'Just a bit,' Will said, frowning and rubbing his head.

'Good. I'm glad. It's your fault for being here in the first place. What's your name?'

'Will. It's short for Willand. What's yours?'

'Never you mind.'

Will scowled. 'Neveryoumind? That's a stupid sort of a name.'

'And you're a stupid sort of a boy. What're you doing here?'

'Looking for unicorns.'

'Unicorns?' She laughed. 'You won't see any unicorns around here.'

'I suppose not. They don't often come this far south.' He tried to sound knowledgeable. 'They wouldn't like it here much either. Not with that mill down there making such a thumping din half the time.'

She gave him a hard look. 'Where do you belong?'

'I . . . I live at the tower.' He wanted to point out his braids and tell her that he was not a boy any more but a man, but her face had taken on a look of deep disgust.

'The tower? I didn't know the Hogshead had a son.'

'You mean Lord Strange.'

'That's what you call him. You're his kin, more's the pity for you. A proper warden would look after the forest, but this one brings men here to cut it down. You can tell your kinsman that he's a pig, his purveyor's a pig, and all the rest of them are pigs too!'

She jumped down and ran from him, but he ran after her. 'Hey!' he called. 'I'm no lordling! I'm a churl like you! Don't be a fool! Wait for me!'

But the girl would not wait. She was as fleet as a fawn and knew the ground well, dodging along the deer runs where she thought he could not follow. But he did, until she came to a slender fallen tree that bridged a ditch of muddy water and, stepping lightly across, reached the far side. Will attempted it, but as soon as he stepped onto it she pulled over a side branch and turned the trunk under him so that he fell off. He landed flat in the mud below, while she stood six feet above him laughing like a drain. 'Who's the fool now?' she cried.

'I'll spank you for that!' he shouted back.

'No, you won't. You'll never catch me! Not here!'

He stood up, slopping the mud from him. He was soaked all down one side in black, foul-smelling slime. 'You know what? I think you're right. Give me a hand up out of here instead.'

She looked down at his outstretched hand, and shook her head. 'Think I'm a fool? I'm not, you know. Anyway, look at your hand. It's filthy.'

'Listen, I'm not Lord Strange's kin. I'm not a lordling. I'm nothing to do with the folk at the tower.'

'You said you lived there. Were you lying then – or now?'

'Neither. What I meant was I'm only lodging there. And I agree with you, the lord is a swine, and he's wrong to have his best trees cut down. It's just wickedness and greed, but he can't help being a pig because there's a spell of magic on his head.'

She looked at him afresh. 'You still haven't told me what you're doing here.'

'The same as you, at a guess. Just walking about, listening to what the birds tell each other.' He clasped his hand round a tree root and began to haul himself up. When he put his hand out to her again she stepped back and made ready to run.

'Oh, come on. You can trust me.'

'I'll decide who I'm going to trust. And you look like trouble. I don't expect you understand anything worth knowing. My father says your sort never do.'

'I told you – I'm not any sort. I'm just me.'

She sniffed. 'Why's your hair all done up like a girl's?'

'It's . . . it's a sign of manhood where I come from.'

'Manhood?' She laughed. 'That's girl hair. You look like a girl.'

Just as he began to think she was not going to help him she made a grab for his wrist. She would not let him clasp her hand. She braced her foot and, with one final effort, pulled him out of the hole.

'Thank you,' he said. 'You see? I'm not going to throw you down – even though I could.'

'Says who?'

'Says me.'

'Try it, then. If you think you can.'

'Oh, this is baby talk,' he said turning away. 'And on the Midsummer of all days.'

She seemed taken aback. 'Do you respect the solstice, then?'

'Doesn't everyone?'

'The Hogshead doesn't. Lords don't. You should know that.'

'Lady Strange thinks it'd ruin her dignity to have any fun. She says only churlish folk go out on Midsummer's Eve. I can't see her standing under elder trees or dancing at fae rings.'

'We do all kinds of things. We sing songs mainly.'

'What do you sing?'

'Mostly the old songs. My favourite's the one about the prince who plants three apple trees that bear him gifts of silver, gold and diamonds. You must know it.'

'Maybe. Sing it for me.'

She hesitated, embarrassed, but then she relented. 'All right. Just one verse.'

But she sang all four, and when she had finished, he clapped his hands. 'That was pretty. You have a sweet voice, you know.' Then he backed away a pace.

'Where are you going?'

'Nowhere. But I'll have to go back soon. I'm in trouble with the Hogshead for backchatting him.' He glanced in the direction of the tower. 'But first, I'd like to know your name.'

She laughed. 'I bet you would.'

'No, really. I would.'

'We live down by the river, so folk call me . . . Willow.' She looked down at her feet. 'I know it's a stupid name.'

'Don't be embarrassed. It's a lovely name. It's beautiful, just like the tree. And it suits you.'

They walked slowly back to the place where they had met, and sat down. She told him she lived in the village of Leigh. Her father, Stenn, was one of the verderers, men whose job it was to tend the forest. He was one of the men who were going to be made to fell the trees.

'But that kind of work isn't at all to his liking,' she said. They crouched down together behind a fallen trunk and looked at the mill and the smouldering heaps nearby. 'A man can't look after a forest all his life as my father has and then be expected to lead a tree massacre. He says the law may say the forest belongs to the king, but there's more to forests than just owning them.'

'And more to trees than just the using of them for timber.'

She looked at him and smiled. 'You do understand, after all. Those big oaks are my father's friends. He grew up with them and delights in each and every one of them. He says there's been an oak grove here since long before the Slavers came. He doesn't like what's happening of late. He says it all stinks!'

'There's certainly something nasty in the air around here.' He looked down at the wreaths of smoke that laced the air around the mill and gave it an acrid tang.

'That's the charcoal burners, stinking the place up with their heaps. They need charcoal to heat the iron and melt it. They cut down all of Grendon copse where that mill pond is now. My dad says there are three blacksmith's hearths down there. Going all the time, they are, with big bellows and everything. And that thumping you can hear all over the forest – that's what you call trip-hammers.'

He looked at her. 'What are they doing?'

'I don't know. Making things. We aren't supposed to go near Grendon Mill, but I know it's where they work iron into shapes. Waggons come up from the Old Road most days and take stuff away.'

'What kind of stuff?'

She shrugged. 'I don't know. Whenever I go down there they chase me off. I don't care. I don't want to be down there anyway. It's a dirty, stinky, smoky place now. Not at all the sort of place I like.'

'That's not what I meant about there being something in the air. It's what that man said – the times are changing.'

She nodded. 'And far too quickly, I'd say.'

'It all seems to fit in with what Master Gwydion told me.'

She sat up and looked at him with sudden interest. 'Who's Master Gwydion?'

Straight away Will regretted mentioning the wizard's name. So much was important and secretive about Gwydion that it seemed almost like a betrayal. And yet when he looked at Willow he felt he could have done nothing very wrong. 'He's the one who brought me into Wychwoode. Can you keep a secret?'

She shrugged. 'I don't know, I've never tried.'

He looked at her and remembered the look on her face as she hauled him out of the ditch, then decided he could trust her. 'If you swear to keep it to yourself, I'll tell you about Master Gwydion.'

'I swear.'

'Hand on heart?'

'Hand on heart.'

He took a deep breath. 'Master Gwydion is a wizard.'

Her mouth opened wide and then her nose wrinkled. 'No!'

'It's true. And I'm his apprentice.'

'And do they all tell such whopping lies where you come from?'

'I'm not telling lies! It's true. I'll swear to it if you like.'

'Hand on heart?'

'Hand on heart.'

She looked at him sidelong, and Will could not be sure but he thought she had decided to believe him.

'It must be very exciting being a wizard's apprentice.'

'It's a little scary sometimes. You'd be amazed at the things I've seen.'

She smiled a doubting smile. 'Like what?'

'Oh, all kinds of things. He makes owls fly so slowly that you can count their wingbeats. He makes falling rain stop, right in mid-air. He can whistle up a storm just like that—' He clicked his fingers and leaned towards her confidentially. 'And he even summons giants out of the earth. Giants as big as barns. They're terrifying.'

'Go on, then,' she said, her eyes sparkling now. 'Do a bit of magic for me.'

That stopped him dead, and he wondered what his boasting had led him to, but then he put on his most serious expression. 'I'd like to, but . . .'

'But what?'

He shook his head and sucked in a breath. 'You must know that magic is dangerous?'

'Surely not if you know what you're doing.'

He drew himself up. 'Oh, no. It's always dangerous. All magic is dangerous because, you see, it affects the harmony, the balance, the . . . the way things touch one another, and so on.'

'Is that right?'

She watched him, waiting for more, while he desperately tried to remember all the things the Wise Woman had told him.

'It's quite hard to give magical knowledge to someone who hasn't had the proper grounding.'

'So I see. But I don't want you to give me any magical knowledge. I just want you to do some for me.'

'I'll . . . I'll think on that.' He nodded his head gravely. 'Yes, I'll think on it. And maybe I'll show you some tomorrow.'

Her glance slid away from him. 'Oh, I see. And what makes you think you'll be seeing me tomorrow?'

'Well . . . I mean I'd like to. I really would.' He felt his composure deserting him so that he couldn't meet her eye now. 'That is, if you're able to . . . if you want to come back here. They say all things come full circle – that's a rede, you know.'

Just then, Will heard two piercing whistles and he looked down the slope. There stood a bearded man with his head tilted back and a couple of fingers stuck in his mouth.

'That's my father! He's going back with the others to make ready for the celebrations. Can't stay. I'm late.'

She jumped up and without another word scampered down the slope.

He was about to call after her, but her father was there and he thought better of it.

'Willow . . .' he said to himself. 'But what about tomorrow?'

CHAPTER FIVE

THE MARISH HAG

For a while Will lay by himself on the fringe of the forest, knowing he ought to return to face Lord Strange's wrath, and that the longer he delayed the worse it would be. But something defiant inside him resisted. He looked out at the still waters of the pool. When the *thump-thump-thump* had ended for the day it had been like the fading away of a toothache. Wisps of smoke still rose up from the charcoal burners' mounds, but there was no other movement. Everyone, it seemed, had gone down to the village to prepare for the Midsummer.

He sighed, feeling truly alone. At home in the Vale, folk would be dancing and feasting and playing festive games long into the evening, but all that seemed too far away now, and a chill touched him as he lay on his mat of mossy grass. He fell into a sombre mood as he watched the pool and saw the doomed trees reflected there.

After listening to the silence for a while, curiosity roused him and drew him down the slope into a forbidden place. He was mindful of his promise to Gwydion to remain within the Wychwoode, but a desire to know the truth pushed him just a few steps beyond its bounds. Around him stood heaps of rubbish, piles of sawdust and the axe-hacked stumps of large trees. Sheds and shelters clustered round Grendon Mill. Piles of small logs were stacked up ready for charring. Where the sluice leaked there was the sound of water spilling down behind the stationary wheel and tumbling through the race.

He looked inside the mill and saw a great square oaken shaft, toothed wheels, trundles bound in iron and bearings set in stone. There were empty anvils at each of the three trip-hammers and an idle bellows by the covered hearth. Long pincers and mallets hung on the walls. All around lay piles of metal that had been cut into different shapes. Most of it was rusty or fire-blackened, though some of it was burnished bright, but there was no mistaking what was being made here.

'War,' he whispered, picking up a half-formed sword blade. 'Just like Master Gwydion said . . .'

Excitement thrilled through him as he looked at what had been fashioned. There were blades of different lengths, all as yet without point or edge. Grim-looking axe-heads and war-hammers stood in rows. And thousands of sharpened arrowheads waited to be attached to shafts. In another shed were iron hats and helms, many roughly-made pieces of armour for limb and body. And in the shelter of a thatched lean-to was a mail-maker's bench with boxes of rivets and pairs of pincers with rags tied round their handles. Thousands of close-linked rings had already been painstakingly fitted together to make hoods of mail like Lord Strange's guards wore.

Every shed Will looked into was the same. There seemed to be enough iron to arm five hundred soldiers, and if as Willow had said waggons came most days taking away what had been finished, who could say how much had already gone into store?

Does Lord Strange know what's happening? he wondered. Of course he must know! The sound of those trip-hammers carries far and wide.

He felt suddenly cold inside. His fingers reached for the comfort of the leaping salmon talisman that hung about his neck. He wished Gwydion was here. This is a fine way to spend Midsummer, he thought as he came away.

He was picking his way past the mill-race when he chanced to look down. The sight that met his eye made him exclaim. Where the water gushed under the sluice and splashed down like a waterfall behind the green paddles of the wheel there was a pale hand. Slender it was, like a girl-child's, and wax-pale in the darkness.

He stared at it, shocked. Unable to turn away, he bent to get a better view. The hand seemed to wave to him and he watched it beckon for a moment. Then, he stood up and looked around in panic. Moments ago he had feared discovery in a forbidden place, now he yelled as loud as he could for help.

But no help came.

I have to do something, he thought, and leapt down into the race. The escaping flow was knee-deep under the wheel and cold enough to make him gasp. The water showering down on him gurgled past in a mass of bubbles. The wheel and stonework in which it was set were slimy and slippery. He reached out to touch the waxen hand, but it was dead and he pulled back from it.

A groan of dismay escaped him. Here was a drowned thing, a body caught up horribly in a wheel. What had the beating and turning of it done to the flesh? He screwed up his face and reached into the narrow gap. There, revealed to his exploring fingers, was a lolling head and a slender arm, trapped and mangled by the tearing of the wheel. His feet kept slipping, but he ducked under the water again, braced his back against the paddles and forced himself up with all his strength against the current to lift the wheel a little and so free the arm from its grip.

It fell away. There was no blood. The body was frail and

light as it came free. He carried it in his arms, looking for a place to lay it down. There was dust and dirt everywhere in the clearing, so he carried the body back up into the forest and laid it on a bed of moss. He was drenched and shivering as he knelt beside the dead, pale thing, but all he could feel was an immense sadness.

He blinked, wiped his face and allowed his eyes to dwell on the body. At first it seemed to be a trick of the light, but then he realized that the skin was as pale as could be, silvery, transparent almost. A tracery of greenish-blue veins showed through. The flesh of the arm was torn where it had been trapped in the wheel, and on the forehead and at the temples there were greenish marks, as if lampreys or sucker fish had attached themselves to draw blood. The hair was greenish too and child-fine, yet the features of the face were adult – sharp and delicate, a pointed chin and wide mouth, and the eyes almost as if closed in sleep. Will knew the creature he was laying out had not been born of woman, but that did not matter.

The poor thing must have died alone, he thought. Caught as it tried to swim in the pool. Dragged under the wheel.

A bout of shivering overcame him and he shed a tear. But he arranged the creature's limbs with dignity and laid leafy branches over it to cover its nakedness until only the face showed. Then he gathered a posy of woodland flowers. Despite its ugly wounds the creature was beautiful. He felt he must lean over and kiss its forehead in farewell. He did so, then fled back to the tower.

As blazing June turned into an even hotter July, Will longed more and more for the return of the wizard. The wild words he had spoken to Lord Strange had brought punishment – work at the slate had been doubled and his long after-noons of freedom were taken away. He was put to do the chores of a kitchen servant to pay his way, which he did not mind. What did trouble him was that he had been stopped from going back to the mill to see if Willow had come to meet him, and now he was no longer allowed to go beyond the moat.

'What about Willow?' he asked the white cat, appalled. 'Shall I ever see her again?'

The cat came and rubbed its head against him, looking up with unblinking eyes.

He hated staying indoors when the sun was shining. The constant squeezing of the quill made his finger-ends sore, but he had begun to see the power of letters, and then the power of words, and beyond it all he had begun to grasp the blazing power of ideas too. Writing, he saw, was not, after all, about the tiresome business of scratching jots and tittles onto slate or parchment, it was about gaining the power to lodge ideas in other people's heads – people who were far away, people who might even be living in another age!

The immensity of the discovery startled him, for no one had yet bothered to warn him what delights all the drudgery would lead to. All he needed now was a book to read, and so far as that was concerned he had already hatched a plan.

Excitement beat through him as he followed Pangur Ban up the stair to the lord's privy chamber. There, he knew, three books bound in old leather stood together on a lime-wood stand. He looked over his shoulder to make sure none of the servants had seen him, then he went in and pulled out the first of the books. It was a book of household accounts and he looked it over quickly and put it back.

The second book looked the same as the first, but the third was quite different. It seemed to be much older than the others and its cover was not secured with an iron clasp and chain. There was something written on the front, and though Will could read the words, they made no sense:

Ane radhas a'leguim oicheamna ainsagimn . . .

The rest had been destroyed by a deep scorch-mark. It looked as if someone had once tried to throw the book onto a fire but had changed their mind. When he opened it, he saw that every other page showed a large picture. There were many lines of careful black writing, with some parts done in red, and lettering so even that Will wondered at the skill of the scribe. The pictures were of animals, all kinds of animals, and one especially caught his eye – a lion, which was the creature on the surcoats of Lord Strange's men, and which he had taken at first to be an odd-looking dog for the only lion he had ever seen before was a dandelion. There was also a leopard, which the book said came of crossing a lion with another, even fiercer animal called a pard. Looking at the pictures it seemed that quite a few of the beasts were crossed with one another, some even with humankind.

Will bent close over the book while Pangur Ban walked on the table and rubbed himself against Will's head. In the margins beside a few of the pictures someone had written several lines. The writing was thin, like beetle-tracks, and looked as if it had been inked by a pin, but again it was writing of a kind he could not read. In the back of the book was more curious handwriting, and this time, as he tried in vain to read it, an idea came to him.

He fetched the lady's looking-glass and then tried the writing again. Now he could read it. But not quite, because although he could spell out the words, still they did not make any more sense than the words written on the cover. He read them aloud – they sounded magical. And when he looked back through the pictures, beside the eagle there was added the word *feoreunn*, beside the bee *begier*, and beside the wyvern – which was a man-eating beast of the air, a two-legged, winged dragon – was the word *nathirfang*.

Will mouthed them aloud for a while, then turned to look in the back of the book where the same small writing was:

> *To have the creature come, say,*
> *'Aillse, aillse, _____ comla na duil!'*
> *To have the creature do thy bidding, say:*
> *'Aillse, aillse, _____ erchim archas ni! Teirisi! Taigu!'*

'They're spells!' Will whispered fiercely to himself. 'And those gaps are where to put the true names.'

I shouldn't be looking at this, he thought, suddenly mindful of the Wise Woman's warnings about the respect that magic demanded. It seemed wrong to be stealing peeks at a book that was not his to look at, and even more wrong to be slyly acquiring spells, but now he had started reading it was hard to stop.

He began to commit the words to memory, and he had made a fair job of it before a sound outside alerted him. He had been so engrossed that he only just managed to scramble back to his own chamber before the housekeeper's maid came past.

After the noonday meal Will took a piece of bread and honey away from the kitchen, and armed with his spells he set about catching a fly. As soon as one came in through the window to feed on the honey he shut it in the room and all afternoon, instead of practising his writing, he called out the words he had learned.

But it was not as easy as he imagined. There were many ways to pronounce what he had written down, and the fly took no notice of any of them. Also, the fly was not exactly like any of those pictured in the book. Was it a *foulaman*? Or could it be a *gleagh*, or a *crevar*? Lastly, he tried *cuelan* with no better success, but when he opened the door a big, fat bluebottle came in and began to buzz round his head.

He let out a yell of triumph. Wherever he went in the room the cuelan followed, flying round his head with the same solid determination that a moth flies about a candle flame. When he walked back and forth, the fly followed. When he stood still, it flew round him in a perfect circle.

'I've done it!' he said, enormously pleased with himself.

He lay down on his bed and watched the fly circling above his face. Then the fly landed on his nose. He tried to waft it away. But it dodged his hand.

'That's enough. You can go away now,' he said.

But it would not go away. It had been called to him magically and nothing he said would persuade it to leave. He quickly tired of it, but it did not tire of him. It kept landing on his lips and bothering him as he tried to write, until finally he dived under the bedclothes to rid himself of it.

When he came out again, it was waiting for him. When he went down to supper it came too, and though three pieces of bread and honey were put before him, the fly took no notice of any of them. It wanted only to circle his head, and when it next landed on him he slapped himself hard on the mouth, threw a fit of temper and almost fell off his chair.

The cook stared at him oddly. He shrugged back at her and scampered off, the fly in pursuit. Lady Strange, annoyed by the fly's attentions when she came near him, asked Will if he had forgotten to wash behind his ears. She set him an evening writing exercise and went away. Will hoped the fly would go too, but it did not.

As darkness fell there was no hope of concentrating on his studies. All evening the fly plagued him, and when the moon rose and every kind of daytime fly might reasonably be expected to go to its rest, this one continued to buzz. It seemed to Will that the only way to catch it would be to let it go where it so obviously wanted to go – into his mouth – then to swallow it whole.

He finally succeeded in killing it – he shot out a hand and slapped it against the wall then trod on it. But his savage joy was tempered with guilt. It was only a bluebottle, but that was beside the point. Working with naming magic could lead to unexpected trouble. He would have to learn a lot more about magic if he was ever going to do it right.

As Lammastide approached, Will planned his escape. It was an unsophisticated plan. Two weeks of obedience had slackened the vigilance of those who might otherwise have watched him with greater care, and when the courtyard next emptied he made a dash for the gate. He went straight down to the river and there he found the Wise Woman's hovel, pitched as it was in the shade of a spreading willow tree.

'Hello, Wise Woman!' he cried as he came up.

She had a basket on her lap and was shelling peas into it, but she greeted him with a kind word and asked him in. He sat down on an upturned pail and said, 'Wise Woman, will you answer me a question?'

'If I can.'

'Do you know a village called Leigh?'

'Surely. I pass by it every third day.'

'Do you know a girl who lives there by the name of Willow?'

The Wise Woman nodded thoughtfully. 'That one is very pretty, is she not?'

'I – I'd like you to take a message to her. If you wouldn't mind, that is.'

'Oh.' She broke open another pod. 'And why don't you go yourself?'

Will knew the Wise Woman well enough to have anticipated that. 'Because Leigh's beyond the bounds of the Wychwoode, and I don't want to break my word to Master Gwydion.'

The Wise Woman's face was like cracked leather, but her eyes were pools. They seemed to see deep inside him. 'That's a fine sentiment when you've already broken faith to come here.'

Will looked down. 'That wasn't any promise made to Master Gwydion. It's only Lord Strange's rule.'

'Does it matter? It's your promise that loses its value when you break it.'

A powerful mixture of feelings welled up inside him. 'But I must get a message to Willow.'

The Wise Woman watched him again in her quiet way. 'What does your message say?'

'I want to ask if she'll meet me in the place above Grendon Mill where we first saw one another at noonday tomorrow. Please tell her how much I want her to come, and say I've got something important to show her.'

The Wise Woman laid her basket aside and hobbled to the doorway. 'What do you want to show her? Let me see it.'

'I can't.'

'Then I can't take your message.'

He squirmed. 'I want to show her some . . . feats.'

'What sort of feats?'

'Just some small magic. The sort you've told me about.'

She looked at him for a long while, then she shook her head. 'Willand, the secrets of magic are not to be vouchsafed lightly. Magic is not a toy. And it is not for everyone to play with as they will. I have told the secrets to you only because Master Gwydion says you are very special.'

'But Willow's special too. If you've seen her, you'll know she's—'

'I know she's pretty.'

Will's cheeks coloured. 'Please, Wise Woman.'

'Oh, I'll take your message to her.' Her eyes twinkled. 'But I'll do it for my own reasons, not yours. You may not think so, but in my time I've known what it's like to burn with youthful fires. I'll do as you ask, but first you must promise not to teach the girl any lessons in magic, for as a famous inscription says "to be curious about that which is not your concern while you are still in ignorance of your own self, that is ridiculous".'

'I promise, Wise Woman. I won't teach her anything at all. I give you my word.'

'Your word?' She laughed. 'Oh, I shall treasure that, Willand. Truly I shall.'

The next day, he rose early and set about completing all the writing exercises the lord's wife had set for him, then he began to watch the courtyard and await his chance. By employing a little craftiness he had managed to get back from yesterday's meeting without being missed. Now, once again, he stole away at the changing of the guard. Excitement churned in him as he sped through the wood. All his worries had been stirred up – what if the Wise Woman had failed to find Willow? What if Willow had got the message but had been given some inescapable chore to do? And, worst of all, what if she had got the message but had decided not to come?

He pushed that idea away. Then, even though he was a little late, he forced himself to stop and calm down. 'There's no point in worrying,' he told an elm tree. 'I'll know what's what soon enough.'

But when he reached the heights above Grendon Mill a terrible sight met him. The entire hillside above the pool had been cut and all the fallen trunks dragged down to the road. Where there had been deep forest it was now a ruinous wasteland. It made his heart sink to realize that the special place in which he and Willow had met was now no more.

All around were crudely axed stumps, broken twigs and chippings underfoot where tree limbs had been hacked off and stacked by the charcoal pits. He looked up suddenly, feeling his skin prickle in warning. Then, as if he was dreaming it, he imagined gangs of men chopping and sawing, and a pair of yoked oxen hauling the trunks away. There were shouts and the cracking of an ancient yew tree as it groaned and split suddenly in half. But then the moment burst open inside his head and the horrible vision was gone, leaving him alone and in silence.

There was no *thump-thump-thump*. The continuing dry weather had, in the intervening weeks, lowered the water in the pool below the level needed to drive the wheel. The mill was deserted, and all the men sent away to other labours. He went down to the pool and called out Willow's name.

His voice echoed, but no reply came, so he sat down on a log and waited, his chin in his hands. An emptiness was growing inside him, though at first he refused to call it disappointment. He got up and walked back and forth across the earth dam. He did not want to go near the sheds or kilns that stood by the mill, so finally he wandered back to the edge of the pool and looked down at his own face in the water. Two fair braids hung down by his left cheek. Without thinking more about it, he took out his knife and cut one of them off. Then he cut the other.

'There! I don't look like a girl now,' he told the emptiness, and threw the braids as far as he could into the pool. They floated forlornly as circles widened around them on the surface.

'Willow!' he called out again. If she had bothered to come at all she would not have waited long. He remembered what she had said: *It's a dirty, stinky, smoky place now. Not at all the sort of place I like*. It was foolish to have tried to meet her here. But how could he have known it would be like this? And where else was there? They had not shared the name of any other place within Wychwoode except the tower.

As his hopes faded he thought of the trick he had learned in the hope of impressing her. He had practised long and hard with craneflies after the bluebottle incident. Before making his promise to the Wise Woman he had meant to do a piece of naming magic for Willow with dragonflies. He had found out the true name of the large kind that wore a dazzling pale blue stripe along its body.

Well, he thought, if Willow's not coming then there's no longer any harm in it.

In an effort to cheer himself up he stepped to the water's edge and called out grandly, like King Leir of old addressing his army.

'*Ealsha, ealsha, sathincarenta comla na duil!*' he commanded.

No sooner had his words echoed out across the pool than a dragonfly swooped in and began to circle before him. He repeated the enchantment five times, and a moment later there were half a dozen of the wonderful insects dancing in the air before him.

'*Sathincarentegh erchim archas, teirisi! Cruind!*' he told them, raising his arms, and they immediately began to fly in triangles. Yet another command, and they began to loop in figures of eight, darting in and out of each other's paths, their great double pairs of wings chattering in time with one another.

'What marvellous skill you have!'

Will turned at the voice. There was a girl standing behind him in the brightness, a girl just like . . .

'Willow?' he said, shading his eyes.

She looked like Willow, but surely she was not, for she shimmered like pale gauze.

He rubbed his eyes. She was tall and slender, and as like Willow as any sister, but her eyes were glowing with a faint, sad light and her voice was deeper and more dreamy. She wore a shining, white gown of such fineness that it might have been made of dragonfly wings. It reminded Will of the one the ghost had worn down by the bridge over the Evenlode, the one he had seen the day he had arrived at the Wychwoode.

'Come to me, Will,' she said. 'Give me your hands and I will show you wonderful things.'

'Willow? Is . . . is it you?' He shook his head, trying to clear it but the whole world was swimming now. 'Who are you? How do you know my name?'

'I'm your friend, Will. I've been searching for you, and now I've found you. You've come to me at last, my own true love.'

'I . . .' He wiped at his face, striving against the weariness that was overpowering him, but there was a cloying sweetness on the air. It was as if his arms and legs had lost their strength.

'Sit down. You're tired. Don't you want to sit down?'

The girl's glowing eyes had lost their sadness. Now they assured him that sitting next to her would be the most wonderful thing there was. He remembered the look on Willow's face when she had reached down to help him out of the muddy hole. How could he not do as she asked? It was hot now and the still, quiet warmth of the afternoon closed in around him like a suffocating blanket. He drew breath, but the air did not seem to satisfy his lungs and he sighed for more.

'Let me touch you,' the girl said, soothing his struggles. He felt a cool hand stroke his knee, his arm, the side of his face. 'Isn't that better? Isn't that so much better than waiting alone? Close your eyes, Will. Rest. Soon we will be together.'

A part of him resisted, knowing there was something wrong, something important, but when he tried to think what it might be it vanished. His eyes felt dusty and sore, and it was getting too hard to keep them open. He fixed his gaze on the dragonflies still turning and circling above the water. The brilliant blue flashes of their bodies swept out the loops into which his spell had locked them. I must release them before I go, he thought. But somehow he could not remember the releasing words, and it seemed not to matter any more if they flew on while he rested.

The dragonflies' weaving patterns reflected in the dark waters of the pool like a mystic symbol. It seemed as if the surface of the water was a looking-glass, a looking-glass that had the power to change him. He would have smiled but the tiredness was too great, and the soothing voice irresistible. 'Close your eyes, Will. Come with me. Come with me into the beautiful, cool water. There is a wonderful world below. A wonderful realm bigger and more beautiful than anything you've ever dreamed. So much. So much you never thought could be. You'll see many things, many wonderful things. You'd like that, wouldn't you? Come with me, then. Come, and we shall be together. Together forever.'

He felt the last shreds of resolve drain from him. The drowsy opal sky burned and seemed to press down on his head. He felt the warm mud seeping between his toes, making the ache in his feet go away, making the hurts of his long journey out of childhood fade. When he looked again he was already knee-deep in the water and the girl was naked beside him. But it was all right. It was how it was meant to be. Velvet smooth mud caressed his skin, inviting him deeper. He sank to his waist, then to his chest, and then he felt the water creeping up his neck and chin. The air above was filled with the lulling drone of dragonfly wings, repeating, repeating, endlessly repeating. And Willow, graceful beside him, walking a watery aisle, her cool hands on his face. Then she kissed him full on the mouth and led him down into the wonderful world that lay below the surface.

PART TWO

THE POWERS
OF THE EARTH

❑ ❑ ❑

CHAPTER SIX

A NEST OF SECRETS

When Will burst into wakefulness he was choking and fighting for breath. A cage of bony fingers imprisoned his face and, as they were ripped away, they tore at his cheeks.

'Be gone, foul hag!' a tremendous voice roared.

He saw a vile creature draw back from him. Its mottled grey skin sagged and fell in slack folds, its hair hung like fronds of stinking pondweed, its mouth hissed and spat as it struggled against Gwydion's grip.

'How dare you exact your revenges upon the innocent?' the wizard demanded. 'This obligation I lay upon you: get back into the slime where you belong and bother the sons of men no more!'

The creature's long fingers grasped for Gwydion's face. Their ends had suckers that tried to attach themselves to him, but the wizard held the hag away. For a moment it seemed that it would succeed in embracing him, but then he laid a mighty word on it, and it collapsed into the water and melted away.

Will was on his hands and knees coughing and spluttering. Every time he tried to draw breath, water vomited from his lungs and he began retching. Gwydion pushed him down and squeezed the water out of him and soon he was able to lie on his back and breathe freely again.

'It was horrible,' he said wildly. 'Horrible! I thought it was a girl! I thought it was Willow!'

'And what of your promise that you would not stray beyond the bounds of Wychwoode?' Gwydion's voice was soft but there was such a power of accusation contained there that Will shrank from it.

'I didn't mean to disobey! The forest got cut down and I sent word for Willow to come to the place we knew and then, and then—'

'And then you fell neatly into a trap set for you by the marish hag! And I hoped you could be trusted.'

Will was shivering and could not stop. 'What . . . what was it?'

'A hag. A creature that preys on fools.'

He put a hand to his throat. 'I almost drowned . . .'

'Oh, you would not have drowned! You would have been kept happily alive for many days and weeks as part of the loathsome larder that all such water hags keep down below. And there all the juices would have been sucked from you one day at a time as you dreamed your death dream!'

Will wallowed in the mush of stinking, black ooze that had accompanied him out of the pond. 'Master Gwydion, if you hadn't come . . .'

'You are lucky indeed that I have returned.' The wizard looked down on him as if from a great height. 'Augh! I cannot abide the stench of dirty magic.'

'But how did you know where to find me?'

'Do you remember your little friends the dragonflies? Your use of naming magic upon them drew me just as it drew the hag. You are fortunate it drew nothing worse, for you were lit up like a beacon!'

'I didn't mean to do wrong. I—'

'You are no better than the child who delights in pulling

the wings from butterflies. Cruelty is a grievous failing, Willand.'

Those words cut deep. 'But I didn't harm them.'

'Of course you harmed them. And after all you were told. Who are you to entrap dragonflies and use them as you did? They are living creatures, with their own concerns and neither the time nor the strength to dance attendance on the will of a lad who merely wants to impress a pretty girl!'

'I never thought of it that way.'

'Indeed you did not!'

The wizard paced up and down the bank and Will looked away in shame. He saw his dragonflies lying exhausted on the surface, their tiny legs moving weakly. He had nearly killed them.

Gwydion reached down and lifted them from the water one by one and whispered words that unbound them, so they revived and flew away whole from the glow that was in his hands. When he had done with them he looked around, his face still grey with anger. 'I hope you now have the strength to walk, for we must be gone from here.' His anger blazed up. '*Na duil!* Look at the desecration they have wrought! They have hewn down an ancient and sacred grove. This is a high crime, the like of which we have not seen since Nis and Conat burned the groves of Mona!' He turned suddenly. 'And you! Where are your braids?'

'I cut them off.'

'Young savage!'

He was shivering, and now he began to babble. 'When the hag came to me she was beautiful, Master Gwydion. She reminded me of the white lady. The one who stood by the bridge over the Evenlode when we first came into the Wychwoode. You know, the one I asked you about. Why was she weeping?'

Gwydion laid his hands on Will's shoulders, his expression hard to fathom. 'That is the innocent form of her apparition. She weeps for a lost love, for she was driven to madness by a jilting.'

'Who was she?'

'Do you not yet know? Did I not tell you that Lord Strange was once the handsomest of noblemen? Before he became a lord he was the younger son of a noble family that lived many leagues to the north, but being without title he greatly desired advancement. While travelling near Wychwoode he met a beautiful girl called Rowen who lived close by. She was a churl's daughter, a commoner, but she loved John le Strange with all her heart, and she was happy when he promised her they would marry.'

'Do you mean his wife? The lady who taught me to read and write?'

'On the day that everyone expected John le Strange to marry Rowen, he announced that he would marry another. That other is the Lady Strange whom you know. Rowen fell prey to despondency. She allowed herself to sink into madness and wandered the Wychwoode, living in the wild for a year before committing herself to the Evenlode. Now she cannot bear to see others who are in love. It is her delight to lure hopeful young men down to their doom to make them pay for her suffering. And meanwhile Lord Strange's foul betrayal left him open to the spell that holds him in its power. Now do you understand?'

Will nodded. He thought again of the figure in white weeds that he thought he had glimpsed floating in Grendon Pool. 'Now I see why Lord Strange must wear his wedding ring through his nose. He is more cursed than ever I knew.'

'Take this lesson from today – bitter grudges corrode the human spirit, while only forgiveness restores it. The same is true of painful memories.'

Will hurried after the wizard until they regained the forest. Had he been a dog, his tail would have been between his legs. He halted and saw how Gwydion drew apart and flushed the anger out of himself. The wizard became as still as stone before he gathered his powers. Then, holding out his hands in an attitude of appeal he focused a thousand brilliant points of light on himself and called forth a staggering thunderbolt.

It was bluer than the flash of a dragonfly, brighter than the noonday sun. It flashed forth with a bang and burst the dam asunder. Out of the brilliance, a cloud of steam boiled up into the air, and the pent-up waters were suddenly relieved. They raged out for a few moments in a dark flood, then the water was gone and all that remained of the pool was a foetid acre of mud in which ooze-worms wriggled and thrashed.

Will followed, both comforted and cowed by the wizard's overawing presence. He was unwilling to break the silence and was still shocked at what had happened. When he closed his eyes he could see crimson spots that the flash had made. A dozen men could not have dug a hole that big in half a day – it was easy to respect such power, and hard not to fear it.

At the tower moat they were met by a guard of alert soldiers. Some of them started in surprise when they recognized Will's companion. They drew weapons, fearing what they called sorcery. No doubt they had heard the thunderbolt, but Gwydion offered only the same words of greeting he had spoken last time he arrived at their lord's tower. But there was no need for the guard to seek permission to admit them, for both Lord Strange and his lady came to the gate.

Will felt wretched. What on earth had made him cut off his braids? He stood before the severe lord and his retinue, his clothes mud-soaked and his face blotched and bloodied. He had proved himself an oathbreaker and a fool, but at least no one was taking any interest in him. All eyes were upon Gwydion.

'You are welcome, Crowmaster,' Lord Strange said stiffly as he halted.

'Welcome?' Gwydion laid aside all niceties: 'I am unable

to forgive you for what you have allowed here, John le Strange. There is a madness abroad in the Realm. But what madness is it that allows the ruining of an ancient grove while the Lord Warden of Wychwoode sits in his tower, turning a blind eye to all that passes?'

Lord Strange's fearsome face was set, his small, pale eyes unblinking. 'Madness, you say?' he grunted. 'You may count the felling of Grendon Copse a grievous loss, Crowmaster, but it means little to me, for I am unlearned in the matter of trees. I was placed here merely for the sake of the king's convenience, and as you must know – I cannot tell a sacred grove from any other kind.'

'Have you learned so little from your misfortune? Even a fool would know that he had no business allowing the cutting of any of the oaks of Wychwoode. You are making preparations for war.'

Will saw a sneer playing at the corners of Lord Strange's mouth. 'Preparations for war I do not deny. But your memory fails you, Crowmaster, for it was you who brought warning of strife to me. Is it not prudent to stand ready for the blow which you say is coming?'

Gwydion shook his staff and banged its haft into the ground. 'John le Strange! I have known you since you were a babe in arms. Once I had great hopes of you and your line, but you have failed me. That foul mill was stamping out swords long before any news of war was brought here by me. Why have you ignored your duty when the king himself set you to command watch and ward over this ancient wood?'

'I did not ignore my duty,' Lord Strange's snout jutted. He put his hand to his monstrous face as if some part of him wanted to preserve the secret still. Then he wiped the foam from his lips then said in a voice that was barely audible, 'for it was the king himself who ordered Grendon Mill to be built.'

It seemed to Will that, behind his solemnity, Lord Strange was laughing. He looked to Gwydion with alarm. The wizard was barely in control of his displeasure as he said, 'I thank you for that morsel of courage at least, but it would have been better for you had you found your tongue sooner, for now you have presided over the murder of the living heart of Wychwoode. This forest is doomed to fail and never again to be as it was. But know this, John le Strange, the circle of fate turns ever upon itself. By your cowardice and negligence you have tainted yourself. Because of this your blood shall fail as the forest green fails. Your firstborn shall be a girlchild, and all who follow shall be girlchildren likewise. Unless you purify your heart of greed and ambition, you will have no son, and your title and worldly wealth will pass to the son of another. I bid you think on that in my absence.'

Gwydion turned away. He was going from a lord's presence without dismissal, which was a great slight, but the curse had stunned everyone, and there was not a soldier in the Realm who dared lay hands upon a wizard.

The guards fell back as Gwydion swept from the scene. Will followed, hoping that the wizard's power would see them safely away from the tower. Whatever happened, it seemed that a dismal shadow had been cast over the future of John, Lord Strange, and that he would not let it go. But, despite the unbearable tension Will felt between his shoulder blades, no call to arms was made, and no order to loose an arrow was given.

'This is bad, very bad,' Gwydion muttered as they passed from view.

'What is?' Will asked, looking over his shoulder again.

'Lord Strange is the gauge that shows the prevailing temper of the nobility. He has grown worse these last few months, I think. And that worries me.'

And now that Will thought about it, perhaps Lord Strange had indeed become more pig-like of late. Seeing him every day might have masked slow changes that were stealing over him.

'If the spell's getting worse, why don't you take it off him?'

'How little you know,' the wizard said, and walked on in silence for a while, but then he added, 'John le Strange was once the handsomest of men. Both his vanity and his ambition laid him open to magical attack. The spell he labours under was not put on him by me, but by Maskull. My ingenious enemy wished to make of Lord Strange a gauge with which he might test the governance of the Realm.'

'I don't understand.'

'Friend John does not know it, but his appearance follows – and depends upon – the state of corruption of his peers. Is that simple enough for you?'

Will scratched his head. 'Do you mean, the worse his fellow lords behave the uglier Lord Strange becomes?'

Gwydion nodded. 'Exactly!'

'Well, you could've said that in the first place! That's nasty.'

'It is a cruel and clever spell, is it not? And all the more cruel for the Hogshead himself already has the means to set it aside – if he did but realize it.'

Will blinked. 'Do you mean that?'

'All he has to do is attend to his own duties selflessly and in good conscience. That would break Maskull's spell-hold over him.'

'You mean, if he started being a little less greedy then he'd start looking less ugly again?' Will blew out a breath. 'But, why didn't you tell him that?'

'Because Maskull's spells are rarely simple. There is a stubborn protection that binds this curse. It makes all assistance deadly to the victim. Did I not say that the spell was constructed by an ingenious enemy? John le Strange must release himself, and I have gone as far as I dare in pointing him in the right direction. If I, or anyone else, were to tell him what to do, then he would die.' The wizard looked back. 'Friend John was sent here to keep him out of sight – sent by one who could not stand to see their own failings portrayed in his features. Unfortunately, ambition convinced him that the only way back from exile is to help the king's weapon-maker.'

The idea that had been forming in Will's mind sought release. 'Is the king a bad man, then?'

'The king himself is a gentle spirit. It is those who surround him whom we must worry about.'

They went on in silence as Will digested the wizard's words, and soon they had passed fully into the forest's green embrace. Then Gwydion produced a bag from the folds of his robes which he gave Will to carry.

'What's this?'

'It is my crane bag, made long ago from the skin of a large wading bird that once lived in the West. The bag is of small size, but you will find it is of surprising capacity. It contains all needful things for the wayfarer. And whatever you put inside, it will always weigh the same.'

Will took it. 'Then I suppose it must be magical.'

'There is a very considerable spell upon it.'

He hefted it dubiously. 'You don't carry much else that's made of leather.'

'I do not like to kill my friends for the use of their hides. What would you say if you knew that a book had been bound in skin cut from a dead person's back? Would you read it?'

'Urgh! No!'

'You may make a face, but that is so with some manuals of sorcery and star lore. However, the hide of this bag is quite different. It was sloughed and shed long ago, when the crane, whose name was Aoife, returned to human form.'

The wizard said no more about that, and Will lapsed into silence too. He began thinking about Willow, appalled now at the way he had endangered her. What if she had been taken by the hag? What if he had seen her body, white and bloodless, at the bottom of the pool when the waters had drained away? It was too horrible. Magic, as the Wise

Woman had said, was mostly about consequences. Harnessing the power was the easy part, what was difficult was managing what happened as a result.

The more he thought about Willow the more heartsick he felt. He had so wanted her to come, but now he would never even know if she had agreed. He wanted to have the chance to explain. He wanted it so much that it hurt to think about it. He tried to put her out of his mind, but there was something that the wizard had said that would not let his thoughts rest – he had said that the hag could not bear to see others who were in love . . .

Might that mean he was in love with Willow? And might it mean Willow was in love with him too?

The idea excited him mightily. He was considering whether he could ask Gwydion about it when the wizard halted and thrust out a hand.

'Did you feel that?'

'Feel what?' He felt only a breeze that shivered the birch leaves.

The wizard braced himself and looked around, as if he expected some great beast to leap from the forest and try to tear him to pieces.

'Feel what, Master Gwydion?'

'A passing danger . . . but we are not its target.'

'But what was it?' Will asked suspiciously. 'I saw nothing. I felt nothing. I never do.'

'That is merely your inexperience. But one day soon, I think, you will begin to feel the warning of such threats.'

Will touched the other's sleeve. 'Master Gwydion, why do you say I'm a Child of Destiny?'

The wizard decided it was safe to go on, then for once he deigned to answer directly. 'Because, if I am correct about you, according to prophecy one day you will stand at the crossroads, at the place where the future of the world will be decided.'

'What prophecy?' he said, fully alert now. 'Tell me.'

The wizard's half-smile faded. 'Have you ever heard the name "Arthur"?'

'You mean like Great Arthur? The king of olden days?'

'Olden days. Well perhaps those days seem olden to you. What do you know about him?'

'Only what the stories say.' Will tried to recall what he had been told, but realized his knowledge was scant. 'Arthur lived long ago, just a little time after the Slavers left the Realm. It was a time of war and so he found a sword in a stone and . . . and when he pulled it out that made him king. And then he had a big, round table made out of a dozen different trees in Waincaister, and his knights came and ate their dinners at it . . . and . . .'

'And?'

'Well . . . he fought battles and always won, except for the last one, because he got shot in the eye with an arrow. But before he died he had to give his sword back to a lady who lived in the pond. And . . .'

The wizard seemed amused. 'Oh, is that what happened?'

Will shrugged. 'So the stories that I've heard say. I'm sure there's more, but I can't remember it all. Valesmen add their own parts to a tale every time they tell it, so the stories about Arthur the King, which were always our favourites, got more mixed up than most. I've heard them told all ways around and can't rightly say what's true.'

'Then I shall have to tell you how it was. Great Arthur was the hundred-and-first king of the line of Brea. He succeeded his father when he was but thirteen years of age, and he lived a most extraordinary life. But you know, his strange fate was hardly that of a mortal king, for he was in truth nothing of the sort.'

'You once said there was no such thing as immortals.'

'Oh, Arthur was not immortal. He was the second coming of a king of old, one who reigned in the time of the First Men, the same who swore to protect these isles in time of peril. What you were told about in Valesmen's stories was Arthur's *second* coming, which was prophesied and watched over by one who then called himself Master Merlyn. But you are right about the manner in which Arthur's kingship was confirmed. When he was just thirteen he drew the hallowed sword Branstock from a stone, which is one of the signs that were to be watched for.'

'Calibor!' Will said. 'I remember King Arthur's sword was called Calibor!'

But Gwydion, who had been watching him carefully, shook his head. 'No, that was much later. The Lady of the Lake granted Arthur a sword called Carabur. But the sword he drew from the stone was quite different. That was called Branstock. And it was one of the Four Hallows of the Realm.'

Will put a hand to his mouth thoughtfully. He had the feeling that something was dimly familiar. 'The Four Hallows . . .' he whispered. 'Wand, sword, cup and pentacle!'

'Now, how could you know that, I wonder?' the wizard asked, very satisfied.

'I don't know . . . I . . .' Will shook his head as if trying to clear it. 'Tilwin! Of course! He brought cards to the Vale and taught me to play.'

'And have you heard of the Sceptre, the Sword of State, the Ampulla and the Crown?'

'No.'

'They are four items of regalia that represent the Hallows when a king is crowned. These four objects must be present at each royal coronation. Unless they are, no man may call himself king. But they are not the real Hallows. Those were once lodged deep underground. In ancient times they resided together in a vault in the Realm Below. The first is the Sword of Might, called Branstock. The second is the Staff of Justice. The third is the Cauldron of Plenty, and the last—'

'And the last is a star.'

'The last is the Star of Annuin. Tell me, how did you know that?'

He shook his head. 'I . . .' His fears suddenly overflowed. He swallowed hard and looked up. 'Master Gwydion, has this got something to do with me being a Child of Destiny, because if it has then a big mistake has been—'

The wizard held up a hand. 'In the same way that King Arthur's second coming was prophesied in the Black Book, so also was another's.'

Will felt another current of fear run through him. 'Whose?'

The wizard looked away. 'It may be that it was yours. What do you think of that?'

Will tried to laugh. 'Mine? But that's – that's silly!'

'Is it? Why do you think I saw to it that you were saved from harm and cared for by loving parents, hmmm? Why do you think I made sure you were brought to adulthood in the carefree bosom of the Vale? That place has long been under my magical cloak, for if you were the Child of Destiny, then you had to be preserved from Maskull. Now do you see? You must be properly prepared to fulfil your destiny.'

The idea was vast, terrible. He wanted to hide from it. 'But . . . but what if I don't want to be *prepared*?'

'It does not much matter what you want. You must be. That is one of my tasks. And it seems to me there is still plenty to be made of you.'

'What does the prophecy say?' he asked, dazed.

'As with all prophecies, the wording is far from clear. It speaks mistily, of "one being made two" and other notions that are hard to fathom.'

Will felt heartsick. 'But it *can't* be anything to do with me!'

'Ah! A further proof.'

'*What*?'

'The prophecy says you would deny yourself thrice. That is the second time you have done so.'

'But I'm not denying myself!'

'And that sounds like a third denial to me.' Gwydion glanced at him critically. 'Still, Lord Strange and his lady have not accomplished as much as I had hoped with you. You have yet the bare means to gain knowledge which is needful, for no man can truly call himself a man until he has stocked his head with a goodly measure of knowledge. You are still far from being sufficiently taught. I think perhaps you need—'

He halted suddenly again and threw out a staying hand. Will froze, then they crouched down together behind a stand of saplings. But nothing showed itself, and the afternoon sun filtered through the leaves until all was still and sleepy again.

'What was it?' Will whispered at last. 'Something evil?'

Gwydion turned, frowning, light upon his feet. 'I have asked you not to use that word. It makes for loose thinking.'

'Then tell me what you felt.'

'A danger. A shadow . . . some piece of malice in hiding. Or so it seemed for a moment.'

'Do you mean Maskull?'

'It felt somewhat like his dirty magic. But perhaps I was mistaken – ah, look there!'

The wizard drew the split hazel wand from his sleeve and began to test the ground ahead. He went on a few paces and pointed his staff at a partly overgrown track that drove through the forest like a green tunnel. It was too wide to jump across, and paved with stones so that its way was clear, for no trees grew along the line where the close-set slabs had been laid. It looked as if it had not been used in a great many years, but still it was a better-made road than any that Will had ever seen.

'If you would know a little of what you call evil, Willand, then mark this scar upon the land.'

'It's a fine path made of stones, Master Gwydion,' Will said, staring up and down it. He wondered where it came from and where it went.

'Do not admire it! It is the Akemain, a Slaver road! Slave-built, laid here long ages ago by a sorcerer's empire. Its main purpose was to take armies of foot soldiers across the land as fast as could be. It was built to aid in the work of murder and the holding down of the people.'

'Sorry.' He scuffed at the grass with his toes. 'Where does it go?'

'It runs fifty leagues and more east to west. And there are many other such slave roads that defile the land in like manner. See how it goes straight and takes no heed of hill or dale? Mark that arrogance well, Willand! For the stones of this long street and others like it have ever been an insult to the earth and are the present bane of our Realm.'

'How so?' asked Will stepping into the middle of it. 'It's just an old stone road.'

'You will learn soon enough what it truly means. Come! Do not stand upon it!'

As he hurried on, the ancient road faded quickly from his mind, and little more passed between them until at last they came to the southern edge of the Wychwoode.

It was a hot and close afternoon, but a change came into the air as the sun reddened and the evening became golden. They were once more among open fields. Gwydion avoided the places where folk might be found, meandering instead through woods and along overgrown paths, and as they crossed over a small stream the wizard asked about the lessons the Wise Woman had told him, and what manner of magic he thought he had learned from her.

Will repeated the first of the Wise Woman's lessons, but then he could not help but admit to having read the book of beasts in which the spells had been written.

'I know I shouldn't have,' he said lamely. 'I know that now.'

'And doubtless you did at the time too. Tell me, were there any words written on the front cover of the book?'

Will nodded. 'A few. But I couldn't read them in the ordinary way.'

'The words were most probably, *Ane radhas a'leguim oicheamna; ainsagimn deo teuiccimn.* That is the true tongue.'

Will marvelled. 'The sound of it rings pleasantly in my ears.'

'It is a very ancient way of speech, the words the First Men learned from the fae. They cause a mighty hunger in the head, do they not? That is why you must take care when speaking the true tongue, for it is the language of stones and it has great power. Now tell me what else the Wise Woman taught you.'

While Will recalled all he could, the wizard nodded or stroked his beard, but he asked no more questions and gave no rebukes, for which Will was grateful. At last Gwydion said, 'Say after me: *Fiel ean mail arh an mailor treas.*'

Will tried. Then he tried again. And then he tried a third time to get the sound just right, and at last Gwydion smiled.

'There!'

'What does it mean?'

'You have spoken the Rede of the Three-fold Way in the true tongue.'

Will smiled back, pleased. 'That was easy.'

'Easy enough for some. But heed me well: magic must always be requested and never summoned. Always respect it, and never treat it with disdain. And when you ask, ask openly and honestly, for the honest man alone has the right to speak the words of power.'

By now they had come to a river bank, and Will saw a small standing stone sticking up out of the grassy bank.

Gwydion said, 'Come here and put down the crane bag.'

Once more, Will did as he was told, and the wizard made him jump up and sit on the stone. 'Do not be afraid. This little stone is called Taynton Sarsen. It is as benign as your own Tarry Stone. It marks an important ancient crossing point over the stream.' He took from his pouch a piece of flint so sharp at the edge that it could have been used to shave with.

'What are you going to do with that?' Will asked, eyeing the flint uncertainly.

'Give you a beggar's head.'

'What?'

The wizard tested the edge of the flint, then began to cut off locks of Will's hair. 'Hold still. The place where your braids used to hang looks like a half-harvested wheatfield and we can't have that.'

Will screwed up his face but endured the indignity and when at last he put a hand to his head he found his hair was no more than half a finger's length all over, and tussocky. He ruffled it and followed the wizard, picking up a stick on the way. 'Why did you cut my hair?'

'It is a disguise.'

'It's not much of one.'

'It will serve to confound those who have been sent to make report on you.'

Will felt renewed anxiety cramp his stomach. 'People sent by Maskull, do you mean?'

'It is not unusual for him to have me watched when he can get news of my whereabouts. It is likely we are being watched now, for he certainly knows my bag-carrier was lodged in the Wychwoode.'

Will's anxiety turned to alarm. 'He found out about me?'

Gwydion smiled. 'I made sure of it.'

'You mean, you told him?'

'I made sure Maskull found out that I had brought an unsatisfactory apprentice lad to Lord Strange's tower for a summer of correction.'

'Wasn't that dangerous?'

'Of course. But far less dangerous than if I had not done so. You see, Maskull does not know who you are. He will dismiss the detail from his thoughts, and once dismissed it will stay dismissed.'

'I hope so.'

'He believes I am a coward. He cannot bring himself to believe that I would dare bring the one spoken of in prophecy into plain view, for were he in my place he would certainly have kept you locked away in a fortress of spells. Be warned, Maskull wants very much to find the prophesied one, and if ever he decided that you were he, then . . .' The wizard's words petered out and he made a lethal gesture.

Will passed a hand over his throat and looked around uncomfortably. Fresh fears bubbled up inside him. It was terrifying to think that his survival now depended on his being mistaken for his own decoy. 'Where are we going?'

'You'll know that when we get there.'

'Well . . . how far is it?'

'About as far as it is to Nempnett Thrubwell.'

Will gave a hard, frustrated sigh. 'Oh, Master Gwydion, why will you never tell me where I came from and what is to become of me?'

'As to the first, I do not know. And I have already told you the second – you are going to be taught.'

'Taught what?'

'What the world is truly like.'

Will snorted. 'Who can know what the world is truly like?'

Gwydion tapped his nose with a forefinger. 'Ah! The world is the sum of what men believe it to be. Now, that is deep wisdom, if you did but know it.'

He liked the idea. 'Do you mean that if most men thought the sky was green and the grass was blue then they would be?'

The wizard smiled. 'Willand, I mean precisely that.'

'Is that why magic is leaving the world? Because people are stopping believing in it?'

Gwydion's eyebrows lifted. 'Why, Willand, you surprise me! That is a very interesting question. Indeed, there is an important rede that says, "Magic alters" and another that says, "Magic to him who magic thinks".'

Will swished at the dust with the stick. 'But what I really want to know is why did Maskull put that spell on Lord Strange if he's not an evil sorcerer?'

Gwydion picked his way towards a mass of brambles. 'Three steps forward, two steps back. How easily you use the word "evil", Willand. Where did the idea come from in the first place?'

'I don't know.' He shrugged and pushed the spiky briars aside with his stick. 'Isn't it right? To use the word "evil", sometimes. I mean, surely Maskull is evil, even though he may not know it.'

'"Evil" is a dangerous idea to have in your head if you wish to understand magic properly. Each of us carries tremendous power for the doing of what you unthinkingly call "good" and "evil".' He drew a deep breath. 'I suppose you ought to be given instruction about this, though you hardly seem ripe for it.'

Will wrinkled his nose at that. 'I don't want to know.'

Gwydion stopped dead and turned so that the charms which hung inside his shirt clattered together. 'Is that truly so? Make no mistake, people are forestalled or led on by knowledge – and by the lack of it. I must be careful what I reveal to you, and what I hide. You must be taught. You must be prepared. But I must not fill your head with so much that your essential nature is altered. Do you see?'

Will thought about that as they followed the banks of the river. The sky deepened and the brighter stars began to appear. Before night fell fully, they camped. Gwydion picked a place close to running water and in the lee of a hill. He danced earth magic around his chosen spot, then produced a cooking pot that was heavier when taken from the crane bag than the bag was with the pot and all its other contents put together.

'What's this pot made from?' Will said feeling the weight. 'Some kind of stone?'

'Correct. That is *cleberkh*, or loomlode as some say, a kind of stone found in the Isles of the Sword, a place that lies beyond even the Orcas in the Far North. At first the stone is soft enough to shape, but the more you cook with it the harder it gets.' Gwydion took out a patched brown travelling cloak much like his own. 'And this is for you. It will help you to sleep.'

He took out a slate blade and cut a yard square in the grass, made nine turfs of it and stacked them up. Then he gathered twigs into the hole and whispered a merry fire into being. In the pot he made a thick, savoury broth in which pieces of roasted vegetable floated. Will could not tell if it was done by magic or the brown powder the wizard spilled into the mix, but the soup tasted wonderfully flavoursome.

As the flames of the fire died down Gwydion lay back and searched the sky.

'What are you looking for?' Will asked. 'A sign?'

'I am simply marvelling.'

Gwydion told him how the dome of the sky was very far away, and how tiny windows in the dome let through the light of the great furnace that was the Beyond. 'Those windows,' he said, 'are the stars.'

'And shooting stars?' Will asked. 'What are they?'

'The Beyond is a place of unimaginable brightness. There are fireballs with hearts of iron that perpetually crash against the outer dome of the sky. Sometimes one of them falls down through a star window. That is what we call a shooting star.'

'A shooting star.' Will echoed. He stretched out his hand in wonder. 'Can a person ever touch the sky?'

He continued to stare at the vast, eerie dome, but soon his eyelids grew heavy and moments later he was asleep.

CHAPTER SEVEN

LAMMASTIDE

They rose early, just before dawn. Gwydion turned about on his heels, tasting the air warily until he was sure that no danger had been laid for them. Then he danced and paced and danced a little more. He spoke words to himself until it seemed to Will that a billowing net of blue gossamer came into being around their sleeping place. As Gwydion spoke, the light was drawn down to his hands and vanished inside him. Then, as if nothing had happened, he raked the ashes out of the fire and scattered them about, while seeming to thank the grass for having made them welcome. Will watched with raised eyebrows.

'And now we must remake the ground,' Gwydion told him. 'Do you want to do it?'

He shrugged, feeling a little foolish. 'What should I do?'

He was told to replace the turfs just as they had been before, and ritually water them. This he did, not really knowing how ritual watering differed from pouring the jug out over the ground, but Gwydion seemed to approve his actions, and when all was done and the ground looked almost as if they had never come this way, they set off.

'What were you doing before?' Will asked.

'I was dancing back the magic that I laid forth last night as our protection.'

'Against Maskull?'

'Against all harm.'

Will's heart felt suddenly leaden. 'Why does Maskull want to kill the one spoken about in the Black Book?'

'Because he was ". . . born of Strife, born of Calamity . . . born at Beltane in the Twentieth Year . . . when the beams of Eluned are strongest".'

Will tried to be withering. 'I suppose that's meant to tell me everything.'

'Perhaps it does not make much sense to you, but Maskull knows that the prophesied one will eventually stand between him and that which he most desires.'

'And what's that?'

'To be the one who chooses the direction of the future.'

'Well, I'll not stand in his way. He can do what he likes with the future for all I care!'

The wizard smiled knowingly. 'If you are the one, then you will eventually confound him. This he knows, and knowing it he cannot rest.'

'And because Maskull is your enemy too, you've become my friend. Is that it?' he said gloomily. It felt like he had been caught between gigantic forces, and that they were fast closing on him.

But the wizard smiled another wistful smile and shook his head. 'I see that you doubt my sincerity, Willand. But I was a friend to you long before I suspected whom you might be.'

They continued south, skirting villages and avoiding the most well-travelled roads. They kept off the fields where golden grain awaited harvest, and Will enjoyed the walking. After weeks of homesickness and stifling study in the tower he felt truly free at last. Still, the wizard's words had unsettled him more than a little.

He took his knife, went to the hedge and cut a bough

from the blackthorn. It was an arm's length from end to end and two fingers around. As Gwydion looked on he began stripping it of twigs and bark, shaping the torn end into a handle, the other into a point. But he felt ever more uncomfortable as he worked, for Gwydion's eyes rested upon him and at length he stopped and looked up. 'Is there anything amiss, Master Gwydion?'

'What is it you are at, lad?'

'Just carving a new stick for walking.'

'Blackthorn is a good choice. Like ash, fine wood for tool handles, a wood that is strong and dense.'

Will smiled back, encouraged.

'But you neglected to ask first if the blackthorn minded.'

'Should I have done that?'

'It would have been the polite thing to do.'

Will looked at his stick, confused. It was just a stick. 'Do you mean I should have asked forgiveness of a *bush*?'

'Not forgiveness, Will.' Gwydion's voice grew mellow. 'Permission.'

'But surely a bush couldn't hear what I said to it.'

'That is quite true. But also quite beside the point. One day you will understand. Meanwhile, tell me: are you versed in any weapon?'

'Only the quarterstaff, Master Gwydion.'

'In the wider world it is important you know how to protect yourself. When next you cut yourself a quarterstaff, make it as long as you are. And remember that you will double its strength if you give thanks for it beforehand.'

Will narrowed his eyes at the wizard. 'They say a quarterstaff is always to be preferred to a sword, but I can't see how that can be true.'

'Can't you?' Gwydion opened his crane bag and drew out an impossibly long staff. 'No swordsman, no matter how fine his weapon, can hurt you if he cannot reach you. You need only learn how a suitable distance may be kept.'

Suddenly Gwydion rose up and danced, stroking the staff about him in eye-fooling twists and thrusts, then, equally suddenly, he halted, pushed the staff back into the crane bag and motioned him to follow on.

'That was amazing!' Will said. 'You moved the staff so fast I could hardly see it!'

'Practice, as the rede says, maketh perfect.'

They pressed on across a river, the broadest yet, which they crossed easily by walking ankle-deep across an eel weir. Will dogged Gwydion's steps three paces behind until, as night fell, they came near to a barn. Gwydion made it safe by crumbling bread crusts in the corners and dancing out an eerie-sounding protection. But for half the night Will lay awake in the straw, listening to every sound. He curled himself tighter in his nest and did not have the courage even to wake the wizard, but in the morning he made his admission.

'Master Gwydion, I heard noises last night. I thought they must be Maskull's spies.'

'I heard them too.'

'You did?' His eyes widened. 'Then I was right?'

'Oh, indeed. They were spies. Three of them, in fact. All in brown velvet coats. All about *this* long.' He placed his hands a little way apart.

Will tutted. 'Rats?'

'Rats. Exceptional creatures. They were looking out for our safety as I asked them.'

With the dawning of the day they went down into the village of Uff, and Will saw the Blowing Stone. It turned out to be only a great block with three holes in it that stood in the yard of the village alehouse. 'It is played like a stone flute every second year,' Gwydion said. 'It calls men to the Scouring. Do not hang back from it, it is not a battlestone, nor anything to be afraid of.'

'Scouring? What's that?'

'You will know all about that by the end of Lammas.'

All that morning while the wizard talked with the villagers, Will waited and waited. The wizard was well liked in Uff, and well used to tarrying there, for it was horse country and he seemed greatly fond of horses. Word soon got about that a famous horse leech had come into the village. Food and cider were brought out for him, but he gave both to Will to offset his fears and forestall his impatience. And after so much cheese and bread and a quart of best apple dash to wash it down, Will lay in a corner and did not get up again until a goodly while had passed.

'When are we going to leave?' he asked Gwydion, feeling more than a little wretched and dry in the throat. 'I thought you wanted to get along, yet you've nearly wasted the whole day.'

'And lying dead drunk on your back all day is wasting nothing at all, I suppose?' the wizard said, ruffling the mane of a fine, white horse.

'Come on, Master Gwydion. You know what I mean.' He rubbed his arms and looked around unhappily. 'Maskull.'

'But first things first. You must learn patience, and understand that old debts must always be paid. Anyway, we cannot go on more urgently if we are to spend Lammas night on the Dragon's Mound. Behold this mare, Willand. Is she not the very image of Arondiel?'

'Who?'

'Have you not heard tales of Arondiel, the steed of Epona?'

When the villagers overheard Gwydion's remark they began to grin and clap their hands as if the wizard had conferred some deep and secret honour upon them. Will had never been told who Arondiel was, nor Epona, though for some reason he had the unshakable idea in his mind that the latter was a great lady who had lived hereabouts long ago. He did not know why, but her name made him think of white horses and a queen of old who delighted to feed her favourite mount apples . . .

He started. 'Hey! Master Gwydion! What's that about a "Dragon's Mound"? You can't trick me like that!'

But the wizard was too busy appreciating horseflesh to pay him much heed. 'There is no cause to worry, Willand,' he said lightly. 'It's just the name of a little hill near here. You will like the place, I think.'

When Gwydion finally took his leave and called Will onward, he said, 'They are faithful folk hereabouts who know their horses. There is a bond between us that I would not deny for they have kept to the Old Ways more than most.'

They pressed on southward through what remained of the day, and soon came to the foot of a ridge that rose up green and round out of the haze. It took longer than Will expected to reach, so that just as the sun was beginning to sink into the west they came to a halt under a great swell of sheep-cropped land.

Gwydion was delighted. 'This is a very special place,' he said.

'But are we going to be safe here?'

'We can do no better than to camp here tonight.'

He led Will up a curious little conical hill and showed him how the flattened top gave a fine view to the north of the plain across which they had walked. The hill stood below a fold of the ridge which blotted out the prospect to the south. Directly below them an arm of flat land swept interestingly halfway around the hill and into a dead-end, while on the other side a well-worn path meandered up into a fold of the scarp as if it was taking the easiest way up to higher ground. It seemed a most ancient place.

Will breathed deep and decided that anyone with both a heart and a head would know that this place was very special, but as he looked up to the south-east he saw a shape cut high on the ridge which put its uniqueness beyond all doubt. Above the path was a strange set of curves, shapes cut out of the turf so that the white chalk underneath showed through. The slope of the land foreshortened the figure somewhat, but the white lines flowed around one another in the unmistakable shape of a horse.

'Behold, Arondiel!' Gwydion exclaimed. 'Is she not most beautiful to your eye?'

Will was awed by the figure. 'She's wonderful!'

'Look upon her with respect, for she is the oldest form made by the hand of man that you have yet seen in the land. On yonder plains there once grew great orchards where a powerful queen once reigned. She rode yearly to this place upon a white mare. Men have been coming up from the village of Uff every second year for thousands of years to keep Arondiel alive. This is the Scouring of which I spoke. Were it not for that effort of care, Arondiel would have vanished under the encroaching grass long ago, and we would all be the worse for that.'

'But what is she?' he asked, staring at the figure like one who finds himself suddenly unable to remember something important.

'She is both a sign to read and a spirit guardian. Some see in her form the idea "horse". What do you see?'

'She looks like a horse to me too,' Will agreed. 'But maybe . . .' He shaded his eyes and studied the figure a moment longer. 'I think that if she's a word she isn't "horse", but rather "gallop", or maybe "speed".'

Gwydion beamed. 'Ah, Willand! How easily you prove yourself again!'

'What do you mean?'

'I mean you are more in tune with the spirit of this sacred place than I had dared to hope. You will be very safe here tonight. Speed! Her name means speed! And such a form as hers cannot be cut in these latter times, for though this is a land of many horses, there are no longer men who know how to draw lines like this upon the land.'

The gift that Gwydion had taken when they left the village was a loaf of new-baked bread. For this was Lammastide, also called in the Vale 'the festival of loaves', the day when the first ripe grain was cut and threshed, ground and baked into bread, all in the space of a day. This was ritual bread-making, a solemn and sacred duty, and done to mark the bounty of the earth. A time to give thanks to the land, and for folk to count their blessings.

They climbed the flat-topped hill and munched their bread, and it seemed to Will that the taste of it was as good as any food he had ever eaten. Festive bonfires burned red across the plains of the old Kingdom of Wesset to the north. As darkness deepened, folk would be attending each of those fires, toasting bread on long forks. There would be butter and honey for the children, and much ale drunk and many songs sung. They sat together and talked far into the night and Will felt himself to be closer to Gwydion than ever before. Tonight the wizard seemed joyous and wonderfully wise and very pleased to be here. He spoke much about history, showing Will to the very the spot where, almost a thousand years before, Great Arthur had stood to address his assembled troops.

The wizard said quietly. 'Shall I tell you the name of this hill in the true tongue? It is "Dumhacan Nadir".'

Will repeated the words as if he half recognized them. '"Dumhacan Nadir" – the Dragon's Mound.'

'You have not slept upon a dragon's mound before, I think. Nor shall you again for a very long time.'

Will patted the ground under him in wonder – there was something too regular about this mound for it to be a natural hill, and nearby was an odd bare patch of chalk, a part where the grass would not grow.

'Flenir was the greatest of the great dragons of old, the

most famous in the land. Huge and fierce was he, the "winged beast with breath of flame" of which many tales were told and many songs sung in a time long before the establishment of the Realm. For long years did Flenir misuse this land, preying upon sheep and cattle across the domain of Angnor. Any man unwary enough to be caught in the open at his approach would be torn to pieces like a mouse caught in the talons of an eagle. Flenir would breakfast in a place near here – it is still called Wormhill Bottom – and when he had rent enough flesh from bone he would return to his lair to lie. The top of his mound is flat because Flenir was accustomed to rest here, rubbing his great red belly free of the lice that clung to it. All dragons had lice, Willand, and dragon lice were as big as a man's hand. In daylight you can see the groove where Flenir wrapped his tail around the mound, and if you look carefully down there you might discover the entrance he used, though it has long since been sealed. It is said that one day, while flying over Angnor, Flenir saw the figure of Arondiel and became enamoured of it. That is why he made his mound here. Though other tales say the site was chosen only out of jealousy.'

Will looked down into the darkness below. 'I think a dragon would have found this a perfect place to launch himself into the air.'

'That much is certain.'

Will scuffed at the turf with his toes. 'So was there once a great treasure buried under here?'

'There was, for as you know the great dragons were like magpies. They would collect any trinket that glittered. They coveted bright metal for its own sake and would always try to make a hoard of it. But in the end Flenir did not much like the bright bronze blade that was forged up on yonder ridge, for that was his bane.'

Will thought of those brilliant, ancient days, all long gone now and impossibly heroic. But what kind of heroes did the world have now? Men who wore the heads of pigs, and lords whose own increasing greed showed in the Hogshead. A shiver passed through him as he sat there, and thoughts of home began to crowd in on him. His fingers went to the greenstone talisman that hung at his neck, and he remembered the song that Valesmen used to sing every year called the Wyrm Charm. Last year it had been Eldmar's turn to sing it. The moment had come when they had all raised their hot, steaming dragon soup together and supped off the flavoursome liquor, then Eldmar had raised his voice and led the others through the verses.

Will felt a tear come to the corner of his eye. He sniffed, fighting the sadness away, knowing very well that it was no use pining for home now. He stood up and went to stand alone and a feeling of such strangeness came over him then that his eyes rolled up into his head and his hands went deathly cold and it was as if all the world was melting away before him. And when he opened his eyes he saw a ghostly army of ten thousand filling the space below, and he knew they were gathering here before starting their heroes' march to Badon Hill where great deeds of war would soon be accomplished.

He saw them clear as day, saw their burnished war gear, watched them shake the charms on their spearheads and clash their spearshafts against shields that bore the device of the hawk. He saw their faces, and heard them raise such a shout that it echoed across a forsaken land like rolling thunder. And he stared back, enthralled, standing at the edge, lifting up his arms, to shout in reply, '*Anh farh bouaidan! An ger bouaidhane!*'

Then Gwydion's arms were instantly around him, and the echoes were rolling around the hill as he shook himself out of the vision and when he came to himself he was cold as death and he could still hear the horns of Elfland faintly blowing.

'Where am I?' he said, falling.

The wizard drew him back from the edge. 'Do not sit here. Do you see how it is bare of grass? That is where dragon's blood once was spilt. Nothing has grown here since.'

He staggered in the wizard's arms as vague fears flashed through him. For a moment he wondered if he had unleashed some unnamed peril upon them, but when he looked up at the sky, only the cold stars shone down, pitiless as the glint in a dragon's eye.

His words came all in a rush. 'Master Gwydion, let me go home. I can't be this Child of Destiny you've been looking for, really I—'

'Easy, lad. The Rede of Foolishness says, "Talk not about things whereof you know nothing." You are what you are. Stop fighting yourself.'

For a moment Gwydion's answer put a stone in his heart, but then he saw a shooting star flare and its beauty so moved him that he wept. The wizard laid a comforting arm across his shoulders and Will leaned against him and soon he began to drowse. It seemed he had been sleeping half the night when he woke up with a start to find that all was still and silent. Gwydion was nowhere to be seen, so he got up and began to look around. This time he was careful to respect the bare patch as if it was a gravestone. He walked around the top of the hill, telling himself not to worry, then he stumbled over something hard and sharp that was half buried in the grass.

When he knelt down to try to discover what it was, it felt cold to his fingers, like metal, and as he scraped the hard earth from around it he saw that it was curved, a metal rim – like the edge of a goblet – sticking out of the ground.

The more he scraped the freer the goblet became, until he was able to pull it out. Then he saw it was no goblet at all, but a horn, clogged with earth, the silverwork upon it battered and tarnished black but a horn all the same. It was not the sort that shepherds blew, but the kind warriors winded to send a warning clear across a valley. Even in the starlight he could see there were words cut in the metal.

He knocked the dirt out of it and tucked it into his bundle. Then, with a heavy sigh, he lay down to sleep.

The next day they travelled onward, following the meandering path that climbed up the ridge. They passed a great bank of bracken that was overgrown with bindweed. It parted before Gwydion's steps, and the many pale pink flowers closed up and seemed to nod respectfully as he climbed up between them. Will saw revealed another ancient earth enclosure much like the one in which they had rested on their way to the Wychwoode. This ruin was round in form, and Gwydion said it was the remains of a *burgh*, a dwelling camp, built in a time when all men raised their homes in timber and thatch and did not arrogantly root out the bones of the earth for the sake of vanity.

'They used only those stones which the earth itself offered up. A great gate once stood here. How wondrously worked were the timbers of that camp, how great the magic knotted into its carven beams. But great though the ancient camps were, all of them fell easily to the iron-girt invader.' Gwydion's eyes flashed. 'There was no defence against Slaver steel and Slaver sorcery once the Isles were betrayed. The Slavers were the beginning of the darkness that has ever since shadowed this land. I do not say such a thing easily, but I would that Gruech had never lived!'

'Gruech? Who's he?'

'A foul traitor! One whose bones lie in a dusty cave far away.' Gwydion grunted. 'Let me tell you how it was: King Hely reigned forty-four years, longer than any king of the line of Brea since Dunval the Great, and his first son was called Ludd. When Ludd became king, he rebuilt Trinovant, the city that Brea had founded near a thousand years before. So great were King Ludd's works that the city was renamed Caer Ludd, in his honour, but on his death the name Trinovant was taken up again. Ludd's body was interred in one of the great gates of the city that bears his name – Luddsgate. It was I who gave his funeral oration, and at that time I made known certain truths that disqualified Ludd's son, Androg, from the kingship.

'This was well done, for Androg was possessed of a weak spirit, and four years after Ludd's death, during the reign of his brother Caswalan, there turned out to be much work for a strong leader. The mighty power from the East that we called "the Slavers" first invaded the Isles. They claimed they had come on the Day of Auspices, one thousand years to the day since the landing in the Isles of the hero Brea. By this boast they sought to terrify the people, for Iuliu, the captain-general of the Slaver army, was a famous seer and he had said that the line of Brean kings could stand only so long.

'But our bards sang well their histories in reply. They countered that the true Day of Auspices must already have passed unmarked during the reign of King Hely, and Iuliu's prediction was therefore false. Thus were our warriors heartened, and afterwards they scorned the claims of the enemy, even when what they said was true. Now as the first Slaver foot stepped upon shingle shore, the lorc awakened. It happened exactly as the fae had always intended it should. Soon a great battle was fought, and one of Ludd's younger brothers, Neni, who was a master of many arts, fought bravely against the Slaver armies that day, though in the end he paid dearly for his enterprise. The Slavers were setting camp on the banks of the River Iesis when the great clash came. Neni's men rushed upon them and he himself captured the Slaver sorcerer's sword, but it cut him and the poison entered his body, so that he died of his wounds fifteen days later and was interred in another of the northern gates of Trinovant. The sorcerer's gilded blade which he took as spoil, and which he named Thamebuide, or "yellow death", was buried with him.

'And that's how the Slavers won the Realm?' Will said, frowning.

'Oh, not so! The Slavers' ill-fated first invasion was ended by their captain-general, Iuliu the Seer. Ever since landing on the shingle shore, he had been troubled. He suffered falling fits and terrible night visions, both of which were conjured in his mind by the lorc. So affected was he that after the great battle fought against Caswalan and Neni, he chose to withdraw his dread army back across the Narrow Seas. He returned with it to his great capital of Tibor where he vowed never to trouble the Isles again. Iuliu the Seer became a despot upon his own people and was murdered by his friends.'

Will scratched his head. 'Then how did the Realm pass to the Slavers?'

'A hundred years later we were betrayed by one of our own.'

Will nodded. 'And that must have been Gruech's doing?'

'Indeed it was. And all the worse for he was one of the druida, and a bard. There could have been no greater betrayal than his.'

Gwydion strode onward in silence then, and a little while later they passed by some ancient stones and the wizard explained that this was the place where Welan son of Wada had forged the exquisite bronze sword called Balmung, the same that had shaved the scales from the dragon's ribs.

'These stones mark the place where Wada was laid to rest by his grateful people.' The wizard's lips pursed wryly. 'Had Welan but known how, he might have charmed Flenir to his will, and then there would have been no need to forge a sword. There is no need to dig earth-iron from holes when you have skill in your hands and in your head. The earth gives up freely all that a wise man needs. She holds fast to that which should not be had by fools. Alas! The earth can never give all that men desire, for men's desire is limitless.'

But Will's mind was already bounding along another path. 'Could the great dragons be tamed by words alone, then?'

'Tamed? Never! But charmed certainly. At least in some measure, for the greatest of the dragons were vain and greedy beasts, and those are failings against which compliment and flattery most easily succeeds. In that, dragons were much like kings.'

Will looked back the way they had come. In the bright summer sun he could see for many leagues, and the view served to make him wonder at the vastness of the Realm and how small was the world that he had hitherto known.

'Where are we going, Master Gwydion?'

'That question again? Over hill and down dale to sup with the king.'

Will sucked his teeth, hating to be so casually talked down to. 'There and back to see how far it is,' he muttered.

Gwydion poked him good-naturedly with the foot of his staff. 'We go to the king to offer him consolation in his time of trouble. But travelling is not simply an attempt to arrive somewhere by the shortest possible route. A destination must be arrived at properly, for there is much more in the going than there is in the getting there.'

'You're not making much sense.'

'Then let me put it plainly – there may be those whom we might wish to meet with on the way, or those who might wish to meet with us.'

Will sighed. The crane bag seemed to be heavier, though he knew it could not be. Then he realized that it was weighed down with a secret. He had not yet told Gwydion about the silver-bound horn. I'll tell him about it when he tells me where we're going, he thought, and swapped the bag from hand to hand. Fair trade is no robbery, and that's a Valesman's rede!

At Lyttenden Hill they came upon ancient, wind-bitten towers and a lake of mist below. The ridge turned south again and they walked on along high ground, coming down at last, late and after dark, into a looming wood that lay across their path.

On the way, Gwydion told him about some of the different sorts of magic. There was 'seeming', which was making things appear to be what they were not. Then there were the persuasive arts of talking people into a state of sleep or enthusiastic agreement. Then came the power of perceiving deceit in men's hearts. 'No motive is hidden from a wizard,' Gwydion said. 'He hears truth in people's voices as others hear joy in laughter or sadness in sobs. Much that folk suppose is powerful magic is really only illusion-weaving. Most people cannot tell the difference, but it is the difference between a person believing he sees a mouse change into an apple and the change actually taking place. True transformations are much more difficult – they are very tiring, and they tend to return to their original state in a short space of time. Which is especially upsetting if you have just eaten an apple that once was a mouse.'

Will laughed. 'Yes, and more upsetting still if you're the mouse!'

As they entered the gloom of the woods Gwydion sang a song of an ambush of shadows that he had met with in the far darker forests of the West, in the land of Cambray, where hidden strings were often plucked and deadly arrows flew, biting deep into the flesh of those who came uninvited into what was the most mystical of lands. The song wrung the blood from Will's heart. And when it was done he thrilled to hear cries in the dark, though they were only owls answering the moon.

They camped and ate the last of their Lammas bread along with some wonderful mushrooms called pig's ears that Gwydion hunted out. Tonight he cut no cooking pit nor did he whisper up any fire, but went to stand in a clearing for a while to ask strength from the earth and fill himself with its potent power. Afterwards he told Will to wrap himself tight in his cloak and take his night's rest under a bush where the moss was thickest. But if the wizard's aim was Will's peace of mind, his words failed, for he also said that this place was shunned by the local folk. It was known by the name of 'Severed Neck Woods', Gwydion told him, and lay under the hereditary wardenship of the House of Sturme. From olden times, it had always been stalked by woses and wood ogres. Perhaps that was why Will was restless and still only half asleep when he saw figures moving among the trees.

At first he thought they were animals, deer probably. Then he thought they were men, then he knew they were neither. They came to him in a ghostly light, pale yet growing to a strange lambency like the shine cast by a slim crescent moon. They came like a tribe gathering from all directions, and he heard a sound on the edge of hearing, like the low hum that rises in a man's head just before he faints. Will felt the back of his neck tingling. He had listened to Gwydion's warnings of pursuit long enough to believe there was a danger shadowing them, and if Gwydion was afraid of it then it must be considerable. Then he remembered the woses and wood ogres and fear jolted him.

'Gwydion!' he hissed. He tried to shake the wizard awake, but he could not. Gwydion slept on, unmoving as a log. The mushrooms! he thought. He must have made a mistake and poisoned himself!

For a moment he sat there in the dark dern, frozen-hearted

and alone, wondering what he should do. Panic began to envelop him, but then he took a deep breath and looked inside himself. To his surprise, he found a calm strength there that he little expected. 'Whoever they are, they'll not take us without a fight,' he muttered, taking up his stout blackthorn stick.

If only Gwydion had not made an uncooked supper, he thought, but then he realized he was feeling well enough himself, and he had eaten far more pig's ears than Gwydion.

The glowing figures swayed as they approached. He watched as the wraith-like gathering came towards him steadily. This was no wood ogre's band. He did not feel threatened. Rather there was a sense that this was their place, and it was his fault for having walked into it uninvited. He heard the tread of their feet on the forest floor, the sound of branches moving aside as they came. He rose up and shook off his cloak and stood as a man stands to meet a stranger, half warily, yet half in greeting, and as the glowing ones came to him at last he began to see their true form.

Astonishingly, they looked like the creature he had pulled from the wheel at Grendon Mill. They had the same silvery pale skin, the same wispy hair and the same delicate faces. Some came mounted and some on foot, and those who rode sat upon the bare backs of unicorns. It seemed that a light came from within them, as if from their hearts. He dropped his stick, all thought of violence vanishing from his mind, and a feeling came over him that this was a moment more beautiful than any he had known.

No words were spoken. None were needed. The shining folk gathered around him, droning softly, and soon there appeared their king, for king he must be judging by his great size. Fearless now, Will was amazed to find that he recognized him – his likeness was painted on the board that hung above Baldgood's alehouse! This was none other than the Green Man. His stout body was twined about with ivy leaves, fronds clothed his limbs, and a crown of holly sat upon his head. Briars issued from his nostrils and from the corners of his mouth, but they could not disguise his wild eyes, nor his smiling strength, nor hide the fulsome power of his nature.

As Will watched in delight and reverence, the Green Man came to him, clasped him hard about the body and squeezed him like a great bear so that the breath was forced from him. Green smells like the earth in spring filled Will's nostrils and the humming drone rose louder in his ears as he felt his feet being uprooted from the ground in welcome. He did not struggle, only closed his eyes against the crushing grip, and when he opened them again he found that the Green Man had let him go.

Everyone had gone. All was now silent in the dern. He looked around, his heart beating fast, his mouth dry, but his thoughts were vivid and he was filled with an over-powering sense of oneness with all around him. There below was the dark form of Gwydion, slumbering still, but the Green Man and his shining host had departed. Will breathed deep, taking in the keen night odours and watching starlight rain silver through the branches of the wildwood. Then he lay down on the moss, pulled his cloak tighter about him and rolled back into slumber.

□ □ □

CHAPTER EIGHT

CLARENDON

The next morning Will awoke covered in diamonds of dew. Silver mists lay over the land, until golden sunbeams put them to flight. He said nothing to Gwydion about what had happened during the night. He found it hard to believe it had not all been a dream, though his heart told him that the meeting had been real enough. But as he packed up and readied himself once more for the road, he noted the glint of bright metal that shone in the top of the bag.

He pulled out the battered horn he had taken from the dragon's mound and stared at it in disbelief. It was now as perfect as the day it had been made, bound at rim and tip in finely-worked silver and inscribed with unknown words. As he polished it with his sleeve a shiver passed through him, and he knew he had been thanked and also, in some peculiar way, accepted.

Gwydion was already dancing out mysterious signs in the air, appearing to cast spells on the trees. When he had finished he collected leaves and threaded them into a wreath which he left by the roadside, then he said, 'Did you sleep well? I hoped you would.'

As they moved off, an encouraging thought struck Will: although Gwydion had seemed to be speaking in riddles the day before, what he had said about walking up hill and down dale and supping with the king had, after a fashion, come to pass. Because the Green Man was surely the king of this place.

'There is a saying that goes, "You cannot make a silken purse from a pig's ear",' Gwydion told him, then added knowingly. 'But sometimes you can.'

As they cleared the bounds of the Severed Neck Woods, Will became aware of larks singing above the cornfields. There were summer snowflakes on the road verge, downy woundwort and meadow cranesbill and the brilliant yellow of ragwort. There were so many pretty flowers growing that Gwydion whispered his regrets over them, pulled up a few and saved them in his pouch. He said out of the blue, 'Something has put a spring in your step today. Have you been feeding ducks again?'

Will smiled. 'No, Master Gwydion.'

'I would say you look like someone who has lately passed an important test.'

Will looked askance. 'Do you think so?'

'I do indeed. Returning respect has settled upon you – I would say.'

Will shrugged. 'Maybe I've been given the freedom of the wildwood.'

Gwydion nodded thoughtfully. 'Maybe. It would be a great honour to be given that. What could you have done to deserve it, I wonder?'

Will felt proud and humble and a little uneasy all at the same time. 'Don't you know?' he asked.

'I know many things. Many more than most, but not quite everything.'

Will smiled again, pleased to find that one so powerful as Gwydion also had the capacity to laugh at himself. 'In that case, I'll tell you why I was given the freedom of the wildwood when I judge it right for you to know.'

Gwydion's eyebrows lifted. 'Are you mocking me, young man?'

'Fair trade is no robbery, as we say in the Vale, Master Gwydion. And they say every man must have his secrets.'

The wizard suppressed a smile. 'Spoken like a wizard, lad! Now let me see what it was that you took from the earth upon Dumhacan Nadir.'

Will reddened, then bent to undo the bag. 'It was just an old horn, all battered and tarnished when I found it.'

Gwydion took the horn. 'It does not look so battered and tarnished to me.'

Will passed it across. 'Whoever visited us last night must have polished it while we slept.'

'Great is the power of that embrace, for all the world is renewed by it each and every spring. Keep this horn with you always, for it is a rare gift. Now put it away from prying eyes, and be more careful with your secrets. Now that you have passed your test and been accepted I must inform you regarding important matters. How much do you know about your king and those who surround him?'

Will gave an empty shrug. 'My king? Not a lot.'

'Then hearken to me closely, for the time has come when you must know. The king sits on the throne which is in the palace of the White Hall. He does so with the approval of the Stone of Scions and without demur from either Magog or Gogmagog, who are, all three, the throne's guardians. Now, if—'

'Whoa, Master Gwydion!' Will's eyes had begun to glaze at this sudden rush of strange names. They meant nothing to him.

'Hmmm – well, do you know what a usurper is?'

Will brightened. 'Is that not a lord who tries to take the crown away from a king?'

'And then becomes king in his stead. Correct. Though you would not know it to look at him, your mild King Hal is the grandson of a most fierce usurper. He had a fearsome warrior father too – also in his time called King Hal – who won lands in conquest across the Narrow Seas from Burgund to Breize. That the fool died of the bloody flux before he had any chance to enjoy what he had won, or even to clap eyes upon the son he had fathered, is down to what his own father did.'

'So Hal the Warrior's father was Hal the Usurper?' Will said, trying to keep up.

'Correct. The first Hal seized the crown unlawfully, which was a very great crime. He starved the true king to death in a castle dungeon. No matter that the true king was arrogant and wilful and trustless. No matter either that the usurper was clever and able and acclaimed by all as the best leader of men. Still it was a crime, for the true king must be appointed by sovereignty, and must be approved by the Stone of Scions. He is only allowed to sit on the throne if there is no word of complaint from Magog and Gogmagog, which are the names of two beady-eyed statues that stand in niches behind the throne. Now do you see?'

'Not really,' Will said.

'It is no matter. All you have to understand is that King Hal is a usurper's grandson, and that he knows very well how the curse of his blighted ancestor has followed him.'

'Is it a magical curse?'

'Judge for yourself. There was once a common saying: "Woe betide the land that hath a child for a king", and, though that saying may no longer be uttered upon pain of death, it nevertheless remains true. The crown came to King Hal in the first year of his life, and though he remains king in name, he has always been the pawn of powerful men. He was purposely grown into a weakling by contending barons. Their aim was always to keep him pliable to their will, and so he has proved, for he never grew much of a spine. If the curse that settled on King Hal's father brought that king's untimely death, then that which afflicts the present Hal is worse, for he lives on in helplessness and sees the Realm plunged ever deeper into the direst distress.'

'That sounds like a curse indeed.'

'The crown that was placed on the child-king's brow thirty years ago was a disputed one. Nevertheless, in the minds of many lords so long an elapse of time has served to make Hal the legitimate king. He is, they argue, the third generation of his line to hear their oaths of fealty. They say that true majesty flows in his blood now. But equally, in the opinion of others Hal is – and always will be – no more than the grandson of a murdering usurper.'

Will could only just follow Gwydion's explanation, but he was disturbed by it. He had never thought there could be so much to consider about kingship. Suddenly, his child-hood notions of what it would be like to be the king seemed simple-minded. 'But what about the true king?' he asked suddenly. 'The one that was usurped and starved. Didn't he have any children?'

The wizard looked sideways at Will, as if he had chanced to raise an important point. 'The dispossessed king left no child. But there remains a living blood line whose claim, according to the strict laws of kingship, is stronger than Hal's – and that blood line has continued all the while and is presently into the fourth generation.'

'Who is it? A great lord?'

'A duke, no less. The royal blood flows now in the veins of Duke Richard of Ebor, he who was sent by the king's council not long ago to rule over the Blessed Isle as Lord Lieutenant there – though what right he has to such a title as that may well be debated. Still, he is a man in all his power, and a most capable governor. In truth he is most like a king, and kingly in his thoughts. When last I spoke with him I saw that it was in his mind to return into the Realm and press his claim to rule.'

'But I don't understand. Surely everyone would be best served by the crowning of the rightful king according to the laws of kingship. And surely, if he's the better leader of men into the bargain—'

'Think again. What did I just say about Friend Hal?'

'Oh, I see. . .' Will nodded. 'You mean there are many lords who prefer to keep King Hal because he's easily handled. While the true king is shunned for he'd be strong with them.'

'Now you see clear to the bottom of the pail. But that is a truth best not spoken aloud, for the man who does so puts his life in jeopardy.'

All that day they walked along through a mellow land that rolled gently across their southerly path. For a league or so it rose up to broad chalky tops, then fell away for the same distance into rolling clay vales. As they climbed higher there were stretches where dense clumps of spiky furze showed off their yellow flowers. Gwydion led Will on sheep tracks that ran among the bushes. For much of the way the sky was hazy and threaded with the warbling of larks, but as the sun declined across the south a chill wind blew in across the high plain.

Gwydion looked into the western sky to where clouds were boiling up. 'Thousands of years ago there were great temples to the moon and sun over there. All are now in ruin and forgotten, and the moon and the sun are both the less for it. One day, if you would know the essential nature of magic, I will take you to the Great Henge. It was once called in the true tongue, *Celuai na Sencassimnh*, which is to say "the meadows of the storytellers". It was built on a node in the earth where three great oaks once stood, and a tower was raised upon them. Later, when the woods around were cleared, a henge of wood was built, then two of stone, one within the other. Many of the tombs of the kings of the First Men are set about it.'

Will listened, hoping to hear more about the battlestones, but Gwydion called him onward, saying, 'Look down there! What do you see?'

Will shaded his eyes and looked into the south. In the distance the land was all a-shimmer with light. 'What is it?' he asked, awed. It seemed like a vast plain, part land, part sky, yet brilliant as a bank of fog.

'That, Willand, is called the sea.'

'The sea . . .' Will echoed, still staring at the ribbon of light. 'I had no idea it would be like that.'

'To the south of us lies the valley of the Bourne. Do you see that grey spire that sits on yonder skyline like a crack in the sky? That is a chapter house, a cloister of the Sightless Ones.'

Will stared at the sharp, soaring point. 'Who are they? They come up every year to the bogs near Middle Norton to take the tithe. I know they come to impoverish honest folk, but it's said their eyes have been plucked out. And do they really have hands that are red?'

'As red as a rooster's comb, some of them. And yellow fingernails like claws. Do you know the saying, "to be caught red-handed"?'

Horror thrilled down Will's spine. He knew that to use the name 'red hands' in their hearing risked the cutting off of a man's lips. 'But are they truly blind?'

'As blind as love and justice. Though they deal in neither of those fine goods. Nor do they believe that all things come full circle. They are mind-slaves, you see.'

Will shivered, and the wind that whipped among the furze bushes seemed suddenly cold. 'Who are they?'

'Clever blood-suckers who have found a way to interpose themselves between lord and churl and so grow fat at the expense of both.'

'Why don't the lords and the churlish folk fight back against them?'

'The churls can do nothing because the work of the Fellowship is under the protection of lordly arms. And that is so because the Fellows relieve the lords of the trouble of collecting tithes and taxes. The chapter house which you see down there is one of many thousands that have been built across the Realm to store their ill-gotten booty in. That spire is second only in height to the great Black Spire of Trinovant, which place you will also see one day. In such places are kept all the tithes taken from the districts round about. Half they keep for themselves, and half they pass on to the lords who rule.'

'What if a village can't pay?' Will asked, thinking of some of the thin years they had had in the Vale. 'What if there's a poor crop or a failed harvest? Or damp rots the grain after threshing? Or pests come and spoil it? What do the Sightless Ones do then?'

'In that case the Iron Rule is invoked.' Gwydion looked out darkly from under his eyebrows. 'When famine comes the only way the Sightless Ones can be appeased is by making an offering of youth to the Elders.'

'Youth?'

'Children. They call it having too many mouths to feed. Did I not tell you that the Fellowship is always on the look-out for new recruits?'

'Are we going down there now?' Will asked, putting a hand to his throat.

'The grey spire yonder lies close by the city of Sarum. But we are going a little way beyond, to the royal lodge of Clarendon, and there, as I have already told you, our host is to be the king himself.'

They came off the high downs, passing on the way an ancient earth circle. Gwydion waved his hazel wand at it and said that these overgrown banks were all that remained of the once-great Figgesburgh Calendar. In times past it had held a huge mirror of polished bronze that had sent beams of sunlight down into the ancient palaces of Sarum on the most sacred of days. And on sacred nights the ancient astronomers had used their great mirror to interrogate the stars. Will delighted in the feel of the place and tried to imagine the observatory that Gwydion described, but so little of it remained now that even Gwydion's words could not easily bring it back to life.

They descended by a wooded valley and reached the limits of Clarendon Forest just as the sun was setting, but tonight there was no beautiful display of pink and gold in the sky to bid the day farewell. Grey clouds that looked as heavy as anvils had gathered, and there was the sound of distant thunder as they entered the forest.

Will soon saw that this was no forgotten forest like Wychwoode. This was a much-visited royal park, and within it stood a magnificent hunting lodge that had become over the years a palace in its own right. Gwydion said that the king's court came often to Clarendon to hunt, and that a hundred foresters kept his herds and managed his chases.

'But the king never liked hunting. He is not a man of blood. It is his nobles who enjoy the killing, lesser men, cruel and brutish – and loud, as you will soon see.'

Will looked up at the leaves of the great oaks. They were in the dark green of late summer, but many had become covered in a white bloom they called in the Vale 'oak mildew', and he knew that meant the trees hereabouts were unhappy. The lodge itself could be seen at the end of a long processional avenue, a green maybe two thousand paces long by a hundred wide. Gwydion saw him looking at it and whispered, 'It was made so to prevent an ambush of the royal party.'

'But who would want to ambush the king?' he asked, shocked.

'Politicking is a deadly and self-serving game. The aim is for one lord to make himself richer than all the rest, and so more powerful. If he owns more land, then he can lord it over more men. If he is rich enough he will have the final say in all things, for he may keep the king himself in his purse.'

Will shrugged, thinking of Lord Strange. 'But what use is all the gold in all the world if a man cannot sleep easy at night and be at peace with himself and his neighbours?'

'Ah, lad! I would that your country wisdom was better understood among the company we are soon to meet. But it is not.'

Will recalled what Gwydion had said about the usurper's curse that lay upon the king, and a pang of fear ran through him.

Gwydion shook his head, 'Chivalry gutters low in these latter days. There is ever the stink of greed and ambition rising over the king's court. Violence must soon follow, as night succeeds day.'

Now they were nearing the lodge, many people were to be seen. The poor and the sick, hearing of the king's presence, had come – as was their right – to petition him, to receive his healing hand. But they had been allowed to approach the lodge only as far as a line of hurdles. Behind these stood a wall and a gate, and beside the gate-posts half a dozen soldiers lounged at their ease.

Gwydion moved unnoticed to the front of the crowd. He murmured and moved his arms, slowly, as if casting a stone towards the group of soldiers. Then, with Will following in his wake, he unhooked one of the hurdles and walked through the gap.

'Hoy!' one of the soldiers shouted. Three of them got up, pushed forward their iron hats and moved towards Gwydion. Their chief carried with him an axe with a long handle. He said, 'And where do you think you're going?'

'To see the king, of course,' Gwydion told him.

'Get back there!'

Two of the three soldiers made to lay hands on what appeared to them to be an old man too bewildered to obey instructions. 'Stay back behind the hur—'

Then their chief came forward. He pulled the others away and bowed an abject apology. 'I'm sorry, your grace. They didn't recognize you. Let Duke Edgar and his kin pass!'

'Come along, Henry,' Gwydion muttered.

'Henry?' Will repeated, looking around, but then he darted after the wizard as he went through the gates. 'Who's Henry?'

'You are. How does it feel to be taken for the young Earl of Morteigne and Desart?'

Will looked at himself but could see no change. The soldiers looked at one another. One of them shook his head while the other tried to argue with his chief.

Will glanced round. There rose a hooting and jeering from the crowd of petitioners.

'But that's not his grace!' the soldier insisted. 'That's a beggar!'

His chief turned away angrily, saying from the corner of his mouth, 'Can't you see, it's meant to be a disguise . . .'

A second set of guards came into view by the inner doors, two mailed and helmeted men, wearing royal tabards of quartered red and blue and embroidered with golden lions and silver flowers. A third man was seated at a high desk. He wore black hose and jerkin and had sharp, watchful eyes and hair cut and shaped like a black mushroom. Will disliked him on sight.

Gwydion began to twist and turn along the passageway, like a man beginning a dance or preparing to throw a heavy weight ahead of him. Though nothing was thrown that Will could see, something appeared to hit the man square in the face, so that he almost fell off his stool, but then straightened.

'Good evening, your grace,' he said smoothly. 'The gathering awaits.'

'Thank you, chamberlain,' Gwydion said, in a voice that was not his own. He whispered words to the guards and made signs above their foreheads so they swept their helm-axes aside and opened the doors for him. Will stumbled as he went past them, but they just looked straight through him. He snapped his fingers under the nose of one of them, but the man did not notice.

As Will entered, what he saw made him gasp: the hall was fifty paces long by at least half that in width, and lit by half a thousand blazing candles. It was the biggest room he had ever seen, and by far the brightest. The roof above was supported by ornate beams between which many flags hung, all in bright colours and all bearing lordly devices. The floor was made of squares of pure black and pure white stone and the painted walls had been plastered to a smooth flat-ness and pierced by tall, dark windows. Between the windows were arrays of trophies, mostly deer skulls, complete with antlers, or huge boars' heads that made Will think of Lord Strange. But this hall outdid the tower of Wychwoode in every way. Two long, finely-wrought elmwood tables set with all manner of mouthwatering foods ran the length of it, each of them seating more than a hundred well-dressed folk, and capping those tables was a third high table, more ornate than the others and raised above them. The high table was set with eight seats, whose backs grew taller towards the middle, where Will supposed, the king and queen sat.

And there was a deal of noise too. Everyone was talking and a band of minstrels was playing music, while a man in sparkling robes of many colours juggled fire in his hands. Will watched him making great boasts and amazing the watchers with the shapes he made in the air.

'Careful you do not catch fire, Jarred,' Gwydion told him. 'They say illusionists burn very well!'

The moment the juggler saw who had entered, he let out a yelp and his leaping flames all dropped to the ground in a smoky heap.

Then the music ceased.

Gwydion's arrival hushed the echoing din, and when the guarded doors banged shut, a profound silence fell. Will felt his palms dampen, and everything that Gwydion had told him about self-serving lords came together.

All eyes were now on the wizard. On the top table a man sitting on one of the two tallest chairs, a big man in blue and white robes, got to his feet. 'Who dares enter the royal presence uninvited?' he demanded, angrily.

At first Will took the man for the king, but then he realized that he could not be, for here was a thick-set man with short, greying hair, a fighter's neck and heavy, black eyebrows. He had limbs that a lifetime of sword practice and riding at the hunt had kept powerful. His hawk nose and hooded eyes gave him a cruel and self-possessed air that was at odds with all that Will had been told about the king. And this man was aged forty-and-some years, which was ten years older than King Hal should be, for the present year was the thirty-first of King Hal's reign, and he had become king while still a babe in arms.

'You know me well enough, Edgar de Bowforde,' Gwydion cried, throwing up his arms, 'though it is not my part to answer to you, nor any of your people. Even so, I will tell you, and all who dare to ask, that I am come here at your king's command, for he did bid me appear before him whenever I deemed an appearance necessary.'

All the while as Gwydion's fiery words rang in the rafters, Will's gaze ran between Duke Edgar and the incredible woman who sat beside him in the other of the two tallest chairs. Will saw right away that she must be Queen Mag.

She was slim and gowned in brilliant crimson, and her headdress was elaborate with what looked to Will like horns sweeping up from the sides of her head and overdraped with the finest of crimson veils. Her hands were ringed and covered in jewels, and her death-white face was set off by a pair of blood-red lips and eyes that were as black as night. If she was beautiful, then it was the kind of beauty that made women proud and caused men to obey. When she spoke her voice was honeyed with amusement. 'Then come in if you please, Old Crow, and eat with us.'

Edgar gnashed his teeth at that, but then the queen picked up a chicken leg and tossed it down onto the floor.

'No doubt, you're here again to beg at my husband's table.'

There was uproarious laughter all around, but it faded somewhat as Gwydion bent down to pick up the morsel. He called a greyhound out from under one of the tables, and began to feed it flakes of flesh while stroking its head. 'Listen to me carefully, Mag, for I shall speak neither loud nor long to you. You should know that, whether you like it or not – whether you believe it or not – privilege always brings with it responsibility. We shall soon see what it has brought to you and your friends.'

Will saw a dangerous-looking youth sit up beside Duke Edgar. He knew this must be Henry, the Earl of Morteigne and Desart, of whom Gwydion had spoken earlier. Henry also wore blue and white, and the badge of a golden portcullis glittered on the breasts of both father and son. Henry was about seventeen, and the way he played with his long-pointed knife sent a shiver down Will's spine.

But the wizard had by now turned to one who sat on the far side of the queen. 'The last time I appeared before you, Friend Hal, I warned that your realm was in jeopardy. It is still so.'

The vacant-faced man to whom Gwydion spoke would not meet the wizard's eye. This is a weakling indeed, Will thought. Narrow of face he was, tall and thin as a sapling, pale and beardless, and plainer of dress than any in the hall. Grey and bloodless he seemed, frightened and wishing he was elsewhere.

Gwydion turned this way and that, pointing with his staff to where lords whispered behind their hands. 'I see you, Thomas, Lord Clifton! And Dudlea! And Scales! And you, Lord Ordlea! So many worthy peers of the Realm. So many that you cannot be gathered merely for the pleasures of the hunt. What are you plotting, I wonder? And I ask you fairly: what have you done to ensure the king's peace since last I came among you?'

Will's eyes were stuck fast on Queen Mag. She was beautiful, but she was fearsome also. Whether it was through terror of her or a loathing for the place he could not tell, but a sickness began to well up in the pit of his stomach. The smell of the banquet became repulsive to him, and now the hall started to shimmer and ripple like the surface of a pond into which a pebble had been dropped. It seemed to him that the hall must be webbed about by tense forces, magics and countermagics, static and invisible, contending in the air all around. If ever there was a dangerous place, he thought, this is it. Master Gwydion surely cannot have it in his mind to leave me with such folk as these.

He felt the hairs on his neck rising and a peculiar drone started in his ears as if in warning. He looked about himself warily, and strange words came into his mind like a minstrel song:

> *A ravening wolf,*
> *A greedy hog,*
> *A crafty fox,*
> *And a shameless dog.*

What it meant he could not say, nor where it had come from, unless it was his own ideas concerning those gathered at the tables. His senses seemed somehow to be magnified, his thoughts jerky and disjointed. He felt he could see and hear everything with great clarity, and yet Gwydion's voice seemed to echo far away. It was, he supposed, the onset of great magic and a special dread stole over him.

He fought down the panic, but the faces of the revellers had already begun to take on a gross and beastly appearance. Their mouths became like the muzzles of wolves as they laughed aloud or ripped at the flesh of the banquet. They would not listen to the exalted visitor who had come before them. Instead they tried to sport with him. Their jeers became snarls, and their faces warty and horrible. Their manners were gross, they brayed like beasts, and their glee was cruel. And above it all sat poor, pale King Hal, remote within himself, a defenceless white hart at bay among so many tearers of flesh. And there, at his back a strange shimmering, like the wind rippling across summer waters – only these ripples were in the air.

Suddenly the disturbance settled and Will saw a figure hooded in black appear. The figure was suddenly standing there where no one had been before, at the shoulder of the king and queen. Will wanted to call out, to warn Gwydion, but he dared do nothing. A bead of sweat started to run at his temple. He tore his eyes away and awoke suddenly to the terrible stillness in the hall. Gwydion stood with his arms cast wide, his staff glowing with a pale blue light.

'Friend Hal, your subjects are forgetting their manners,' the wizard warned the king softly. 'I deserve better than this, for I have come urgently to lay before you a weighty matter which touches you all. May I not speak of it and be decently heard?'

The king gave no answer, but managed a feeble sign with his hand.

'I thank you.' Gwydion bowed with great dignity in acknowledgement, then he began. 'I have come concerning certain signs that speak of approaching war. There will be a slaughter of innocents such as this land has never before seen. The stars above do speak of it. Blood shall flow in torrents until the very rivers of the Realm shall run red. Brother shall do murder unto brother, father shall war against son! All men shall wish themselves dead and freed from the bondage that suffering brings! All this will come to pass unless a remedy can be found.'

As Gwydion's calamitous portents rang out, Will's eyes remained fast on the figure that stood between the king and queen. It was a ghastly form, dressed and hooded in a black habit, its face – if face there was – hidden in deepest shadow. Will shook in terror, wondering if this could be one of the Sightless Ones. He looked away and back, trying to dispel his fear. The figure's power to haunt him was stubborn. But suddenly, Gwydion's voice recaptured Will's attention.

'There is a deadly canker in the land! I say to you that unless men of conscience stand up for what is right there will be a terrible price to pay in blood. The Realm is sliding, and by degrees this slide will become a rush. Only the true king of this realm has the power to give me what I need if I am to protect his people—'

'Ha! It is as your queen has told you, sire!' Duke Edgar shouted out. 'This crow who calls himself "wizard" is nought but a beggar come to have what he can of us. Begone, Old Crow! His grace knows your tricks! He will no longer be gulled by your ghost tales and fairy stories!'

Gwydion stood straighter. 'A most useful rede of magic I have for you, Friend Edgar. If you would one day be a greater man than you presently are, you should make this your watchword: "I shall lack before the poor man lacks".

Naked greed is but one reason why you are a lesser man, lesser even than the poor folk who wait patiently at your king's gate. If you do not change your ways you will be struck down and die a violent death, but I would rather that you made your peace with this world.'

'Fearmongering carries the penalty of death, Old Crow, though your words have lost the power they once had to terrify!'

'I did not come here to bandy words with you, Edgar. But I do most diligently desire to save your king and his people from a conflict that will in the end cut the blood-line of every nobleman here!'

'Seize the doomsayer!'

But Gwydion gathered himself dangerously and no man dared make a move toward him. 'Pity the one who lays angry hands upon an Ogdoad wizard! Tread softly, Edgar de Bowforde, for I call you to silence!'

It seemed to Will then that the blue light which still glowed in the head of Gwydion's staff flared up and strove to reach out like a pale ray towards the duke, but the hooded figure who stood by the queen sent forth some contrary power to surround the light and keep it at bay.

'I will not be silent!' the duke roared. 'You see? He has no magical power against those who stand up to him! He dares tell me to tread softly, but he is nothing more than an old conjurer! An interfering busybody from a forgotten age! A madman, yet one with enough wit to try to wheedle silver from any fool prepared to indulge him! Get you home to your cave in the West, Old Crow! Tend your herbs and mix up your potions there, for we'll have none of your witchcraft!'

Braying laughter thundered through the hall, but Gwydion paid it no heed and instead fixed his eyes fast upon the king.

'Friend Hal, how is it that I bring you this timely warning, yet you have nothing to say to me? How is it that you are called king of this realm? Have you no shame? Look how your nobles sit at table gorging on roast swan and haunches of venison, swilling down your finest wines. Do you not hear how they are laughing at you? Where is their respect for the ancient ways? Why, if you are king, do you allow these insults from worthless men? And why do you fear to admit the sick who cluster at your gate? Is it that you are so far corrupted that you care not even for justice? Or is it that those close to you fear to admit such persons into your presence lest they test the healing power of kingly touch?'

'Enough!' Duke Edgar bellowed. He leapt to his feet in fury, threw his flagon of wine at Gwydion's head. The jug missed its mark, but the ruby liquid flew through the air and spattered the shoulder of the wizard's cloak.

'Where are your charms and protections now, Old Crow?'

'Have a care, Friend Edgar, for I am no motley conjurer like Jarred.'

'I care not what you are. Go from here before I take my dagger and slit your scrawny gizzard!'

Will flinched as the blade was drawn. He willed Gwydion to cast a thunderbolt at the duke before it was too late, but no thunderbolt came. Instead Gwydion's wrath flared out. 'Edgar de Bowforde! I lay this prophecy upon your head: *beware castles on pain of death*!'

A gasp of rage escaped the duke, for he thought it a curse aimed squarely at his ambitions. He leapt up onto the table and jumped down before Gwydion, menacing him.

'Your time is past! Your magic will not work here! The druid world you come from has long since failed, and the powers you once kept have faded from the world. You are the last of your kind, and soon we shall be troubled no more. And now you have tried our patience enough. Get out, Old Father Time, and take the beggar-child with you!'

The air shook with cruel laughter and shouts of, 'Out, Crow, out! Out! Out! Old Father Time!'

Jarred jumped up onto a table and blazed up a swaggering show of juggled fire to mock the wizard's powers. Gwydion gathered his dignity, clenched his staff and prepared to leave the hall.

The guards flung the doors wide and were about to drive the unwanted visitors out at spear-point when a piercing shriek split the air. It came from the high table. Even the duke turned, and every eye went to the queen. She had risen from her seat and was staring down with horror at her husband.

All triumph ceased among the onlookers as the king's head lolled against his shoulder. His face had turned ash grey, his eyes bulged and a single trickle of blood rolled down from nostril to lip. Suddenly, as they watched, his mouth began to twitch.

'Help me . . .'

And then his limbs began to jerk.

Queen Mag, her eyes wide, screamed again. 'Do something! For mercy's sake, somebody do something!'

'Upon whom do you call?' Gwydion demanded. 'For I alone can help him here.'

'Do not let him back!' Duke Edgar shouted. 'This is one of his own enchantments, a spell he has set upon the king!'

Gwydion's voice remained soft. 'The harm at work here is none of my doing. This is a cup of deception, spiced and tempered to King Hal's bane.'

The duke raised his dagger to strike. Will was about to spring forward when he felt a grip close on his arm and an irresistible force wrenched him away. The duke's son had come up behind, seized him and now held his throat at dagger-point.

'Stay your hand from murder, Edgar!' Gwydion cried. 'And you, Henry! Or your king will die – that much is a certainty.'

The duke hesitated, knowing where all his hopes rested. 'Hear what treacherous threats he uses!'

'You fool!' the queen shouted and her eyes flashed fire. 'Don't you understand? It doesn't matter what the Old Crow says. We need his leechcraft!'

Reluctantly, Duke Edgar let his dagger arm fall. He ordered his son to stand off. Will was released, then kicked down so that he went sprawling. Gwydion ignored him and moved instead to the king's aid. He cleared the banquet from the board and asked for Hal to be laid flat on the table. Then he bent to listen for a heartbeat.

He muttered words in the true tongue, then said to those who crowded anxiously around, 'Fetch me hot water. And give your liege lord air!'

But still the knights and nobles pushed in close with apprehensive faces, though Will saw they were more concerned for their privileges and positions than for the life of their king. Gwydion swept them angrily back to their benches and cleared a space for himself.

'Come here, bag-carrier!' he called out, and cast about for Will. 'Where's my apprentice boy?'

But as Will got up beside him he saw how Duke Edgar whispered furiously with his son, then sent a servant away on an errand.

The queen stood close by, her hands white and wringing one another. 'He must not die yet,' she repeated over and again, as if saying it would make it so. Will noticed how her tight red gown bulged in the middle – and suddenly it dawned on him that she was with child.

Gwydion worked purposefully on the unconscious king, whispering spells and making signs and sigils above the royal brow. He dissolved a pink powder into a bowl of water that was brought to him. It smelled of strawberries, and Will could almost feel the wholesomeness of it rising through the air. The king's shirt was opened and his throat, chest and belly washed.

At last Gwydion raised his head and drew Will towards him as he addressed the hall. 'I have completed my work here. There is nothing else that can be done for him save to make him comfortable, which I am sure the queen will see to after her fashion. His recovery will begin as soon as he leaves this place. But it will be slow, for his body has been poisoned and his will-power is even now being sapped away by—'

His words were drowned by the gasps that came from those who thought they had heard an accusation.

'Poisoned!'

The duke, whose page had secretly brought his broadsword, exploded in wrath. He had made his calculation. He had decided that, now the king's life was no longer in danger, there should be a reckoning. He launched out his sword and sprang at the wizard all in one movement.

But Gwydion was ready. He pulled out a small white object that hung at his neck, and mouthed a powerful word, enfolding Will in his mouse-brown cloak at the same time.

The heavy hand-and-a-half blade tore through the air.

'Aaaaaaaaaaaaaaaaaaaaaaagh!'

Will howled in horror as the sword sliced down through his own body from shoulder to hip, and rang sparking on the chequered stone floor. Then everything went black.

CHAPTER NINE

A BARROW ON THE
BLESSED ISLE

When Gwydion swept his cloak away, Will saw he was clinging to a jagged ledge in what seemed to be a blasting gale. The wind was cool and fresh and full of moisture, and there was bright sunshine all around him. A wall of grey rock pressed hard against his cheek, but he knew without looking down that he was poised over a long and precipitous drop.

That knowledge alone almost made him fall, for he had more than a little terror of heights.

All round he heard echoing screams and he tried to turn.

'Easy, there!' Gwydion gripped his shoulder hard and drew him in a little from the edge. 'Step towards me, Willand. Now the other foot. That's good. Tread softly now.'

The ledge was narrow and the fall deadly. But there was soft turf close by his hand, and the hope of safety. The wizard guided him upward and shoved him over the lip of grass, where he lay exhausted among the sun-warmed blades, tingling with gratitude and astonishment.

The wind ruffled him. 'What happened to us?' he said after a moment. 'Where are we?'

'The edge of this hill is the edge of the world.'

'But . . . how?' He stood up and stared around. A few paces away there was a grassy rise, and below it a path, and woods beyond. But to windward there was – nothing. Nothing except sky and a grassy brink where the land fell straight down into – what?

'They are the rocks where the song of the drowned breaks forever upon the shore,' Gwydion said, breathing deep. 'This is the sea, Willand. The same glittering silver band that you saw from the heights above Sarum. We are at the uttermost end of the land here.'

Will continued to stare out into the emptiness, until suddenly a great grey-and-white stormbird with a yellow bill sliced up from below the cliff like a sword stroke. It screamed at him and he flinched.

'She will not hurt you. She is the *faoilenn*,' Gwydion said, laughing. 'The bird of joy and hospitality. She makes her home here and comes only to see who approaches her nest. Have you never seen a sea gull before? But of course you will not have done. Yet you should thank her for one of her kind has just saved your life.'

But it was not the bird that had made Will start, so much as the memory of the duke's blade. He was so certain that Duke Edgar's sword had passed through him that he dared not move in case he fell into two parts. To drain away the fear he looked out at the purifying sea. Far below, a crawling carpet of dark blue stretched away as far as his eyes could see into the distance. A swell, born somewhere in the Great Sea, rose and fell, crashing wave upon wave upon the adamant shore. With the sun on his face and the wind's freshness carrying tears from the corners of his eyes, he felt lifted up. The sea! There was just so much of it!

'Behold the Western Deeps!' Gwydion said. 'This is what was called in the true tongue the *Fairgge*. The word is still used in the North to mean "the ocean in storm". It is a marvellous sight indeed! Do not fall down there, now. For there will be no getting you up from the rocks if you go over. I am quite spent for the moment.'

At last Will sat down, and asked, 'How did we get here?'

'This is the reason.' Gwydion kissed the bird's skull that hung at his breast. 'Come sit with me upon the barrow while I receive that which the earth would offer me, and I will tell you how this bird's skull has kept us whole.'

They went to sit on the small hill, where the turf was fine and green and the remains of pink flowers stood browning on their stalks. Back from the edge there was not quite so much wind, and Will listened with amazement at what the wizard told him about how he had prepared a vanishing-spell upon the bird's skull some seasons ago in this very place.

'But how has it become daytime?' he asked suddenly. 'At the royal lodge a moment ago, night was falling, yet by the sun—'

'If you change place, then you must also change time. It works that way, for the one is connected to the other – and contrariwise – if you see what I mean.'

Will's eyes opened wide at the idea that time had jumped. 'I don't think I do.'

'Well, worry about it when you have a quiet moment to yourself, and perhaps you will see how it goes. It is now the equinox – or as you would say, the twenty-first day of September.'

Will blinked. 'But that means you've robbed us of six weeks! Are we ever to get them back?'

'You will,' Gwydion said. 'But not until the end of your life.'

'Master Gwydion, I meant the war? What about that? Can we afford to lose so much time?'

'We would have lost a great deal more had it not been for the vanishing-spell. Nor was it so small an undertaking – such a spell is never used casually, for its outcome is never quite sure. And only one may be prepared at a time. We have travelled a long way, for this is the westernmost point of land in the world.'

'In the whole world?' Will repeated, thinking over what must have been the result if the range of the spell had been just a fraction longer. 'Then we must have come to the Blessed Isle! Who would have thought I would ever come here, and in such a fashion?'

'And how do you like it here?'

'Tilwin told me it was very . . . green. And so it is.'

Gwydion looked to him sharply. 'But do you feel anything?'

'Feel anything?'

'How do you like the taste of a sea breeze? Do you feel it filling you with the stuff of life?'

Will breathed deep until he was quite dizzy, then he said, 'How did that spell bring us here?'

Gwydion lifted up the bird's skull he wore. 'I wove the spell's trigger upon this. You are right to think that a vanishing-spell must have a destination. They are usually woven upon a spell of possession, therefore I designed it to bring me back from where I invoked it to the place where the hand of man first touched the trigger upon which it was woven. A vanishing-spell, once woven, waits to be sprung at time of need. Once a single subtle word is landed upon the trigger, the spell vanishes everything alive within its compass!' Will blinked as Gwydion snapped fingers in his face. 'Vanishing-spells are useful for they are paid for ahead of time, so to speak. They are a power stored and set. Such has been the danger of this summer's mission that I have been ready to fly here like a bolt from a crossbow for over a year now. Yet at Clarendon Lodge even this stalwart piece of magic almost failed to save us, for we were standing in a finely wrought trap. So fine that I did not at first perceive it, yet in the end it was all I could do to pull the trigger that released us.'

Will stretched himself. 'It's a pity you didn't pull the trigger a bit sooner. That sword scared me half to death and back.'

'It is the back that matters most. But I had little choice. That hall was wrapped tight, and thick with spells! All those antlers – and every point of them glowing with dirty magic. Could you feel anything in your feet? I could not. There was nothing crackling in the floor. Dead marble is the worst kind of hewn stone, Willand. It is not like having live rock underfoot. There was precious little for me to draw upon. No wonder they meet in that place to plot their schemes. And no wonder King Hal fell into a swoon under the pressures stored up there. Have I not said before that the king has a sensitive spirit?'

'Is that why King Hal's nose bled?' Will asked, thinking suddenly of the hooded figure that had shimmered into being behind the royal chair. 'Dirty magic? You mean like Maskull's magic?'

Gwydion looked to him suddenly. 'Why do you speak that name, I wonder? Maskull was certainly at Clarendon some little time before us. I am troubled to think that our moves might have been so closely anticipated by him.'

'And perhaps your deceptions too?' Will said, watching the slender thread of his own safety fraying to almost nothing.

The wizard got up and planted his feet firmly in the turf. 'Willand, I'm going to explain to you what I did not have the chance to explain to the king. Pay attention to me, for it is important you understand it well. You have already heard me speak of the fae folk, have you not?'

Will nodded. 'Yes, Master Gwydion.'

'Then you will know that the fae were an ancient race who once had the stewardship of the world. They matured their worldly wisdom over many hundreds of centuries, and so came to understand much that was true. They were the keepers of the wild, the ones who planted the first forests of birch and pine in the Isles, seeding trees ever further north as the ice melted before the power of their earth magic. After their victory over the cold and at the ending of the Long Night, they began to plant groves of oak and lime, hazel and alder, but by the time the First Men came, their stewardship was already coming to a close.

'By then their knowledge was at its peak, and their greatest achievement was the nine ligns of the lorc that channelled enriching earth power to all parts of the Isles. But there was a darker side to the skills of the fae. They found that all things in the world might be thought of as vessels that contained two contrary kinds of spirit – "bliss" and "bale" as we call them in dealings magical, though you may wish to think of them as "kindness" and "harm". Everything that exists in the world – every rock, every blade of grass, even the air – contains nearly equal measures of each kind of spirit, churning and boiling constantly together. But in the end, the fae found a way to part these spirits one from the other and use them separately.'

'How did they do that?' Will asked, awed by the idea.

'By their magic.' The wizard stopped walking up and down, and spread his hands. 'The arts of the fae were so profound in the end that they could stand two stones beside one another and shift all the bliss into one, and all the bale into the other. And in this way, one stone became a vessel of refined, unblemished kindness, and the other one of pure, unrestrained harm.'

Will chewed his lip. 'I think I begin to see. You're speaking of the battlestones.'

'Indeed I am, Willand.'

'And it's the harm in the stones that would make all the suffering happen.'

'Correct again.'

Will thought about that in the light of what he already knew. 'Can't it be brought out a bit at a time and set to the four winds?'

'Not without cost. Think of the harm that resides in a cup of poison. If someone drank that cup, then he would die. And if the cup were passed between two people then perhaps neither would die, but both would suffer serious illness. But if the cup were to be passed from mouth to mouth around a whole feast, five dozen folk might suffer the bellyache.'

'So if the harm that was inside a battlestone were let out all in a rush, there would be a battle.'

'And should a battlestone's harm be got out and dispersed into the world today, then tomorrow there would be many breakages and falls, lost coins and spilled milk. Do you see? All the men in the Realm would wake up a little bit weaker, and all the women of the Realm would turn a shade uglier.'

'Yet that seems a cheap price to pay when set against a war.'

'Perhaps it may come to that in the end. But do you see the vastness of the idea? Huge powers of destruction and preservation were brought into being when these stones were wrought. At first the harmful stones were kept closely paired with their sisters and housed together, each pair within a roofed chamber. How many pairs there were, I do not know, but their barrows were said to lie scattered throughout the North and West. Some are known to me, for three great ones have survived almost whole. One is at Maeris Howel on the Isle of Orcsay, which lies beyond the northernmost coast of Albanay. Another is within the Grange of Buyenn, here in the Blessed Isle.'

'And the other?'

'The other?' Gwydion looked him over. 'You cannot guess?'

'Should I be able to?' The moment grew awkward. 'Should I know, Master Gwydion?'

'Perhaps you should, for you are sitting upon it!'

Will marvelled. 'You mean this little hill?'

'Do you feel nothing at all?' the wizard advanced on him, his exasperation showing now. 'The Black Book says that the barrows were chosen most carefully. They stand at important places, where powerful earth streams come together. Stand up! Can you feel no tingling in your toes?'

Will got up. He rubbed his feet back and forth across the turf, then shrugged. 'It feels to me like . . . grass.'

'But these barrows were given to the First Men. They have been known in later times only to the druida, the wisest of the men of a later age. There can be no mistake! Try again!'

Will looked down at his feet uneasily. He hardly knew what was being asked of him. 'I don't know what else to do, Master Gwydion.'

The wizard sat down heavily. 'Oh, never mind,' he said, waving away Will's concern. 'Perhaps I have been wrong about you, after all.'

Will lingered, anxious now. 'Master Gwydion, have I displeased you?'

'Oh, Willand, sit down. The fault is not yours. There is no fool like an old fool, and of all the old fools the worst is the one who wants to believe.'

Gwydion's gloom had settled in for the rest of the afternoon. He sat in silence on the barrow and Will let him be, thinking that the dirty magic of Clarendon Lodge had perhaps sapped more of the wizard's strength than he had imagined.

Yet it seemed to Will that Gwydion was also wrestling with some great disappointment and trying to adjust his plans to take account of it. But he decided not to ask for he thought that the disappointment might concern him and if it did, there was no sense in stirring it up.

After a while the wizard gave up his brooding and returned. He seemed to have cheered up and he began to speak of the ages that had passed since the time of the ice, how when the ice had withdrawn the Drowned Lands had become ocean and the Isle of Albion had been left. Then he began to tell of the Age of Trees, and the time of the First Men since when a dozen-dozen times seven-dozen years had passed. And this time Will found that his mind did not wander from the wizard's words, and it seemed that there truly was something special in the air of the Blessed Isle for when the stories of elder days were told they were made more real.

And so Will learned about the departure of the fae, and of the three hundred generations of First Men who dwelt peaceably in the Isles and lived according to the ways of the fae.

'But then, three and a half thousand years ago the world changed,' Gwydion said, his eyes now filled with fading light. 'The Age of Trees came to an end, and there began the Age of Giants, when there were no men in the Isles. And that Age, which was a time of desolation, lasted for a thousand years. Then began the third Age, which was called the Age of Iron, when the hero-king Brea came and defeated the giants and proclaimed the Realm, and there were men in the Isles once more.

'Ah, those were high days, Willand, but by then the sorcery that had arisen in the East was driving westward vast migrations of folk, and the fae's gift to the First Men began to stir.'

'The battlestones?' Will asked. 'But why?'

'Thousands of years before, while the fae were still living in the world of light and air, the barrows of the North and West were opened and every stone, harmful and kind, was brought forth. Each pair was sent over to its own special place of strong flow along the lorc. No battlestone could be sent alone, for without its sister in attendance it would have been a most dangerous cargo. On its own each harmful stone would have attracted strife like a lodestone attracts flecks of iron. Turmoil would have been summoned, for the stones have the power to affect the minds of those who are drawn to them. But the fae said that once these harmful stones were set like coffins into their graves in the lorc and the array tuned and shaped by the power that flows there – ah! – then they would become a powerful guardian force.'

'And the sister-stones that came with them? What happened to them?'

'The word for them in the true tongue is *amhrainegh*, which means "wonderful". Once the battlestones were set in place the sister-stones could be returned. And they were. To these, their barrows, in the Blessed Isle and the isles of Albanay and elsewhere. Here they have remained as a source of comfort and wonder for all the world.'

'But I don't see,' Will said. 'Surely harm was spread all over the Realm when the battlestones were left here. How could that have worked as a protection?'

'It is true that each battlestone contains purest harm, but in the same way that a killing edge may be set into a handle and becomes a tool or a protection, so a battlestone – when directed by the lorc – serves in the same fashion. Remember that the places where the battlestones were buried were chosen with great care. They were always special places. For many dozens of centuries the stones protected themselves by repaying malice with malice. "Malice to him who malice thinks". Have you never heard that saying?'

Will shrugged. 'No.'

'It is today the motto of a certain order of knights, but it is a sentiment more ancient than any of them knows. The battlestones drove anyone who came maliciously into these isles towards insanity and self-destruction. Those who came in a spirit of honest friendship were not troubled by these terrible sentinels. Brea established the Realm unopposed by them. And later, when the Children of Nemeth came fleeing persecution and sorcery in the East, they came to these shores and found succour also without rousing the battlestones.'

'But Lord Strange told me the Nemethians were chased out of the Realm by one of the kings of the old days.'

'John le Strange's view of history is shallow and serves his own view of the world. In truth the Nemethians were received unscathed by the battlestones. They lived peaceably in the Land of the Lakes for many years until they fell out with the tyrant, Memprax, after which they wisely decided to depart for the Blessed Isle. I know, for I conducted them there myself. But whatever befell the Nemethians, there was many another peaceable folk welcomed here – folk who set down roots and fully mixed their blood and so helped to invigorate the Realm in the best way. So long as the newcomers did not try to keep themselves haughtily apart, they were welcomed and never once was the lorc inflamed by their coming. Never once in all the reigns of the Brean kings down to the time of Caswalan was there an awakening of the lorc, for there was no threat to the land.

'And so in a thousand years and more since King Brea reigned, the battlestones were all but forgotten. There grew up among the people a legend about certain stones hewn by the fae from the Pillars of the Earth and brought out from a place now deep under the sea. But that was an idea believed in only by those given to fancies, for in those days only the druida knew the truth about the lorc, and only the highest of the druida were vouchsafed the full secret.'

Will gazed out at the endless sea and at the glory of

sunlight that played through a cloud, turning the waters silver. He asked, 'How was it that King Brea was able to come and proclaim the Realm? Did the battlestones not try to destroy him too?'

'Why should they? When Brea came to the Isle of Albion there were no men there. The First Men had long since vanished and the land had fallen under the sway of monsters. But then Brea and his people came, and since giants are hugely strong but not especially clever, Brea inherited the land of Albion and the lorc made no demur at that.'

Gwydion spoke then of King Brea and the warriors aboard his seven ships who landed at Dartness and declared the Realm. He told how Canutax, a bold captain in Brea's host, had brought down the giant, Godmer, whose chin was seventeen feet above the ground, how Debon slew Coulin, and Corinax bore down the mighty Albion.

'At last, the giants were scattered and their line failed. In the end, Magog and Gogmagog were all that remained of them. These chieftains were taken captive and brought to Brea's oaken palace, the White Hall in Trinovant, there to do service as porters. That was many reigns ago, a thousand years and more before the coming of the Slavers.'

'Well what about them?' Will said, rapt. 'Surely the lorc should have thrown the Slavers back into the sea.'

'It happened like this, that one of the contending sorcerers in the distant East grew greater than all the rest. He began to put out searching fingers westward, to grasp and to conquer, one by one, the lands of the Gadel, and to bring them all into slavery. This, Iuliu, by then the mightiest and most ambitious general of the Slaver empire—'

'Ah! Iuliu the Seer!' Will interrupted.

'Iuliu the Seer, who—'

'—who was troubled by terrible night visions.'

'Quite so. Iuliu ordered to the Isles a fleet of many-oared ships. On board was an army that landed in great force and marched inland. They fought a fierce battle on the banks of the Iesis against an army led by Caswalan and his brother, but soon afterwards, prompted by the—'

'Now come the terrible night visions . . .'

Gwydion raised an eyebrow. 'Are you going to tell the story, or should I?'

'Sorry.'

'Soon afterwards, prompted by the power of the lorc, a dismal spectre came to disturb the Slaver-general's dreams. Mightily did it convince him that the invulnerability of his army was but a clever illusion, and the next day he took his steel-clad troops out of the Isles again.

'No Slavers came here after Iuliu left. Not for nigh on a hundred years, for none dared try to face down the protection they knew was buried in these Isles. But then it happened that the foulest renegade who ever lived, a man named Gruech, brought calamity upon the Isles.

'Gruech was one of the druida. He had taken the vows and had read much that was in the Black Book, but he fell into weak and desperate ways. He sailed his coracle across the Narrow Seas into Galle – which was the old name for Nestria and Breize – and so carried a great secret out of the Isles to be sold for a pittance of silver. Thus it was that the sorcerers and Slavers of the East found out how to disrupt the lorc by laying out roads of stone across the land. When their steel-clad army came again they knew what magic of their own to employ that they might quickly subdue the Realm and make it their own.

'Straight away they went about their unwise work. Attacking and burning down the great fortified hill towns, pinching off the power of the earth streams, breaking the bones of the land, tearing out her beating heart! Risings there were, of course, and rebellions aplenty. War flared, the brave Queen of the East fought the invader back as fiercely as only a woman can. I can see her now – tall and terrible to look upon and gifted with a leader's voice and mien. Her two grown daughters stood to left and right of her the day she roused her army to march upon Caer Malydion. Her bright red hair flew like a cloak about her shoulders and she wore the golden Torc of Sovereignty, and when she raised her spear aloft such spirit was kindled in the hearts of all who set eyes on her!'

Gwydion fell silent and it seemed to Will that a tear was bedewing the wizard's eye. 'What happened to the brave Queen of the East?'

'In the end, the Slavers killed her with poison. They had brought the secret of how to grip these isles, and grip them they did, ever tighter in a fist of steel. Every season that passed their eagle claws would sink a little deeper into the land, tearing up rib and knuckle, tearing away chalk and flint, until they had built stone fortresses for themselves, and connected together every quarter of the land.

'They told lies and made maggots of the people, Willand! Killed the honourable, drove out the strong, enslaved whoever they caught. They burned the sacred groves in acts of barbarous cruelty. They dwelt not in homes of living wood, but as dead men dwell, in tombs of quarried stone. Soon, high-walled city began to talk with high-walled city. Stone roads were sent like knives, cutting straight across the land, severing the pathways of the lorc, polluting and weakening its flow. Those roads are as looking-glasses, or as dams, turning back the earth power that runs up against them. They fractured the spirit of the land into tiny pieces. They even raised a great wall across the Isle from coast to coast – that was done to hold back the mighty magic that dwells in Albanay. These roads, these walls and other works of naked stone, they made the battlestones rage in lonely impotence, isolated and forlorn, each stone no longer part of the knitted web of power that was able to keep watch and ward over the sacred land, but now a tainted flow stored up in so many solitary kernels of malevolent fury.

'And so you see, Willand, the Realm that had once been protected by the battlestones came wholly under the sway of a sorcerer's empire, until the Old Ways were at length practised only in the West in the places where the sister-stones lay buried in their barrows, and cast a kindness over the land that the Slaver sorcerers could not penetrate. And trapped under the sway of the Slavers the folk of the line of Brea were beaten down unless they took themselves away to hidden places. Thus was the wisdom of the druida talked of eventually as half-truths and then let to rot away.'

'What happened to the Slavers in the end?' Will asked spreading his fingers in the thriving turf. He had sat on one buttock too long and his leg had gone numb.

'Like all things built upon sorcery, the Slaver empire was devoured by its own child.'

Will narrowed his eyes. 'Who was that?'

'The slavery of the body was in the end conquered by the slavery of the mind. When the Slavers brought their armies here they had not yet been bedazzled by the blinding light that overcame them in later times. It was a blinding they were powerless to resist for all their soldierly might.'

Will thought about that as he tried to rub the life back into his left leg. 'You mean the Fellowship, don't you? The Sightless Ones.'

Gwydion closed his eyes, remembering. 'It may surprise you to know that the Fellowship began as a small group of well-meaning spirits gathered about a single far-seeing man. A rebel he was, a fighter against Slaver tyranny, and his people infected by a terrible belief that would in the end make them the most hated of races. But, as with so many rebellions, this leader was ruined by the weaknesses of others. Jealousy, hatred and fear, Willand. Those are the three great enemies of men. Do not forget their names, for they are within us all and they are what confound our best intentions. The original Fellowship was a fragile flower. It did not long survive its contact with Slaver sorcery in the Tortured Lands. Its leader was hanged upon a tree and his following dispersed. Some fell silent out of fear. Others out of hatred took his name in vain. But the worst of them were driven mad by jealousy. They twisted all that their leader had taught them, until it was the very opposite of what he had intended. This new Fellowship became a secret society, one that dwelt in the shadows and gloried in its own persecution, for the surest way to enlist fools is to make them believe they are threatened, and every now and then to send one of them out to die a glorious death.

'Yet all the while the Elders of the Fellowship were gaining a taste for Slaver wealth and Slaver luxury and Slaver power. In place of the charity and poverty their first leader had espoused, they preferred gold. And so the Fellowship began to attract to itself exactly the wrong kind of man, and in time these full-fed princes bloated fat. They grew as parasites grow, inside the Slavers' great city. And by the time they burst out of their host, they had found a new way to own the world. It is called the Great Lie. It works, not by shackling bodies in iron, but by forging invisible chains that grip the minds of men.'

Will shuddered. 'How do they do that?'

Gwydion lifted his hand and tightened it into a fist. 'The Great Lie uses the victim's own natural hopes and fears to enslave him. Now you see why the tide of Slaver power ebbed just as the Sightless Ones were gaining their stranglehold over the Empire. When the Sightless Ones devised their improved method of slavery, it was bound to supplant the old. Here in the Realm, the regime of Slaver days was broken – their towers tottered, their cities crumbled, their palace roofs fell. The new invaders who came from across the seas lived in the Old Way, and in time, all that the Slavers had done returned broken into the damp earth.'

'Except the roads.'

'Except the roads. Those have outlasted all the rest, but even the work of giants decays, Willand.' Gwydion shifted, drew in a great breath and fell silent. By now the sun had slipped lower, sculpting the wizard's face as if it was stone. At length he stirred. 'Since the Slavers left, the Realm has been invaded many times. Dozens of armies landed, year upon year, until the greatest conqueror of all made the Realm his own and began a fresh wave of stone building. But Gillan the Conqueror built castles, not roads. And now the Slaver roads are a thousand years old and are fast being broken up.'

Will suddenly saw the point at last. 'So the land is no longer quartered and the battlestones are no longer alone in their malice. That's why the lorc is awakening!'

The wizard nodded gravely. 'I believe that sparks have begun to pass along the limbs of the sleeping giant once more. He is twitching. Whispers are travelling anew along the lorc, and for the first time in half a thousand years one battlestone has begun to sense another and thereby to rediscover its purpose.'

'But what does that mean?' Will said, turning over. 'Surely only that the Realm will become safe from invasion again?'

'It is as I have already told you.' Gwydion sighed deeply. 'The lorc is now tainted. The flow has been fatally warped. It has been turned brackish and is malign with poisons. We cannot dismantle every castle that stands in the Realm. We cannot return every stone to its quarry. Think of the many years in which invaders have been mingling in these isles. Which folk now have hearts warmed purely by native blood? Now everyone is descended from an invader! And so everyone will be touched by the insanity that will be inspired by the battlestones.'

Will felt a spot of rain on his face. There were grey clouds above now, though the sun was shining gold far over the sea. 'Is that really going to happen? Are we all going to be driven mad when the lorc wakes up?'

'It has already started. Do you not yet see how foolish decisions plague us? How lords flap their mouths endlessly, yet do nothing to solve the real problems that beset the Realm? No one knows what to do for the best, and worse, no one seems to care. Oh, the battlestones are certainly talking one to another! And to stop them now seems an impossible task.'

Gwydion got up and walked slowly down the slope of the barrow. Will watched him gaze into the West. For the first time he saw how great was the problem, and how high the price of failure.

But what has any of it got to do with me? he thought unhappily. I'm not a lord. I can't do anything. I'm just a wizard's lad – apprentice and bag-carrier. As Gwydion himself said, 'The fault's not yours'.

He left the wizard to his dismal contemplation of the sunset, and rubbed at his leg until the pins and needles went away. Then he took himself off, making a half turn around the barrow. To his surprise he found that it had an entrance. There were stone walls and stone posts and a stone lintel making a low doorway. There seemed no harm in going inside and so he ducked under the lintel and shuffled forward into the darkness within.

At first it was hard to see anything. There was a dank smell and he could feel hard-packed earth underfoot. Slowly his eyes grew accustomed to the gloom and he saw he was in a round chamber with walls made of stacked, unmortared stone. There in the centre stood a great rough-hewn plinth. It was squarish, though a lot taller than it was broad and a little broader than it was deep. He reached out to touch it and felt something pleasant pass through his fingers. He wanted to hug the stone tight, for it seemed as if it could heal hurts and give a mighty comfort to anyone of troubled mind.

Then Will found himself shading his eyes because a narrow beam of light had somehow found its way into the barrow and was now falling square on the stone. His eyes were drawn to the stone and he saw something that made him shout out loud.

'Master Gwydion! Master Gwydion, come quick!'

A moment later the wizard entered the chamber, staff in hand, ready to face whatever peril Will had found. 'I am here!'

'It's the stone, Master Gwydion! Look at it!'

And there, revealed by the light of an equinox sunset, were dozens of markings. They ran along the edges, and the stone itself was glowing with a dull light that seemed to rise and fall, as if it was breathing, or perhaps drinking in the sunlight.

Gwydion's eyes opened wide with delight, 'It has drawn you here after all! Or you have found it. Then, this is a sister-stone and maybe all is not yet lost!'

'But those ridges and furrows! What are they? They just came up in the stone's edges while I watched, like . . . like whip weals.'

The wizard examined the marks. 'They are called ogham. It is an inscription. I should have known!'

'You mean a kind of writing? Can you read it?'

Will touched the stone again and felt a power coiling and uncoiling within. He drew away his hand again quickly, then he felt something rubbing itself against the back of his legs and he turned. There was a beautiful white cat looking up at him with big golden eyes. Its tail was up as it wound itself about Will's shins.

'Pangur Ban!' he called out. He picked the cat up and held him. 'How did you get here all the way across the sea from Wychwoode?' He cradled the cat, then let him ride his shoulder. 'Look, Master Gwydion! He's called Pangur Ban.'

Gwydion tore himself away from his study of the stone, enough to say distractedly, 'Oh, I know him well enough. He travels much and always seeks good company, though the Blessed Isle is much more to his taste than the Wychwoode ever was. But look at the stone! The inscription seems to be in the form of a question: *Si ni ach menh fa ainlugh?* It means loosely, "But whose light am I?" Or perhaps, "Am I the brilliance of the Lord of Light?"'

He moved round the stone and examined the next side, pronouncing one word at a time, '*Tegh brathir ainmer na.* Which might mean something like, "The name of my brother is Home".'

Will wrinkled his nose at that. 'It doesn't make much sense, does it?'

'It is written in a very old ogham, not the later oghams of the revival. This inscription was wrought by one who knew well the language of stones. *Tilla angid carreic na duna.* "Here in the morbid stone city".' Gwydion moved further round. '*Aittreib muan nadir si a buan.* "Has my dragon returned to dwell." But we do not know the order of the lines. Or for certain where the verse begins or ends.'

'Does it matter?'

'Of course it matters. Let us suppose it begins with the sunlit side then proceeds sunwise around the stone as it should. And ogham, I might say, is always read from bottom to top.'

Gwydion stroked his beard and spoke the whole verse:

> '*Si ni ach menh fa ainlugh?*
> *Tegh brathir ainmer na.*
> *Tilla angid carreic na duna,*
> *Aittreib muan nadir si a buan.*

'But whose light am I?
The name of my brother is "Home".
Here in the morbid stone city.
Has my dragon returned to dwell.'

He mused. 'Perhaps not "morbid", perhaps it is "malicious".'

'I told you it didn't make any sense.'

'Look!' Gwydion growled. 'The sunlight is now almost halfway across the face of the stone. If I do not find the key to it soon the chance will be lost for at least another year – and that almost certainly means for ever.'

Will stepped back from the stone, chastened. He watched as the wizard's long fingers played over the pillar, checking the translation again. Then he watched the square of light track across the carved face as the sunbeam moved. When it reached the edge of the stone it slid slowly but irresistibly onto the far wall. Gwydion moved round the stone as the light faded from it. When the last tiny glimmer left the stone, the ogham vanished. Gwydion stood up straight and said, 'Come here . . .'

Will moved in closer, awed. 'What?'

'Look at the stone, Willand. Tell me what you see?'

'I don't see anything, Master Gwydion.'

'But you will. In time, you will see such a thing again, and you will read it, for you are he, and I mean to teach you the language of stones!'

Something about the wizard's fierce triumph scared him, though Gwydion's mood now was the mirror of his earlier despair.

'Are you all right, Master Gwydion?'

'Oh, this is an art I have learned and forgotten and learned again. Did you see how the marks were set along every upright edge? They were like that because they carry two meanings. The first was there to be read plainly: he who stands opposite each corner in turn may read the meaning and be satisfied. But there is a second meaning which is not to be read so easily. It may only be followed by one who walks sunwise around the stone. It jumps from edge to edge, then up to the next row. That is an old druid trick, and one they may have learned from such stones as these!'

'Then this truly is a sister-stone?'

'What do you think?'

'How would I know?' Will tried to take a turn about the stone but Gwydion put out an arm and stopped him.

'Sunwise, Willand. The way you are going is called "widdershins". It is disrespectful. You must always walk sunwise about a standing stone, you must always turn to your right hand.'

Will looked at the stone wonderingly as the last of the sunlight died in the chamber. 'So, what does the other reading say?'

In the gloomy confines Gwydion's voice was deep and resonant, yet the true tongue sounded in Will's ears like harpstrings.

> *Si ni tegh tilla aittreb,*
> *Ach menh brathir angid muan,*
> *Fa ainmer carreic na nadir si,*
> *Ainlugh na duna a buan.*

'In the plain speech of today we have:

> *I am Here returned Home,*
> *But my Wicked Brother,*
> *Whose Name is "Dragon Stone",*
> *Dwells yet beneath the City of Light'.*

They left the barrow and stood under a sky that had turned to the colour of embers. Gwydion planted his feet in the grass and tasted the air again to test the weather.

'City of Light!' he cried. 'I know that name. The wind is backing somewhat. Maybe fortune favours us, after all, for it will soon be set fair for a crossing. Come, my excellent young friend, we have a ship to find!' And with that he went striding away.

'Wait!' Will cried. 'What about Pangur Ban?'

But the cat was nowhere to be seen. Will was suddenly unsure if he had dreamed him. By now Gwydion was almost gone from sight too.

'Hey!' he shouted. 'Wait for me!'

CHAPTER TEN

LEIR'S TREASURE

Their 'ship' turned out to be no more than a cockleshell. They found her in the port of Cauve, and she was given to Gwydion for a song by one of the masters who suspected a sinking spell had been cast over his vessel. Unlike the big trader ships that were tied up at the mole, Gwydion's boat was no more than a narrow basket with two benches set across and oiled hides stretched under and over. There was a sapling tied like a whipstaff, and pulled back taut for a mast, and a bellying sail of canvas.

At first Will was afraid to go in her. He found it hard to believe that such a vessel could succeed without magical aid. Sometimes water slopped over the low sides and into the bottom, and it became Will's job to bale. Gwydion said little and did nothing but stare ahead and work the steering oar from time to time. Nor was it the most comfortable way to go upon the sea, yet it skimmed along, and Will was astonished to find how the little boat conquered the great grey waves with ease.

He had thought that it would be in the nature of large stretches of water to lie flat like the pool at Grendon Mill, or like the sea he had seen from the clifftops, but it turned out that when seen close to the sea was anything but flat.

It was made of great hills of water that in a moment became valleys. The rolling of the waves made his stomach turn at first, but he soon got over that, and found that so long as he was able to fix his eyes on the distant skyline his belly would be stopped from complaining.

Once he cupped his hand like a dipper and lifted a handful to quench his thirst, but quickly spat it out again.

'Urgh! It tastes of salt!'

'Indeed it does,' Gwydion chuckled. 'Did I not warn you of that? You will not see me drinking of it, for I have sailed with Manannan, son of the Sea.'

The wizard drew the boat first close in to the rocky coast, then he steered far out across the ocean's deep, so they almost – but not quite – lost sight of land. Out there in the watery wastes there were sometimes dark shapes down below, a giant fish as big as a man, a monster perhaps. And there were other wonders that made Will smile, things almost as transparent as the water they lived in, round they were, with bodies of jelly that pulsed and throbbed upon the waves and trailed long ribbons beneath.

Will drowsed at times, but Gwydion's head never dropped. They had bread, cheese and fruit with them for their journey, and on the first day even a piece of smoked fish that Gwydion would not eat, and a skin of fresh milk. Will saw two sunsets behind and two sunrises ahead before the last of the land disappeared into the final sunset and they found themselves alone on a black sea overspread by a sky of jewels.

Will pointed out the star pattern he knew as the Plough low in the northern sky. Gwydion called it *Liag*, and said that was a fae name because to them it had looked like a water ladle. He showed Will how to steer by the Pole Star, which was a star that lay near the Plough, and how to keep a steady course as the boat bucked and splashed under them and the stars wheeled serenely overhead. No sooner had the sun gone down in the west than a bright star rose up in the east ahead of them. Gwydion said it was a good omen, for the star was king of the sky wanderers, known in the true tongue as *Riannana Lugh*, or Lugh's Star.

When Will asked about the song the wizard had sung to gain the boat, Gwydion sang it in full, an ancient song of the sea, but his words were not of summer's joy, rather he sang of the hard watches that the ocean rovers of old endured at winter's night upon the deeps, of places in the Far North that were hard and grey and ever as cold as ice:

> '*Hearken to this truth I tell you,*
> *Lost, we sailed the stark salt wave.*

> '*Dealing days of bitter hardship,*
> *Steering straight, our lives to save.*

> '*Strange the seas and mischance many,*
> *So far the fathoms, so deep the swell.*

> '*Of frosty, fearsome waters travelled,*
> *No landsman, haven-safe, can tell . . .*'

And so it went on, and Will's mind's eye saw a great wave sweep a warrior from his ship, saw men in the bleak watches of the night chipping frozen spume from the planks, from rigging ropes grown thicker than a man's leg, chipping with unfeeling fingers until the dawn came, chipping without cease so the weight of ice would not turn the ship under. On and on the wizardly words rolled, like the wind, like the sea. They made a song of deeds done in a far place, in a time that long ago had passed out of mortal ken, but deeds that should ever be remembered by those who came after.

'You will go there one day, I think, Willand,' Gwydion said when the song was done. 'One day, a long time from now, you will travel into the Far North, to the place where stands the icy mountain that is called the Baerberg.'

'Are you making another prophecy?' Will asked, unsure if he was happy to be the subject of such a forecast.

'Some might see it as such, though I would not, for this has not the strength of definite promise about it. It is but a fair likelihood in my estimation.'

On the morning of the fifth day, Will noticed that the sea had changed colour. He was pleased to see a green coast coming up to the north. There were cliffs and pale strands and purple hills behind – the magical land of Cambray, Gwydion said. And in the other direction lay an island far distant and soon passed, an isle the wizard said was named Inysh Lughnasad. There was a misty coast beyond it.

'Why is the sea brown now?' he asked.

'Because the water we are in is not so much a sea as the mouth of a huge river – the Great River of the West. Cambray lies to the west of it. That is a most favoured land!'

Soon the coast began to enclose them from both sides, and an inrushing brown tide picked them up. It bore them headlong into the estuary, and they rode a magical wave that Gwydion said was no magic of his but a natural memorial to Severine, granddaughter of King Brea, who was drowned nearby.

They beached the boat at high tide, and as soon as Will stepped ashore he knew for certain that he was back in the Realm. There was something about the way the air tasted, something about the way the ground felt under his feet. They breakfasted on blackberries that grew above the mudflats. Will boiled a pail of mussels too. Then he took a long-needed sleep until the waters turned again and they were able to ride another surge of water up along the broad reaches of the muddy river, which Gwydion now called 'Severine's Flood'.

When he asked about Severine and how she had drowned, Gwydion said it was a sad tale. 'I told you how

King Brea conquered the giants and how Magog and Gogmagog were brought to Trinovant to serve as porters. After that, Brea took to him Inogen, daughter of Pendrax. She bore him three sons, Loegrin, Alban and Cambaer. When the Realm passed to Loegrin, he took to him Gwendolin, daughter of Corinax, yet King Loegrin lay with the Lady Estril, and this was his undoing for Gwendolin warred jealously upon him and killed him. And in this very place, below the city of Caer Gloustre, Gwendolin drowned both Estril and her daughter Severine, so that, even to this day, the men of Cambray call the Great River "Severine's Flood" and give good respect to the swans, which you may know are the creatures that guard the mysteries of all rivers.'

'Swans? Why?'

'They are the mystic guardians of all rivers.'

'I didn't know,' Will said.

'Then you do not know much.'

Will looked down the track ahead. 'I suppose that now we're back in the Realm we'll have to be careful and start watching out for trouble again.'

Gwydion cast him a sharp glance. 'I expect you are right.'

'Your enemy will be on the lookout for us, won't he?'

'From now on we must take even greater care not to attract his attention.'

'What does he look like, Master Gwydion? It would help if I knew how to recognize him.'

The wizard shook his head, his manner once more grim. 'In truth, these days he has the look of a death's-head about him. But you would not be able to recognize him if you looked for that, for he goes abroad most often in hand-some disguise.'

'Handsome?' Will undid the crane bag and drew out his silver horn. He polished it again with his sleeve. 'If he comes, shall I blow upon this?'

'I think you should not blow upon that without reading it first.'

Will looked closely at the words carved around the rim. 'But I can't read what it says. These letters are not in any shape that I was taught.'

Gwydion took it and looked closely at the inscription. 'This is written in the true tongue,

> *'Ca iaillea nar oine baiguel ran,*
> *Ar seotimne meoir narla an,*
> *Aln ta'beir aron diel gan.'*

'I'm none the wiser for that, Master Gwydion.'

'Let me show you: Here – *iaille*, a moment of time. And here, *baigullar*, which is not quite a verb, might mean to imperil, or a need. Then we have *seotiem*, a gust of wind, and *morhne*, me, myself, but only when talking of the me which is to come. And this word *ta'beir* means to carry upon your own shoulders, or ownership in coming time, or perhaps the colour of a possession or the way in which you carry something you like—'

Will sighed and took the horn back. 'If that's the true tongue, then I'll never begin to understand it.'

'—and *ediell* is haste, of which you have too much.' Gwydion raised his eyebrows. 'We say, *fa nah aron diel* for "make haste" or "go speedily". But if you want the meaning plainly, then,

> *'Should you stand in time of need,*
> *Blow me, and you shall have . . . speed.'*

Will put the horn away, satisfied. 'Well, why didn't you say so in the first place? That's easy enough – whenever we've need of haste, I'll blow the horn.'

The next day the wizard surrendered the boat to a merchant he met along the riverbank. Though a piece of silver was offered for it Gwydion would take nothing more than half a dozen crab apples from under the merchant's tree and the promise of a future favour. He engaged the man in lengthy conversation which Will did not overhear, then they set off across country on foot, travelling always south by east.

'Where are we going now, Master Gwydion? Not back to Clarendon, I hope.'

'The bee knows, lad.'

'And what's that supposed to mean? If the bee knows, he's not telling.'

'The virtue of wayfaring is not always just to get somewhere. It is to gather enough nectar for a man's thoughts to feed upon. That is how the best honey is made. But if it will satisfy you better to know, we are going to find the City of Light.'

But the answer did not satisfy Will, and perhaps it was not meant to. He was prickled enough by it to ask another question, this time about something that had been bothering him.

'Would it not have helped us to have taken what that merchant offered for the boat?'

'Do you mean silver coin? I do not carry smelted-earth about with me.'

'What harm can a little silver do? And anyway, I could carry it for you.'

'Could you, now? What is the harm in silver?' The wizard tossed him a crab apple. 'Here! I was given leave to gather these. Eat if you are hungry.'

Will looked at the wizened apple, bit into it and made a face. 'It's sour. I don't want it.'

Gwydion grunted. 'Nothing is sour but that which we take to be so. And do not confuse wants with desires. A song given to a friend paid for that boat. It was given away on a friendly promise likewise. The man who has friends is always richer than the one who has silver.'

'Tell me why you don't carry metal with you. What's wrong with smelting it from the earth? No birds or animals die to make silver or iron.'

'It is not true that I carry no metal at all, for I always wear this.' Gwydion drew a short-bladed knife from inside his gown. He pulled off the canvas sheath and Will saw how the polished iron gleamed with an unusual pattern like straw scattered across a threshing room floor. 'It is most precious, for it is true star-born iron. It comes from the days when iron was rarer than gold, stronger than anything that was known, prized, handed down from father to son, and always named. In those days men had not yet been taught the sorcerers' secret of how to squeeze the liquid essence of iron out of stones. The only iron was that which fell to earth from the skies inside shooting stars. All the greatest tools of wizardry were once made of star-iron like this.'

'It's a nice knife.'

'It is not a knife, Willand. It is a ritual blade. There is a great deal of difference.'

'I still think you should have taken some coin for the boat.'

'Are you suffering?'

'No.'

'Then be content, and let your feet take you where they will.'

It was not long before they entered a pleasant wood, and soon happened upon a glade and in it lay a sinister pond in which it seemed that nothing lived. The sight of it sent a murmur of fear through Will and he stepped back from its edge. Gwydion seemed to sense what was amiss also. The water was perfectly clear but the bottom was as black as charcoal. A shaft of sunlight penetrated into its depths, and in a far corner, where the breeze had blown across its surface, a fine web of scum floated. Will thought he saw the silvery-white bellies of fish dead among it. Instead of pond water alive with many green twitching things, this water was barren. Moreover, it seemed that everything had been killed at a stroke. Gwydion prodded the mud at the edge of the water and examined the scorch marks on the trunks of a stand of sad-looking pine trees. 'Maskull,' he muttered at last, his grip tightening on his staff. 'This is certainly his work!'

Will looked around, half expecting Gwydion's enemy to appear, but no movement broke the stillness.

'Death and destruction has lately been wrought here. Even so, Willand, let me show you a reason for hope.' Gwydion tossed a tiny pebble into the water and Will watched it plop and saw the rings spread out from it. 'Do you see how those ripples reach out to touch all parts of the surface? And do you see how, in a very short time, the ripples die away? Fate is like that.'

The wizard rooted up a much bigger stone. It was as big as Will's head. With a whisper he launched it into an arc high over the water. Will stared as the stone lurched up to the top of its path then miraculously slowed and stopped.

'How do you do that?' Will said, in awe.

'It takes a great deal of effort. But it is worth it. Watch!'

Will saw the rock falling slowly towards the water now, turning as it fell. He watched it fall as few others before him had ever watched a rock fall. He saw it push its way down into the clear water and throw the surface up in a great glistening crown. Then the crown broke up into shimmering drops that also fell back. Now, where the rock had fallen there was a great hole in the water and Will could still see the top of the rock until it sank and the water gradually closed over it. For a moment everything stopped again, but then it quickened until all was as it should be.

The surface of the pond was covered in little waves and water swilled in the black mud at its edge, but eventually, just as Gwydion said, the waves died away and stillness returned so the pond was much as it had always been.

'Do you see how the water heals itself?' Gwydion said. 'In the same way the fate of the world closes up after a violent blow. It finds its own level again in time. Things return to the true path, to what was always meant to be, so that everything that men do – be they selfless acts of charity or repugnant crimes – all is eventually swallowed up by time and forgotten.'

Will stared at the water. 'But I thought you were going to tell me a reason for hope.'

Gwydion smiled and leaned on his staff. 'Now you see how Maskull can say, "What does anything matter that men do? Men live and men die, and all they do becomes in time dust before the wind." But perhaps you also see that he is wrong, for who would say that flowers do not last and therefore do not matter? And who would say that since the end be known, the journey does not matter? In great wisdom there may lie great sorrow, and in the end, for some, there must be madness.'

Will gasped, for a huge thought had struck him. 'What if Maskull in his madness could find a stone so large that the pond couldn't heal itself?'

'Oh, you are wise beyond your years, Willand,' Gwydion turned to him and his eyes flashed. 'The boulder that Maskull wishes to throw into the pond of the world is so big that we will be thrown forever from the true path. If Maskull wins, the world will never be the same again.'

As Will contemplated the dark surface of the pond the waters began to foam and boil and he drew back in fear, thinking that Gwydion's rock had awakened some writhing thing that lurked in the blackness under the waters.

'It's a marish hag!' he shouted, fear crawling over him.

But Gwydion merely spread his arms and whispered subtle words. His eyes closed and a weird light came from him. The water in the pond began to cloud. Reeds sprang up and green weed appeared. A shoal of tiny fish turned as one in the shallows and damsel flies fluttered above, chased now by a wagtail. Then Will saw a smiling frog at his feet. It was as green as grass with two fine black stripes along its sides and big yellow eyes that closed and opened again as it swallowed. The frog leapt into the water and swam away, and when it had gone Gwydion stepped back from the water's edge and bowed long and low to the pond which he had restored to life.

Will felt a great bubble of joy well up inside him and lodge in his throat. 'Oh, that's beautiful,' he whispered.

'So it is.' Gwydion put his hand on Will's shoulder. 'Come along, bag-carrier! It is time you tried to forget about the marish hag. Remember what I said about doing away with painful memories – what's done and cannot be undone must not become heavy baggage for tomorrow.'

They tracked eastward, walking up hill and down dale, and Will learned much about the earth as he watched the leaves begin to yellow on the trees. All was fine and the season was just as an autumn in the Realm should be, yet Gwydion paused at every crossroads they came to and sniffed about like an old dog. Whenever they topped a hill or emerged from a wooded break Will felt threat simmering in the air. And when next he caught Gwydion peering narrow-eyed into a clear blue sky he said, 'What is it you're searching for?'

But the wizard said only, 'Eyes of a hawk, ears of a hare!' And after a moment he added, 'Did you know that hawks have no liking for the autumn? It is their least favourite season and makes them bad-tempered.'

'Hawks, Master Gwydion?'

'Think about it! Hawks earn their meat not so much by

the sharpness of their beaks and talons, but by the sharpness of their eyes. And a bird who spends his time watching for small movements in the grass – now what would annoy him more than countless brown leaves blowing across the land?'

Will ignored the wizard's whimsy, knowing it was aimed at forestalling his fears and his endless questions. 'If we're not going to Clarendon again are you taking me to another secret place like the Wychwoode? Somewhere to be put for my own protection? If you are, can I go to a place where there are many people? We say in the Vale that the best place to hide a tree is in a forest.'

'You may have something there. But I believe it may be best to hide you by not hiding you at all.'

Will sighed. 'When will we get there?'

'I have told you once that we are going to find the City of Light. Be patient, for there is much for you to learn on the way.' Gwydion put hands on his shoulders and turned him about to look northward. 'See that? We say that land has "good aspect".'

'Good aspect – isn't that what you told the Hogshead about once?'

'Indeed I did. I had forgotten that you were eavesdropping. So, good aspect, plain to see.'

Will looked at the cabbage field and nodded. 'Good aspect, Master Gwydion.'

Then the wizard directed him to face east. 'Whereas that meadow over there has bad aspect. Can you feel it? Can you feel the sluggishness in the earth?'

'No, Master Gwydion,' he said in a monotone.

'But it's as plain as a pikestaff, lad!'

'That field has cabbages in it, and that one has rabbits,' he said helpfully. 'Is that it?'

The wizard sighed heavily. 'Sometimes, Willand, I am driven to doubt that you could possibly be the one I have taken you to be.'

'I'm sorry, Master Gwydion. But I am trying.'

'I know. And that is what worries me.' The wizard pointed out a furrowed field. 'There is a reason why the crops do not do well down there. All farmers know that plants grow by the moon. Always sow on a waxing moon, they say, for plants of all kinds love the moon!'

'I'm hungry,' he said flatly. 'Do you think we could pull up a few of those moon plants and make a salad of them?'

'Hungry again?' Gwydion gave him a hard look. 'Very well, we shall rest in a little while. Choose a spot you like.'

But it was not until they had passed by Leirburh that Will said he wanted to sit down.

'Here?' the wizard asked, looking carefully at him.

'No. Over there. It looks like a nicer place to eat.'

'Then let your feet lead us to it.'

Will steered them towards a small knoll by the side of the track. It was not far from a crossroads, and Gwydion hunted about there and found a string of leaves. It was just that – a string onto which a hundred twigs and leaves had been threaded. Beside it was a feathery wreath twisted together expertly from the heads and stems of wild barley. Gwydion examined both objects carefully then broke them up and scattered them.

'What were they?' Will asked, recalling an earlier time when he had seen Gwydion make a similar wreath and leave it by the roadside.

The wizard sounded unusually thoughtful. 'One was a letter, the other a signature. Eat your fill quickly. We must go on.'

'But I want to rest here on this little knoll.'

Gwydion's eyes narrowed. 'Why have you brought us to the Tump, I wonder?'

The wizard seemed to sink into melancholy, as if he was wrestling with difficult news. Will picked a hatful of black-berries and took out a little of the cheese he still had in his bundle. Then he chewed the last of the small, wrinkled apples that Gwydion had got for the boat. They had been getting sweeter each time he ate one, and he had been saving the last. It was so deliciously sour that it made his mouth go dry, but as he sat back on the grassy rise he fondly remembered the surprise visit of Pangur Ban in the Blessed Isle, and he lay back to enjoy the sudden blaze of late sunshine.

He thought of Willow then, and brought to mind the Midsummer song she had sung for him about the prince and his three apple trees. He wished she was here now, and wondered how long it would be before he returned to the Wychwoode. One day I'll go back there and find her, he thought. One day. Whether Gwydion likes it or not, and that's a promise!

The wizard was still nosing around anxiously. He could not settle, and all the while his hawk eyes were scouring the far hills, looking for signs of danger. Will tried to ignore the prickling he felt in his own skin. He spat out three pips and planted them each a finger's depth in the soil of the knoll. When Gwydion saw him do it he danced down from the barrow and began to grovel on hands and knees until the earth itself trembled.

'What are you doing?' Will called to him in alarm.

'Quickly! Get down off the Tump!'

Will needed no second telling. He dashed down off the little knoll and panic-fear flooded him as he saw Gwydion raise his staff and begin to shriek out in the true tongue. But though the ground had trembled, no great upheaval followed.

'Master Gwydion, what's amiss? Did I do wrong?'

For a moment Gwydion gave no answer, then he cried, 'Maskull! Are you here? Show yourself!'

Will stared around, bristling, but again seeing nothing. Then Gwydion went down on his knees again. 'Aggggh!'

'What's wrong?'

'Wrong?' Gwydion's eyes were swimming and rimmed red. A rapture seemed to be upon him, but then he steadied. 'Nothing is wrong. That was a fine gift you made to a great king. To have made it in kindness, an offering made upon a tomb! You are the one! You must be, else how could you have known what to do?'

Will pulled at his arm. 'Master Gwydion, get up.'

The wizard jumped to his feet. 'How did you unlock the tomb? Hmmm? Tell me!'

'I didn't do anything . . . I was just putting apple seeds into the ground and then—'

'Apple seeds! The fruit of Avalon! And behold the consequence!'

Will spun round. His mouth opened as he saw the little knoll begin to shimmer like heat over a dusty summer road. He looked to where his feet had stood just moments before. The knoll seemed suddenly to turn to vapour so that now he could see to its very centre.

It was a tomb! Inside there was a chamber, but it seemed to be empty. As Will approached the shimmering began again and a glitter of brightness flashed through the empty chamber.

'*Arh twydion iy dionor, Semias-baigh!*' Gwydion shouted. He danced aggressively forward as if in challenge to Death himself. But then the wizard gave out a great yell of triumph. 'This is no sorcery! The tomb is truly undisturbed! Can it be that there is no more than one simple spell upon it? The one cast by Semias so long ago?'

'What have we come to?' Will asked, following uncertainly.

'Oh, gaze in awe, Willand, for this surely is the tomb of King Leir of old!'

'A king?'

'Great Leir! Do you really know nothing of that illustrious

name? He was eleventh king of the Realm. Leir, who reigned for sixty years! So great a warrior was he that he lived to be an old man, and few warriors do that! Come with me, Willand. See old Leir, who at the leaving of his life was so much troubled in his mind by his three daughters.'

They went deep into the barrow, which was now filled with an eerie blue-white glow that came from a point that hung in thin air. Gwydion reached out to it and threw back a shroud of white feathers. It was a mantle that had been laid upon the king, and the moment it was taken away his skeleton was revealed. He was dressed in battle gear, and surrounded by an array of weapons the like of which Will had never seen before. He thought he heard warrior shouts, the gigging of shields, the gnash and gnaw of horses all fleet and frisk for battle. When he looked again he saw the chamber was filled with similar treasures, glittering darkly and in an unearthly manner. Terrified, he bent over the skull that lay grey and loose within a helm of bronze. Its toothless grin accused him and he recoiled.

'Show respect, Willand! Your clever feet have brought us to a place that has long been hidden from the world, though many have wanted to find it.'

Will stared at the great shield with its boss of bronze, at the spears and swords that surrounded the bones, at gold and jewels that were enough to bemuse the eye.

'I . . . I wouldn't bring us to a place like this, Master Gwydion,' he stammered.

'But you did! Though you asked me a hundred times where I was taking you, it was your own feet that were leading us.' The wizard took the shining sword from beside the king and stooped to kneel before Will. 'Take this kingly blade in your hand! Wield it! It is yours!'

Will backed away. 'I don't want to take it.'

'But you must!' the wizard urged.

'No!' He turned again to look at the other treasures, but

he would not touch any of them. 'Master Gwydion. If I've brought us here, then oughtn't I be the one to decide what's right to do here? You may take what you will, but I don't want to touch anything, for as I see it it belongs to Leir and I'd let him keep it all.'

But the wizard's eyes were already hungrily examining the cloak of swan's feathers and now such a note of awe came into his voice that Will turned to him. 'Never in this world . . .'

'What now, Master Gwydion?'

'If I am not deceived, this very cloak was brought out of the Realm Below long ages ago by a king far greater than Leir. *Whomsoever wears his mantle shall remain unseen by mortal eye* . . . Now I understand how Semias could have hidden King Leir so easily. Look at the jewel that secures his shroud! Oh! This bauble I have long wished to gaze upon!'

Will saw the clasp of intricately wrought gold and silver, and the great blue-white diamond that decorated it. Gwydion took out his knife of star-iron and whispered subtle words, then he broke the stone free from its setting. He admired the colour for a moment, then replaced the cloak over the king's body. Will gasped as the bones and the array of treasures vanished away once more.

They fled from the tomb as the earth of the Tump reappeared and the barrow became a grassy knoll once more. Will rubbed at his eyes as if he was waking from a dream.

'Come, Willand!' Gwydion said, striding away. 'Little do you know what you have done this day, for it could be that you have delivered us from the one who would destroy us!'

On they went to north and east for many days, crossing now into the Middle Shires, heading ever towards the well-ordered Earldom of Warrewyk, yet tacking back and forth, it seemed, to no great purpose, while Gwydion became ever more urgent and excited. At Tollton they found a bridge over the Stoore, but the purple-faced bridgeman stopped them. He wore a faded red coat and a tattered badge – the chained bear, which was, Gwydion explained, the family device of the Earl of Warrewyk, Captain of Callas port and the richest man in the Realm.

'Now, then. It's a penny each, or the long way around for you beggars,' the bridgeman said.

'Since when has the Earl Warrewyk's men stopped honest folk at this crossing?' Gwydion asked, looking at the man's badge. 'Why does he seek to take money from them?'

'War's coming. It'll be paid for by the likes of you,' the bridgeman said, and Will grew aware of other figures in Warrewyk colours coming out from the shed behind them. There were six men, armed with clubs and ready for business.

'Trouble?' one of them said.

'No trouble at all,' the bridgeman replied, and without warning the nearest man swung his club at Will's head.

He was only just able to duck a braining, but the next moment he was thrown down by a crunching blow to his back. Then everything boiled up inside him and his senses became a blur as he and his assailant rolled over along the egde of a roadside ditch. The clubs flew fast and furious about Will's head, and he knew that soon a murderous blow must break his skull and he would be done for. But he grappled the man close to him as best he could and tried to use him as a shield until he could tear away. Feet scuffled all around him, a blow landed on his back and he yelped. The man's grip was rough and his strength overpowering, but just as Will thought he had been pinned, to his astonishment the man's grip on his jerkin failed.

As Will broke free he saw Gwydion standing apart from the fighting, quietly watching it all happen with his arms half raised.

'Run!' Will shouted, and readied himself to fend off further blows, but everything had fallen strangely quiet. Three of the men had begun looking at one another as if the attack had all been a joke, the others behaved as if they could not understand what had come over them. The one that had borne Will down was being helped up. Will ran up and tore the club from him, then swung it but the blow swerved wide of the man's chest.

One of the other men laughed. 'Look at him!'

'You think it's funny, do you?' he shouted, outraged.

'Now, then,' the bridgeman murmured backing away. 'Pack that up, youngster. There's no need for that.'

'Master Gwydion, run!' Will tried to swing the club again, but this time it slipped from his fingers. The wizard came up and looked over the nearest of the men with close interest. 'Well, if that was not the sorriest fight I've seen in a long time,' he said, plucking at the white bear on the man's chest. The stitching gave way easily. 'I thought as much.'

Will's fear dissolved, but he was shaking and sweating from his efforts. 'I've a good mind to knock them all down while I can!'

'Hush!' the wizard said, his eyes roaming with interest over the bridgeman. 'Tell me, if you do not serve the white bear, then whose man are you?'

'I'm my Lord of Mells' man, sir.'

'And you were sent out to look for the Crowmaster and his young friend?'

'We've been waiting for him here these three days, since report came to us he'd been seen upon Foxcote Hill and was like to try the crossing here sooner or later.'

'You were charged to waylay him?'

'Aye. He's a warlock who's lost his powers. He has to be found and killed.'

'So says Duke Edgar?'

'That was his order.'

'Do you not fear the Crowmaster, then?'

'Some. But we has charms.'

'Let me see yours.'

The bridgeman opened his shirt and showed the sign of a ram's head tattooed on the man's left breast. Under it was the legend, 'ecipsuA .nretarF.'

'Under the guidance of the Fellowship,' Gwydion muttered.

He touched the man lightly upon the forehead so that he forgot about everything for a while.

'You have a disorder of the blood,' Gwydion whispered in his ear. 'Take dandelion root. And if you know Good Sister Knit-bone ask her kindly if she will spare you some of her best plantain. The boils will go away in five days.'

'You have a strange way with folk on bridges,' Will said, dusting himself off as they crossed over the Stoore. 'What did you do to them?'

'Nothing so very serious. They will recover what wits they possess before dark.'

'I thought I was nearly done for.'

'It is not an attack by Duke Edgar's bully boys that so greatly concerns me, it is that they were able to find us – if they can do that then so can others.'

As they marched onward, Will could not stop turning the attack over in his mind. It had unsettled him, and he began to see shapes and dangers lurking in every shadow. What Gwydion had said was true: if they had been seen going over Foxcote Hill, then spies must have been out there watching them. How many times had they passed within view of the many spires of the Sightless Ones? More often than he could remember, and the Sightless Ones had hirelings among the common people – hirelings whose eyes had not been plucked from their heads. Next time an attack came, it would be worse, for Duke Edgar was no small power in the Realm. As the queen's ally he could use the king's name to get anything he wanted. Perhaps Gwydion had already been declared an outlaw and a general bounty placed upon his head. But worse even than that was the thought that if the duke had found them, then it should be no great matter for Maskull to do the same.

At last they came to open country and Gwydion called Will to look out as he had often done across a broad run of land.

'There is much I do not yet understand about you,' the wizard said as they halted by a hazel tree. 'Some things do not fit with you, and now I must try to find out why. I have told you there are strong places and weak places in the earth, yet you seem to have no clear sense of them, no aptitude. Why not?'

Will shook his head. 'I don't know, Master Gwydion. I don't even know what you're talking about.'

'The finding of the flows is called "scrying". Watch what I do.' The wizard put his hands together and knelt down at the base of the tree, muttering and whispering. Then he took a fresh wand from it, stripped and split it halfway down and held it out ahead of him in the same inside-out sort of grip that Will had seen him use before. He seemed to be reading the movements of the wand as he walked.

'What are you feeling for?'

'Flows. I am feeling my way along a green lane. There are streams of power in the earth, stagnant pools, sinks and springs, all these flows lie beneath our feet. You ought to be able to feel them too.'

'When you say "flows", do you mean those great channels the fae made to move earth power to the battlestones?'

'Not the ligns – the lorc is an artifice that lies deep underground. I speak now only about the natural flows that pattern the surface of the land. When these flows are like running streams they make a place healthy, a place where folk like to linger. But when the flows are sluggish, folk want to hurry past.'

'Can all people feel them?' Will asked, feeling suddenly left out.

'Of course.'

'Then why can't I?'

'Perhaps you do, after a fashion. I have watched your moods change as you go along. I saw you recognize the great upwelling that pours from the land by the White Horse and again as we came by the Calendar of Figgesburgh, which is the earth ring that stands above Sarum. I watched your heart leap as you passed by that place. But your grasp of the land is quite different to that which moves in the bones of growers and herdsmen. It seems there is some interfering talent in you, one that is not in other folk. At present, I can say no more than that.'

Will felt even more uneasy as he set off again after the wizard. He thought of the verse they had read on the sister-stone, and remembered the benign power that had tingled in his fingers. He hated feeling different and wanted more than anything just to be like everyone else. He was suddenly filled with a feeling of futility. 'We're never going to be able to find the City of Light,' he muttered. 'Never!'

'I have high hopes still,' Gwydion said evenly, playing the hazel wand over the ground once more.

'*I am here returned home. But my wicked brother, whose name is Dragon Stone, dwells yet beneath the City of Light.*' He shook his head, no closer to solving the mystery. 'What is *that* supposed to mean? We're never going to find a battle-stone, Master Gwydion.'

The wizard turned to him, weighing his words. 'Twice in twenty paces you have uttered a counsel of despair, and yet this land is of fair to middling aspect. I wonder why?

Is there something about this place that bothers you especially?'

Will looked around him, and then inwardly at the hollowness in his heart. 'I . . . I just think it's like looking for a needle in a hayloft, as we say in the Vale.'

'Do not give up hope yet.'

'But the Realm is so big! And there's just the two of us, and we have so little time and you drag your heels all the while, Master Gwydion! You do, you know.'

'All the more reason for us to tread softly. More haste is less speed, as the rede says.'

Will tutted. 'What a poor pair of stone hunters we make. I don't know where we are, and you don't know where we're supposed to be going.'

The land they began to pass through now was heartland, as rich and as fat as any that Will had yet seen. The folk they met on the road from time to time spoke with a burr that reminded him very much of the Vale, and he wondered how close he was now to home. He dearly wanted to ask if they might go by way of the Vale. It would be wonderful to call in at Nether Norton, to see his mother and father again and to tell of his adventures, though he was sure they would have a hard time believing the least of what had happened to him. The pang he felt when he thought of home was painful, and made all the more painful by knowing that Gwydion had set the Vale under a magical cloak and that he would never be able to find his way home, unless the wizard showed him how.

'I never thought the Realm was so huge,' he said as they crested another rise and saw the land rolling away endlessly to north and east yet again.

'It takes many days to walk from one coast to the other. Tell me, have you never heard of the Great Book of the Realm?'

'Do you mean the Black Book?'

'The *Sgraiet na Taire*? Oh, not that. The Black Book is lost, though it was once a parchment scroll, and far more ancient than the book of which I presently speak. The Great Book of the Realm is not yet even five hundred years old. It is bound in red leather and sits in the king's palace at Trinovant. It lists all the towns and villages and hamlets, and records what wealth might be had from each of them. It is there so the Elders of the Sightless Ones know what to demand in tithes of each place. There are many thousands of villages in the Realm, and in my time I have visited each and every one many times over. I try to visit every place at least once in a generation.'

Will whistled softly. 'No wonder you're known wherever you go.'

The wizard stopped and leaned on his staff. Then he pointed into the distance towards a ridge of land. 'See there, Willand. I believe our quarry must be close now, for that hill not far away was of old a great burgh. Today it is called simply Burgh Hill and nothing stands upon it, but long ago it was the fortress city of Lugh. The Gadelish warriors who issued from that fortress joined with the Queen of the East and together they came within a whisker of throwing the invading armies of the Slaver empire back into the sea. But, by then, the power of the lorc was already broken and the men of Lugh's city were finally overawed and destroyed.'

'I don't see how that helps—'

'Lugh was also called "Lord of Light".'

'Oh.' Will threw up his hands in frustration. 'Yes, but even if you're right about Burgh Hill being the City of Light, even if a battlestone is somewhere in this district, how shall we find a single buried stone in such a wide spread of land? It could take months and months. Years even.'

The wizard turned a maddeningly unreadable gaze on

the land. 'At times of greatest flow I have sometimes fancied that I might sense the lorc myself.'

'I think that's no more than dangerous wishfulness, Master Gwydion.'

Soon they had come to the fringes of Badby Chase. Will looked out across the fields and saw by the margin of the woods a line of about a dozen figures walking along a path. He screwed up his eyes and saw they were wearing tall, masked headdresses and long grey robes. Each was following along with a hand placed on the shoulder of the man in front.

'Sightless Ones,' he whispered, sure of it.

Gwydion steered him under the shade of an oak. 'The Fellows come out from their chapter houses more often in autumn, when the full brightness of the sun has begun to diminish.'

'But they can't see us . . . or can they?'

'Not if we take care.'

They crept quietly round the brow of the hill and saw what place they had almost stumbled upon. There was a small chapter house, complete with attendant acreage worked by hirelings. There was also a garden lying inside a low wall, and three or four men could be seen watering rows of plants, while two more attended to one of the many bee hives. Robed figures were nowhere to be seen, except one who stood sentry at the gate.

At that moment, the line of Fellows reached the door and their leader halted. He seemed to gauge the moment, then led his line indoors. The feet of those that followed were at first unable to decide left from right, for as they came to the threshold they seemed to want to go the wrong way.

'They are recent recruits, new to the Fellowship,' Gwydion said. 'They are as yet unused to finding their way about.'

Their helpless obedience made Will grimace. But the

Fellows had soon passed from view, and Gwydion led him down from the hill on the far side towards Badby Chase. Tall oaks were close to the track and sent thick branches snaking overhead, making a tunnel of autumn colours.

As Will followed he thought again of the figure wrapped in a black mantle, hooded and cowled, the one he had seen standing by the king and queen.

'I saw someone who looked much like a Fellow at Clarendon Lodge, but he was dressed in black.'

Gwydion looked sidelong at him, yet he seemed preoccupied. 'Black, you say? Black . . . I do not recollect any Fellow of the Dark Order being present at Clarendon. Nor could that be so.'

'But I *did* see a man in black.' He sighed and trotted after. 'Tell me, Master Gwydion, is there really an Old Father Time? They shouted that at you at Clarendon.'

'There is an Old Father Time. Though I am not he.'

Will grinned at that and fell silent for a while as they passed deeper into the woods, but then he asked suddenly, 'Does the figure of Death really appear whenever some great personage is going to die?'

'What makes you ask such a thing?'

'I was just thinking.'

'The answer is: it is rare for anyone to see Death, and rarer still to see him attending another. Nor does his appearance herald only the fall of the great. Some hold that those who see his form will themselves soon be visited.'

Will felt a shiver run through his flesh, and when it had passed an uneasiness remained with him. He looked at the dark woods of Badby Chase, and saw too late that there was movement all around.

'Master Gwydion!'

'Stand you there!'

Will was jerked out of his daydream by the challenge that came from behind them. Gwydion halted.

'Show us your hands, or you'll die!'

Three men appeared ahead of them, and others carrying pitchforks and hammers came out of the bushes. At least four figures hung back in the shadows, bowstrings pulled taut to their lips.

Outlaws! Will thought. A deadening fear unfolded inside him as he saw the deadly arrowheads pointed at him. His hand crept past the bag and the silver-bound horn that lay within, but the crane bag was shut and he knew that one hasty move might cost his heart a skewering. He did as Gwydion had already done and raised his hands, suspicious now that they had been caught by Duke Edgar's men.

A woman of middling age was led forward by two younger women. She raved and her eyes rolled. She seemed to Will to be hopelessly mad.

'Is he the one?' a hollow-faced man asked her.

'Look! He has a different lad with him now!'

Gwydion waited for the older woman to answer, but she merely gurgled and tossed her head.

'It was him,' one of the young women urged. 'It was, wasn't it?'

The men brandished their weapons, grim-faced yet unsure what to do as the mad woman still gave no answer.

'We have urgent business,' Gwydion murmured. 'Tell us why you will not let us pass.'

'Keep quiet!'

'Bring them!' the other young woman shouted.

'Where's my Wale?' another cried. 'What have you done with him?'

One of the men stepped forward and reached out roughly to Gwydion, but the wizard stayed him. 'I will come with you willingly,' he said. 'You may put up your weapons.'

'No one will touch you if you're innocent,' one of the men said. He was trying to see that the situation did not get out of hand, but Will could see that matters were poised on a knife-edge.

Another of the men was white-lipped with rage. 'And if you're not innocent, you'll soon not be caring about anything! Do you hear me?'

As Will hurried alongside he whispered, 'Master Gwydion, who are these people?'

'Steady, Willand. They are just the good folk of Preston Mantles.'

He lowered his voice, very scared now. 'Good folk? But they're waylaying us.'

'It would be a calamity for all concerned,' Gwydion said quietly, 'if I refused to be brought into their village.'

Will looked around at the men who led them through scrubby woods. They were in real agitation, and Will saw that some were guarding them from the rest. He whispered, 'You're going to let them take us wherever they want? What about—?'

'They will not touch you. The folk of Preston Mantles are honest. But they are also in distress. I cannot ignore their pain.'

They continued along a track that was scattered with fallen leaves, going deeper into the dark woods. When they reached the hamlet, white and brown yard-fowl scattered before them. They were taken to the house of a man and woman who stared ahead and did not greet them.

'Tell me, what is amiss?' Gwydion asked.

Instantly, his words had a calming effect, but one of the dirty-faced women who had come to the roadside scowled at Gwydion and threw a handful of earth at him. 'Listen to him! What's amiss he says!'

The man who had challenged them on the road stepped

forward, his eyes narrowed. 'Their son went missing three days ago. What do you know about that, stranger?'

Gwydion ignored him and turned instead to the anguished man. 'How old is your son?'

The father blinked. The pupils of his eyes were like pin pricks. 'Thirteen years. And a half.'

'He's a good lad!' the mother shrieked. Her eyes were bloodshot from crying.

Gwydion laid a hand on her head and muttered some hard-to-hear words.

'His name is Waylan,' the woman said, looking up. 'We call him Wale.'

'Tell me what happened,' Gwydion said.

'Just upped and vanished,' the husband muttered. 'We've hunted high and low for him, but we can't find him. He's a good lad. He wouldn't have just gone off. Not by himself.'

'Think now,' Gwydion told them. 'Did any stranger come by here beforehand?'

All those who were gathered at the door tried to recall if a stranger had passed through the village, but they said that nobody had come to Preston Mantles in over a week. Then the compulsion in Gwydion's voice rose irresistibly. 'I ask you: did any stranger come by here?'

The villagers fell back from him, their faces awed. 'No! No!' they cried. 'There was no one!'

But then the mad woman blurted something out. She fell down strangling, frothing at the mouth.

'Wise Woman!' someone called out. 'The maggots are in her brain!'

Gwydion knelt over her, made a sigil over her forehead, then commanded, 'Speak to me, Sister!'

'The old yew!' she gasped, her lips blue. 'It's bleeding! Bleeding!'

Gwydion tended the woman briefly, seemed to tear

something unseen from her throat, then he straightened. His face was as pale as moonlight. 'Take me there.'

A yew tree bleeding, Will thought as they were led to the green. How can that be?

They reached the great sombre tree, surrounded now by fifty or more folk. At about head height the yew split into two main trunks, and thereafter it spread its dense dark foliage into a soaring spire above the ground. Under its shadow no grass would grow. Poisonous red berries glistened all over it. It was very ancient, the sacred tree of Preston Mantles. Gwydion approached it with careful respect. A little below the place where the trunks separated a deep red resin oozed and ran from a fold in the wood.

'Which of you has broken the heart of this venerable tree?' Gwydion demanded turning angrily upon the gathered crowd.

His words resounded with great power now, and the villagers backed away from him.

'Who has been dancing here?' Gwydion demanded. 'Tell me!'

The people looked guiltily to one another, still denying all with shrugs and wide eyes. They quaked with fear at the wizard's wrath. All weapons were cast down and children hid behind their mother's skirts.

'Tell me who was dancing here!'

Despite himself, Will shrank back also.

'Fetch a team and chains,' Gwydion commanded. 'This must be settled!'

As the oxen were being yoked together and led up to the tree, the villagers muttered among themselves, but their complete obedience to Gwydion surprised Will. They seemed to accept his anger and his authority for they responded without demur. The parents of the missing child watched as he took up a mattock and began to hack away the lower branches. Then a chain was looped around one of the two main trunks and the oxen set to haul.

'Gooo-on!' one of the men shouted. He held a rope attached to a ring in the nose of the lead ox. The great beasts strained as they were urged on. Hooves stamped into the ground. The chain tautened and then tore into the red bark as it strangled the bough. Then a shudder passed through the tree and with a crack the timber of the trunk split clear to the ground and the tree thundered apart.

The man leading the oxen yelled. The broken half of the tree lurched and fell to the ground in a cloud of dust and leaves. Then Will saw the white heartwood of the ancient tree revealed to daylight, and he turned away in horror.

Embedded in the wood was a perfect skeleton. Maggot white, maggot soft, glistening, curled up like a sleeping child. The sight of it made Will gasp. All who witnessed it reeled back, groaning. The mother screamed and the father cradled her so she would see no more.

Gwydion went immediately to them and laid healing signs upon their foreheads. Will looked away from the horror. He could not move or utter another word for the shock of the moment held him in its grip. But then Gwydion turned his attention back towards the tree and directed a stream of blue fire into it. Then the wizard's grip tightened on his staff and he turned upon the old woman who shrank down to her knees before him.

'Tell me who did this, Sister!' Gwydion ordered, his eyes blazing like smelted iron.

The Wise Woman fell down again and began to writhe. Her blue lips were flecked with foam and she groaned as if her spirit was fighting to leave her body. Then the wizard laid both hands upon her upraised face and made his irresistible demand.

'Tell me his name!'

And her frothing throat gave up a single word – 'Maskull!'

◙ ◙ ◙

CHAPTER ELEVEN

THE STONE OF
CAER LUGDUNUM

Will said little the next morning. What had passed in Badby Chase now seemed like a horrible nightmare and perhaps also an ill omen for the future. For the moment he wanted only to put the terror of it out of his mind.

But what did the dead boy signify? Under powerful compulsion, the poor Wise Woman of Preston Mantles had told Gwydion everything he wanted to know – the monstrous deed had been the work of the wizard's great enemy. And though Will was not directly touched by what had happened, yet it hardened his heart against the dishonest use of magic that was called sorcery.

The sight of the dead boy had shocked him horribly. He had not understood at first, or perhaps he had not wanted to understand. But Gwydion had not left it there. 'His name was Waylan, but they called him Wale. He was thirteen-and-a-half years old, and Maskull came into his village and killed him. I think you can work out why.'

Last night he had felt pity for the parents as they had watched their son's sap-softened skeleton crackle and hiss among the flames. He had listened to the village women keening and his heart had been broken by that unforgettable sound. But to hear that the boy, Waylan, had been murdered in his place – that brought the horror down full upon him, and fear crept into his belly.

'Can I ask a question, Master Gwydion?'

'Of course. And if you are lucky you may even receive an answer.'

He did not react to the wizard's attempt at levity, but said morosely. 'Last night you asked the villagers if they had seen a stranger come by, but they were lying. They were lying, and you saw that and punished them for it. That's not like you, Master Gwydion.'

'They were not lying,' Gwydion said softly. 'They could not fully remember what had happened because they had been told to forget it.'

With that the wizard reached into his pouch and took out a grey powder. It looked like some of the ash left from the burning of the yew. He tried to make a sign over Will's forehead but Will pulled away. 'What are you doing?'

'Giving you comfort. What did you think?'

'I don't want comfort, Master Gwydion,' he said tonelessly. 'I want to remember how today feels.'

The wizard put away his pouch. 'As you wish.'

As day followed day in the open air and meetings with others grew seldom, Will lost track of time, but judging by the colour of the leaves and the strong webs and great round bodies of the orb spiders among the hedges it must have been near the end of October by the time they broke off their fruitless searching and came at last into the village of Eiton.

Mice fled from them as they crossed the stubble fields and coneys bounded out of their path as they climbed the hills. In time they came to a huddle of oak-framed dwellings whose lime-washed walls of wattle and daub and roofs of thatch seemed most homely to Will. He best liked the look of the Plough Inn, whose sign-board showed seven stars.

'*Liag*,' he said and made Gwydion smile. 'You see? I'm not a teasel-head. I do remember some things.'

By now Will had become used to sleeping out of doors, and he knew how to make himself comfortable, be the weather fair or foul. He had learned how to choose the best ground, how to make himself a leafy bed, how to weigh down his cloak with stones and to prop it up over him with sticks. Several times now that the weather had begun to turn cooler he had stuffed his shirt with straw, or filled their cooking pot with ashes and red embers, put on the lid and curled up close around it. In the mornings he had often awakened to find his cloak sparkling with rain or fallen dew, but himself dry and warm within his little cloak tent and nothing to do but shake out the earwigs to fend for themselves.

He was now so strong from all the walking that no matter what ache was put into his bones from sleeping on open ground, a league's journeying could always put it to flight. In the last week, though, the ground had begun to lose much of its summer warmth, so the prospect of indoor hospitality at the Plough was greatly to Will's liking.

When they entered they found a cheery place with a stair that led up to a second floor. In the downstairs parlours there were several folk warming themselves by the fire, mostly waggoners and carriers and other men of the road.

'Now then, Master Gwydion!' said Dimmet, the Plough's keeper. He was a big man with a strong chin and bewhiskered cheeks. 'What a pleasant surprise. Ought I to pour you a tankard of my best?'

'That you ought, Friend Dimmet.'

'And what about you, my lad? The same for you, is it?'

'We have no payment,' Will said, putting his hand to his pouch while a big black dog sniffed at him.

'Nay, lad. That will not be needed. Any companion of

Master Gwydion's is welcome here, freely and as my guest. Duffred! Come on out here, you sluggard! You'll see a change in my lad, I'm thinking, Master Gwydion.'

'Indeed! He's a well-fed lad.'

Duffred, who seemed to be growing into the image of his father, gave a wink and a beaming smile and went to draw off the refreshments.

Gwydion leaned over and whispered to Will, 'Now do you understand what I told you about the man who has friends being richer than the man who has silver? You see, I have travelled this way once or twice before.'

'You get a fine welcome here,' Will said.

'There is a reason for that. Folk come from all around to taste the ale that comes out of Dimmet's brewing vats. He always asks me to put a word or two upon them when I'm here. And I do, though Dimmet's ale is hard to improve upon.'

Will thought about all the spells and favours that Gwydion gave out. It would be marvellous to be like him, he thought, to be carefree and do naught but good wherever he went, giving away boats and doing honest magic and helpfully curing horses that had come down with the fives or the yellows. A wizard left friendships and debts of gratitude behind him all over the place. It seemed a fine way to live. But then Will remembered the confusion that Gwydion inspired when he had appeared in the Vale.

'Master Gwydion? Nether Norton isn't a place of bad aspect, is it? So why do Valesmen fear you so?'

'Fear?' Gwydion said quietly. 'Perhaps that is too strong a word. Nether Norton's wary welcome is due to the spell I used to cloak the Vale. I chose it carefully some time ago – the Vale is a naturally out-of-the-way place, and Valesmen are naturally quiet and self-reliant folk. But if they like to stay at home and do not take kindly to strangers who rudely come among them – especially practitioners of magic – then you may blame my spells for that.'

'Master Gwydion, why is Tilwin the only one who ever came in from outside? Were you sending him to check up on me?'

'Tilwin the Tinker is not necessarily what he seems.'

'Master Gwydion?' He met the wizard's eye. 'Where did I come from? Who left me to die when I was only a day or two old? Was it my parents? Are they to blame?'

But the wizard put a long finger to his lips, and Will fell silent as Dimmet returned with the brew that his son had drawn. Though Dimmet's good cheer was fulsome, a chill had fallen over Will's heart.

'Now then!' Dimmet said, seeing his guests' glumness. 'Let us drink a health to his grace the king. May he get better and rule us for many a long year to come!'

When they did not lift their ale, Dimmet blinked at them in a surprised way and asked in a low voice, 'Have you by any chance picked up any fresh news about the king's ailment?'

'No word about the king has come to my hearing in the last few weeks,' Gwydion said with perfect truth.

Dimmet shook his head sadly. 'Then perhaps you'll not have heard what I have – he's as sick as a Nadderstone man, or so they say. A carrier who comes through here once a fortnight says his grace was laid flat on his back by an ailment and without the use of either his limbs or his wits.'

'Is the carrier a man whose word you trust, or one of the usual wagtongues who trade loose talk in the back parlour?'

'I never forget a face, Master Gwydion. And I generally read what's in them. And if I don't like what I see I don't let a body linger under my thatch for long. It's out in the road and on your way!'

'Oh, is that so?' Gwydion allowed himself a half smile. 'When did this fountain of truth speak about the king?'

'Oh, 'twould be just three days back. It's fresh enough

news, no more than a week old, I'd guess. They say his grace has been poorly nigh on two months now. They say—' Dimmet leaned in close '—they say it were a shock to his heart to see that swelling come up around the queen's middle. Now, then! What about that?'

'You mean the king did not know the queen was with child until he saw the swelling?' Gwydion asked, his eyes fast on Dimmet's face.

'Seems not.'

Gwydion's murmur was a mild caution. 'Why, Dimmet . . . that is treasonous talk.'

'That's as maybe,' Dimmet sniffed. 'But between you and me and the roof beams, you know how unworldly his grace is. Always at his studies and his devotions, or so it's reported. The king is otherworldly, as you might say. Now I'm not a great one for gossip as you know, but the gossip everywhere is that the child is not his grace's own.'

At that Will looked in surprise to Gwydion, but the wizard gave no hint of his thoughts on the matter. Instead he changed the subject. 'You said just now his grace was "sicker than a Nadderstone man". What did you mean by that?'

'Oh, there used to be a place up yonder and over Chapter House Hill, a place name of Nadderstone.'

'I remember it. I was there once, but it was a very long time ago.'

'It would have to be, for it's a hamlet as used to be but ain't no more. Everybody there took sick of the Great Plague back before my great grandfather's time. But before that they used to say it had the worst luck of any place hereabouts. There were all manner of stories about it, and the saying lives on yet – if you hear of a man going mad, or cutting his own throat, or falling off his horse, or getting struck on the head by a thunderbolt, then you'd say: "He must be a Nadderstone man." There's nothing left of the place now. Nothing at all, except ruins.'

'Is that so?' Gwydion said thoughtfully. 'Well, now, that is worth a word or two spoken over your brewing vats.'

They retired to a corner and as evening fell they warmed themselves by the fire in a small back room that Dimmet called 'the snug'. It seemed to be at the back of the great hearth and was approached through one of the inglenooks. Gwydion said that the entrance to the snug had a magic about it that only certain people were able to fathom. It had a low-raftered ceiling, a small grate stacked with a few sawn boughs ready for burning, and a tiny, lead-glazed window that opened onto the yard. There was an oak table, several benches, and it was lined with carved and polished wooden boards so that it seemed somewhat like the inside of a big barrel, or one of the tiny cabins Will had seen aboard the ships along the mole at Cauve. The snug seemed like a place where most cares could easily be forgotten, but despite the good food and drink, Will did not feel wholly at his ease. At last he asked why they were tarrying in comfort if there was urgent work to be done.

'We must await the moon.'

'The moon? But what's that got to do with anything?'

'The moon has a lot to do with most things.'

'If you say so, Master Gwydion.'

'I do say so. Indeed I do.'

There was another question Will wanted to ask, but he was more tired than he had realized and a quart of ale had made him drowsier still, and when his eyelids began to droop, Gwydion ruffled his hair and said that with a restful night in prospect they should take to their beds.

The wizard was up again before first light. When Will came down the stair he found him sitting in the parlour next to the kitchens. Will yawned as Bolt, the Plough's big, black dog looked up at him expectantly. Its tail wagged as Will fed it a piece of bacon rind. 'Where are we to go now, Master Gwydion?' he asked.

'To a place Dimmet spoke about yesterday. Did I never speak to you of Caer Lugdunum?'

'Not that I recall.'

'Do you remember watching the bonfires of Lammas?'

'I'll never forget that night. Or that place.'

'The name Lammas has been warped and worn down over the centuries as all names are warped and worn down by time. Long ago it was *Lughnasad* for, as I have already told you, Lugh was a great hero among the Gadelish folk and known by them as the Lord of Light. Lammas was Lugh's favourite festival. The word *Dunum* is an old term for a fortress, and *Caer* means city.'

'So,' Will said, remembering the inscription. 'The City of the Lord of Light's Fortress . . .'

'Correct! Now, what about the dragons?'

'As in Dragon Stone, you mean?'

Will thought hard, but try as he might he could not see what Gwydion was trying to tease from him. Then an idea came to him. 'Wait! I remember *Dumhacan Nadir* – the Dragon's Mound. So Nadir must mean either "dragon" or "mound".'

'Which is it?'

'*Dumhacan* makes me think of *dunum*, and you said that meant a fortress. And fortresses always used to be on hills. Also, *Nadir* makes me think of adders, and adders are snakes, and thought of as baby dragons by some. Also, according to Lord Strange's book of beasts, snakes are sometimes called "wyrms", and so are dragons. So my guess is that we're going to Nadderstone!'

Gwydion smiled. 'Quick as a young stoat! I must confess, Willand, sometimes you do surprise me.'

'I think I'm getting more into your way of thinking at last, Master Gwydion.'

'It takes time. But then most things that are worthwhile take that.'

Will wolfed down the rest of his breakfast of bacon and eggs, and then they set off eastwards, walking over gently rippling country. The prospect to the north was hillier, but to the south the land ran down to a broad plain. Woods occupied the high ground and ploughed fields extended a league or two from Eiton. The soil here was thick brown clay, and on the slope was a pond – no more than a round depression filled with water and fringed with bushes. Gwydion took out his hazel wand and walked back and forth beside it. He said it would be a likely place to wade in and feel in the mud for star-iron, for the hollow was surely no man-made dew pond or any other sort of earthly mere, but had been made by a falling star hitting the ground in ages past.

'Do you feel anything about the land here?' Gwydion asked.

'Uh . . . no.'

'Are you sure? Do you not feel the least prickling in your feet?'

'Nothing like that, Master Gwydion.'

'Then let us go on.'

They descended into the valley half a league and saw a ridge where a large stone tower stood. Will began to smell smoke. It was rising up greasy and acrid from the walled yards of the chapter house below.

'That stink is their lard vats,' Gwydion said. 'Do you know they destroy every animal they collect in the tithe?'

'Oh, no! Is that true?' Will said, not wanting to believe. 'What do they do that for?'

'They eat the livers and drain the blood to make puddings. Then they grind the bones to make bread. But they keep the fat to boil up and make soap and candles for their rituals. They burn candles by the hundred.'

'I can see why they would have to wash,' he said,

disgusted. 'But why would men with no eyes want to make candles?'

'Their washing is not simple cleansing, Willand, for they are trying to wash away guilt. That is why folk call them "red hands", for they wash endlessly. The longer their devotions, the redder their hands, for there is a kind of soda in their soap that breaks the skin and turns their fingernails into yellow claws. It is a sign of honour to them. As for the candles, they use them to light up vile pictures that hang inside their chapter houses. Those tall windows are glazed with obsidian, which is a black glass that admits only a dark brown gloom. It hides many horrors.'

'But if they are sightless, why do they hang pictures up at all?'

'It is thought they have some dull sense that replaces sight. It turns left into right as does a mirror.'

'How do you know?'

'Because when recruits are first taken into the Fellowship they confuse right and left, as if their minds have been scrambled up by what has been done to them, or they are not yet used to their new way of seeing.'

Will shivered, and Gwydion steered him down and past the quiet fishponds that stretched out to their left. Their path wound onto the ridge and ran close by a square tower on which four small stone spires had been set. The tower had been raised in the soft local stone, which was a dark brown colour and it had become fantastically patterned by pale green lichens, so that now the very fabric of the building seemed leprous. The chapter house beside it was also unwelcoming. Tall, blind windows rose over the high walls that surrounded it, and an ornate iron weathervane stood above the roofs, showing the sign of a white heart and the letters A, A, E and F for the four directions. Above the main door was a large letter E. And Will saw a series of other letters cut into the right side of the stone arch:

NISLIN

And into the left side:

EROBAL

He felt a wave of disquiet pass through him. 'I don't like it here.'

'Have no fear, they will not approach us.'

'I still don't like it.'

Gwydion looked with narrowed eyes at the rich estate. 'Once they went as beggars, but now their poverty is in name only. A sham to deceive the churlish folk, for in truth they are feverish collectors of gold. Their houses and cloisters are most richly endowed, more richly than the lords whom they both serve and seek to control. Look how far these confiscators of the common treasury have led us from the true path!'

Will followed Gwydion onward past the ghastly walls. He had heard enough tales of the Sightless Ones, and the memory of the dark-garbed Fellows who had groped about near those walled yards had already begun to make the hairs rise up on his neck. Nor was the feeling soothed by Gwydion who seemed determined to walk openly down their road and to pass as close by their front gate as he could. Will wondered why the wizard did not go the long way around, but he remained silent until they had left the place far behind.

'They stole all the places of best aspect in the Realm for themselves and polluted them,' the wizard said bitterly. 'Too many sacred groves, cromlechs and dolmens did they lay to waste. They have no understanding or love of the land. They have succeeded only in making fine places ugly. They care only for gold and self-enrichment through the advancing of loans and the selling of empty promises. How greatly do I oppose and pity them.'

As Will came to the top of the hill he saw they were standing on a watershed. From here the land drained eastward. Gwydion pointed to a grey smudge in the distance and said that was where the unfortunate village of Nadderstone had once stood. The village was no more than a ruin now, sinking back into the green earth.

Gwydion studied the sky. 'It is growing near the time,' he said, and took out his Y-shaped hazel wand.

'Can you feel anything?' Will asked.

'The natural flows of the earth are here. The patterns are strong. Feel them for yourself.'

'I'd rather not,' Will said. This seemed to him to be a place of bad aspect, and the nearness of the chapter house had unsettled him.

Gwydion inclined his head and said firmly, 'Here. Take the wand and do not be afraid. Scrying is harmless and I am here by your side.'

He let himself be shown how to hold the hazel wand in the special inside-out grip that Gwydion always used, a branch held in each hand to make it point ahead. When he twisted his wrists the wand turned either up or down. He felt sweat begin to break out on his forehead as he stepped forward uncertainly.

'Turn your elbows out. That is much better.'

For the first few paces he felt nothing, so he stopped. Gwydion motioned him on, and he moved a little further, then he began to feel annoyance that there was nothing at all coming from the wand. 'I don't know what I'm supposed to be trying to feel, Master Gwydion. Perhaps I should just stop now.'

But he went on for a few paces more. Then a few dozen. Then a hundred. At last he let out a curse and said, 'This isn't working!'

'Calmly, lad. You cannot see for looking! Do not force it. In scrying, serenity is your best friend.'

Will took a deep breath, feeling a long way from serene. He took a dozen more self-conscious steps. Nothing. And again nothing. He held his arms just so, and fixed his eyes on the skyline ahead. He tried again, but then his mind began to wander more than his feet had.

As soon as he stopped trying to feel, something odd moved inside him.

'Oh!' he cried. 'I think . . . I think that was it!'

Gwydion smiled and nodded at the way the wand had curled upward. 'Ah! At last!'

But whatever had made it happen had now disappeared. Will flexed his fingers and tried to compose himself once more. Having had the first experience he now knew what to expect, and was eager to feel it again. The sudden excitement had knocked him off balance. Then he noticed the faintest sensation, a tension rising across his chest. He held onto it very gently. It rose and fell as he walked a straight line, then his arm twitched and he lost the feeling. 'It's gone. But that was quite strong! I could feel it for fully six or seven steps!'

'Now turn and come back towards me,' Gwydion told him.

He did, and felt the tension rise and fall once more. The trick, he realized, was not to try to feel for the earth flows directly, but to sense them as they were reflected as a pattern of feeling in his arms and chest.

He yelped. There was no mistaking it now, nor the pattern it made in the meadow. After about twenty more steps he stopped. 'I've walked across a flow!' he said, grinning. 'I could feel its edges! I could feel it flowing! It's just like a stream!'

Gwydion laughed with delight. 'Now try to go along it.'

'There it is again,' he said, wandering away. 'Now it's going – but if I come back towards you again it rises.'

'Ha ha! Now you are scrying!'

Will felt hugely pleased with himself. The feeling was that

of a flow coming up the wand, into his right arm, across his chest, down his other arm and back into the wand. If he concentrated too hard he lost the feeling. Too little, and it faded away. Only when he was in just the right frame of mind and bodily tension could he detect the flow properly.

As he walked along the earth flow the feeling slackened a little. It felt something like the time they were in the boat and moving up the river on an incoming tide. When he turned around he felt the flow in his chest reverse, and he knew he was walking back against the current.

'This is wonderful!' he said, marvelling at the feeling and how it seemed to move strongly in and around his heart.

'It just takes practice.'

'Are you sure this feeling isn't anything to do with your magic?' he asked, looking up.

'It is none of my doing.' Gwydion smiled, though he seemed thoughtful. 'But you have a strange talent. Let me tell you – I have never seen anyone scry the way you do.'

'But it's fun!' Will said, lost to the thrill of it. 'I hope I'll be able to remember how to do this tomorrow.' He shaded his eyes and looked along the direction of the flow he had scried. 'And this big one feels quite different to what's going on above and around it. It's . . . I don't know how to explain it.'

Gwydion looked to him. 'Big one? Where? Show me.'

But Will was more interested in what the hazel wand was telling him. 'Do the deep flows always run in so straight a line?'

'Deep you say?' Gwydion asked, staring at him. 'Straight? Are you sure of that?'

'Why, yes, Master Gwydion. It's as clear as clear can be. It's like when you look at water when autumn leaves fall on it – you can see the leaves floating, but if you adjust your eyes you can see the bare trees reflected there too, as if there was another world upside down through the water.'

'And the deep pattern? The trees? You can see them?'

'It's not so much trees, just a single straight line. The little pond back there, the chapter house and Nadderstone, all stand exactly on it – or so it seems to me.'

'Straight . . .' Gwydion said, his face unreadable.

Will looked back the way they had come. 'Stand over here. Feel it yourself. What's the matter, Master Gwydion?'

But the wizard did not move. He put a hand to his head like a man who had received a dazing blow. 'I cannot,' he said looking piercingly now at Will. 'I cannot feel it. For there is no straight flow in nature.'

'What do you mean, Master Gwydion?'

'In the Black Book it was suggested that the ligns of the lorc run as straight as the rays of the sun, and by this we may know them.'

'You mean . . . this is a lign?' he said, disbelieving it. 'Are you sure? But it's easy to feel!'

Gwydion's face began to light up. 'Oh, this is good. This is very good!'

Will whooped and took the wizard's arms and they began to dance around each other like mad men. But then Gwydion seized him. 'Quickly!' he said looking up at the sky. 'We must make use of the time of power while it lasts!'

'Do you think my talent might go away?' Will said staring after him.

'No talent is ever constant. But that is not the reason. Come! The sun and moon move faster in their courses than men are accustomed to think!'

Will hurried after the wizard. They went towards Nadderstone, following the line that he was feeling. Enormous confidence was running through him now, and Gwydion was exultant.

By now they had come close to the ruins. Ravens cawed in the treetops nearby. Flies buzzed up from the tall grass as they approached. It was a sad and deserted place. The frames of the houses had been broken or burned black, and the last remnants of them were mouldering now in decay and overgrown with brambles.

'Not much of the Black Book survives,' Gwydion said. 'But the fragments I have gathered have taught me a great deal. The battlestones were not made equal in power. There are greater and lesser stones among them. Not all mark the site of future battles. Though the task of the greater stones is certainly to bring men to strife, the lesser ones may serve only to link the greater, for the Black Book is clear that they must have knowledge of one another. It is also written that they may be made to tell what they know. Of the greater stones there is certainly one of monstrous power, which is called the Doomstone. It was planted last of all. It will, I think, be the first to kill when war comes, and it is said that it will exact a heavy price in blood before it is satisfied.'

'Unless we can find it and destroy it,' Will said.

'We?' Gwydion turned sharply and looked at him intently for a moment as if gauging him.

Will wandered among the broken buildings and felt his own mood darken. It seemed to him that somehow Gwydion had tested him and found him wanting. The wizard's words had sounded ironic. They had slighted him, so that he felt put in his place. He heard the cawing of rooks in the distance and hated the sound. Despite the sunshine, this place had a chill to it.

One of the biggest buildings, once the inn perhaps, seemed to have been burned down. Many years of weather had left the ruins a mass of thorns and weeds, but there were no flowers blooming here. He stooped to pick up something from the ground and found it was grey and finger-like and pointed at one end.

'Let me see that,' Gwydion said, putting out his hand.

Will polished the dirt off, but held it back. 'Why should I?' he murmured. 'I found it.'

'Because it may be an important clue,' the wizard said, snatching it from him.

'Clue to what?'

'These little knick-knacks are often called thunderbolts. Unlearned folk call them elf-bolts and say they are goblin arrowheads. Others claim they are what kills when a man is struck by lightning. Yet others say they are what is left when lightning strikes the ground. When folk hereabouts find them they bore a hole in them and wear them on cords about their necks for good luck, or else they put them in their thatch as a protection against fire.'

'Do they work?'

'Sometimes.'

'Only sometimes?'

The wizard's lip curled. 'It depends on how much they are believed in.'

'Does magic work that way? Do people have to believe in it for it to work?'

The wizard sighed heavily. 'See! This bolt carries a charm mark upon it. It came from the thatch of the burned house. You can see where the fire started. Those discoloured stones. I have noticed the same thing often enough. Lightning was the culprit here.'

'So your thunderbolt charm didn't work?'

Gwydion looked at him with hooded eyes. 'That is the point. If this charm did not ward off the lightning, then something else must have been at work here too.'

Will stared around, oppressed now by the eerie emptiness. The wind rustled in the long grass nearby, but no birds flew or sang. Gwydion passed the hazel wand to him. 'Go and try to pick up the lign again.'

Will took the wand, but then his courage failed him and he tried to give it back. 'I told you, this place gives me a bad feeling.'

'You must take the wand and do as I say!'

'Why must I?'

'Do it, Willand!'

The wizard's words carried such sudden force that he felt his belly turn over. He took the wand again and began to walk back and forth, but he did so reluctantly.

'Will you please engage with your task?'

'I am engaging with it!'

'You are not!' Gwydion watched him darkly. 'The knowledge of where each lign runs has long been lost. The Black Book said the flow rises and falls with the season, the weather and the phases of both sun and moon – though it is always at its strongest on sacred days. How does it seem to you now?'

Will had the distinct feeling that Gwydion was using him, exposing him to dangers that he would rather not face himself. It was a feeling that was impossible to ignore. He stopped and put a hand behind his neck as if to stroke down the hairs that had risen there. When he tasted the air it seemed sour.

'Go on with your scrying, I said!'

He swallowed hard and went on, but his trust in Gwydion had dimmed while the sense that he was in mortal danger surged. He felt the scrying sensation rise in his arms and chest as he moved back and forth. 'I've found it again,' he called unhappily.

'Good. Now follow along in the direction of the flow.'

'But I feel . . . Master Gwydion, it's *dangerous*!'

'Pay no attention. Just do as I say.'

Why should I? he asked himself as he trod the green lane. Why should I trust him when he's sending me where he fears to go himself?

He's putting you in harm's way, came an answering thought. Using you as a boar hunter uses his dogs. The old coward only taught you to scry to save his own skin. What has he done but bring you pain and hurt? He almost got you killed when Duke Edgar's sword came flashing through you. Do you want to die through one of his mistakes?

He stopped in his tracks and gave the wizard a hard look. And what about Willow? the thoughts in his head asked. You wanted to see her again more than anything, didn't you? You couldn't stop thinking about her. But you have now. Curious that Gwydion turned up just as you and she were about to meet again. Maybe he feared you'd prefer to stay with her instead of going off on one of his wild goose chases. That was why he conjured up the marish hag. It was all to scare you . . .

He walked on through a nettle patch, fearing the thunderbolt that he was now sure the wizard was about to throw at him. Then he came to a well, a stone kerb and a round wall of brown stone with an iron handle still attached above it. He looked down the well and saw a disc of light and himself looking back up the hole from four fathoms below. He found himself fighting an overpowering urge to tear the hazel wand in two and fling the pieces down into the water. Instead he dropped it to the ground, walked over to an old doorstep and sat down. There he hid his face in his hands and tried unsuccessfully to hold back a flood of tears.

'You have done excellent work, Will,' Gwydion muttered. 'You have felt the despair that lies in the ground here, but you have taken enough for one day. Go over there. If you do, the bad thoughts will go away and you will begin to feel better.'

But Will felt only dizziness and a cold fear creeping over him as he stood up again. He watched Gwydion pick up the wand and begin grimly scrying the ground near the well. Suddenly the wizard seemed to be a loathsome grave-robber, sniffing for prey.

'Why are you doing this to me?' he shrieked, angry that things should have come to this. 'I have no business in this place! I'm going home!'

'It is not pleasant, but it is necessary,' Gwydion told him. 'Get off the lign. Go and stand over by the trees. You would do well to climb up into their branches until you feel a little more in your right mind.'

Will's head felt as if it was ready to burst. He staggered to and fro, but stubbornly refused to do what the wizard asked. 'I hate you! Do you hear me?'

'Be of good courage, Willand. And examine that which you are presently feeling with care. Understand the way the influence seeps into your mind. You must not give in to it, but learn how to fight it! The Dragon Stone is defending itself, as we knew it would.'

Will's feet took him unwillingly out into the tussocky meadow. There he came somewhat to his senses. He went over to the trees. They were whitebeams. They still had their leaves but were clothed in red berries. He climbed up and perched among them in the steep, uncomfortable branches, and as he did so he began to feel the character of his thoughts change. Within moments he was ashamed that he had ever doubted the wizard.

Gwydion was right after all, he thought, marvelling at how much better he had begun to feel. What a foul place this is! No wonder everyone left!

He watched the wizard move among the ruins. The green lane was no more than a dozen paces across in the village, but it broadened as it emerged, soon growing twice as wide.

'Stay there!' Gwydion called, raising his staff. 'This is the place. I am sure of it.'

As Will watched, the wizard knelt down and began to cut away the turf as if he was preparing a fire pit. Then he stacked the sods and began to scrape up the soil.

I must help him, Will thought. He jumped down and ran towards the place where Gwydion was digging.

'I told you to stay where you were,' Gwydion growled. His face was haggard and a sneer was twisting his mouth.

'But I feel better now.'

'That, I fear, may be a temporary condition. If you must come, then try to remember the way the fearful thinking sneaked over you. You must stand guard against it, for the battlestone knows we have come for it.'

'How deep is it buried?'

'It cannot be more than a little way below the surface.'

He watched the wizard scoring the compact soil with his ritual blade. 'Maybe we should go back to the Plough and fetch spades. We'll never get it out this way.'

'It will not be necessary to fetch spades.'

'No, of course not,' Will said, realizing the source of his sudden faintheartedness. 'My mistake.'

Gwydion kept scraping and digging, and though raked by a dozen fears Will helped him. The noonday sun clouded over and it began to look as if it would rain. Will threw the thought away and told himself with all the optimism he could gather that it would not rain, and that even if it did they would keep working. He pulled a handful of soil out of the hole each time Gwydion broke enough loose. After a while their pit had reached a depth of half a fathom.

'Why don't you magic it out?' Will said at last, wiping the sweat off his forehead.

'Why do you have to ask such foolish questions?'

'Don't call me a fool!' he cried, springing to his feet. But just as quickly he bent down to the task again and forced himself to apologize. 'Forgive me, Master Gwydion. Forgive me. I am a fool. I let it get to me again.'

'It is you who should forgive me,' Gwydion said, though his words sounded tight and insincere. 'What I meant to say was this: it will be best if no magic is conducted near the battlestone, except that which may tend to suppress or contain malign power. A holding-spell will have to be applied to the stone, I think, but a binding-spell should only be applied when the stone has been brought out of the ground.'

'But how can we move it? If it's anything like its sister it'll be a couple of hundredweight or more. Far too heavy for us to lift without magic.'

Gwydion stopped digging and peered at Will from under his bushy eyebrows. Will got the point almost straight away. 'Sorry,' he said again. 'Of course we'll get the stone out. We'll cross each bridge as we come to it.'

'Well done, Will. Laugh and you will win through. But this time you are correct: we may be able to lift it, but we will not be able to carry it far. Let us go back to Eiton and ask Dimmet for a horse and cart.' He stood up and patted the dirt off his hands. 'First, though, we should make absolutely sure this is the Dragon Stone and not some decoy set down to mislead us.'

'Now who's being got at?' he asked wryly.

Gwydion sat up. 'Do you think so? Well, perhaps you are right. I am being a little premature.'

They returned to their digging and Will felt hunger stirring in his stomach. He thought it must be another attack of weakness brought on by the stone as it searched for a fresh way to deflect him, but then he realized that the sun was sinking. The afternoon had worn away and they had not eaten since the eggs and bacon he had finished off at breakfast.

Gwydion was apt to forget about meals. He ate very little, and when he did it was vegetables or fruit or bread or oatmeal gruel. He drank ale and cider and sometimes wine, but neither flesh nor fish ever passed his lips, and it seemed that whenever the wizard ate he did so to put others at their ease rather than to satisfy any appetite of his own. Will had wondered at that, for he had never heard of anyone who purposely went without the pleasure of meat. But just as he was about to suggest they break their fast Gwydion's knife struck something hard and a tremor ran through the ground.

'We have it!' the wizard said grimly. 'Stand back.'

As Will watched, Gwydion danced three times sunwise about the grave. He cleaned the soil from the stone and they saw that the battlestone was similar in size to its sister-stone and of much the same appearance. It lay on its back like a coffin with only the lid showing. But there were no marks on it.

The sight of the stone discomfited Will and he could not help the shudder that passed along his spine. 'What now?'

'Undo all that we have done.' Gwydion began to scatter the exposed stone with handfuls of soil. 'We must put it back to bed. Then you can have your supper.'

They arrived back at the inn well before sunset. The wizard found a water trough and cleaned off his hands and the broad blade of his knife, then enclosed the precious star-iron in its sheath, before putting the cord around his neck and hiding it once more inside his robe.

'What are you going to do?' Will whispered.

'I must read the inscription as soon as possible.'

'But there wasn't any inscription.'

'If I am right, then there soon will be. The moon will rise somewhat before sunset. It is almost at the full. I shall whisper such words to the stone that it will have no choice but to betray itself. Where are you going?'

Will had strayed halfway through the door into the parlour. 'You said I could have supper—'

'We cannot afford to leave a stone such as that unguarded for long!'

'Oh, Master Gwydion, it's been buried for all these centuries. What harm will—'

'But we have unearthed it! Ask Dimmet to give you something for the ride back.'

Just then, Duffred, Dimmet's lad, came out of the stable

and Gwydion went over to ask if he could take the bay cob for a few days along with the four-wheeled waggon and the block and tackle used to lift barrels out of the cellar.

Duffred scratched his chin. 'Take Bessie? I'll have to see what my old dad says about that.'

When Duffred fetched Dimmet out, he looked unhappy. He kept sucking his teeth and saying, 'It'll throw things out.' But after another quiet word with the wizard he finally nodded his head and the cob was put in harness, and some sacks and spare ropes and a pick were thrown in the back of the waggon too.

'At one time this old dray were a tithe waggon,' Dimmet told them. 'You might get funny looks off of some folk at this season of the year whilst riding upon it. Don't let the red hands catch you!'

Will's stomach tightened to hear Dimmet use those words so openly. He looked around. Gwydion had said that the Sightless Ones regarded the term 'red hands' as insulting, that their spies reported all such utterances among the churls. By this means, they cowed the common folk and forced a semblance of respect upon them.

'What we really want is a mason's hoist,' Gwydion said, looking in the corners of the old stable. 'But I daresay we shall be able to make do without one if we must.'

'I don't know what you're up to, Master Gwydion,' Dimmet said, 'and I'm sure I don't want to know neither. But I'd deem it a favour if you'd bring Bessie back to me as soon as you can and in good fettle. She's a good, strong mare. Best as we ever had, and I'd hate for to lose her.'

'You shall have horse and waggon back with my thanks,' the wizard said, seizing the brewer's hand. 'May your barrels never leak, my friend!'

'They won't now!'

Will just had time to draw himself a cup of water and tear off a hunk of bread to chew before they began their ride back towards the stone. He asked, 'You said there were greater and lesser stones. Which kind is this?'

'We would do well to assume it is one of the greater sort.'

Will felt a flash of excitement. 'Do you really think it's one of those that call men to battle? How many are there?'

Gwydion did not turn to look at him. 'There may be as few as seven, or as many as seven times seven, or any magical number in between. The lorc is certainly coming back to life, but the song it plays is plucked upon strings tuned by sorcery so that its once-lovely music has been made into a clashing din.' He flapped the traces and clicked his tongue encouragingly at the horse. 'We must hurry, for although this stone has lain in the earth for many centuries, it has not been exposed to moonlight for almost as long, and tonight is syzygy.'

'Sizzy-what?'

'Syzygy. When the moon culminates in the south at midnight it will pass across the prime meridian. Because the moon is exactly at the full this means that the sun will also stand upon the same line, though it is in the part of the sky that is presently below the ground.'

Will looked up. He had no idea there was a part of the sky below the ground and he could not imagine it. 'How can it be below the ground if it's sky?'

'It must be below the ground if the sun is in it and yet we have night.'

'I'm sorry I asked.'

Gwydion glanced at him. 'The part of the sky below the earth is where the sun and moon and all the stars go when they set, do you see? Syzygy is much like when an eclipse happens – only in one plane instead of two, of course.'

'Of course.'

'The effect is the important thing. It is much like a high tide. Today the flow in the lign is strong. It will continue to increase until midnight. And since the stone already feels itself to be under threat it will serve us to lift it before then.'

Will's head swam as he tried to follow the twists of Gwydion's explanation, but he understood one thing – no matter how much they might dread it, the stone had to be got out before midnight.

He asked, 'Does the evil rise as the flow increases?'

'It is beginning to annoy me that you persist in using that word, Willand. It means so many things that it means hardly anything at all. It is only a sign of loose thinking.'

'Sorry.'

'Remember: the lign is not the cause of what happened in Nadderstone. It is merely a channel. The battlestone itself is the source of harm. One of the reasons I put you in the Vale was the nearness to the Tops and to what you call the Giant's Ring. It is the broken doom-ring of a long-forgotten folk, but I have often suspected that a lign runs somewhere near it. A form of protection seems to emanate from the ring itself. Why else would shepherds have, for uncounted generations, driven their flocks many leagues out of their way across the Tops just to touch the King's Stone?'

Will recalled Tilwin's improbable tales, but they seemed thin fare compared to what Gwydion was now telling him.

'Tilwin once said that shepherds always broke off a piece of the King's Stone as a good luck charm.'

Gwydion frowned. 'He has been far freer with his lore than I might have hoped.'

'You mean he shouldn't have told me about the Giant's Ring? Why not?'

'Because it puts ideas in your head, ideas your imagination will no doubt embroider upon. What you call the Giant's Ring is a place of solitude, a place where three dreams were buried. It is a perfect circle of eighty-and-some ancient stones. Only forty paces or so across, yet it is a centre of enormous power. I do not know if it serves the lorc, but it stands close by the tomb of Orba, Queen of the Summer Moon. Long ago, in an age before that in which King Brea lived, Orba was the wife of Finglas, first king of the Ordu. He came from a lake-strewn country far to the north. This much we are told in the Revelations of Cherin, the child-seer, who was fifty-third king of the line of Brea.

'The tomb of Finglas, which also stood near the Giant's Ring, was torn and robbed in later days by the black dragon, Fumi. There is nothing left of his tomb now save patterns in the ground. But Fumi left the tomb of Orba untouched. If you go there you will see the five stones of the fair Moon Queen's resting chamber. They are standing yet, though her mound and all its riches have long since perished.'

'Are we going there, when we've dug up the stone and broken it?' Will asked, suddenly bright with hope. 'Are we? Oh, please! Can I visit my . . . can I visit Eldmar and Breona?'

Gwydion faced him patiently. 'Willand, it is not your task to break the battlestones.'

'But I'm helping you, aren't I? I'm not an encumbrance like you told Lord Strange I would be.'

'I must admit that your talent has helped to find the Dragon Stone, but great hazards attend this task, and your safety is at least as important to me as dealing with the stones.'

'Oh, how can that be? I'm just one person, and the stones will kill thousands if you let them.'

'But you are the Child of Destiny.'

Will folded his arms stubbornly. 'Anyway, you can't send me away. You won't be able to find another battlestone if you can't feel the ligns. You need me now.'

'Do I indeed? I have done far more than you to locate this stone, Willand.'

'No, you didn't! I found the sister-stone just in time, and I—'

'That is as may be. But did I not tell you that the stones have knowledge of one another, and that they may be made to reveal one another by magic? I will wrestle with the Dragon Stone and draw from it a verse much like the one that appeared in its sister-stone. That will be my clue to finding the other stones. As for you, I have thought deeply on what must become of you. You said yourself that the best place for hiding trees was a forest. I have a very good forest in mind.'

Will sat in the slowly descending darkness as the cob's hooves clip-clopped along the track and the landscape rolled by. He felt crestfallen and empty. He tried to console himself that one day he would see Eldmar and Breona again and that when all the dangers were done with he would know who his real parents were. He wanted to be thankful and pleased that there was one such as Gwydion who had taken so much trouble with him, but he felt neither thankful nor pleased.

'So, you *are* going off again.'

'By old New Year's Day you will be free of this cantankerous old wizard's company. It is an apt time for you to be making a new beginning. You must be prepared for what is to come.'

A hard knot of resentment formed in Will's belly then. 'But I don't want to be prepared, and I don't want to be any old Child of Destiny. I want to stay with you and go a-roving after the stones!'

'Willand, listen to me! You are as yet greatly ignorant of the world. For the moment you must let wiser heads prevail and do as you are told.'

The words pricked painfully at his pride, and he fell into a reticent mood as the waggon trundled up and over the ridge. He stared at the gloomy buildings that belonged to the Sightless Ones, their chapter house with its high walls and tower. It was all still now and silent as if the occupants were attending to some ghastly devotion. Nothing stirred. Darkness had fallen almost completely.

As they crested the rise Bessie began to pull with less effort. Will looked into the east and watched a fat, yellow moon lift itself painfully above the eastern horizon, and before the yellowness had turned to silver they were back among the ruins of Nadderstone.

If it had been hard to keep good cheer near the stone while the sun was shining, now it was almost impossible. Gwydion would not allow lanterns, and the glow of the sky had faded, to be replaced by the starlight twinkling sluggishly above. A mist had seeped up from the ground, a boneless presence in ghostly white. As they came to the disturbed ground Will's gorge rose and he almost vomited. But he breathed deep and got a grip on himself and forced the feelings away.

They cleared out the loose earth around the stone, working grimly as syzygy approached. They dug deeper around and under it, then bound it in rope and hitched thick cords to Bessie's harness. Gwydion applied much soothing magic to the wounded earth, stopping every now and then to mutter and dance and sing out in the true tongue. Even so, Will felt the power in the stone stir and test the bonds that were being set around it. In his mind's eye he saw a great boar confined in a rickety pen, wanting only to gather sufficient rage to begin to break out.

Gwydion wanted to pull the stone upright. His idea was to lower it onto beams laid on the heap of soil, from where it could be hauled up onto the bed of the cart. Will saw that was wrong. He could sense the brooding malice waiting to burst free. Lifting it up would crack the stone's fragile temper. He said so, but Gwydion dismissed his warning and sent him away to steady the horse.

'There Bessie,' Will said in her ear. The animal was

terrified, and only his close attention prevented her from bolting. 'He's a wizard, and he thinks he knows everything.'

'I heard that.'

'Good.'

But in a curious way, settling the horse made Will less fearful too. He mentioned it to Gwydion. 'It's as the Wise Woman told me,' he said. 'Caring for another's worries makes you forget your own.'

The wizard nodded in the half-darkness. Once again his voice sounded burdened with a tiresome need to discuss the obvious. 'That is why they call her "Wise Woman".'

'I know that,' Will said waspishly. Then, 'I'm . . . sorry.'

'I accept your apology.'

Will made a face back in the darkness.

'Willand . . . you're doing very well. Hold on.'

He forced himself to reply with humility. 'Thank you, Master Gwydion. I will.'

At last they drew the stone up and Gwydion danced light, fantastic steps around it, calling forth powers to enfold and mute the stone. Will's eyes blazed as the land around began to glow in eerie green, but the stone remained stubbornly dark, a nothingness cut out against the sky. Will crouched under it, re-tying a rope that had come loose. For a moment the stone seemed about to topple upon him. He cried out in panic, scrambled out from the hole and ran like a rabbit. When he sat down in the dry grass he was a long way away from the lign. He felt cold sweat slicking his skin, sharp salt pricking at the corners of his eyes. He felt like sobbing, and was greatly ashamed of his cowardice. He watched the wizard working on alone and thought over what Gwydion had said about not needing him.

'I'll show you you're wrong about me,' he muttered, then drove himself back to help.

He stood next to Gwydion, helping silently, patiently, until the moon, sailing high now, began to cut across the mid-line of the sky. Then Gwydion danced and spoke subtle words, and ogham rose for a moment like gooseflesh in the battlestone's surface. Gwydion circled the stone, menacing it, reading the marks and tracing out the strokes with his finger to be sure of their meaning among the shadows. Then the marks weakened and vanished, and they carefully laid the stone down again on two timbers taken from one of the ruined houses.

Will chocked the waggon's wheels, then reeved the block and tied the end of the rope to Bessie's harness. The cob's strength easily drew the stone up the shallow ramp. He heard the stone complaining against the wood, and while Bessie pulled steadily under Gwydion's whispered encouragements, Will fed three old rake handles under the stone to act as rollers, managing everything with great care until the battlestone tipped safely onto the bed of the cart.

Then Will became aware of a trembling in his legs and a pain in his spine. He felt suddenly like a man who was standing at the middle of a rope slung over a mighty river that was roaring in spate.

'What is it?' Gwydion asked.

'My knees are wobbling,' he said, sitting down suddenly. 'I can feel something rushing along the lign.'

The wizard circled and sang and said at last, 'I think a dam must have been broken.'

Will began to feel better. The stone seemed to lose much of its terrible hold on his mind now that it had been lifted. It was as if its connection with the lorc had been severed and its capacity for malice undercut, but Gwydion said this was probably just another feint on the stone's part. 'It wants us to believe its power is diminished, but it is not. I have applied temporary binding-spells, but they will not endure long. We must move it as quickly as these poor axles will allow. We should go now if Bessie can find her way in the dark.'

'Where to?'

'I have a suitable place in mind.'

'Why don't we take it to the sea and throw it in? It would never be found there.'

'What? And have a hundred shipwrecks at the place it was left? And a thousand poor mariners sunk and drowned in the bottom of the sea? Such would be the result of that plan, I fear.'

'Then where are we taking it? If it can't be buried under the land or thrown into the sea?'

'We must imprison it,' Gwydion said. He got up beside Will and urged the horse on. When Will asked what the ogham had said, Gwydion gave the translation at once:

> *King and Queen with Dragon Stone.*
> *Bewitched by the Moon, in Darkness alone.*
> *In Northern Field shall Wake no more.*
> *Son and Father, Killed by War.'*

And after a thoughtful pause he added the cross-reading.

> *Northern King's Bewitched Son,*
> *Queen of the Moon in her Father's Field.*
> *Dragon of Darkness, Awaken and slay!*
> *Lonely Stone take War away!'*

They rumbled on towards an unseen track, sailing now on an ocean of moon-frosted mist, and Will shivered.

'What does it mean?'

'I do not know.'

'But we did a good job tonight, didn't we, Master Gwydion? You and me?'

'That, Willand, remains to be seen.'

CHAPTER TWELVE

ALONG THE BANKS
OF THE NEANE

By late afternoon on the following day the land to the south had become a broad plain, rich, filled with pasture meadows and dotted with hamlets. To the north there was the great dark swathe of the Forest of Roking with its tangled oaks. Through this prospect the River Neane wound like a serpent towards the east as Will and Gwydion sat high on the four-wheeled waggon and watched Bessie patiently draw her baleful load onward.

The Dragon Stone lay in the back of the cart, hidden by a covering of sacks. Will did not want to look at it: his eyes ran instead along the track towards the town which they were skirting. It seemed to him an immense collection of houses, like Sarum, the distant city he recalled seeing on the way to Clarendon. This place was a blue-grey sprawl of buildings, and around the centre of it rose a towered wall, while over all hung a haze of autumn smoke. The town stood on a rise that overlooked a reed marsh where the River Neane seemed to lose its way. As with Sarum, there were many towers and sharp spires sticking up above the thatches, but this time there was no Great Spire to dominate all.

As they came closer still, he saw many mills and began to smell the tanneries along the river. A great traffic of trade there was within the walls and crossing the bridges.

'What is this city?' he asked.

'It is not a city, it is a town.'

Will frowned. 'What's the difference?'

'A city is only so called if it holds a royal charter and tithe warrants. This town is called by the locals "Corde", or in full Cordewan. It is famous for the making of shoes.'

Will knew that a man who made shoes was called a 'cordwainer', so that made sense, but it did not improve his feelings for the place. He shivered and said, 'I don't like it here. Is there a . . . plague?'

Gwydion glanced at him curiously. 'Why do you say that?'

Will screwed up his face. 'I can smell it.'

Gwydion weighed his remark. 'How do you know how plague smells? There is nothing unusual in the air here. Corde has always been a place of good aspect, and the folk who live in the town are known for their helpfulness to strangers.'

And now Will came to think about it the smell was just the tang that came from the oak-bark pits and tanneries. He forced himself to look again at the town and the mystery deepened for there was nothing, after all, that was unpleasant about it, and he could not say why such a powerful dislike had come over him.

Of course! It's the Dragon Stone, he thought. It's getting into my blood. I mustn't let it.

Soon fields began to spread away to the south, and Will closed his eyes and began to nod into sleep, but such a powerful sense of riot came to him that he started awake again. When he looked out over the fields he saw a crowd of people streaming out over the land. At first they seemed like a wretched crowd, but as he looked he saw they were no more than harvest stooks of grain.

But then he seemed to start awake a second time, and

he knew that they could not be wheatsheaves. These were meadows, and what he had taken for stooks were standing stones. There were hundreds of them, carved into fantastical shapes.

'What are those?' he murmured, pointing them out to Gwydion.

'They are the Hardingstones. I should congratulate you, Willand. You have just felt a premonition, and genuine premonitions are rare. Perhaps being so close to a naked battlestone has woken something more in you.' And when Will looked to him questioningly, the wizard said, 'I saw you shiver – it was as if someone was standing on your grave.'

'My grave? I don't understand you.'

'A figure of speech. As for the Hardingstones, I will tell you they are tombstones – Cordewan lost many folk in the days of the Great Plague. Many fled in fear to the Cloister of Delamprey. In centuries past it was a royal manor house, but the Sightless Ones gradually took it over. The tombstones of Delamprey are not set to mark graves in the usual way, they are the petrified flesh of those who most feared the plague's coming.'

Will stared at them, queasily fascinated and unsure if he could see human forms in the shapes or not. 'Do you mean the people were turned to stone by the Sightless Ones?'

'I do.'

'But I didn't know they used magic.'

'They abuse it. They dabble in a kind of sorcery.'

He glanced at the stones again. 'Can't you turn them back?'

'When they came here to be turned to stone of their own free will?'

A thrill of revulsion passed through him. 'But why would anyone do that?'

'Because false promises were made to them. Folk who are in the grip of the fear of death will do strange things.

Those who came here cast off their shoes and waded barefoot across the river. They gave themselves to the Sightless Ones of Delamprey rather than be taken by the plague. It is said they still wait to be restored to life by a great healer, but he has not yet come, nor will he until three times three dozen and one years have passed.'

As Will watched the ghastly fields and the cloister beyond, something seemed to kick inside his head. It felt as if the battlestone they were carrying was sliding from its bed. He steadied himself, like one who comes awake and feels himself to be falling.

'What is it?' Gwydion asked, putting out an arm to steady him.

'Nothing,' Will murmured, realizing he had fallen asleep. He had been dreaming. He asked, 'Master Gwydion, what did you mean by "premonition"?'

Gwydion chuckled. 'You have a strong imagination, lad. I never mentioned premonitions.' And then he laughed again, out loud, as if amused at some joke, while Will struggled to understand.

'But you did! Didn't you?'

'Did I? Or did you dream it?'

He scowled. 'Don't joke about it, Master Gwydion.'

The wizard laughed. 'It seems you have little taste for philosophy. Go back to sleep. Or if you are already asleep, maybe you should wake up.'

After another moment of wondering Will looked back. There were the sad stones, hundreds of them laid out in rows, as if keeping a long-remembered vigil. 'Can you do nothing for them?' he asked.

'For the Hardingstones?' Gwydion flapped the traces and made an encouraging noise to Bessie. 'They are stones now, weathered and worn these hundred years and more. What would you have me do with them?'

*　　*　　*

The shades of night began to fall, and the star they seemed to be following put on a mantle of blue light for them. Gwydion pulled the waggon to a halt and listened out. Then Will too heard the faint peal of bells that rolled out of the south. Another added its voice nearby, then one that was more distinct rang out to the south-east, and then a clangour began in the town of Cordewan itself. In moments there was a wash of complicated, clashing rhythms. Gwydion listened closely to it until full darkness had fallen and the sound seemed to sweep away to the north again as the town fell silent.

'What was that?' Will asked. He had heard bells rung before but only to summon village folk or to mark the time of day. This was certainly not like that. A deluge of noise had swept over the land like summer rain, then disappeared as fast as it had come.

Gwydion said. 'The last time that happened was more than thirty years ago. The curfew towers are passing special news from one to another. They are sending it up the spine of the country as fast as may be.'

Will's mouth opened, fearing a calamity. 'It's the rumour of war.'

'Not so, lad.'

'Is it an invasion, then?'

'If it was that then there would be beacons fired also.'

'What, then? Could you read the message the bells carried?'

Gwydion gee-ed Bessie up and the big solid timber wheels started to roll forward again. 'This was a royal matter.'

'The king is . . . dead?' Will guessed, and was suddenly consumed by the implications.

'Quite the opposite,' Gwydion said, and just as Will began to fear the wizard would say no more he added, 'King Hal now has himself an heir.'

* * *

All next day they headed towards Geddenhoe Chase, a tract of unruly land where beast and bird were bred for the hunt. Will thought a lot about the arrival of the heir and the shimmering, hooded figure that he had seen at Queen Mag's shoulder.

He now realized an unpleasant thought had been lingering at the back of his mind for some time – that the apparition of Death had meant the queen or her baby would die in childbirth. But now here had come the joyous news, with no mention of any tragedy. But then Will recalled what Dimmet had said about King Hal not being the child's father, and he saw that that must entail dire consequences for the Realm – though what those consequences might be he was not yet able to foresee.

His thoughts left him feeling cold. He pulled his cloak tighter about him, and asked, 'What's to be done with the stone?'

Gwydion was ready for the question. 'According to the Black Book it seems that the power of a battlestone may be broken in three ways. The best course would be to take it back into the presence of its sister-stone – the one with which it was originally paired. The stones need only be set a hand's width from one another for their spirits of bliss and bale to flow back into balance.'

'Do the battlestone and its sister not have to touch?' Will asked.

'I think not. For then there would be too quick a flow, a violent disintegration, and the substance of both stones would be turned to dust along with much that was nearby. If it was let free, the spirit of harm would have nowhere to reside. I do not yet know what would happen in such a case. But the finding out of this riddle must soon become my quest.'

'You don't sound as if you know too much about what to do with it now you have it in your power.'

'But it is not in my power. Far from it.' The wizard sighed. 'My knowledge of the battlestones is in fragments, and all that I say to you about it must be regarded as uncertain. I believe that if the spirits were allowed to drift between the stones in a slow and controlled way, then two ordinary stones would be yielded once more. But there is no time to scour Cambray and Albanay and the Blessed Isle to discover every sister-stone that may be hidden there for they reveal themselves only at certain times of the year. I suspect the whereabouts of certain sister-stones, but in no case except one do I know it for certain. Nor, even if I did, would I know the battlestone to which each sister was linked.'

Sunlight dappled the road ahead and the forest trees were alive with birds. Will's thoughts felt equally hard to gather. 'You said there were three ways to deal with a battlestone. What's the second?'

'To drain the harm from it magically. That is a skill that may have been known of old, but one that is now long forgotten and must therefore be rediscovered. I have consulted many wise heads who live in the remoter parts of these isles, and I have tried to piece together how such a draining might once have been done, though it was never attempted upon a stone of the lorc. I fear that it would be most dangerous, for the harm that dwells within the battlestones is so pure that it would have to be brought into the world a little at a time and each tiny poison drop fully dispersed before the next was drawn out.'

'Would it be easy to make a mistake?'

Gwydion resettled his staff by his side. 'Draining a battlestone would be too dangerous. If it was done rashly and the harm were to get the upper hand, well then it might release itself all in a rush and there would be a disaster.'

Will shifted to look at the shape that crouched in the back of the cart. 'What sort of disaster?'

'If all the harm in this battlestone were to be released in a single hand clap?' Gwydion shook his head. 'In that case, I am sure that all my powers could not prevent it from coalescing. The stone at our back weighs many hundred-weight, yet it might have only a few ounces worth of the spirit of bliss. If even half the harm it contains was let loose and not properly dispersed that would be enough to torment the Realm beyond endurance.'

Will chewed his lip. 'And what's the third way?'

'The third way is the one that is being forced upon me. Since I cannot ship the Dragon Stone alone into the Blessed Isle, I must store it safely against the time when I might fetch its sister-stone here to stand beside it.'

'Store it safely? How? Can there be any place of safety for such a thing?'

'Not absolute safety. But I think if it was mortared into a chamber in the foundations of a great castle keep, if it was oriented correctly and confined within massive masonry, if its chamber was put under lock and key and watchfully guarded by no less a man than a loremaster – well, then and only then, might its malice be contained and no one killed.'

Will stared gloomily ahead. 'Well, there's a cause for celebration.'

The wizard laughed shortly. 'On the other hand, we are not in that happy position yet.'

'Are loremasters wizards? Like you?'

'They are men of great learning, but they are not wizards, for that was a term properly kept for those of the Ogdoad. Each loremaster has his own special learning – Lord Morann is the Jewelmaster, Gortamnibrax is the master of lore concerning green growing things, Barinth is master of the salt wave, a steersman of incomparable wisdom, and there are others.'

'But none versed especially in the ways of battlestones,

I suppose.' Will rested his elbows on his knees and his chin on the heels of his hands. 'I was quite pleased when we found this one, but it seems we've uncovered a nice mess along with it. If only the lorc had never been made.'

'The lorc is not to blame. Nor should you think badly of the fae. The wonderful works of old have been abused and broken by the greed and sorcery of later ages. Would you blame the ash tree for arrow shafts?'

Will thought about that, and decided that the wise ones of old had not perhaps been wise enough. They had not counted upon the three weaknesses and the seven resulting failings of humankind that Gwydion had once mentioned. He watched the trees as they passed. 'So we're taking the Dragon Stone to a castle,' he said, pursuing the subject. 'Which one?'

'Foderingham,' Gwydion said. 'It is not the closest, but I believe it is the most secure for it lies within three broad circular flows, though one of them is a little weak. Also Richard of Ebor, the lord of that place, is a friend who has recently returned home.'

'Am I to stay with him?' he said, already knowing the answer.

'Willand, Duke Richard is not at all like Lord Strange, and is as reasonable a nobleman as may be found in this Realm. After I have spoken with him I shall in all likelihood have to ride on to Trinovant, for it is in that great city that my struggle will best be carried on.'

'I'll be sad to see our paths part again,' Will said, feeling a profound regret creep over him.

Gwydion laid an arm on his shoulder and said quietly, 'Be brave. You must watch over the stone for me in my absence, and this time I shall be gone for quite a time. Learn what must be learned, though it will not be easy for you.'

'I wish I—' He was about to say that he wished he had

been left at home, but he saw that would have been childish. He saw clearly now that the first part of his life had come to an end the day he had followed Gwydion out of the Vale. On that day he had left his happy boyhood behind. The second part had been his learning of the power of words and his coming into a knowledge of the main redes of magic. But now what lay before him?

As if in answer, Gwydion said, 'It will soon be time for you to learn the ways of the men of power. You must learn how it is with lords and lordlings, and there is no other way to do it than to grow up among them. Foderingham Castle is a place of good aspect, and it is my hope that you will grow to regard it as your home.'

'I doubt that will ever happen,' he murmured.

'Manners, Willand. According to the rede they maketh the man, for no one but a fool takes what he wants by demands when a quiet word might charm him all that he needs. Foderingham is not a cheerless place like the Tower of Wychwoode. Richard of Ebor has many sons and daughters, including an heir who is much the same age as you. At Foderingham you will learn to hawk and to hunt. You will understand what it is to be a lord. I have a feeling that the duke's people will take to you, especially the lord of the gardens, whose name is Gort, which means in the true tongue "ivy" or "a wheatfield" depending how you say it.'

Will looked askance at the wizard and folded his arms. What about the special talent I'm supposed to have, he thought. Isn't that important any more? I've no interest in hawking or hunting, and now it sounds as if I'm about to be apprenticed to a compost-maker!

Gwydion said gently, 'I would rather have you go willingly to your new home.'

'I don't know what to think. The stone's making my moods rise and fall like the sea,' he said, trying hard to master his down-spiralling thoughts. 'I'd say your holding-spells are allowing that monster in the back there to leak ill-humour.'

Gwydion cast the stone a dark glance. 'That is quite possible. No one knows what methods these stones use to carry forward their harm. Have you ever heard folk speak of a twist of fate?'

'Yes. Why?'

'Because that may be an apt phrase here. It may be that the battlestones work by warping people's destinies.'

A thrill of terror ran down Will's spine. The idea was nightmarish, for how often had the wizard called him 'Child of Destiny'?

He went back over all that Gwydion had ever told him, searching for a clue, but found little to guide him. At last he asked, 'Master Gwydion, what's a phantarch?'

The wizard's voice remained level, but he could not cover his surprise. 'Where did you hear that word?'

'You spoke it to me once.'

'Did I? "First there were nine, then nine became seven . . ." And have I ever spoken those words to you?'

'No.'

'Then perhaps Tilwin has not spoiled you completely by speaking out of turn. The words come from a prophetic song that tells of the Ogdoad.'

Gwydion began to sing:

> *'First there were nine,*
> *Then nine became seven,*
> *And seven became five.*
> *Now, as sure as the Ages decline,*
> *Three are no more,*
> *But one is alive.'*

When he had finished he said, 'You cannot be a phantarch, Will. You can only be the Phantarch. And I am the last.'

'Does it mean "wizard"?'

'It means more than that,' Gwydion stroked his beard. 'Celenost was the first Phantarch. He headed the Ogdoad of Nine. But Celenost is long departed.'

Will's thoughts settled on the word 'ogdoad'. He had once asked Lady Strange its meaning, since Gwydion had used it in both their hearing. 'We wizards of the Ogdoad,' he had said, and so Will had at first supposed it to be the name of some brotherhood or order of wizardry, but the Hogshead's wife had corrected him.

'Lady Strange told me that "ogdoad" meant a group of eight. But surely you can't have an ogdoad of nine any more than you can have a pair of three.'

Gwydion inclined his head knowingly. 'The Ogdoad was ever a group of eight – plus one more. One who was not wholly of us.'

'Why was he not?'

'Because he was aways destined to betray us.'

Will scratched his chin, seeing for the first time that wizardry, no less than kingship, was far from a straightforward matter. 'You mean it was prophesied all along? You knew that one of your number was going to betray you all, but not who it was? That must have been very hard.'

'It was. It affected our thinking, and our work. We began as other men begin. We were born in the Age of Trees, and drawn from among the First Men. Those who might choose the path were born with a mark upon us that only others who bore the mark could see. But having the mark and choosing the path did not mean a man would become a wizard, for the way was long and arduous, and there were destined only ever to be eight of us plus one. Many carried the mark, but few could endure the tests, and so in time the marks upon all but the Ogdoad faded away.'

'But if there was no mark upon a man in the first place then he knew he could never become a wizard?'

'Correct.'

Will's thoughts glittered with dangerous questions. Had any of the wizards been women? Most of all he wanted to know what a wizard's mark looked like, but did not dare ask in case Gwydion showed it and he discovered that he could see it. Instead, he said, 'You once told me not to call you immortal. Does that mean you'll die one day?'

'Folk say: "A wizard is as changeless as the Northern Star" but they are wrong on both counts. Even that star is not constant. It moves in its course over the ages, and so do we. Wizards were born as mortal men, but we do not die as mortal men. We do not age as other men age, but we do tire. Your spirit is lodged within your body, but that is not so with wizards.'

Will's eyes widened. 'Then have you no spirit?'

'Of course I have a spirit. But it does not reside within me as my consciousness does. It is elsewhere. This was done as a precaution against magical attack. Our spirits were kept in philosophers' stones, which each of us hid away in the Far North.'

Will sat up. 'Philosophers' stones – I've heard of them, but never known what they were! What do they look like?'

Gwydion smiled. 'Mine is a little bigger than a chicken's egg and looks much the same, though it is almost black and veined through with colours. You see, there comes a time when every wizard begins to fail. Then he must recover his philosopher's stone and become one with himself again.'

'Fail?'

'Only phantarchs fail, Will. A failing phantarch becomes harder to see, not because he is fading away, though it may sometimes seem so, for mortal men must concentrate harder and harder to notice him. It would be difficult for you to recall what had passed if you had been in a failing phantarch's company. He leaves an impression of meaning behind, but you would not be able to remember the words he used. To talk with a phantarch who is failing is an unsettling experience, like talking with someone who is forever drifting into the blind-spot of your eye. A failing phantarch is already going ahead of himself, you see. And when the day comes that he is ready to depart on his last journey, he goes into the Far North and all memory of him fades from mortal minds.'

Will thought of the sadness of going on the last journey all alone. 'Does no one go with him?'

'During his office the Phantarch has two deputies. One always departs with him.'

'And the other?'

'The other stays and becomes the next Phantarch.'

'So who are your deputies?'

Gwydion drew a deep breath. 'I have none, for the Nine are now One. When Celenost failed, Brynach and Maglin both looked into their hearts and Brynach saw that he was not to be Phantarch. So Celenost departed with him, leaving Maglin to head a new Ogdoad of Seven. So it was again when Maglin began to fail, for Urias chose to go with him, leaving Esras to head the Ogdoad of Five. And lastly, Morfesa departed with Esras leaving Semias in charge of the Three.'

'Lastly?' Will said. 'But I thought you said you were alone now.'

The wizard's eyes darkened and his long face set in an expression of unfathomable sadness. 'When Semias began to fail, both Maskull and I looked into our hearts, but Maskull refused to depart with him.'

Will felt a bolt of fear run through him. 'Maskull? You mean . . .'

Gwydion looked into the far distance. 'Maskull was ever destined to become the betrayer. We are First Men, the last of a stock that came into being long ago when the world was full of magic. Once we were Ogdoad brothers, Maskull and I, pathfinders and guardians, but he has become convinced of another way. He disputes that which ought to be – and so he has become a sorcerer.'

By noon they were coming to a wide, flat country. To the north, the great oak forest of Roking stretched away dark and drear, but just here the land sloped down gently to the river, and soon a shining castle came in sight ahead of them.

It was the greatest fortress that Will had ever seen. Earthworks and high ramparts rose above the river on which stood a tall mound surmounted by a keep. White walls stretched between round towers, and the river was crossed by a bridge built under the castle walls. On the nearer bank there was a small settlement.

'A league beyond this castle a plain stretches away to the east,' Gwydion told him. 'The Great North Road lies out there, and beyond it is the Deeping Fen. It is that vast marsh that makes this such a useful place to put a castle. Armies marching the fastest route into the North must come under the scrutiny of the men who guard Duke Richard's walls.'

Soon the cart came to a sturdy timber bridge. The path led towards, and then through, a protected barbican. The quartered livery of the guards who waited there caused Will's suspicions to grow for they were blue and white, the same colours worn by Duke Edgar and his son at Clarendon. But when Will looked closer he saw that the guards carried on their breasts no golden portcullis but instead a golden fetterlock enclosing a silver falcon.

'What are we to make of a lord who uses a handcuff as his device?' Will asked. 'Is that not a sign of servitude?'

'Look again, Will,' Gwydion told him. 'The falcon is freedom, and freedom is trying to break the bonds that bind it. Duke Richard is head of the House of Ebor, a house that is somewhat in exile within its own land. He cannot speak of his hopes for fear of the headsman's axe, but by signs and symbols do lords show their secret desires. What the falcon-and-fetterlock means is this: whether it be legal or no, in his heart Duke Richard believes himself to be the rightful king.'

Will took the news in his stride. 'Didn't you once tell me that the king had made Duke Richard his Lord Lieutenant in the Blessed Isle? Was that not an honour? And if the king is so much under his wife's thumb, why would she want to reward her husband's rival?'

'That is no honour, but an empty title, for the Blessed Isle is not ruled by the Realm. Some small port properties and grants of land have been given over for the sake of trade and other practicalities and it is to these that the overblown title refers. By conferring it upon Richard the queen and Edgar have tried to exile him across the water. Their idea was to keep him as far away from Trinovant as possible, and so in ignorance of their doings.'

'You mean they thought that while he was in the Blessed Isle he wouldn't be able to interfere in their schemes to use King Hal as they do?'

'Correct.' Gwydion tapped his earlobe. 'But not long ago a little bird told me that the good duke had found his way back into the Realm.'

Will looked wryly at the wizard, not knowing if he really meant that the news had been carried to him by a bird or not. It seemed more than likely.

As they came to the gate the guards stopped them and examined the waggon. One of them peered mistrustfully under the sacking that hid the Dragon Stone. 'What's this?' he asked.

'A gift for your master,' Gwydion told him.

'And well may my lord thank you for it,' the guard replied, pushing back the rim of his kettle-hat. 'I say to you that if the choice was mine I'd not let an evil-looking block like this ride across my bridge. But I know you well enough by sight, Crowmaster, and I've standing orders never to hinder you in your errands – however strange they may seem to me.'

'I shall remember to thank your lord for his confidence, Jackhald, and for the courtesy of his servants,' Gwydion said warmly, and flapped the traces so that the waggon rumbled across the sluggish waters and into the shadow of the gatehouse.

In an effort to raise Will's spirits the wizard said, 'I have a tale about Castle Foderingham that might help you feel more at home here. As you know, the lowest grade of true magical skill is called "seeming", or what some call illusion-weaving.'

'That's making things seem to be what they're not.'

'Indeed it is. Now, seeming is very useful for lords and ladies, who are apt to forget humility and must at times be reminded they are of no more importance than you or I. I remember a time when I was here at this castle. It was about the Ewletide, and a cruel east wind had been blowing up out of the Great Deeping Fen for half a week. A thin covering of snow lay over the gardens, and every roof-ridge and every wall-top looked as if it was wearing an ermine collar. After the feast was over, at the duke's command, everyone went out into the gardens to walk and talk and take the air, but all Duke Richard's people did was complain of the cold, so he asked me if I might make the sun shine a little warmer for them. But as the snow seemed to vanish away the ladies began to tell one another in loud voices what a shame it was there were no leaves on the trees, and no blooms in the flower beds. So I called forth beautiful roses for them, delicate they were and white as the vanished snow. But then the little lordlings began to complain and ask if it wasn't time for them to go inside where they might have some more gooseberry pudding. At this I made the bushes bring forth delicious, juicy gooseberries, and I told each who heard me to draw out his knife and take in their fingers a rich, round fruit and make ready to cut it off – but to wait until I gave the word!'

Will broke his silence. 'And did they?'

'Indeed they did,' Gwydion said. 'For who would refuse a delicious gooseberry when such a thing could be found in deepest midwinter? But then, when all was ready, I snapped my fingers and took away the spell of seeming, which was one of the finest seeming spells that ever I wrought, and each person saw that he had in his hand no gooseberry at all but the end of his neighbour's nose. Ever since that time the garden has been called "the Garden of the White Rose".'

'Not "the Garden of the White Nose"?' Will said, smiling now.

'Oh, not that,' Gwydion told him as the cart came to a halt. 'For, as you will soon discover, when lords and ladies are obliged to learn a lesson in humility they rarely wish to commemorate it.'

'Is Duke Richard a fair man to look upon?' Will asked, betraying a small fear. 'Will I like him?'

The wizard smiled. 'Duke Richard is a glamorous man. Be careful you do not come to like him too much.'

Will looked up at the steel-shod fangs of the portcullis which being down for repairs had to be raised especially for them. He thought of the men hauling on the bars of the windlasses above him, and began to panic. He imagined them losing their grip and allowing the great barrier to fall down on him. A shiver passed down his spine and made him gasp. He felt like jumping from the waggon, but he steeled himself, and soon they had come inside the castle's outer defences and the dreadful feeling passed.

'Steady, Will.'

He wiped the sweat from his forehead, embarrassed that

the wizard had noticed his inexplicable terror. 'I'm sorry, Master Gwydion. I suppose I'm just a bit overwhelmed by the grandness of this place.'

'That must be it.'

Now all that Gwydion had told him about castles began to make sense, for here was power realized in stone. Inside was an outer bailey, or yard, surrounded by a high wall that was manned by guards. The outer bailey contained stables and other outbuildings. It was filled with hundreds of people of all walks, many in the Ebor livery, but many more plainly dressed and going about their daily business. An arched gateway led beneath a second gatehouse and opened into an inner bailey, but the oaken gates were closed and Will could not see what lay within.

Gwydion was met by more liveried men to whom he gave careful instructions about what was to be done with Bessie and the waggon. Will jumped down, put his hands on his hips and began to study the castle keep. That alone was bigger than the Tower of Wychwoode. The donjon was eight-sided, each side being thirty or more paces across, and it was built on top of a steep, grassy mound. From where Will stood he could see three of the sides and all had slit-windows so that defenders could retire inside and still command the Outer Bailey if it was overrun by an enemy. Like the Tower of Wychwoode the top was battlemented so that defenders could shoot arrows and crossbow bolts at those below from behind stout wooden shutters. And above the keep flew a long white and blue battlepennon with two tails like a swallow. It carried the same device which the guards wore on their breasts along with a scattering of white flowers. Will felt unaccountably pleased to be here. Gwydion had said it was a place of good aspect, and so it seemed.

'And what marvels have you brought for us this time, Master Gwydion?'

The voice made Will start. He turned and saw the question had been asked by a tall, able-looking man about forty years old. Will could not help but look at him admiringly. The man's eyes were as grey as the slate of the Blessed Isle. He wore a brown velvet hat, trimmed with otter fur, and his coat, which was a sumptuous blue, fell from his shoulders all the way to the ground. The coat had a pair of elaborate sleeves which also carried an otter fur trim, and was clinched at the waist by a buckled belt of red and gold. The end of the belt looped over and was pushed down through itself, and supported a broadsword on the man's left hip.

The duke – for who else could it be? – stood with five or six of his people. There was no doubt in Will's mind who was in charge. The man's every gesture was decisive, and he seemed to Will to be someone whom others would follow to the death. Where Lord Strange trod down those around him in an effort to raise himself up, Duke Richard stood effortlessly above the men of his household. Will thought about the sorry weakling that was King Hal, and saw immediately why there should be many in the Realm who would prefer Duke Richard as their king.

'Friend Richard, well met!'

Gwydion and the duke clasped each other by the upper arms for a moment, and Will saw a gold signet ring glitter on the duke's little finger.

'Master Gwydion, you are welcome. But how did you know I was here? I am rarely at Foderingham in these troubled times, nor shall I tarry here long.'

'Important news travels fast. I myself bring tidings that cannot wait. And in return I must ask a favour of you.'

'Ask freely, Crowmaster, but if the tidings you bring concern the birth of a royal prince then we are already aware of that.'

Will heard the unspoken comment that attended the

duke's words. Gwydion said, 'I have no doubt you are kept abreast of events for your messengers are swift and your sources generally sound. But my news is different – and for your ears alone.'

'Come, then, for we must speak now if we are to speak at all.'

'Friend Richard, perhaps the Wortmaster should hear my tidings too, if he can be found quickly enough.' The wizard turned to Will and winked. 'Willand, you must remain here. Take care to do just as you are told now.'

'I will—' He was about to add more but Gwydion had already swept the duke away. There was a strange peal of bells that stopped almost as soon as it had begun, then the gates to the inner bailey parted and both wizard and duke were gone.

Will waited, unregarded, as folk went about their business all around him. He felt awkward, and wondered what he should do. Of late he had spent hardly a moment out of the wizard's company, and it felt strange to be waiting alone like this. After a while he sat down on a bench by the wall, and eventually one of the duke's followers, a huge knight attired in blue and yellow, found him and took him to the kitchens.

The knight was in his mid-twenties, with a broad nose and built like a great captain of war. 'My name is Sir John of Kyre Ward.'

'And I am Will of . . . of Nether-Norton-in-the-Vale, sir,' Will replied, unsure what was the proper form of reply to a knight of Sir John's rank. The knight seemed hardly to regard his answer, but he did not ignore the question that followed it. 'Are you a kinsman of the duke?'

Sir John shot him a narrow glance. 'My father is Sir Hugh Morte of Morte Hall, who is the natural uncle of his grace, and guardian of Foderingham in his absence.'

The kitchen was hot and steamy and filled with iron

pans and copper cauldrons. A great quantity of logs were stacked up at the hearth. The air was warm and smelled of new-baked bread. 'You're to be taken in as a page with all the duties that entails. You look like a handy enough lad and keen-minded. You'll need to be, for there's much practice and learning involved.'

'What kind of learning?' Will asked with sinking heart. He hoped there would be no more of the solitary copying out that he had stomached between Beltane and Lammas.

'Etiquette and the histories, I expect. Though Tutor Aspall will hardly teach you which way to face when you climb on a horse. Do you have anything of the doctrine of letters?'

'Some. I can write out a hundred words or more and—'

'Well, that's not my affair. I'll teach you all there is about the killing arts.' He grinned and sat Will down. 'How to kill without being killed yourself, that's more important than scribe's work. But eat now if you have an appetite, for you'll be spoken to about all things presently.'

After clearing a huge trencher of beef and dumplings, Will was taken by one of the kitchen servants to a tiny room in a building attached to the wall of the inner bailey and told he was to live there. When the servant left him alone he wandered around the garden, supposing it to be the Garden of the White Rose of which Gwydion had spoken. There came the tantalizing tune of striking metal again, and a strange clanging floated over the walls. He stopped to listen to it, then saw that the garden was overlooked by a gallery. Two young girls, about seven or eight years of age, watched him from its shadows. As he saw them, one leaned to whisper something to the other and they both giggled.

Will was about to wave to them when a mild-mannered man, tall and thin and dressed in black and white appeared. 'Ahem! You may call me Tutor Aspall,' he said in a curiously high voice. 'I am tutor to his grace's two elder sons. I will show you your duties.' He began to take Will on a tour of the castle, but then he saw the girls. 'Do not pay Lady Elizabeth and Lady Margaret any heed.'

'Ladies?' Will said, thinking them too young to be called that. 'Those two girls?'

'"Lady" is their title. His grace the duke and the Lady Cicely have seven children in all. Four boys and three girls, though Lady Anne is not a child any more, she is going on sixteen. The two youngest children are George and Richard. You will see little of them for they are still both in the care of Nurse Rose, but the two elder boys reside here.'

Will looked in. There was no one in the chamber, but it was as chaotic as any room lived in by two boys.

'What are their names?' Will asked.

'Sir Edward and Sir Edmund.' The tutor gave a smile which quickly vanished. 'Sir Edward is about your age, I would say. He is his grace's heir. Sir Edmund is three years his junior. You will wait on them.'

Will asked uncomfortably, 'Do I have to call them "sir"?' It seemed wrong to call anyone his own age or younger 'sir'.

'Sir Edward is Earl of the Marches,' the tutor said as if that explained all. 'And Sir Edmund is Earl of Rutteland. You are not allowed to go down that passageway. That leads to the chamber where the Lady Elizabeth and the Lady Margaret sleep. Nor are you permitted to use those stairs. Come with me now, and I will take you to meet Wortmaster Gort – if he can be found.'

All the new names but one had begun to swim together in Will's head. 'Wortmaster Gort,' he said as he left the chamber. 'That's an odd sort of name.'

Tutor Aspall tutted. 'You must never say that in his hearing. It is a most venerable title for a most venerable old – ahem! – personage. He is lord of the gardeners and a healer and also, after a fashion, one of the tutors here. I was told your name is Willand and that you are used to the company of wanderers. Is that so?'

'Er . . . I suppose so.'

'Then I trust you will not find the Wortmaster too strange.'

They followed a twisting passage that came out at last into the inner bailey once more, and an empty bench. Will asked, 'Where's Master Gwydion gone?'

Tutor Aspall turned. 'What concern is that of yours?'

Will hesitated at the oddness of the question. 'Because I have need to speak with him. What do you think?'

One of the guards passed them, and Will recognized him as Jackhald, the same man who had let them across the bridge.

'Hey, Jackhald! Do you know where Master Gwydion is presently?'

The guard stopped, pushed back the brim of his iron hat and addressed his answer to Tutor Aspall. 'Sir, if it's the Crowmaster the lad wants then he's out of luck.'

'Why's that?' Will asked.

'Because he's gone off with his grace.'

'Come along now—'

Will held back. 'Gone off? Where to?'

'It's not your place to be asking questions,' Tutor Aspall said.

'Where to?' Will insisted. 'I need to know!'

And despite his shock at the wilfulness being shown to him the tutor said, 'His grace has taken a guard of men. They're riding urgently for Trinovant. Did you not hear them leave?'

'Gone? Already?' Will looked from one face to the other. 'But . . . what about Bessie? The horse isn't Master Gwydion's. Nor the cart. They belong to—'

Jackhald laughed. 'No doubt the Crowmaster left a mess of instructions. He always does.'

'But when's he coming back?'

The guard laughed. 'Neither his grace nor the Crowmaster account their doings to old Jackhald, that's for sure!'

And Will sat down heavily on the bench. A wave of hopelessness overwhelmed him. Well, how about that? he thought. Master Gwydion's had time enough to arrange for Bessie to be sent back to Eiton, but he's left without so much as a word of farewell to me!

PART THREE

THE DUKE OF EBOR'S PLEASURE

CHAPTER FOURTEEN

A WINTER OF DISCONTENT

Once Will's resentment faded what was left felt like loneliness. A new jerkin and hose in Ebor colours were brought to him, along with two shirts and a pair of leather shoes that at first felt very strange.

He wrapped his own clothes around his precious silver-bound horn, took his other belongings from his bundle and put them into the small chest that had been provided for him. No sooner was he dressed than he was sent down the long passage to meet Duke Richard's two elder sons. It was not long before they had his measure, and he theirs.

After the fashion of princes these young lords wore their hair cut to just above their shoulders. Their doublets were of the best quality, though well used, and they sported matching green velvet hats that gave them a lofty air. Edward was certainly his father's son: tall, blond and determined to be a leader. Edmund was more studious and kinder to a newcomer.

'Can you use a sword?' Edward asked as soon as they met.

'Maybe,' Will replied warily. Something about Edward troubled him.

'Either you can use a sword, or you can't. Which is it?'

Will shrugged. 'It's maybe.'

Edward met his eye. 'You'll have to learn good manners if you're going to serve as my page. And swordsmanship. I'll show you some moves. Here, hedgehog!'

Will silently caught the blunt steel practice sword that was tossed to him.

'My name's Willand,' he murmured.

'What's wrong with your hair? Had a fight with a lawn mower, did you?' Edward laughed, then his brother laughed also. 'What other weapons do you know?'

Will had no idea what the other was talking about. 'I can shoot a bow. And where I come from men use the sporting quarterstaff. I can wield one, but we don't use them as weapons.'

Edward looked down his nose and scoffed. 'A quarter-staff? Did you hear that, Edmund? He fights by waving a wooden stick! So, Willy Wag-staff, let's see how you fare with a sword!'

Will parried the sudden blow and began to wonder about his welcome. Edward's next wild swing threw Will backwards so that he jarred his elbow against a table.

Edward's third blow was intercepted by a large man in knightly garb. He and Sir John were as alike as two peas, except that this knight was grey-haired and Will realized he must be father to Sir John of Kyre Ward, which must make him Sir Hugh of Morte Hall.

The knight cuffed Will's ear, then Tutor Aspall who had entered behind the knight, asked him what he thought he was doing.

'Here for less than an hour and already you're behaving like a barbarian. You will go without supper tonight.'

Edward smirked at him from behind the tutor's back.

Will looked back defiantly, but said nothing. It seemed to him that if Gwydion had wanted him to have his under-standing of the lordly world tested, then he had picked the right place, for this was in its way as much a madhouse as Clarendon Lodge or the Hogshead's dismal tower. It seemed an ill-advised place to have brought the battlestone.

But it was not long before Will had completely forgotten about the captive stone. At first he was taken up with getting used to his new lodgings, and making a truce with those who were to be his new companions. After life on the open road, the days at Foderingham seemed like torture. The lessons were endless. Everything at the castle was ruled over by a strange iron engine that sat inside the small tower overlooking the inner bailey. Every now and then the bell near the engine would clang out. The tower had a wheel on it, marked with 'I's and 'X's and 'V's, and a pointer that moved when no one was looking at it. There were times when nobody took any notice of the clangs, but at other times the guard would rush to change, or a meal would be served or some other sudden alteration in the rhythm of life would happen. At those times Will hated the engine, for then conversations would finish without ending properly and people whose company he was enjoying would hurry away as if some insult had been passed.

And it was not only the ebb and flow of the day that was closely controlled at Foderingham. Here, as in Lord Strange's tower, the folk were divided into family and retainers and servants. The servants were of many different kinds, all ranked one above another, and some had been made miserable by being put to lowly duties and never given anything better to do. But there was never any complaining, for servants were treated roughly if they complained, or even if they did not defer. It was a long way from life in the Vale, where everyone looked after one another and a man's respect – and his self-respect too – depended largely on how helpful folk said he was.

Nor were these the only shocks that Will's view of the

wider world suffered. There were Sightless Ones among those who were let into the castle. Their nearest cloister stood not half a league distant from the castle, and when he enquired about it he was told that the duke's family had paid for it to be built, and that it was maintained there at great annual cost to him.

The Fellows came into the castle from time to time to perform their strange rituals. They refused to celebrate the eight great days of the year that Gwydion had named – the two solstices that marked Midsummer and Ewle, the two equinoxes that marked the days of equal light and dark, and the four festive days of Sowain and Beltane, Imble and Lammastide. At Foderingham the duke's family celebrated lesser days, not the important ones that were set by the great motions of the sky, but ones named after men, and mostly dead Elders of the Fellowship at that, men such as Ilbyn the Perfect or Swythen the Martyr.

And when the day of a true festival did come around, it was called by another name, one given to it by the Sightless Ones to glorify themselves, and none of the proper observances were kept. There were no jolly games, no feasting, just hunger all day long and a dull parade of Fellows decked in golden robes who moaned as they walked along. Will suspected that the fasting days had been deliberately set down to supplant what had gone before, so folk would come eventually to forget the Old Ways altogether.

As for Will himself, there was little at Foderingham that he could call fun. He missed Gwydion's company more than he could say, for after the time they had spent together the wizard's going away felt like losing a part of himself. And though Edward and Edmund were not as bad as he had first thought, neither of them seemed to know anything worthwhile about the world.

Though Will was called a page he was not treated much differently from the duke's two elder sons. When they went riding so did he, when they ate supper so did he, when they endured their long lessons so did he. Yet, in some hard-to-grasp way, they managed to remain aloof from him. He did not dislike them for it – this was their home and he was an unwanted guest in it – but he wondered why Edward remained so suspicious of him. And why Edmund, who allowed himself to be ruled so easily by his elder brother, refused his friendship as if attending to some expected duty.

Edward was as tall and strongly built as Will himself, but he was as changeable as Edmund was constant. Edward's moods rose and fell, and his manners or temper could not be relied upon. Edward could be generous, but he also liked to be in charge. Will quickly realized that to annoy him he only had to challenge him in some detail. It did not matter how unimportant the detail, Edward would insist to the point of violence if he found that Will disputed it with him.

Will soon recognized that whenever Edward was trying to insult him he would always call him 'pageboy'. At such times, Will would put on an annoying smile and tell himself what Gwydion had told him very firmly, that pity was as demeaning and useless an emotion to feel about another as was envy.

Ewle came and went without snow. There was a feast of sorts, but it was mostly a gloomy time with mournful songs and another grim procession of Fellows. Will watched from what he hoped was a safe distance. Again there were long tapers and droning speeches made by men in golden cloaks and tall hats. Pale light glinted on their ritual fleshing knives. When they spoke they did so in a halting language that Will could not understand. A severed pig's head was put on a platter, lifted on high and brought into the Great Hall. Salvers of blood were poured into golden basins. And speeches were made wishing a health upon Isnar, the present Grand High Warden of the Fellowship. Only after they had left the castle precinct did Lady Cicely call her children to her and take them down to the Lesser Hall where there was a juggler dressed in red and yellow, and a tumbling dwarf who had bells on his hat, and a man like Jarred, the one who had worked fire at Clarendon Lodge, who blew flames from his mouth and conjured for them and made bangs and sharp smells with sorcerer's powder. After having seen the real thing, Will thought it all very poor fare.

But in February, news came that raised everyone's spirits. The duchess gathered her children and brought in all the heads of the household servants and told them that Duke Richard had lately won a bloodless victory. His patient diplomacy in Trinovant, she said, had convinced many of the lords that he should be allowed to open the Grand Council in the king's name. And since King Hal continued weak and speechless and unable to handle public affairs, Duke Richard had been awarded the title 'Lord Protector and Defender of the Realm'.

To Will's chagrin, no mention was made of Gwydion, and when he asked the Lady Cicely if there had come any news of the wizard she smiled at him in a kindly, regretful way and said that she had heard no word of him at all.

'The Crowmaster is always late,' Edward said, believing himself to be funny. 'Just like you, he doesn't know what a clock is.'

'He comes when it pleases him and he leaves when it pleases him. That's what you mean,' Will said.

'Don't tell me what I mean, pageboy. I know what I mean and I mean what I say.'

'But you don't always say what you know,' Will said cryptically, then he added a bit too loudly. 'And half the time you don't know what you say.'

'I heard that, pageboy!'

'Good.'

'Take it back!'

'If you like. Consider it taken back.' He offered his insin-cerest smile, hoping it would enrage Edward further, but this time Edward was minded to accept what he supposed was an apology. He barges about like a bull in a bottle shop, Will thought, amused. What an idiot, when there's no need for it.

As the icy blasts of February gave way to the rain of March everyone found themselves longing for more good news, but what came next was more disturbing. Parties of armed men had clashed in the Northern Marches. The queen's men and friends of the Duke of Mells were riding about like reivers and robbers, stirring up trouble for anyone with links to the house of Ebor. Now the rumours spoke of orders sent out across the land telling the most powerful lords to raise troops for duty on the king's behalf. And what that portended Will could easily guess. While winter's icy touch lay upon the land, he found that good cheer remained hard to come by. More than once he saw columns of men marching by the castle and soldiers foraging the distant fields. Numerous lordly retinues travelled up and down the Realm on the Great North Road, coming in sight of the highest tower of Foderingham and causing the guards to stand vigil in doubled strength all night.

Throughout the long weeks of cold Will endured the simmering dislike of Edward. But he had learned by now to hold himself in check. Each time the duke's son made a remark calculated to rile him, he would shrug it away like water off a duck's back. He tried to be a man about Edward, tried to do as Gwydion would have counselled – to see things from the other person's point of view and to make broad allowances for his failings. But it was not easy.

Gwydion had said that the seven human failings were built on the three weaknesses, though he had not really explained what those were. The failings were, so far as Will could remember: pride, vanity, tyranny, wrath, sloth . . . and a couple of others which he could not readily call to mind. Edward was certainly prideful and vain. He was also apt to be tyrannical when he thought he could get away with it. As for wrath, he was quite hot-tempered, and if sloth showed itself as a lack of conscientiousness in lessons, then Edward was that too.

But Edward was also hard to despise. In truth, Will genuinely felt sorry for him. Duke Richard was so much the master here, and so much at the centre of everyone's thoughts, that no one else seemed to matter. During the duke's absence everything fell silent and dark, and it was not just the inactivity of winter that was the cause. There was a noticeable emptiness, a sense that everyone was waiting for their lord's return. And no one felt that loss as keenly as Edward.

It was no way to live. News was hoped for daily, and when some snippet came it was treasured and mulled over and looked at from every angle. Only Lady Cicely knew the real contents of the letters that came by exhausted rider under the duke's personal seal and signet. Will had once seen impressed into the hard red wax the shape of a four-leaf clover and three flowers. But though the duchess often broke the seal while they watched, she would never read out the duke's letters in full. And when it came to it she did no more than tell of inconsequential things and then assure everyone of their father's continuing good health and best wishes.

But if time spent gathered in the Great Hall was bitter-sweet, then that spent in the school room was gall. Tutor Aspall insisted they study great books. He made them learn and recite the names of the thirty-nine earldoms of the Realm. He told them in his high, precise voice about valorous deeds. 'A knight must ever seek to avenge wrongs,' he assured them. 'He must protect the weak and give charity unto the needy. Neither does a knight knowingly abandon a friend, but shows courage in the fray and gives quarter to all who cry for it. Always he fights with honour, and is mindful of his oaths.'

And of honour their tutor told them: 'A knight must always keep his word. No secret and no comrade may he ever betray. Never shall he tell a lie, for this is called chivalry and it is a code that applies to all men of sufficient rank. Now hearken to me, while I read to you from the Lay of Sir Tristrem . . .'

Will considered the rules of chivalry, but he was unimpressed by them. It was obvious that all those complicated regulations could be thrown out and replaced by just one simple rede – the Great Rede, or if not that, then perhaps the special one that counselled, 'Do not do unto others what you would not have done unto you.' That was something that never entered anyone's head at Foderingham, least of all Edward's. Little of the chivalric code had rubbed off on him despite all his pretences. He's riding for a fall, Will thought, as he watched the duke's heir casually defacing his father's property with the point of a dagger.

'What are you looking at, pageboy?'

'I don't know,' he said. 'I've never seen one before.'

Edward held out the dagger. 'What? It's just an old doorframe. And anyway it'll be mine one day.'

And Will took himself off, saying under his breath, 'Everything comes full circle in time, Edward. And you've yet to learn that.'

But for all Will's difficulties, there was one great compensation – Wortmaster Gort.

The Wortmaster was so called for his knowledge of worts, or plants, of all kinds. Here was a man who though seeming only middling old in years was very ancient. In wisdom he seemed unsurpassed. Yet he was young enough in spirit for he danced through forest and fen like a child. The guards – whom the duke's children called 'jacks' on account of their padded jackets – swore that the Wortmaster had not pruned his badger-streaked beard nor cut one hair of his head within living memory. They said he was a wizard of some kind, though Will knew the jacks had only the haziest idea of what a wizard might be.

Will knew that Gort was no wizard but that he did understand much that Gwydion taught about magic and the wild world, for he was a loremaster. He could charm blossoms from the bud, and like a Sister of the Wise he had a 'familiar' – a fat, white, red-eared rabbit called Osric which could fight cats and win.

Gort liked to cook for himself, and he liked to brew. The shambles that was his shed contained much that burbled yeastily or stank of decay. Gort stored huge, smelly fungi there and kept rank cheeses wrapped up in cloths. He saved crusts of bread until they went so mouldy that mice would not eat them. And he hung dried herbs from his rafters. Whereas most people's tongues could make out only the five principal flavours, Gort said his own tongue could distinguish two dozen, and his long nose could smell bluebells in a wood three leagues away. He always wore a long, dark green robe and a grey hat on his head that was as shapeless as a pastry – though with something of the squareness of a scholar's about it – and embroidered with a leaf.

He was often to be seen in the gardens, helping to push a barrow of manure, or basking in a corner of the castle grounds that had trapped a little winter sun. He said that whosoever could make two ears of corn, or two blades of grass, grow upon a piece of ground where only one had been before, did more for the Realm than the whole tribe of disputatious lords put together. Gort really came alive when he was in a meadow. Then walking with him was a joy. He would go into the beechwoods and slap a hand on one of the great rising silvery-skinned trunks and say, 'Is

this not like the leg of some great grey beast? Ha-har!' or
'"The beech he be a sacred tree, good for you and bad for
me," quoth the villain!' And away he would dance until he
came to another tree, when he would say something else
like: 'Shelter not beneath the oak, for he attracts the lightning stroke!' or 'Oh, sweet woods how much I do like your
solitariness!' or 'Elm tree graceful, elm tree tall. Elm tree
never let me fall!'

'Is that a spell?' Will would ask at such times. But Gort
would say, 'Phial, philtre and fiddlededee! Why, no, pilgrim!'
in a way that at once made Will feel foolish for asking, and
sure that Gort had said something much more interesting
than anything that was as ordinary as a magical spell.

Inside the castle, Gort's manner was generally as unas-
suming as a snail's, but in the fields it was all dancing and
prancing and song:

> *'U for the alphabet,*
> *Ewe for the show,*
> *You for the archer,*
> *And yew for the bow.*

'Ha-har-har!' or any of a thousand other pieces of sense
and nonsense that happened to flitter through his head.

From Wortmaster Gort Will learned all about the world
of living things, all except the hunt, for matters of blood
were reserved for the brusque and stoical Huntmaster
Tweddle. Tweddle came from the hard dales of the North.
He had greying unkempt whiskers and stub teeth and hard-
to-see eyes. He wore a raven's wing in his hatband and his
hands were large, hands that had wrung many a game bird's
neck and heaped up many a quarry. But for all that, he
also kept the falcons and hawks, and to them the huntmaster was like a doting father.

The hunting birds were a delight to Will's spirit, for they

were fierce creatures and touched with a powerful glamour. They led unknowable lives of wing and wind and had in them a keen understanding of the middle airs that no man could ever share.

Still, time spent in the mews was time out of the company of the Wortmaster. Gort and Tweddle avoided each other, for they had a mutual loathing which was rich and rare. Will saw straight away that they pulled at the opposite ends of most ideas. Somewhere in between them came two men who taught about the world of men: Sir John Morte, who could show how to do most things but could never explain it in words, and Tutor Aspall who could tell the whys and wherefores in his high, reedy voice, but could not actually do anything himself.

'Ahem!' Tutor Aspall would begin. 'Today – ahem! – we shall consider *The Jeaste of Sir Gawain . . .*'

But after the romances it was Sir John who showed them how to ride and to shoot like a real knight. He taught them much that Will did not want to know, like how to slit a man's gizzard, or how best to burn the thatch off a house. But there were compensations, like country horsemanship and how to hide a whole company of spearmen in the woods without them being seen.

It was from Tutor Aspall that Will one April day learned about lordly rank. The lesson was in the garden, and they were all enjoying the warmth of early spring sun. In the centre of the garden was a neat patch of turf called a 'lawn'. All year it was kept closely mowed by two men with reaping scythes and stiff brooms. Will wondered why these lawn mowers did not use sheep to crop their grass and save men the trouble as happened with the bowling green in Nether Norton. Every Valesman knew that what sheep left behind did the grass no end of good, but Tutor Aspall tutted at him for making low suggestions and Edmund whispered that lawn mowers and those who attended the duchess's

wardrobe and all the other servants had to be allowed some
way to make their livings.

'Still doesn't make sense . . .'

'Willand! Attend to your lesson!' Tutor Aspall pointed
to the scroll he had opened out. It seemed he was unhappy
teaching this lesson, as if he thought there was something
indelicate about it that he thought he had to tread carefully
around.

'As you can see, the king is of highest rank,' Tutor Aspall
explained. 'After the king come princes. After them, the
king's brothers and uncles, though King Hal has none.'

'King Hal – ha!' Edward murmured scornfully, his arms
folded.

'Ahem!' The tutor tapped the corner of his table
smartly with his finger, then he went on. 'After the king's
brothers . . .'

After the king's brothers, Will discovered, came men
of curious title: the Lord Great Chamberlain, the Lord
High Admiral, the Earl Marshal of the Realm. Below
them were dukes, then marquesses, and then earls.
Viscounts and barons came even lower down, and so,
Will thought, must hardly figure even though they still
came above knights. Right at the bottom of the list were
people called esquires and gentlemen-of-coat-arms. Pages
were not mentioned at all, nor were farmers, blacksmiths
or swineherds, which seemed odd for they did all the
useful work.

'That's because everyone else is a commoner,' Edward
said, poking Will in the ribs. 'Like you, Willy Wag-staff.'

'All right then, what about wizards?' Will asked,
unmoved.

Tutor Aspall said, 'Wizards do not appear either.'

'I don't think much of it, then,' Will said, 'if wizards
don't appear.'

'Wizards! Ha!' Edward said.

'How do you know when you've even seen a wizard?' Edmund asked.

'Wizards have big eyes, long ears and short tongues,' Will said archly, sounding, or so he thought, a little like a wizard himself.

Tutor Aspall tutted at him, and Will knew he would soon be ordered out of the garden, but just then Wortmaster Gort came by with a bunch of freshly-picked charlock in his hand. He said he was looking for his rabbit, and moments later there was uproar as Rock, one of Huntmaster Tweddle's lurchers, bounded into the garden. Will saw the great grey hunting hound make for the far corner where Osric was sunning himself. Will jumped to his feet, put out his hands and shouted.

'Nooo, Rock!'

The sun flashed on the hound's bright steel collar. Just as its jaws were about to close on Osric, Rock crashed to the ground as if his forepaws had been swept out from under him. Then he rolled under the rose bushes and began yelping, more from surprise than hurt.

Edmund ran forward then, but Osric bounded away from him until Gort snatched him up and away from the dog.

'Master Tweddle! Take this hound of yours out of the garden! He's been lapping at the brewhouse beer drippings again, by the looks of him. And you too, come to mention it.'

The huntmaster and Sir John came for Rock. Once the lurcher had trotted after them the peace of the garden returned. Or almost, for Will sat down heavily on the bench, his hands by his sides.

Edward stared down at him dispassionately. 'Are you unwell? You're as white as a miller's boy.'

'I feel . . .' he said, trying to think of a word for the odd empty-chested discomfort. 'It's . . . passing.'

'Look into my eyes,' Gort said, peering closely at him.

'He's just afraid,' Edward said, hands on hips and grinning. 'He imagined the dog was biting that coney's head off and all the blood squirting out like a fountain. That's what made him want to faint!'

Tutor Aspall's finger pecked the duke's elder son on the shoulder. 'Sir Edward, please. You too, Sir Edmund, attend to the chart.'

While Will sat and regained his strength the engine of time made its clangs and the lesson came to an end. Will did as he was told and remained on the bench. The Wortmaster said, 'Clench the fingers of your right hand as hard as you can around my wrist.'

Will did so, but his effort was weak. He was still dazed. 'What's the matter with me, Wortmaster?'

And Gort smiled his healer's smile. 'Nothing to worry about. I'll mix you a powder. That will have you feeling better in no time at all.'

That afternoon it rained for an hour, during which Will had his hair cut and the back of his neck shaved. Now his hair was more in the style of the duke's sons, and his neck tingled as they leaned over parchments painted with heraldic banners and badges. Tutor Aspall explained the complicated 'rules of tincture' that told which colours could go with which others on a knight's banner. They pored over other scrolls, on which were painted all the long, swallow-tailed war standards that knights and lords flew in battle. They learned why some carried the red sword and others the white heart, and what all the different badges were meant to signify until Will found them running together before his eyes.

When the inside studying was over, they went outside again, and stood there mutely while Sir John barked at them.

'According to the laws of chivalry a knight must live in

a way that is worthy of respect! With honour and valour, pride and faith, and with courtesy to all! He must be unselfish, charitable and loyal! He must respect women and protect the innocent! This is the ideal for which all knights must strive! Any questions?'

There were none.

'Good,' he said, then he added with a dark gleam in his eye, 'That kind of learning you'll get from Tutor Aspall and no one else. From me you'll hear how to render due respect to your betters, how summarily to dispense justice, and how to survive in a dirty fight.' A brief smile fleeted over his lips. 'All fights are dirty, by the way. And don't let anyone tell you different.'

He showed them some rusty pieces of armour and they were taught the names of each and where on the body they were meant to be buckled.

Will picked up a pauldron and looked at it dubiously. 'What's this one?' he asked.

'It's back to front,' Edward told him.

'Why am I learning about armour?' Will asked, turning to Sir John, 'Am I to be a knight too?'

'You?' Edward said witheringly. 'A knight?'

Sir John told him, 'You're here to learn all the duties of the page, and that involves accoutrement.'

'You need to know about armour . . .' Edward smirked, '. . . because you'll be scouring mine clean over the cinder bucket.'

'I'd make a better knight than you would.'

Edward showed his disgust at the idea. 'Knighthood is a great honour, something only a lord may bestow on a favoured vassal. Who'd bestow it on *you*?'

'I'd be a lot more use in a real fight.'

'Says who? Anyway, knighthood is a matter of blood and birth. It's not meant for one of your station.'

Will felt stung enough to cuff Edward around the ear

with a gusset of chainmail when Sir John next turned his back. Then they fell to furious scrapping, until Sir John roared at them, pulled them off one another and then sat them down long enough for their tempers to cool.

Then he taught them lovingly about his own favourite weapon, the falchion. It was an ugly-looking sword, axe-heavy, with a one-sided blade and a handguard that curved down over the fist. A little later he called in a young jack and showed how a man ought to be buckled into a full – though battered – harness of armour. Then Sir John tried hard to kill the jack with ringing falchion blows to every part of him: head, body, arms and legs.

> 'Sallet . . . head!
> Bevor . . . throat!
> Pauldron . . . shoulder!
> Breast! Back!
>
> 'Rerebrace . . . upper arm!
> Couter . . . elbow!
> Vambrace . . . lower arm!
> Gauntlet!
>
> 'Tasset . . . hip!
> Cuisse . . . thigh!
> Poleyn . . . knee!
> 'Greave . . . lower leg!
> Sabaton!'

There was a sabaton missing, but fortunately when Sir John chopped at the man's foot he turned the blade aside at the last moment. Finally, he let the jack out of the armour and gave him a silver penny for his trouble. The man staggered away uncertainly.

'Do you see how curves deflect blows? Never prefer a

sword against plate, no matter how heavy the blade. Prefer this!'

They watched as Sir John brandished a spiked mace. He took them to an old breastplate that had been strapped over a sack of sand and mounted to a post. A heart had been crudely chalked over the centre of the armour. When he swung the mace the weight of it drove its two-inch spike straight through the flattest part of the plate. And when he pulled it out a trickle of sand fell to the ground.

'Dead!' said Edward.

'As a door nail!' said Sir John.

Will saw the sand and imagined how he would feel if it was his own heart's blood pouring from a wound. The thought made his mouth dry.

Sir John took them out to a tree stump and showed them his own broadsword. It was sharp enough to pare fruit. Then he showed them how, in the hands of an accomplished swordsman, it could cleave a fresh boar's head in two with a single blow. Will did not faint at the sight, though Edward watched him closely to see if he would. And for the rest of the day he had to be very careful not to give Edward any hint that he might have a weakness about blood, for he knew that if he did he would never hear the last of it.

That night Will had a monstrous nightmare. It began well enough, walking hand in hand with Willow in the Wychwoode, but then there appeared an armoured man who was many times his own size. His adversary had a falchion just like the one Sir John had used, and it was held in an arm of irresistible strength. When the warrior swung his axe-sword at a tree, the tree fell apart and inside was Will's own skeleton. And Willow ran away crying and there beside the tree, weeping, were Eldmar and Breona, but also, laughing at him now, were his real parents – the duchess and the figure of Death.

When he woke up he was drenched in sweat. He threw off his covers and got up to fetch some water, but his feet froze on the cold, wet stone of the floor. What had made him stop? The water cask was leaking. Drips splashed his feet. Water soaked and seeped into the spaces between the stones. But he fancied he heard something else outside, and all at once he remembered the Dragon Stone.

The stone had been buried, locked away in some damp cellar in the care of Wortmaster Gort who had neglected to speak a word about it. But Will could hear the stone's whisperings now. It was calling to him. There was no doubt that it was the Dragon Stone, nor was he surprised when he looked out and saw the spectre that haunted the inner bailey.

He knew its name.

It was Death who walked there in the cold moonlight. Death, reeking like graveyard soil, foul as coffin liquor in the night mists. Death. There could be no mistake. And Will crouched down because he felt fear flowing in his bones, and because somehow he knew the spectre was blindly searching for his only begotten son.

He awoke again to a wet and windy spring day and found Gort poking around on the castle mound. There were Fellows in the castle and Gort would have nothing to do with them – whenever they came he made sure he was elsewhere. When Will quizzed him about them, he straightened up, rubbed his back and said spookily, 'He who goes to the Sightless Ones of his own free will and claims sanctuary in a chapter house will always be admitted. Oh, yes! But there's no leaving it. Oh, no! Remember that!'

'I will.'

Gort blinked at him, an appalled look on his whiskery face. 'Once their High Warden has laid hands upon a newcomer's face his eyes begin to wither like grapes upon the vine. Fhhhhh! A blindness comes upon him and he must remain in the Fellowship forever.'

'Master Gwydion told me the . . . the red hands admit thieves and even murderers to their number. Is that so?'

'When has Master Gwydion ever told an untruth to you? Many a Fellow is recruited from among folk who are staggering under an unbearable burden of guilt. And there are plenty who've done wrong yet feel no guilt – they sometimes give themselves up to the Fellowship too.'

Will was horrorstruck at that. 'But why would anyone give themselves up freely?'

'Not freely! When they're cornered! All that is required are the words, "I claim the sanctuary of the Fellowship!" Whosoever says them must be admitted, and he who enters the sanctuary of the Fellowship moves beyond the king's law. Don't you know that?'

Will looked at Gort and narrowed his eyes. 'Beyond the law?'

'Beyond the law. But surely not beyond punishment, for once a man has surrendered he becomes sightless in every way. All that he was, and all that he is, must be forgotten. He can no more leave his chapter house than the honeybee can abandon its skep. Indeed, the honeybee has greater freedom, for those Fellows down there may go outside only by permission of their Warden, and only then in the company of older Fellows.'

'Can't they ever escape? Not even if an army comes to their rescue?'

Gort's laugh was fluting. 'Haw! Not even then. No lord of this realm would dare to send an army against the Sightless Ones. Such an affront would never be made – the reach of their influence is too long and enduring. And their memory is limitless.'

The Wortmaster began wandering the grassy bank upon which the keep was built, looking at the wildflowers that grew there. He seemed less than pleased with what he found. 'Spearplumes on the north side,' he said. 'Spearplumes coming up everywhere.' He pointed to the offending plants which Will knew as thistles. They were already knee-high and spiky with leaves like halberds. 'They'll grow to three times this height by full summer.'

'What's wrong with them growing here?' Will asked. 'I rather like them.'

'I like them too. They're cantankerous and wilful, but proud in the best way, and there's nothing wrong with any plant growing in its proper place, eh?' He scanned the lowering, leaden sky. 'The goldfinches eat spearplume seeds, so they won't be sorry about these. But spearplumes have never grown here before. Not never ever. So I'm wondering why they've come here now.'

'Must there be a reason?'

Gort peered under his eyebrows and began momentously, 'In this world, Will, there's a reason for everything. And in everything there's a cause for wonder . . . Roses are red, and violets are violet, but nothing much rhymes with violet . . .'

Will smiled. 'I never thought of it like that before.'

Gort bent over a bud that was to his liking. 'Arise, little celandine, spring is here!' he intoned in a surprisingly melodious voice, and out came a lovely flower, yellow and star-shaped. 'See how she shrinks from the weather, but afterwards she comes out bright as the sun! We call her the wayfarer's favourite for she mostly grows in hedgerows and puts herself forth for the wanderer's pleasure. Ah, me! What beauty there is in green life.'

Joy welled up in Will and he began to sing.

> *'First there were nine,*
> *Then nine became seven,*
> *And seven became five.*

Now, as sure as the Ages decline,
Three are no more,
But one is alive.'

Gort had joined in on the last two lines. Smiling, he took one of the spearplume leaves between his fingers and stroked it, despite the spikes. 'That's a prophetic song, you know. I expect it was Master Gwydion who taught it to you, hmmm? Do you know what it's about?'

Will looked sidelong at the Wortmaster, undecided if he should mention the Ogdoad. 'Do you know, Gort?'

'Wizards! There! Now I've told you, even if the Phantarch himself didn't.' He scratched his cheek and then threw his head back. 'I don't suppose that Master Gwydion told you that I was once put up to be one of the Ogdoad of Nine, did he?'

Will looked at the Wortmaster with great surprise. 'You? You had the mark?'

'Oh, yes, me! Poor old Gort! What a different world it would have been if they'd had old Gort instead of that monster, Clinsor. But that was a very long time ago. That was back in the days even before Celenost became Phantarch. You won't know much about that, I don't suppose.'

'Not much. Clinsor? You mean Maskull?'

'That's the name he goes under these days, is it? He was the betrayer all along, and didn't I always think it was him? I told them. I had a funny feeling about it. Oh, way back in the days when Maglin was Phantarch, that was. But Maglin drew himself up like he used to and he said to me, "We can't go around making accusations on the back of funny feelings, Gortamnibrax".'

'I suppose Maskull wants to rule the world and live forever,' Will said. 'And if he can only get Master Gwydion out of the way there'd be nothing to stop him.'

'Clinsor? Rule the world? Live forever?' Gort sniffed the air. 'It's probably something foolish like that. It always is. That's what vainglory does to you once it sinks its fangs in your flesh. All you want to do with your life is to make a monument to yourself. Now isn't that mad? And some folk are quite blind to the daftness of it, you know.'

Will wanted to hear more, but Gort's mind wandered away again, and he was now squinting up at the sky. He held out his hand. 'Ah me! Taproots and tubers! Medlar for the pedlar, but quince for the prince! There's more rain coming. Oh, how wonderful!'

A little while later the rain did come again, and it was good refreshing rain, the kind that Gort said trees delighted in. They walked together through the drizzle, enjoying it as much as the swans on the river enjoyed it, and Gort told him about the various uses of lady's mantle and wild strawberry, and what wonders could be done with yarrow and frogbit and viper's bugloss, but Will was still thinking about the significance of thistles on the keep mound and whether they might have some sinister connection with the Dragon Stone.

When he went back to his lessons, Will found Edward listless and staring mournfully at the grey sky. 'I want to know when father's coming back,' he said to his brother. 'He promised to present me with Dalgur.'

'Father will come back when it pleases him, I suppose,' Edmund said with sparing belief.

'Your father will be away for some while yet,' Tutor Aspall said, then added with unusual tenderness. 'He loves all his children, Edmund, but these are turbulent times, and a duke is wise to heed the crow's warning.'

'What's Dalgur?' Will asked.

Edward's eyes flashed. 'His second best broadsword. His best is called Fregorach, which means Answerer.'

'What does Dalgur mean?' Will asked, thinking it

sounded very like the word in the true tongue for the pin of a buckle.

'Smiter of fools.'

'You just made that up.'

'I did not! Father was given both swords by a famous smith in the Blessed Isle when he was made Lord Lieutenant there. The steel they're forged from is very rare.'

Edward leapt up to the base of the high window and raised a great, flanged mace heroically above his head. 'Father is in the great city of Trinovant, contending even now against the villains and false friends who gather about the king's person! These are my father's enemies, and he must deal with them before he can return! But never fear, Edmund, he will set all things to rights for the good of the Realm, and we will see him again just as soon as he's done. If I was my father I'd take Fregorach and cut off all the king's enemy's heads!'

'I think you would not,' Will said, unmoved by Edward's savage theatre.

Edward turned on him. 'I would do it in a moment!'

'And I say you would not, for King Hal's chiefest enemy is his own wife, and your rules of chivalry don't let a nobleman murder a woman, much less a queen, only to lock her up in a cloister until she dies of unhappiness.'

'What do you know about chivalry, Willy Wag-staff? You're just a lowly pageboy.'

'I am not a page, and I'm not a boy,' Will said, meeting his eye. 'I'm here at Master Gwydion's pleasure. And as for what I know, I was at Clarendon Lodge when the king was there. I've seen the king and queen with my own eyes, which is something I bet you've never done.'

'That wormy weakling, Hal?' Edward said. 'He's not a real king!'

'Sir Edward, sit down!' Tutor Aspall's reedy voice rang out angrily. 'And you will be pleased to hold your tongue!

By your father's order, there are some things you may not say!'

Edward seemed to realize that this time he had gone too far. He subsided, but he flashed Will a superior glance as he sat down. 'You're still a pageboy.'

Will smiled to himself and chose to say nothing, which by now he knew would only serve to annoy Edward all the more. Privately, he imagined beating Edward until he was truly humbled. On the one hand imagining Edward being mashed felt good, but on the other hand it felt like a betrayal of what Gwydion had taught him about treading softly in the world of men, having compassion for fools and maintaining inner strength. But that's a hard path to tread, he thought, still relishing the violent impulses that had begun to spark inside him increasingly of late. One of these days Edward'll go too far with me, he thought darkly. I'll lose control of myself, and he'll rue the day he was born.

Eventually, Tutor Aspall reached the tedious end of the *Lay of Brea and Inogen* and it was time to go. Edmund lingered as the lesson ended.

'Why do you always have to goad him?' he asked.

'Me? I don't goad him.'

'Yes, you do. Even when you don't say anything. It's your manner.'

'I can't help that. And anyway, he's the one who's always goading me.'

'But you should pay him respect.' Edmund seemed embarrassed to have to point it out. He was far cleverer than his elder brother, though he hid it well. 'Take my advice: give in to him. That's all he really wants.'

'Edward's asking for more than that.'

'Can't you see? It's . . . it's because he misses his father.'

'So do you, Edmund,' Will said, and added, 'And . . . so do I.'

'Maybe, Will. But, it's different for Edward. You see, he's the heir.'

And at that moment, as Edmund left him alone in the room, Will realized a crucial truth about Edward. His father was not just a great lord, he was a great lord who considered himself the rightful king of the Realm and, where any lord's son was concerned, being the heir made a very great difference indeed.

The death that Will expected at Foderingham did not come. The duchess and her family remained in thriving good health, and Gort continued on, lively as pond water.

To Will's disgust Beltane came and went unmarked by celebration. The Sightless Ones called it the Day of Abstinence, and the rite they performed in the castle felt as if every last drop of joy had been wrung from the ritual centuries ago. No news had come from Gwydion, and Will began to feel that he had been truly abandoned. Surely, he thought, no matter how busy he is, or how important his work, he could have found time to write a message of some kind. But it was not to be.

Added to that, the stone had been whispering in the night again. He had lain awake trying not to listen to it, but his body had begun to feel strange. He was changing, he knew that. His voice quavered and croaked by turns, hairs began to sprout on his upper lip and in a ludicrous clump in the middle of his chest and down in his groin. He felt restless and prone to sudden irritation, as though there was a new kind of hunger lurking inside him that could not be fed, but there was also a heaviness that he knew must be coming from the Dragon Stone.

Throughout the months of May and June the summer's heat slowly mounted. He found himself day-dreaming and lost sight of what he was supposed to be learning. Sir John's weapons exercises were turning him into a monster. They took up first two, and then three, hours of every day. Will and Edward took their instruction in sight of one another, and the urge to compete grew. Though Will took to the labours more easily, Edward would never allow himself to be bested. Their necks and wrists began to thicken with all the repeated movements, and their thighs and arms and chests became corded with muscle. Will began to have a strange dream that his own spirit had begun to inhabit someone else's body. As he and Edward completed their exercises with practice swords, each eyed the other and wondered when Sir John would set them to see who would fare the better in combat.

Finally July came, and one hot morning Edmund cut a finger on a quill knife and Tutor Aspall had no choice but to leave Will and Edward to their studies unsupervised. That proved to be a mistake.

Edward sprawled with his feet up on a chair, looking bored. 'I'm sick of being locked up in this place!' he shouted and threw the flanged mace he had been toying with across the room.

It clanged down heavily near Will and made him start, so that the ink spattered from his quill and across his work.

'Why don't you go down to the Garden of the White Nose?' he said, prickled. 'Go and trample down a few flowers until you feel a little better!'

Edward turned, equally prickled. 'Don't call it that! I hate it when you call it that.'

'Why not? It's a better name for it than the idiot name it's got now.'

'You're the idiot!'

'I'm certainly next to one.'

'Take that back!'

'Or what?' he said, looking up. 'What will you do, eh?'

Edward disappeared and moments later he came back with the contents of Will's private chest. He scattered them on the floor, and his silver-bound horn fell clattering to the boards. 'Let's see what the beggar has got wrapped up in his filthy shirt, shall we?'

Will felt a cold current of rage run through him unstoppably. This went far beyond the routine jibes that Edward made at Will's lowly origins, this was war.

'Oh, look! What's this?'

'Put it down! I'm warning you!'

Delighted by Will's anger, Edward brandished the horn. 'Who is that little boy dressed up in blue?' he asked, meaning the blue-and-white Ebor livery clothes that Will was obliged to wear. 'Tell me now, who can that little boy be?'

'I said, put it down!'

Edward pranced away. 'Little boy blue, come blow up your horn! The sheep in the meadow, the cows in the corn!'

When he put the horn to his lips, Will swung at him. But Edward was ready. He threw down the horn, moved aside and shoved Will down hard. As he went over he fell awkwardly, banging his head. The injury was slight but it hurt, and his eyebrow bled, and that enraged him. They pushed and shoved. Then Edward came at him, arms flailing, until one of the blows caught Will in the bloodied eye. Will swung back and felt bone bite against his knuckles, then he tried to break away and recover his belongings. But Edward was up and on him again. He threw Will back to the floor. Will fended off the punches as best he could, but Edward rained powerful blows against the side of his head. They were meant to do damage, and Will knew that the moment when they might have quit and still kept their pride had come and gone.

There was now a fury upon Edward that was frightening. He had little natural mercy in him, and when Will broke away he could taste blood in his mouth. He could feel it welling from beside his left eye and he knew this was not just play that had got out of hand. They had both been trained to fight and they were ready. He saw Edward glance at the mace. If he reached it, Will knew, he would have his skull opened. Edward would not be satisfied until Will was hurt. And then what? Nothing would be done, because Edward was the heir. There was no alternative – he had to meet the onslaught with craft.

As Edward went towards the mace, Will dived under the table and rolled over onto the weapon. He felt several kicks aimed at him before one connected with his back. He anticipated the next and made a grab for the heel. Edward tried furiously to wrench his foot away, but that only overbalanced him. Will dumped him on his back, and that bought enough time to find his own feet. As Edward came at him again, Will flung ink pot and quills into Edward's face. The rim of the pewter pot caught him on the bridge of the nose. Then a wax writing board was warded off by a forearm, and it clattered to the floor, splashing ink across the stones like black blood. They came together again and as they wrestled, Edward's foot slipped in the ink and down they went together.

This time Will was on top. One hand gripped Edward's throat, until Edward tried to pull himself up. He hauled on the chain that secured a heavy book to the table. When the book slid off, the iron binding slammed into the back of Will's head. It sent a jab of pain through him. Their heads clashed together. Dazed, Will let go and was easily pushed off. When he tried to straighten up Edward aimed a kick at his jaw, which, if it had landed, would probably have killed him. Luckily, Edward was blinded, half by ink, half by rage, so his foot slammed instead into Will's shoulder.

Both were now at bay. They shook with fury and exertion as they stared at each other. Edward's face was scratched and bloodied and sweating, his fair hair besmirched with ink. He was gasping and snorting. Will tried to staunch the red flow that was pouring from his nose. In the hiatus, Will tried to pick up Tutor Aspall's big book and jerk it free from its chain. The idea was to throw it at Edward's head, but the chain would not come free, and the effort of trying to yank it loose pulled it out of his hands.

They advanced on one another again, all lessons but one in the way of war forgotten, grimacing, roaring, artlessly tearing at each other's heads, gouging, poking, pushing and falling down. 'All fights are dirty.' The wisdom sounded in Will's head like a rede of magic. Then, suddenly, Edward was on top of him and choking him. The mace-handle was hard across his windpipe. No matter how Will struggled he could not work himself free. He was fighting for breath. He needed to throw off the weight that was killing him, but he was unable to find purchase, until a great surge of panic-strength welled up into his arms and chest. Something snapped in Will's head like a flash of lightning, and Edward was flung bodily across the chamber. He slammed into the wall. Then the door opened and Sir John Morte was in their midst and his mailed hands were round Will's neck and dragging him backwards.

'Outside if you want to do that,' he barked. He hauled Will out of the room and all the way down the passageway.

'Gmmmmmh!' Will yelled. He coughed and spluttered and spat out a mouthful of blood and spittle when Sir John dumped him in the corner. Edward came roaring out after him, his face streaming with blood. He could hardly see to start the battle again, but that did not stop him from trying.

'Yaaaaaagghh!'

Edward's teeth were bared, his face pressed hard into Will's own, but the flurry was short-lived, for Sir John pitched them both headlong down the steps and into the yard, and when Will got up to swing at Edward again Sir John slapped him to the floor with an effortless backhand.

'You – stay there!' He raised a blunt finger at Edward. 'And you – do you want the same? Well, do you?'

Edward thought he did at first . . . but then he decided he did not. And suddenly the fight was over. Both combatants sat on the ground, panting. Will wiped his swollen lips, tried to blow the blood from his nostrils, and Edward tested his jaw with both hands.

Half to make a joke of it, but half to show he still had fight in him, Will said, 'I told you we should've gone down to the Garden of the White Nose.'

Edward got to his feet, still glowing like a coal. 'That's the last time you'll insult the badge of this house in my hearing!'

'How do you know? You're too thick in the head to be a seer!'

'You will be quiet!' Sir John roared, poking him in the chest. 'And you, Sir Edward . . . what would your father think of you if he could see you now?'

Will tried to grin as Edward too was restrained.

Sir John slapped Edward, then slapped Will too for good measure. Mail gloves closed over both their scalps as Sir John took them down to the well. He threw a pail of water over each of them in turn. Then he sat them down and asked Will what the fight was all about.

'I don't know,' Will said stubbornly.

'You don't know.' Sir John nodded slowly, and turned his broad, hard face towards Edward. 'And I suppose you don't know either?'

Edward nodded tightly. 'Forgotten.'

'Then I shall have to tell you. Come here.'

Will grew wary of Sir John's quiet tone and the way he beckoned them closer. But the knight put a hand on each of their backs, showed a row of big, even teeth and said, 'This is what always happens when two evenly-matched young bucks are set together. They feel the need to knock heads. The velvet on your antlers is shredding away fast, my lucky lads. It's time I doubled your exercises. From now on, you'll rise an hour earlier and finish an hour later. And next time you meet in battle, it won't be a nasty little brawl on a school-room floor. You'll fight with naked steel.'

■ ■ ■

CHAPTER FIFTEEN

AGAINST BETTER JUDGMENT

Gort saw them in turn, to check their bones and sting their wounds with punitive medicine. When Will and Edward met again it was at the supper board. As Will tried to sit down, Edward immediately – and uncharacteristically – made room for him.

'Thank you.'

'You're welcome.'

'Here!' one of the serving women screeched, seeing their uncommon civility and their marked faces. 'What's to do with you, eh, young masters?'

'Fight,' Will said proudly, and slapped Edward on the back.

'Good one, too,' Edward said, inclining his head to shovel a spoonful of pease into the unbruised side of his mouth.

'Aahh!' The serving woman grinned as her big arms scraped out a pan. 'You'll be blooded as friends then now, I expect. That's the way it always is after a scrap, eh? I got seven brothers, so I knows!'

It was odd, but true. Will felt as if a great barrier had been torn down. That he had been lifted up in a way that made whatever pain he felt seem wholly unimportant. Something – he couldn't say quite what – had been settled between them. It was something to do with being tested and something to do with winning respect, and it worked in both directions at once. Before the blood was even dry he had begun to feel closer to Edward than ever he had before. And Edward seemed to feel the same.

As Will pushed the empty trencher away from him and Edward got up and poured him out a beaker of Callas wine, the castle clock chimed the sixth hour of the afternoon. Will winced at the acid touch of wine against his split lip, but he delighted in the honest feelings of brotherhood that had come out of the violence. He thought guiltily of the promises he had made to Gwydion, and realized he had not given the wizard much thought in a long while. His quest to find the stones of doom and stop a war, a quest that had just a little while ago seemed all-consuming, seemed far away now, an echo of the past that did not matter any more.

'Hey, Willy Wag-staff!' Edward called, grinning from the far side of the table.

Will grinned back. Amazingly, the taunt no longer bothered him. He wore it with pride. 'What?'

'Do you want to see something?' Edward drew an ivory rod out of his jerkin. It was about a foot long and twisted in a spiral, but the ends were roughly sawn. 'One good horn deserves another, eh?'

'What is it?'

'What do you think? A unicorn's horn.'

'Let me see!' Will looked at the prized object with bedazzled eyes. 'Where did you get this?'

'It's from my father's treasury.' Edward turned it over proudly. 'Don't touch it. It's very old.'

'How did you get it?'

'I can get the keys for every door in this castle.'

'And everyone's locked chest too, it seems.'

Edward took the point wearily. 'I promise I won't mess around with your things again. Is that fair?'

'That's fair enough.'

Will looked closely at the twisted white rod. It was as long as Will's forearm, heavy and hard as a tooth and a little browned with age in the grooves. There was a worn patch on it, as if someone had been scraping at it with a blade. It made him think of the powders that Gort made.

'You should be careful. Unicorns are magical beasts. You ought not to tamper with magic.'

'Who says?'

'Gort says.'

'The Lord of the Earthworms? I'll do what I like around here. When my father's away, I'm head of the household, not Gort.'

Will was about to argue and say that he should have more respect for the Wortmaster, but he stopped himself. Edmund was right: arguing with Edward was a waste of time – and the warm glow of their new-found friendship was too good to jeopardize unnecessarily.

Some days later, in high summer, Huntmaster Tweddle took Will and Edward aside and walked them down to his lodge. He was a man of short temper, narrow interests and base humour, but what he knew about he knew very well, and all of it concerned hunting.

Outdoors, his eyes were slits. Indoors, they were the same faded blue as cornflowers. He told them, 'At fourteen years the young knight goes first to the field to hunt the hemule, but that's not to feed his stomach on venison, that's to learn what death may be. Aye, and to find out what courage is too. He must learn to have his wits about him, and how to take heed of signs. You're ready to put on your first harness, to learn to wage war on men, to joust and to ride. In course of time you'll learn how to take castles by force, how to skirmish, how to call up the courage that lies in other men's bones, how to set watch for perils, how you might defend yourself, and what might be the correct use of weapons. But first, you'll learn about blood. Come with me, and I'll show you how to draw the guts from a deer and spread them for the hounds.'

And so they learned how to stalk deer and shoot good arrows into thickets. All that month they spent with their hands bathed in blood to the elbows. Often they were bloodied from head to toe amid a mire of dismembered animals as the hounds gathered at the quarry and the flies buzzed afterwards. Will put arrows into a target so well that Edward walked off and would not shoot alongside him. At fifty paces only three in thirty of his shots went astray, yet under Huntmaster Tweddle's gaze none of Will's darts hit hind or buck.

As the huntmaster had predicted they were soon handed sword, mace and war-hammer and made to practise hard under Sir John's ungentle tutelage. The knight showed how armets and sallets and barbutes and helms of many other shapes were most easily opened. He demonstrated how mace blows delivered to the heavy pauldrons that covered an armoured knight's shoulders were worse than useless. He explained how bodkin arrowheads could burst open links in the chainmail that protected the gaps that all plate armour needed for movement's sake. And what were the deadliest mistakes to make on a field of battle.

Soon it was time to put on expensive arming doublets, which were tight jackets of red fustian lined with satin, re-inforced with strips of leather and set with holes here and there. Through the holes bowstring twine rubbed with shoemaker's wax was passed to hold the armour plate in position. Their armpits and the insides of their elbows were gusseted with mail. And there were thick worsted hose for their legs, reinforced in a similar way at knee and groin, and special shoes of thick leather, over which flexible steel sabatons could be strapped. The arming suits were hot to wear, but wear them they did, and for a whole summer week, while the material 'sweated in' against their bodies.

Then for a second week they had to wear leg armour to all their lessons with Tutor Aspall. In between the lessons two armourer's smiths came to ask if they felt sore in any part and to beat and bend the metal to a closer fit. When the blains on their ankles and knees began to heal, it was time for their arms and upper bodies to suffer. Will found to his surprise that although armour was very hot to wear, it was surprisingly comfortable, and not especially heavy because the weight of it was borne over the whole frame, and after a while his muscles became well adjusted to it. Two weeks after putting on his first arming doublet Will could run and climb and turn somersaults in full harness, and most important of all, he could ride in it with confidence.

And so the long summer and autumn passed, in lessons and hunting and sparring and tilting. It was interesting for Will to see how the wearing of armour changed the way folk looked at him. The mirror shine of steel was meant to turn arrowheads, but it just as easily turned the heads of the girls who came to sell eggs in the outer bailey. The glint of steel made the jacks straighten their backs as he passed. Wearing costly armour made a lad feel like a lord, and despite himself Will started to enjoy that feeling. It made him brusque of manner at times and a little swaggering in his walk, and though he was not aware of it, others noticed him changing.

But for all the changes, Will never lost sight of his true self. And whenever the girls in the outer bailey turned to look at him, he could not help but imagine how Willow would look at him if she was here. But never once did he have the arrogance to wear armour or carry a weapon when he went down to see his friend the Wortmaster. One day, in the mellow month of October, one of Huntmaster

Tweddle's beaters came into Gort's shed while Will was with him. The beater had taken a gash from a boar's tusk, and Gort made a drawing poultice to take the poison out of the wound. Will watched the way Gort scraped the blue patches from mouldy bread and bound it hard against the man's calf with dock leaves, common mallow and wood sorrel.

'In healing,' Gort said when the wounded man had hobbled away, 'you must remember that the life force has a flow of its own. Magical cures heal unnatural breaks in the flow – as with that man's wound.'

'What's that in the jar?'

'Best graveyard basil.' Gort narrowed his eyes. 'Basil thrives best on the entrails of dead men, don't you know that?'

Will looked around the untidy shelves with burgeoning interest. He peered up at a great globe of blown glass that contained the heavy liquid metal Gort called 'quicksilver'. It showed the whole room as if in a looking-glass; only strangely warped and turned back on itself.

'If you can change the flow of the life force, Wortmaster, does that mean you can make a man live forever?'

'Whoooh! Who in his right mind would want to do that?' Gort was quietly horrified at the idea.

Will flicked a glass tube with his fingernail and made it ring. 'Most folk would like it, I suppose.'

'That's because most folk don't know what it's like to outlive their proper span. When the life force rightly fails, when a man's time has come, then meddling with it is against the grain of Nature, against that-which-is-meant-to-be. It's contrary to all oaths and vows that I've taken. I'll not do that kind of meddling.'

'But what about yourself?' Will asked, unimpressed. 'And how old's Master Gwydion?'

'He's as old as the hills, and then some more. But then

he is a wizard, and you wouldn't want to wish wizardhood on yourself.'

'What about you, then? You're not a wizard.'

'I'm not a wizard. Oh, no no no.' Gort smacked his lips and looked at the doorway. 'I'm not.'

'But you're as old as the hills too. How is it that you loremasters can make yourself live so long, but you won't give the potion out to others?'

'Potion, he says!' Gort returned his attention to the bundle of bittersweet from which he had been stripping the red berries. 'I've lived many lifetimes, but you can be sure I've paid the price for it.'

'You look fine to me. And anything's better than being dead.'

Gort grunted. 'If you say so.'

'I suppose you must do it by upsetting the balance,' Will said loftily. 'I heard Master Gwydion speak of it more than once.'

'Ah, yes, the balance. It's a long while since last I heard that term used. I have no dealings with great matters such as that. I know only that upsetting the balance always costs more than it's worth, and except in very special circumstances it shouldn't be attempted. You'll only ever see me take from the green world that which the green world freely gives.'

'And only as much as you need,' Will said. He stared around the interior of the shed, which was filled with all kinds of oddments that served no obvious purpose except to satisfy the Wortmaster's curiosity. 'I suppose you need all this stuff? What do you want it for?'

'This and that. You never know when something might come in handy. All loremasters have a powerful need to know, Will. It comes with the job, but it's a curse as well as a kindness, I can tell you. Clinsor even cut off a piece of himself to gain knowledge, do you know that?'

'Clinsor? You mean Maskull?' Will said with sudden interest. 'What knowledge was he after? And what did he cut off?'

Gort shook his head.

'Oh, tell me, Wortmaster!'

'It wasn't his little finger, I'll say that much! I can't speak for Maskull, but all other magical practitioners have big scruples over our dealings. We dislike waste, and we abhor greed. No loremaster would ever gather more of a herb than he could use. Nor would he take so much of it that the plant was caused to fail in the place where it was found growing.'

'What about poisons?' Will said peering into an earthen jug that contained a rotting greenish liquid. 'And fireworks. Tell me about them.'

'Oh, my, how you're growing. I hope Master Gwydion's right about you. In these sad days there are only two things every youngster wants to know about magic: poisons and explosions. When it comes to explosions, Will, I know nothing at all.'

'But poisons, you must know lots about them!'

'About poisons – being a healer, I probably know all there is to know. Everything from adder venom to *zzzzzzzt* . . . hornet stings. Though for poisons of great potency the worts win every time: aconite, baneberry, bloodroot, toadstools of ten dozen different kinds, bryony, hellebore, dwale . . . there are thousands, hundreds of thousands, of wort poisons.' He cleared his throat and sat up with a surprised look on his face. 'But no Wortmaster would ever deal in them, of course, except to use them to make people better, d'you see?'

'Poisons can heal?'

'Oh, yes! Didn't you know? It's a principle of magical healing that a very tiny bit of something nasty often turns out to be very nice . . . if I may put it that way. Walk with me and I'll show you.'

Gort led him out into the fields and on a long ramble to a distant wood. He told him how herbal infusions helped digestion in many different ways, and how even deep wounds could be made to heal with a fine fungus poultice. 'Even a passing knowledge of wortlore is as useful to a land traveller as a lodestone is to a mariner – any loremaster can lie face down in a meadow and know exactly where he is in the Realm to within half a league.'

'How?'

'Simply by listening to the accent of the birdsong, by smelling the soil and by spying out the tiny flowers and mosses that carpet the ground. Did you never see Master Gwydion tasting waters or rubbing a bit of soil between his finger and thumb? But tree lore, Will – ahhhh! That is the most wizardly of the virtues connected with the green world. Many trees are ancient, and many are old friends to wizards. Do you know that all trees talk when the wind blows through their branches?'

Will folded his arms. 'Do they?'

'Have you never listened to their conversations? Each of the thirty-three ancient kinds of tree has its own sound. The elder tree makes the sound *rrrh* – written down of old as five straight cuts on a stone's edge, like this.' Gort made the lines across his outstretched finger. 'Whereas the alder has the sound *ffffff* – two straight cuts the other way. That's why leaves are left by loremasters at the roadside: they're spell-warnings – messages that only other loremasters can read.'

Will thought of the ogham marks on the Dragon Stone, and of the leaves Gwydion had so often arranged on the ground. 'I once saw Master Gwydion putting out wreaths like that as we passed out of Severed Neck Woods. And again when we came back from the Blessed Isle. I think he used them to leave messages for Tilwin the Tinker.'

'Tilwin the Tinker, you say?' Gort paced around the clearing. 'More than likely he did.'

'Do you know Tilwin?' Will brightened. 'Does he ever come to Foderingham?'

Gort got down on hands and knees, distracted by the delicate bells of a group of pale toadstools that grew by a fallen log. 'I've heard the name spoken, of course.'

'He's very learned in matters of gems. And he grinds knives. He's probably a loremaster too.'

'Oh, my . . .' Gort stopped by a graceful willow tree that dipped its weeping fronds in the Neane's waters. 'A bitter juice distilled from the bark of this tree will take away headaches and pains in the chest.'

'I knew a girl called Willow,' Will said. 'She once gave me a headache and a pain in the chest. But it was an odd kind of pain. And I got it when I wasn't with her.'

'Has it gone now? The odd pain?'

'Not when I think of her. It comes back. I can feel it here, in the pit of my stomach. I'd like her to be with us now. You'd like her. You'd like her a lot.'

'I suppose she's pretty.'

'Oh, yes. But I don't know when I'll get to see her again. Master Gwydion will have to come back first.' He sighed and looked out of the glade along the lane that led back towards the castle. 'Do you think the thistles blooming on the keep mound are anything to do with the Dragon Stone? Do you think it's a portent of war?'

Gort shuddered. 'I don't know about such things as portents. Oh, my, no. Master Gwydion should never have brought that thing here. I haven't had a good night's sleep since it came.'

'Do you feel it too?' Will asked. 'I have horrible night-mares some nights. And I saw a figure walking in the garden a little while ago, and then in the Great Hall. I think it was . . . Death.'

Gort blinked like an owl. 'Death, you say? Oh, my!'

'I thought that at first, but now I don't see how it could

have been, because nobody's dying, or at least they haven't yet.' He walked under one of the trees and shivered, feeling its eerie starkness.

'Take care, Will! The elder is a witch tree, for her bones are pithy and hollow, and many an elder has been found to imprison a lost spirit.'

Will folded his arms. 'Wortmaster, tell me straight: did Master Gwydion ask you to teach me about plants and birds and such for a reason? Is he coming back? Does he want me to be his apprentice, or not? Does he want me to become a loremaster, because if he doesn't—'

Gort tutted. 'So many questions. Master Gwydion said nothing at all about me teaching you. It's just as plain as a pikestaff to me that you're ready to know a thing or two.'

Will swatted at a fly. It seemed that Gort was not telling the whole truth. 'What did you mean when you said back there that you hoped Master Gwydion was right about me?'

'Oh, did I say that?'

'Yes, you did. What did he say about me? He kept calling me a Child of Destiny. What does he mean by that?'

Gort blinked at him. 'You are what you are, Will. You have the talent, just like one of the First Men. You can't escape that.'

'But what exactly is this talent that I'm supposed to have?'

Gort grunted. 'It shows in lots of different ways . . . You're sensitive. You keep seeing things – that alone bespeaks a talent. I once watched you think two dozen arrows into a target one after the other without any training or practice. How did you do that? I bet you can't tell me, hey? Bet you didn't even know you were doing it, hey?'

Will laughed. 'I wasn't.'

'Ho! You may laugh it off, but I know you were. What's more, you did it to put Edward in his place, which was wrong-headed of you, and a misuse. But there's another side to it – you wouldn't think your arrows into killing a deer for Tweddle – that kind of fellow-feeling for flesh and blood comes from your talent too. Look at the way you saved Osric!'

'Osric? You mean that fat rabbit?'

Gort grinned and wagged a finger. 'Oh, no, Will. You can't tell me I don't know a spellcast when I see one. I watched it happen. And it was beautiful. Precise, wonderfully timely, and you didn't hurt that stupid hound at all.'

Will screwed up his face. 'Wortmaster, I did no such thing!'

'They say it takes one to know one, but that's not quite right.' Gort sighed then, and his voice seemed suddenly far away. 'You're more different than you know. Some quite knowledgeable folk can't cast spells at all. They just seem to go to pieces when they try.'

Will suddenly felt the timidness in Gort's heart and knew what had stopped him from becoming a wizard.

Gort nodded sadly. 'It's why I could never progress. Everything else was fine, but when it came to casting spells I just couldn't do it. In great magic I'm about as much use as a swordsman who can't bring himself to cut.'

On their way back to the castle, Gort told Will more than he wanted to know about corn cockles and ragged robin and the plant called treacle mustard that was good for gout. As they passed under the shadow of Foderingham's walls once more Will said, 'Master Gwydion said there was a prophecy about me, something about "one being made two". What do you think it meant?'

Gort threw up his hands. 'Prophecies? Who knows about them? I expect some are not worth the stone they're graven on. But when the trumpet of ancestral voices pours its spirit into the bitter urn of all flesh, then watch out!'

Gort gave a confused sigh and Will had to laugh. 'Oh, Wortmaster, what's to become of me?'

'I don't know the answer to that, Will, really I don't. But you know what I wish?'

'What do you wish, Wortmaster?'

'I wish that I'd tried just a little bit harder to find my way through the nettle patch of magic. I was never as good as Master Gwydion, of course, but I think I might have gone further than some of the others, and a lot further than I did. But I gave in to my fears, you see.' A long silence stretched out, then Gort cheered himself up. 'Still, if "hads" and "coulds" were pies and puds we'd none of us go hungry, heh?'

Autumn came and the swallows which had screamed and swooped in May gathered to fly away to a hot land that Gort said lay on the very southern rim of the world. The leaves browned and fell. The equinox passed unmarked, except that wild weather came to sing the dirge of the dying year. Will remembered dimly how in years gone by the wind had rattled the thatch of home and he shed a tear, for that life seemed far, far away now.

As the darkness and cold of November began to close its grip on the land, the penitent Fellows came in procession in identical hooded robes to the castle to start one of their fasts. Thirteen of them were meant to stand still in a line all day long, and the trial was meant to continue until all of their number either died or demonstrated 'the Miracle of Sustenance'. But this ferocious austerity claimed no one. Will realized that it was secretly broken each noon and midnight when the Fellows embraced and twirled round together and so changed places one with another in a dance that was meant to deceive the eye.

After Sowain, fragile hoar-frosts came. Foderingham's walls loomed and the intrigues of those who were enclosed within began to deepen. One cold night Will and Edward whispered together in the half-darkness, and Edward spoke about Duke Richard's hopes of restoring the throne to what he called 'proper blood'.

'That's all been ruined by the birth of the queen's bastard,' Edward said. 'Had it not been for that, when Old Hal died like he probably will soon the crown would have fallen back onto the head of the rightful king. But this has changed everything. Now when Hal dies we'll have another child-king instead of a good, strong, capable leader, and that'll be a disaster for the Realm.'

'If Hal dies soon.'

'He will.'

'Do you mean . . . war?'

Edward laughed shortly, but made no immediate reply. Will could not recall ever having heard the word 'usurper' openly spoken at Foderingham. Nor did anyone ever mention the right of Duke Richard to be king. To have spoken such a thing aloud would have been an act of high treason, and high treason, Will knew, was at least a beheading offence.

'Of course, war. War is a rightful king's last resort, the only thing that prevents him from being crushed by his enemies. They want to force my father to trial, but they dare not push him too tightly into a corner, for they know he will raise arms against them, and they do not want to risk an open fight.'

'Does your father want war?'

'My father would not easily lose a war, but the law is another matter. He is far better born than the king, but such are the jealousies of a royal court that if it came to a trial things would go badly for him. If the queen and her friends could persuade the lords to convict him of high treason, then they'd use "attainder" and the "corruption of blood" to snuff out the line of Ebor forever.'

'What's attainder?'

Edward sighed so that the light of their single candle

writhed. 'A law. It means that lands and titles held by any lord who's executed for high treason can't be inherited. Everything would go straight to the Crown as forfeit.'

'I see.' Will whispered. 'So, if your father was beheaded for treason you'd never become Duke of Ebor? And you'd lose this castle.'

'We'd lose all our castles. And all our lands and titles. Everything.'

Will nodded in the gloom. 'Then your father has to be very careful. And everyone else too, I imagine.'

Edward looked at him, gauging him from the shadows. His voice was low but full of passion. 'We must all be vigilant. Even here. Every castle has traitors and spies. At Foderingham we know there are paid eyes and ears, vermin in every corner.'

'Master Gwydion says that even the best cloth may sometimes have a moth in it.'

'The Crowmaster is one of the few men beyond our own kinsmen that my father dares to trust. Now – since I've trusted you, perhaps you'll trust me, and tell me what was that great stone you brought here?'

It was the last question Will wanted to be asked. He knew it was a mistake to believe that one important confidence necessarily deserved to be repaid by another, so he chose his words with care. 'It's called the Dragon Stone. Master Gwydion says it's a powerful engine of harm that was wrought long ago. Beyond that I don't know much.'

Edward's eyes glittered. 'I watched it being taken down into the cellars under the keep. It was the same day my father left for Trinovant. Masons came at Gort's bidding. They took that stone and placed it exactly according to instructions left by the Crowmaster. It stands upon two blocks of sandstone. They're fitted into a tomb in the foundations of the keep. Shall we go down and look at it?'

'What?' Will hissed. 'Are you mad?'

'What's the matter? You're not scared, are you?'

'Only a fool wouldn't be.'

'Why? What does the stone do? Tell me.'

Will decided he must say no more. Uneasiness stirred in him as he lay awake and alone in the darkness that night, listening to the cool, fetid wind drifting in off the Great Deeping Fen. In the uncertain land between sleep and waking he fancied he heard curlews, but then the sound became the voice of violent forces screeching and groaning within a stone tomb, straining against slowly decaying binding-spells. A feeling of dismay rose up inside him, a feeling that made him smell again the reek of Death and look out across the inner bailey in expectation of an unwelcome visitor.

The morning after next Will noticed an excited whisper running between the duke's two younger daughters. It seemed to him they had heard a rumour.

'Tell me,' he asked Margaret. 'Is your father coming home?'

'Father?' Margaret said, her eyes suddenly opening wide. 'Have you heard something about him?'

'No, but I thought you had. There's some kind of secret. You and Elizabeth are whispering like mice. And Edward's acting strangely too.'

Margaret shifted her gaze. 'I shan't say.'

'Why not?'

'Edward said not to tell.'

'Then, I'll have to go and ask Edward myself.'

He left the girls to their embarrassment and went to look for Edward, who only laughed when Will confronted him. 'Yes, we're all going down to look at the magic stone tonight. I didn't mention it to you because I knew you'd not want to come.'

'The stone?' Will said, shocked. 'But you can't do that.'

Edward smiled as he produced a big iron key. 'Can't? Why not?'

'Because it's dangerous!'

'It's just an old stone, Willy Wag-staff. Oh, I knew you'd be like this – boring!'

'It's not just an old stone. It's . . .'

'What?'

'It's . . . evil. Well, no, not *evil* exactly – that's a word Master Gwydion says we shouldn't use. What I mean is . . .'

'Magic!' Edward snatched the key away as Will made a grab for it. 'One of the cooks says it has powers. It can tell fortunes.'

'That's nonsense. What do the cooks know?'

'Plenty. All cooks know lots. Will, don't worry. We're only going down to look at it. If it's not evil, then where's the harm in it? There's no guard on it even.'

'No guard? But I thought—'

'A lot of the jacks are in a bad way. Two dozen of them have gone down with the gripes. Sick as dogs and shivering. Sir Hugh's not going to waste good jacks on a stone in a cellar when the news is so uncertain and there's a full circuit of walls to look after.'

'Oh, no.'

'You're worrying about nothing. We're all going tonight. Look, you might as well come too.'

Will thought about the offer, knowing that he could not stop Edward. 'I'll come, but you must promise me, on your father's life, that you won't try to touch it.'

'I'll swear to that,' Edward said easily. 'Now you swear by the sun and moon not to tell anyone where we're going.'

'I'll swear by the moon and stars.'

'If you like.'

He looked at Edward, wondering at the other's curious charm. He had a disarming directness, and Will saw his father in him, but this time in the bone and not in any studied way.

That night, the early winter darkness fell along with a drizzling rain, and they all went obediently to their beds before the eighth chime had struck. But they did not sleep. Instead they listened to the wind getting up for a long time, and when everyone else had retired and left the castle to the care of the night watch, they rose and dressed and gathered together in secret in the shadows of the inner bailey.

The night was wet and blustery, which kept everyone else indoors and so played into Edward's hands. With determined stealth he led his brothers and sisters up the steps to the keep, then produced the key and counted them all inside and down the dark stair that led into the cellar below.

At Edward's insistence, every one of the duke's children had come on the adventure. Even two-year-old Richard who was in the care of the Lady Anne, and five-year-old George who now held the Lady Elizabeth's hand. Lady Margaret and Sir Edmund brought up the rear. When lightning flashed outside it made them all jump, and the low rolling of thunder made them uneasy. They stood breathlessly in the dark. Then brilliant yellow flashes came from Edward's steel as he struck sparks into his tinder box. There was a small red glow as he blew gently onto the kindling and the smell of smoke drifted in the dank cellar air. Then the wick of a new tallow candle caught in flame and a feeble light began to pierce the gloom.

The lime-white walls were cold and moist all around, the ceiling vaulted with arches of stone and, where the jointed flutes met their supporting pillars, grinning goblin heads were carved. They seemed to watch, greedy-eyed, from the shadows.

There, set on end in the centre of the floor, was the Dragon Stone. In the flickering candlelight Will saw the ogham standing out clear along its edges. The visitors stood huddled before it like petitioners who had come before their lord. They waited and watched with bated breath until George mewed unhappily and said, 'I want to go home.'

'Watch this,' Edward told them, and drew the wand of unicorn ivory out of his sleeve.

Will said, 'You shouldn't have brought that!'

'Why not?'

'I told you before: the stone's dangerous. You'll rouse it. Take it away!'

Edward ignored him, but stared, unimpressed, at the marks that shimmered as they appeared in the surface of the stone, though his brother took keener notice.

'It's some kind of writing,' Edmund said, approaching the stone more closely.

'Edmund, keep back,' Will murmured. The hairs had risen on his neck, and he knew for certain now that he should have found some way to stop this foolishness.

Edward used the wand as a pointer, running it dangerously close to one of the stone's edges, making the ogham sparkle. 'It's probably a prophecy. I can't read it. You're the wizard's apprentice. What does it say?'

Will repeated the straightforward reading he had pondered on the way to Foderingham:

> 'King and Queen with Dragon Stone,
> Bewitched by the Moon, in Darkness alone,
> In Northern Field shall Wake no more,
> Son and Father, Killed by War.'

'It's just poetry then,' Edward said, disappointed. 'Is that all?'

'Look!' Anne said, her eyes widening. 'Look at it now! What's happening?'

They all stared, not knowing what they were supposed to be looking for, scared yet rooted by their fear. The two younger girls clutched one another, wondering if their eyes were playing tricks on them. George began to snivel again, and the echoes set baby Richard crying. Edmund grasped Will's arm. 'What's it doing?'

'Quiet! All of you,' Edward hissed. 'Do you want us to be found out?'

'We ought to leave now,' Will told him.

But the stone cut off his words, for it had begun to pulse in a long, steady rhythm as if it knew how to play on their fears. It glowed with a brick-red light of its own, and then the surface began to shimmer again, as solid stone turned into velvety liquid.

'Look at that! It is a prophecy! Words. Real words,' Edward said. He took the candle closer and began to read. '"My first in the West shall marry. My second a king shall be. My third upon a bridge lies dead. My fourth far in the East shall wed. My fifth over the seas shall send. My sixth in wine shall meet an end. And my seventh, whom none now fears, Shall be reviled five hundred years." A prophecy and a riddle too!'

'We must get out of here,' Will said, feeling the nausea beginning to roll in his belly. It was just how he had felt the day he had found the stone. And he knew that, despite the powerful bonds holding it, it was coiling itself like a serpent ready to strike.

'Get out! Save yourselves! Now!'

He did not know if his words broke a spell, but two things happened: the candle blew out and they all made a dash for the steps up to the door. For a panicky moment they were in darkness, amid piercing screams, all clambering over one another. It seemed forever before they tumbled out into the rain, scrambling down the wet grass, sliding among the spearplumes, shaking with terror. Only after the Lady Anne had rushed the crying younger children away down the mound did they realize that Edmund was not with them.

'Where is he?' Edward demanded.

'I don't know,' Will told him.

They went back together towards the door. It was now hideous with light, and they soon saw why. The Dragon Stone was glowing red now, bright as a horseshoe held in a blacksmith's pincers. And Edmund was embracing the stone. His arms were around it, clasping it as a sleeping child clasps its mother.

Edward made a move towards him, but Will held him. 'No! Stand back!'

'He's my brother!'

'No! You don't know what you're doing!'

He pushed Edward aside then steeled himself fiercely, concentrating his mind, ready to oppose the stone's malignant power. He called to mind the effort that had drained him the day he had saved Osric. Then he reached out to lift Edmund away.

Immediately an almost unbearable tingling began to pass along his arms. Will hung on grimly. The tingling tried to enter his chest, but he found he was able to use his scrying skills to hold the surge in check. He knew he must not let go of Edmund until the boy's grip on the stone slackened, yet he lacked the strength to oppose the stone directly.

'Dragon Stone, release him!' he ordered sternly.

But there was no response. Despite the binding-spells that held the stone's power in check, an impression of massive force confronted him, a malign force that was blind and hampered, yet still aware of the disparity in their strengths. It refused to waver. Then the tingling inched further up his arms, as if testing him. His failure to order the stone to obedience dismayed him. He felt the stone feed on that dismay. As another wave of uncertainty passed through him, he felt the tingling consolidate in its wake. It was a deadly force, a venom seeking to enter his chest. He must not let it reach his heart, yet he saw how his fear helped it.

He called upon all the disciplines he had been taught. He thought he must make a fist of his mind, hardening it, making it proof against the battlestone's probing. Already the tingling had reached cold fingers down inside his ribs. He switched his attention away from himself, concentrated instead on Edmund. The boy's eyes were open but his body felt as slack and heavy as a sleepwalker's. He pulled, but Edmund's hands remained locked around the stone.

But, yes! The true tongue! There was his defence!

Some instinct or shred of memory made him realize that he must employ the stone's true name. But what was it?

He tried the command again, this time in the language of stones. '*Acilui beithirei, scaiol!*' Dragon Stone, release him!

But once again, the monstrous stone refused. Instead, a vicious surge of power jolted from it, making Will gasp in pain. Edward jumped back as blood-red light pulsed from the stone.

'What's happening?' he shouted. 'Will, tell me!'

But Will gave no answer. He could not, for he was locked in a death struggle. The lethal tingling had now closed a loop around his chest and was threatening to strangle his beating heart.

He forced his thoughts elsewhere. A bright emerald began to blaze in his mind. He latched onto its pure light and the colour took him back to the green barrow of the Blessed Isle, and to the sister-stone's eerie verse. The verse that had seemed to make no sense at all . . .

> '*Si ni ach menh fa ainlugh?*
> *Tegh brathir ainmer na.*
> *Tilla angid carreic na duna,*
> *Aittreib muan nadir si a buan.*'

He let the words form dryly on his lips:

> *'But whose light am I?*
> *The name of my brother is "Home".*
> *Here in the morbid stone city.*
> *Has my dragon returned to dwell.'*

and suddenly all became clear.

'The name of my brother is "Home"!' he cried.

The power of the stone faltered. Will's mind strained to the limit to remember the word in the true tongue. The battlestone's true name was 'Home', which in the true tongue was . . . was . . .

'*Tegh!*' he cried. '*Tegh, scaiol!*'

And in a moment it was as if all power had been thrown back inside the stone. As its light withdrew, Will pulled Edmund backwards and they fell together onto the floor. The red light surged back. It seemed angry to have been thwarted, but contact was broken and its rage was once again spell-bound and impotent. Edward, blank-faced and shaken, helped Will drag his brother up the stairs and out into the open air. The drenching rain was still falling. It was cold and sharp and very welcome.

'Quickly!' Edward hissed. 'The night watch! They're coming!'

The guards had been roused. There was a clatter as a file of men passed them, heading in the wrong direction. Edward held back in the shadows until the way was clear, then he motioned Will out. They took Edmund between them and managed to get him back to the Garden of the White Rose and into their quarters without being seen. What they found there was almost worse than being caught. Edmund's face was cold to the touch. He was weak and it took more than a little effort to wake him from his trance. When he came to, he was barely able to speak and wholly unaware of what had happened. He could only say that he had stumbled in the darkness and had put his hand on the stone.

'You shouldn't have done that,' Will said.

'He knows that!' Edward spat back. 'And you shouldn't have brought the evil thing to Foderingham in the first place.'

'Master Gwydion brought it here, not I. And it was put under lock and key for a reason. If anyone's to blame for tonight, Edward, it's you.'

'My hand hurts,' Edmund whined.

When they looked at his palm they saw an ugly burn.

'Don't worry,' Will told him. 'I'll bring salves from Gort. It'll heal. The pain will go, I promise you.'

'We can't wake Gort,' Edward said.

'We must! We'll say it's a kitchen burn.'

'No. The guards are out. He'll guess the truth. We'll wait till morning.'

Will helped Edward get his brother undressed and into bed, and as they parted Edward said, 'You're not to say anything to anyone about this. Do you understand?'

'I'm not a fool, you know.'

'Still, I want you to promise!'

'All right, I promise! But only if you promise to put that unicorn wand back where it belongs among your father's things and never touch it again.'

Three days later Will and Edward were in harness and facing one another again, this time with practice swords. Each blamed the other for what had happened in the chamber under the keep, and that made for an unusually vigorous fight.

Steel rang against steel. The blows were full-blooded, unforgiving. Will drew deep, moist breaths inside his iron mask, taking cuts and bruises without noticing. Their clashes rang in his ears, loud groans of powerless frustration for both their defences were stronger than their unedged weapons and neither could hurt the other decisively. Plates clattered as they wrestled and tumbled and rolled on the ground. Fingers, sweaty and numbed by many layers of protection, struggled to tear off pauldron straps, to rip at exposed mail, to force a way into one another's armour. And though neither carried a war-dagger, each imagined he might have and so played the game of killing as if for real.

In the end their dignity was all used up and the jacks who had watched with interest began to laugh. Sir John stepped between them to call off the combat, saying that stirring the dirt like that was unseemly and served only to put dust on the crusts of the pies that cooled outside the kitchen window.

Will met Edward's eye unafraid as they took off their helmets. The skin of Edward's face was bruised and scraped where Will's swordblows had pressed the helmet's unpadded interior against it. His hair was sweaty and bound up inside a dirty linen skullcap. Will knew his own face was bruised and his nose was bleeding at the bridge, cut where his helmet had been momentarily forced forward.

But as they faced one another with less than their usual friendliness, there came a sound they had long waited for. A horn blowing from the barbican – two rising blasts that told of the approach of mounted men from the south.

Instantly, Edward threw down his helmet and bolted for the gatehouse. Will ran after him, tearing off his own skullcap and gauntlets, clattering up the stone steps to the ramparts.

'It's Father!' Edward said as they stood side by side in the narrow space. 'It has to be!'

'Move up. Let me see.'

Others were now caught up in the excitement. Jacks were gathering in knots along the walls. Word began to pass swiftly that the duke had returned.

'Look,' Will told him, pointing. There were standards flying, and now they could make out the livery of the riders.

'Argent a fess gules in chief three torteaux a molet azure for difference,' Edward said in heraldic as he peered at the column. Will knew exactly what he meant: a red-and-white banner with three red discs and a blue star on it.

'I hope they're friendly,' he said.

'It's Sir Walter Deveron – Lord Ferrers. He's one of my father's personal retainers.'

And Will heard the disappointment in Edward's voice, for the duke was not with them. They hurried down to the gate, then took the reins of the lead horseman, a knight accoutred for travel in time of war. Will guessed this must be Lord Ferrers. At his back were perhaps a couple of hundred riders, and behind them came a long line of covered waggons each with an outrider to act as escort.

Once across the Neane Bridge, Lord Ferrers dismounted from his muddy horse and looked around, alert as a jerfalcon. He was big and headstrong, an iron-fisted man of war, and he was exhilarated. He and his men had been in an engagement, and they had come off best.

'Booty,' he called out, pleased with himself. 'And what stuff it is! Sixteen waggons arrested on the road to Trinovant, packed to the ribs with the tools of war.'

'You've captured all that?' Edward marvelled.

'Aye, Sir Edward, we sent their escort running like hares! The drovers said they were under orders not to let it be known where this train was headed, but they told us soon enough once we were masters of it!' He laughed. 'This is a burden of weapons that Lord Strange will no longer have to shoulder!'

Will started at the mention of Lord Strange's name. But Edward took Lord Ferrers' helmet and together they headed for the gate of the inner bailey, to where Lady Cicely had appeared amid a gaggle of waiting women to bid the newcomers welcome.

While Will watched from the outer bailey, the waggons

were brought across the bridge and marshalled together nearby. By now, his blood had cooled and he was beginning to feel all the cuts and bruises he had taken. His lip felt puffy and fat, one of his eyes was almost closed, and there was a lump the size of a duck's egg on the back of his head. He knew he ought to go down and ask Gort to tend him, but he did not relish Gort's disappointment at the sight of him. Instead he made his way among the newly-arrived waggons when something made him look up, for there, sitting beside one of the drivers was a girl with fair hair and fear in her eyes.

Will looked once and then again. The girl saw him but turned her gaze quickly away, as she would from any armoured man.

'Willow?' he called, his heart thumping loudly now. 'Willow? Is that you?'

She turned back, surprised to hear her own name, and when she looked at him again the fear turned to confusion.

'Willow, it's me. It's me, Willand!'

'Will?' she said in disbelief. Then she put a hand to her mouth and whispered, 'Whatever have they done to you?'

CHAPTER SIXTEEN

COLD COMFORT
IN THE WEST

When they met next day, Will was dressed more plainly in the blue and white of Ebor livery. He went down to the empty waggons that now served as a camp for the waggoners. They were drawn up close together in a field by the river and the oxen set to grazing nearby. He decided to say nothing about how his face had come to be so cut and bruised, nor did he explain why he had been wearing armour. He was already wise enough to know that to Willow's way of thinking the study of war was not something to be admired.

Willow shared her makeshift home with her father, Stenn, a capable-looking, bearded man of middle height, who was very careful about what he said. He greeted Will genuinely enough, but there followed an uncomfortable silence. At last, Will saw a reassuring look pass between daughter and father before Willow led Will away.

'Does he mind me coming to see you?' he asked once they were out of earshot.

'He doesn't know who you are,' she said. 'Only that we met once at Grendon Mill. He thinks you'll have us sent back to Wychwoode and we'll have to face Lord Strange's wrath. I told him I'd ask you not to do that.'

He looked out over the river where a pair of beautiful swans were dabbling at the grassy bank. 'It's not up to me to send anyone back. I'm—'

'I know. You told me once before. You're no lordling.'

'Well . . . I know it looks . . .'

His words petered out and she looked at him uncertainly. 'Will, you've changed.'

'Don't be scared.' He smiled, trying to reassure her.

But she would not smile back. Instead she looked away from him as if she was not able to cross the gulf that seemed to have opened between them.

'Don't be put off by these clothes. They make me wear them.'

'I hardly know what to say to you,' she said quietly. 'After all . . . all you said back in Wychwoode about magic and . . .'

'I think we'd better have a talk,' he said. He sat himself down on a low wall and told her what had passed since they had parted. He told her everything, except about the finding of the Dragon Stone.

Willow, in turn, told him what had happened to her. She had received a message from the Wise Woman to meet at Grendon Mill, but her duties had delayed her and as she had come along by the brook she had heard a great crack of thunder and what looked like a blue lightning stroke coming from the edge of the forest. A few moments later a great torrent of muddy water had gushed along the ditch. That had scared her so much that she had run all the way home. Later she had plucked up the courage to go to Lord Strange's tower, but one of the guards had told her that the lad who had come with the wizard had gone away.

'Until then I never believed in any Master Gwydion,' she said.

'You mean, you thought I'd made him up?'

She nodded. 'My father says boys often tell girls things that aren't true, just to impress them.'

Will reddened. 'I suppose they do.'

'But you do just the opposite, don't you?' She looked at the way his hair was cut now and at the richness of his clothes. 'You told me you were no lordling. But it seems you're going to be one, after all.'

'No, these things are not mine. I'm just a page.'

She touched his hair. 'I liked it better long, when you had the two braids in it.'

He scrubbed fingers through his hair, remembering how he had cut his braids off because she had said they made him look like a girl.

'The truth is,' he said, 'I don't really know what I'm supposed to be doing here. Master Gwydion dumped me on this lordly household like so much old baggage. He just wiped his hands and went off without even saying so much as goodbye.'

'What did you do to annoy him?'

'I don't think that was it. He just said he had important work to do, work I couldn't help him with.'

'Why did you stay here?' she asked, looking gloomily at the stone walls that rose up around the outer bailey.

'It's not so bad here once you get used to it.'

'You could have run away.'

'I made a promise to do whatever Master Gwydion wanted.' He looked down, thinking of the magical cloak that covered the Vale and how much he should tell her about it. 'In truth . . . I probably couldn't go home.'

She chose not to pry. Instead she said brightly, 'Well, in the end, Master Gwydion's thunderbolt made no difference at the mill, because every man who could be spared was set to rebuilding the dam. Even my father was sent to it. It wasn't a month before the autumn rains started to fill the pool up as high as it was before. Then the wheel was set to moving again and the trip-hammers began thumping out again.'

Will nodded, wondering if Gwydion might not have told the Duke Richard's men to set a watch over Wychwoode and wait for a train of waggons to appear. 'You must have been afraid when Lord Ferrers' men came down on you like that.'

'At first I thought we were all going to be killed. My father took out his bow, but I made him put it down.'

He smiled. 'I'm glad you did.'

She took his hand and squeezed it. 'I was never so pleased to see anyone as you, Willand. A friendly face in such a place as this. You don't know what it means. Thank you.'

He blushed and could not think of anything else to say. His left eye was still bloodshot and there was the remains of a purple ring around it. 'But I haven't done anything.'

She looked into his eyes. 'You say that, but last night I lay awake thinking and it seemed to me it must have been magic that drew us here.'

When he thought of her lying awake thinking of him, embarrassment overwhelmed him. 'Willow, the truth is, I don't know any magic. Not that kind anyway.'

'If it wasn't magic, then I'd like to know what to call it. Maybe a twist of fate.'

'Yes,' he said, wondering again what part Gwydion might have played in her arrival. 'Maybe it was that.'

But as they sat together, it all seemed a bit too good to be true, and Will could not wholly put out of his mind what Gwydion had said about the way the battlestones might work their harm by warping people's destinies. Perhaps it was the Dragon Stone that was playing with them. Perhaps enough of its power had reached beyond Gwydion's restraining spells to draw Willow and her father here.

Perhaps all was not quite as fortunate as it seemed at first glance.

He saw young Edmund limping near the gate, watched over by a servant. His hand was still bound up and he seemed dazed. Horse hooves clattered on the cobbles and Will recognized Edward's powerful chestnut destrier. Edward was in the saddle. He had concocted an unchallengeable tale about his brother having fallen down in the hearth, having put his hand into the fire and cracked his head. But the effects of what had happened to Edmund half a week ago had still not gone away. Perhaps, Will thought, it was time to tell Gort the truth.

Will's thoughts were interrupted by Edward's approach. The easy manner he had lately begun to adopt whenever he was in the presence of young women seemed to suit him. In his velvets and jauntily-set hat he looked manly and almost as glamorous as his father. His horse sweated and stamped.

'What goes, Willywag?' he asked, nodding a breezy greeting. 'Ah, you're busy, I see!'

Willow bowed her head and looked demurely away.

'Hello, Edward.' Will jumped down from the wall and touched Willow's hand in parting. 'I must go.'

As she made her way back towards camp, Will turned. 'Edward, listen, I've been thinking about going to see the Wortmaster.'

'You're always with him.'

'You know what I mean.' He took the bridle and began to lead Edward's horse into the inner bailey. 'About Edmund.'

Edward continued to watch Willow over his shoulder until she passed out of sight. 'I think not.'

'Look – Edmund was never like this before. There's something wrong. He doesn't even smile.'

'He never did smile much. His hand is getting better. Leave him be.'

'It's not his hand I'm worried about. He's losing himself. It'll be best if I tell Gort—'

Edward's flinty smile fell away. 'He's my brother, Will, and I'll say what's best for him. It'll pass.'

Stenn turned out to be a more agreeable man than Will had at first feared. He was level-headed and calm and he had the strongest handshake Will had ever felt. The other men from the Wychwoode saw him as their spokesman, and Will promised to petition the Lady Cicely on their behalf. To everyone's great surprise the duchess came herself to the gates of the inner bailey the next day to give her decision.

'You are free to go home,' she said, looking from bowed head to bowed head. 'However, Willand tells me that some of you are reluctant to leave. He says you are honest verderers who were pressed into a service that was distasteful to you. Is this true?'

No one moved. Then Stenn spoke up. 'It's true, your ladyship. Every word of it.'

The duchess eyed them, deliberating for a moment, then she said, 'Anyone fearing the retribution of Lord Strange has leave to remain here. I will not have churls unjustly blamed.'

When she retired, Will stepped forward to recognize the waggoneers' gratitude on her behalf, and after a moment Edward appeared and drew him aside.

'Where's the girl?'

'Willow? What about her?'

'I came to tell her she should attend my mother to receive her duties. She's to serve the family.'

Will felt a warning pang. 'But she knows nothing of castle life. Surely her place is with her—'

'Will, it's an honour.'

*   *   *

In the days that followed, trumpet blasts were blown several times upon the walls of Foderingham. For some time the garrison had been swelling with men who had come down from the northerly parts of the duke's domains. Rumours circulated of armies seen marching along the Great North Road, and reports were heard of levies assembling in distant towns. But a curious false peace settled over the Realm as the cold hand of winter tightened. Whatever combination of magic and politics Gwydion and the duke might be working out in Trinovant, they seemed, for the moment, to be holding back the terrible tide.

As it turned out, Willow was put to helping care for the two youngest sons of the duke. It was a task that brought with it much responsibility and she longed to be free of it, for the infants were wilful and given to tantrums. Will knew that she would have preferred to visit the butts to shoot arrows or walk the meadows with Gort to learn about herbs. But, as Edward had said, it was an honour to be taken into the duchess's service, and in truth Willow had no choice.

The days grew shorter, and the weather colder and greyer, but on a rare bright winter's morning several days before the Ewletide, horns sounded from the walls of Foderingham, and this time there were three long notes.

They were enduring a lesson, but as soon as Edward heard the warning trill he was up and out of his seat, hauling himself up to the iron-barred mullions to catch sight of the looked-for return.

'He's back!' he shouted. 'I knew it!'

'Sir Edward!' Tutor Aspall's voice fluted. 'You must not rise at every alarum. Sit down again if you please, you have not asked permiss—'

But the helpless tutor could only look to where two brothers had been sitting and where now only Will stood alone. Edward had already dragged his brother from his seat and was leading him along the passageway.

'He really has no discipline,' Tutor Aspall muttered, then, 'Now, Willand . . . Willand?'

But Will had already eased past him into the passageway and was heading for the far door.

He followed the brothers down the worn steps of spiral stone, out of the solar and down to the gatehouse. A body of mounted men, two or three hundred in number and flying the duke's personal standard, were approaching the barbican. Horses were already clattering across the inner drawbridge and through the open gate. The whole castle was in uproar as the duke and his lead riders came in, gear jangling. Will saw the horses were lathered and that the duke wore a neck-piece of shining steel and leg armour. It seemed he had travelled quickly and in expectation of trouble. Following along behind him were thirty men also part-armoured, and others in mail-shirts and brigandines. All wore swords, several were men of significant rank, the rest their attendant knights. Will looked for Gwydion among them, but of the wizard there was no sign.

Duke Richard dismounted and threw back a mud-spattered riding cloak, plainly delighted to be back among his family. Edward and Edmund were already close at their father's side. The duke ruffled their hair and smiled at them and took them with him inside to be greeted by Elizabeth and Margaret and George. Then the Lady Cicely appeared with the duke's two-year-old namesake in her arms. He exchanged a serious word with his wife as everyone went inside.

Willow picked Will out of the crowd and beckoned to him. 'So that's the duke,' she said.

'That's him,' Will said. 'Isn't he a fine lord?'

'I don't know about that.' Her eyes drifted among the various members of the duke's family. 'But he certainly looks to be a fine man.'

Will saw that Edward was standing close by the duke's

side, and for an uncomfortable moment he could not be certain if Willow had meant father or son.

That night, after the excitement had died down, Will sat with Willow in the buttery and took a simple supper with her.

'I was hoping to see Master Gwydion among the arrivals,' he said glumly.

'It must be that he hasn't yet found a way to break the power of the Dragon Stone,' she said.

'How do you know about that?' he asked, shocked to hear her mention it by name.

'Sir Edward told me all about it.'

'Did he now?'

She looked at him blithely, her blue eyes unblinking. 'Yes, he did. Anything wrong with that?'

'No . . .'

She inclined her head. 'Why do you think he won't take me to see it?'

'Did you ask him to?' he said, fearing the worst now. 'I mean, do you want to see it?'

She shrugged. 'I was hoping he'd offer.'

He tore off a hunk of bread and dunked it in his stew. 'It's best you don't think about that stone.'

'Why not? Maybe you'd like to show it to me. I want to see what all the fuss is about.'

'Well, you can't. It's locked in a vault under the keep where it's safe – or as safe as anything like that can be.'

Willow bit her lip. 'Is it very dangerous, then?'

'Oh, yes. I don't know much about it, but I do know that. And I'm beginning to think the harm inside it has found a way to get out. It's already done something to Edmund.'

'Edmund? You mean Sir Edmund? The son who limps? The one with the crippled arm?'

'He wasn't like that before. And it's not just his arm and leg. He behaves as if he's trapped in a maze and can't find his way out. It's hard to explain, but I met him feeling his way along a wall yesterday like a blind man. "What are you doing?" I asked him, and he looked at me all kind of hollow and replied, "Looking for the light." I tell you, Willow, the fates of all of us are getting twisted up and ruined because of that old stone. I hope Master Gwydion comes back soon.'

Her look seemed oddly cool. 'Willand, you think too much.'

'What do you mean?'

'You should count yourself fortunate. Yours is a fate most country lads would swap theirs with as soon as blink. All that high living – leather shoes, and riding and shooting and wearing of armour. Living like a lord you are. What have you got to complain about if your Master Gwydion never comes back?'

'If I'm living like a lord, then lords are welcome to it. If I could be anywhere now, I'd be away from here, eating apple pie back in Nether Norton where I belong, bare feet and all.'

She folded her arms. 'Oh, that's very nice! Don't you like my being here?'

'What's that got to do with it?' he asked, not realizing what he had said. He sighed. 'Look, all I'm saying is you mustn't take that stone so lightly. It affects people. And it's not just this one. There are others planted out there, quietly working the downfall of the Realm. Very soon now there'll be a tiny little change somewhere in the land – a Slaver bridge will fall down or a cartload of stone will be stolen out of the old Slaver wall – and that'll be that. Crack! Like the last straw that breaks the mule's back.'

'I don't pretend to understand all that stuff. It sounds like nonsense to me.'

'Well then, don't concern yourself with it!'

'I shan't!'

'Good!'

Will left the buttery then and went to watch the lords gathering at the entrance to the Great Hall. Look at them, he told himself. They're excited about something. Maybe the mule's back is closer to breaking than I thought. By the moon and stars, I wish Master Gwydion had come back with them!

After a moment hanging back, he decided it would be better to find out than to wonder. He went past the familiar-faced jacks and slipped into the hall among the many servants and guests who were going in and out. As soon as the moment favoured him he asked Sir Hugh about the noblemen who had arrived.

'Don't you remember your standards and badges?' Sir Hugh asked. 'Over there – in the red, with the device of the white bear?'

'Uh . . . Earl Warrewyk, the Captain of Callas.'

Sir Hugh nodded. 'Lady Cicely's nephew. Mark him well, for he owns more land than any earl in the Realm. Your friend the Crowmaster says he pities him, for even a gift of ten thousand marks of money is not enough to make the Lord Warrewyk smile. To his left, in the red-and-black coat, that's his father, Earl Sarum. Over there, the badge of the red lion signifies Lord Falconburgh, a natural brother of Earl Sarum. And here, in green, is Lord Bergaven whose badge is the black-and-white bull, a brother also of Earl Sarum. See Lord Scrope de Belton, there? He is their cousin.'

'Are they all such close kinsmen?'

'Of course. And kinsmen of mine. How else could it be, for is not blood thicker than water?'

'It is when shed.'

Sir Hugh looked hawkishly at him, saying, 'You're a sharp lad, Willand, but then what should we expect from the 'prentice of a crow.'

'I meant to offer no insult, sir. Truly.'

'And none was taken from you. The power of the Warrewyk clan is very great. Of all the earls, Warrewyk and Sarum are our chiefest allies. And allies are sorely needed now, for you must have marked how the days have darkened.'

'Is the news so bad?'

Sir Hugh slapped him on the shoulder. 'What news there might be is not for your ears. That way is the short way to the door.'

He had been dismissed, but he poured more wine into Sir Hugh's flagon and said, 'At least tell me what's become of Master Gwydion? That's surely news to concern me.'

'Who can say? The Crowmaster's business is rarely apparent. We do not pretend to understand what he does, unless it be the spinning of spells which push and pull and maintain the Realm in a great web of good and evil. State magic it is called, though I have never thought much upon it. It was once explained to me in my younger days as much like the way ropes and poles hold up a tent. Your Master Gwydion has crawled tireless as a spider these last thirteen months all over Trinovant, pegging down influence here, propping up persuasions there, tirelessly manoeuvring until no one knows which side he really speaks for any more.'

Will felt a little put out that Sir Hugh should liken Gwydion to a spider. 'You scarcely speak of him as a friend.'

'What should I call one who sups with the enemy?'

'Does he do that?'

'He has certainly gnawed upon every bone of contention in Trinovant of late – but now he has made a great mistake.'

'What mistake?'

'He has revealed his true heart. He has made a priceless gift to Queen Mag. He has given her a beautiful blue-white diamond. Planted it upon her forehead publicly when last the lords were assembled together in Great Council.

Everyone knows that she loves jewels above all things – except perhaps the pup she swears is King Hal's.'

Will was stunned. He recalled quite clearly the precious gem that Gwydion had prised from the clasp of the swan cloak in Leir's tomb. It seemed astonishing that the wizard would have given it away at all, let alone made a gift of it to Queen Mag. 'But . . . why would he do that?'

'You must ask him yourself, for I do not know the answer. He tells us he seeks to bribe the vixen so that she will tolerate peace, but such a diamond as that? Our good duke does not see why she must be paid at all before he may have his rightful say in government. And nor does any man here!'

Will could think of nothing to say to that.

Sir Hugh cracked no smile, but remained fierce. He pinched finger against thumb. 'Beware, young fledgling crow – the duke has come this close to declaring your wizard an enemy. And when he does there will no longer be a place for you among his own.'

'You'd drive me out?' Will asked.

'We'd treat you like any other spy in our midst.'

'But I'm no spy! You'd drive out one who had never done you any harm?'

'Drive you out? No!' Sir Hugh let a murmur of amusement escape him. 'Make no mistake, at a word from the duke I or any other man you see here would cut your throat from ear to ear.'

Will looked for some sign that Sir Hugh was joking, and was appalled to find that he was not. 'But you can trust me, can't you?'

'Trust? I say again – the only true friends are made through blood. Kinship is the only trusty bond. Everything else is moveable.'

The grey-haired knight rested his hand on the hilt of his sword and moved away. Will blinked at him, not knowing quite what to do. For the first time he saw from what a slender thread his life dangled, and he began to understand how it truly was with lords – and how their minds, being already so fixed on fierceness and suspicion, would fall as easy prey to the battlestones' influence.

Will sank into the shadows and gave his attention over to the duke's sons. He watched how Edmund's distracted twitching went unremarked, and how Edward hung on his father's every word. The reasons for the latter were plain enough. The duke was a glamorous man. Glamour shone from every pore of him. Despite all that Sir Hugh had said, it was easy on the one hand to regard Duke Richard as a great lord, and on the other to like him as a man. He captured the eye, and Will could see why some men had no choice but to follow certain other men in battle.

When the duke stood up, a hush fell. He said simply, 'My mind is made up. This household will commemorate the sacred season of Ewle at our stronghold of Ludford.'

It might have been thought a bland enough thing to say, but when Duke Richard said it the effect was almost magical. Immediately everyone in the Great Hall fell to cheering and banging their hands on the tables in approval.

Only Will's heart fell, for he too knew what it meant. He turned on his heel and withdrew without being noticed. Then he went to tell Gort.

But first he found Willow in the kitchens.

'Commemorate?' she said. 'Doesn't he mean celebrate? Oh, I hate it when lords call a fast and let the Sightless Ones parade about in their high hats and golden cloaks.'

'No, you don't understand,' he told her. 'It's not about Ewle, the duke's moving his family to a stronger castle. Ludford's deep in the Western Marches and all the lands round about it are loyal to him. It's where he can gather his strength. This really does mean war.'

'Maybe that's not such a bad thing,' Willow said.

He frowned at her. 'Oh, think what you're saying.'

'I heard they pay soldiers a penny a day. That's good money for sitting around mostly.'

'Yes, and it's not the fall that kills the man who dives off the top of a tower, but the sudden stop at the bottom.'

'If it's soldiers the duke wants then he'll be glad of my father and the other men from Leigh. They're all good archers. And who knows, maybe the Hogshead'll be killed and the Wychwoode'll get a new warden and we'll all be able to go home.'

Will made no reply, thinking at first that she must be taking leave of her senses. But then another, more sinister thought struck him – that whatever was leaking from the Dragon Stone must have got inside her head too.

The next few days were hectic as preparations for the duke's move were set in motion. For all that, Will was pleased to be leaving Foderingham, though he fretted about the battle-stone and what would happen to it when the household had gone and the castle was left in the care of a much smaller garrison. Gort was suddenly hard to find, and when Will did track him down he refused to talk about the battle-stone, and so Will set all his hopes on Gwydion returning before they departed.

But Will's hopes were dashed, for the wizard was neither seen nor heard from, and none of the newly arrived nobles seemed to know what might have happened to him. In the event, the move to Ludford was a great undertaking, yet it seemed to Will to be a dreary task. There was much fetching and carrying and making ready to be done before they could set off, and when they did the weather refused to smile on them. For three days it rained and rained. The winter roads were turned black with mud, and the horses churned up the way so badly that other folk were forced to take detours. In the valleys there were bogs and on the hilltops driving sleet. Then an icy snap set in and the mud froze into ruts that hardly thawed by day before darkness came down again.

A bare four leagues a day would have been steady going on that week-long journey westward. Most of the horses walked ponderous and slow alongside a travelling household of three hundred. Carts and waggons and teams of oxen ploughed through cold mud or stumbled over frozen ruts as the stark grey winter misery of the Realm took hold.

Five hundred foot soldiers and men-at-arms made the journey with them as they struggled against the grain of the country. The knights and nobles rode on ahead, roaming the country meadows with their lance tips bared. Each morning, hunting parties left camp, and scouts rode out to see how the land lay and to watch for enemies and look for signs of their spies. But the horse soldiers would not leave the household waggons for long, and never all at the same time. At first Will thought it was through fear of outlaws – bands of lawless men were said to infest some of the remoter parts through which they passed – but no outlaw band would dare attack so well-guarded a train no matter what riches were in prospect, and Will realized that what the duke feared was an ambush laid by a far greater enemy than reivers – the queen herself.

Having fallen once to an attack upon the highway, Willow was quietly watchful. The men from Leigh had been dressed all in blue and white and equipped with stout yew warbows. When she was not attending the Ebor infants, Willow sat beside her father on the ox-cart that carried a portion of the duke's stores. At other times, she would grow tired of sitting and would walk for a while, so long as the mud was not too deep. Will saw how she talked with Wortmaster Gort and lent a hand in everything she could. He also noticed that whenever Edward rode by she would look up and smile. Will did not have a horse to ride. Horses were needed for the escort, and he did not qualify. What was worse, a bad cold had come over him, spots had appeared on his face and he ached in every bone.

'How much longer are we going to be travelling?' he asked when Edward next galloped up.

'The days are too short to get anywhere,' Edward said expertly. 'And this mud's worse than I've ever seen it.'

'Then why did we leave Foderingham so soon? Surely we could have stayed until the weather improved.'

Edward looked at him as if he had asked a foolish question. 'The days would only have got shorter.'

It was a fatuous answer, and Will cut straight to the point. 'What I mean is, I suppose your father wants to get to his heartland while he may.'

Edward's eyes narrowed. 'My father fears no man.'

Will coughed thickly. 'War is coming, and when it does it will stamp everyone down, even your father – especially your father. Doesn't that worry you? Don't you want to find a way around if a way is to be had?'

'It's nothing to me. Let war come.' Edward's chin jutted, then he looked around. 'Where's Willow?'

'Why do you want to know?'

But Edward made no answer.

A camp the size of a small town sprang up each night where they rested. There was an hour of chaos at the appointed site, then a calmer mood settled as tents were raised, smoking fires lit and the daylight died. He would sit with Willow in the gloaming and eat a delicious supper of spitchcock eels and listen to Stenn tell stories of happier days in the Wychwoode before Lord Strange came.

Later, Willow would go to sleep and Will would wander over to the soldiers' camp, or go over to where the painted tents of the nobles stood in a tight circle, luxurious inside with carpets and sheepskins and charcoal braziers and clever pegged furniture that could be taken apart for the journey.

The circle was guarded by helmeted jacks whose breath steamed in the freezing air, jacks who leaned on their spears for long, patient hours as quiet conversations droned inside the candle-bright canvas and a wild world stretched out for league upon league on every side in the cold and the dark.

On the third night, by chance, Will saw Edward call Willow to his tent. The duke's heir remained closeted with her for quite a while, and it pained him to know they were together. When they came out he saw Edward take the ring from his little finger and give it to her. That stabbed him through the heart and made him want to go over and show them he had seen it all, but he realized that such an urge, though powerful, was not helpful. It would not be wise to give in to it, and so he fought it down like a man ought to, for why shouldn't Willow and Edward speak if they wanted, even privately? And if Willow preferred Edward's conversation, then whose fault was that?

He had hoped that once away from the influence of the Dragon Stone, his mood would brighten, but it had guttered lower. Jealousies played on his mind. He drank the powders infused in hot water that Wortmaster Gort said would help him throw off his cold, but three days of winter misery had already passed, and it was not until the fourth day that he began to breathe a little less tightly. 'Ah, Master Miseryguts,' Gort said. 'So you've finally decided to co-operate with the cure, have you?'

'What do you mean by that?'

'Don't you know that's how cures work? You have to help the goodness in the herb along. Give it permission to heal you.'

That sounded absurd, and he said darkly, 'I'll try my best.'

As they camped late that afternoon Will grew ever more restless. He felt an odd excitement that he had not felt since before coming to Foderingham. There was something about the land hereabouts, something strange in it. He had learned to recognize that much. A lign. A battlestone maybe. A glimmer of light burning on the edge of sight. A whisper in the shadows. An unplaceable stench. The thought came to him to cut a hazel switch and try to scry it out, but the very idea made him shudder, and at once he knew the reason the Wortmaster's powders had taken so long to work – while at Foderingham the battlestone's harm had been slowly seeping into him. Now, away from it, his mind and body were gradually expelling the poison as pus wept from a healing wound.

He emerged from his tent, coughed and spat, then crept away and went alone beside the muddied road to a place where wildness reigned. He breathed deep, making an effort to shield his heart from the strange power in the earth, but to draw in the strength that Gwydion found. He liked it best when the stars came out and the wind dropped, so that stillness lay over the dewy land. Tonight it was going to be very cold – cold enough to freeze fishponds so they could be walked across by morning – and quiet enough a little way from camp to make his ears hum. Tonight the blackness of night was frosted away by the light of a full moon and the tautness inside him was tingling.

He went out knowing that these hills that hunched their backs all around were in the Earldom of Salop, and so quite soon – maybe tomorrow – they would arrive at their destination. For a while at least there would be no more wide-open nights like this. If only Gwydion could be here, he thought. If only someone would tell me news of him. I'd give everything to know if he's succeeded.

A blazing halo of coloured light stood out from the high winter moon and Will counted the faint rainbow colours, bands through which the brighter stars shone. There, in the south almost overwhelmed by the moonlight was a line of three middling stars. A bright blue spark stood below them and a fiery red one above: this was the star-group that Gwydion had said was called by the princes of the North 'the Ell-wand', and by the ancients 'Belatucadros, the Horned One', and by later peoples 'Cernunnos', a hunter whose form rose over the land every winter with his two brave dogs to see what prey might stir below. A shiver passed through Will as he stared into the sky. He coughed again, wishing he felt better, less vague in his thoughts, less tired and remote from the world. Gort was right – something heavy was lying upon his heart like a haunting.

Nor could solitude heal this ill. He feared to take off his shoes and plant his cold toes in the hoar frost because that would make the sickly feelings sharper. Memories of scrying for the Dragon Stone still lingered in the muscles of his arms and chest. But, though little more than a year had passed, his body had changed. Overhead the moon was trampling down the truceless armies of the stars. The sheep in the fields stood motionless. All was colourless. Nearby, a stream gurgled through shingle banks, but here at the crossroads mud trodden by a thousand hooves had hardened. A journey stone declared this place was called Morte's Crossing and that Trinovant was seven times seven leagues distant. Slaver figures cut in the stone swam into ogham as he squinted at them. They had gone when he looked again. Opposite, in the shadow of the trees, stood a terrible gibbet. It loomed upon him as he staggered over the frozen hummocks of the road. An oaken post, rough-hewn, square and three times as tall as a man stood as a reminder. From its high iron arm horror hung suspended – the body of a criminal, condemned to hang in chains, caged at this crossroads for a year and a day as an example, as a warning. By night this sentinel waited still and silent, a lonely shepherd keeping his flocks.

Who was he? Will wondered, trapped by the grim need to look up at the frosted head of the corpse. The shock of seeing flesh for what it was reverberated inside him. But who had this stranger been, this man dressed now in his ice-whitened rags? A poacher perhaps? A murderer? A stealer of cattle? Had he been guilty or innocent? Had he ever loved? Had he been loved in return? What error had ruined him and brought him to this? Why had he not been saved? And what brutality had hung him here to be displayed like so much rotten meat?

There were no answers in the ghastly smile. The glint of moonlight on teeth revealed under stretched, wind-dried lips gave nothing away. A hand, withered and slim, lay composed against one of the iron bands that enclosed the dead man. And the empty sockets of his eyes, all pecked away by crows, looked down with a knowing sort of assurance. He seemed to Will like a man who had been on a journey, but to a far place of which he could never tell.

Unnerved by the stillness, Will reached up and pushed the cage a little. It moved as easily as a sweetheart's swing in a summer garden.

'War!' the figure told him rustily. 'They hung me high . . . and I did die!'

And Will, who had never seen an executed man before, put his hands over his ears to shut out the words.

'War!' said the cage's hinge. 'I would not go . . . and so you see . . . they made a show . . . of me.'

For all that they had tried to teach him at Foderingham, his inner spirit still understood that war was not about bright swords and brighter armour and swallow-tailed flags that floated in the breeze. It was about lordly greed and common suffering – and it was about pain and fear and death.

'War!' cried the corpse's empty jaw. 'It's coming! It's coming . . . It's coming . . .'

He closed his eyes to shut out the sight of that horrible,

moonfrosted flesh, and in that moment he grasped precisely what Gwydion had sent him to Foderingham to learn.

They made their approach to Ludford late the next afternoon, two days before Ewletide. The low sun, dilute and unwarming all day, was now only just clearing the woods that stood out above the furrowed lines of misty fields. Skeletal trees held rooks' nests, and there was the kind of cold in the air that sent woodsmoke straight up to fan out flat in a breathless sky.

'What do you think?' Will called out, gesturing at the sad beauty of a watery sunset where the sun slumped into a wispy haze of yellow and red.

'That?' Edward called back, misunderstanding. He was ruddy-cheeked from his ride. 'Good heavy horse country. And a very strong fortress.'

'I meant the sunset, not the castle.'

Edward controlled his horse and slapped himself on the chest. 'Did you know Ludford was mine?'

'Yours?'

'I'm the Earl of the Marches. Didn't you know? The castle of Ludford belongs to me.'

'Let me ride,' Will said, suddenly wanting to swap places with Edward.

But the duke's son turned the mare's head and walked her away, saying, 'Not today. She's blown.'

Such was the day: cheerless and miserable in the dead of the year, despite what the merrier folk of the train said to try to make it otherwise. Will brooded, watched the way Willow picked dainty steps over the ridges and ruts of the frozen road. He saw the way her skirts swished as she lifted them. The way she moved bewitched him.

Why had Edward been talking privately with her?

'Now, then, Will!' Stenn said, coming up. 'What ails you? You've had a face as long as a lute for days.'

'Bad cold.'

'Is that all? Double portions for you tonight, then. They say to feed a cold and starve a fever.'

Will liked the older man, but for all his solid cheeriness he kept a vigilant watch over his daughter. 'She's the only person I've got in the world,' he had said at supper last night, and it had sounded like a warning.

'Why don't you go see the Wortmaster?'

'I already did.'

But he knew the cold was no cause – it was an effect.

They went by Wyg Moor and then by Leint Hall, where the great family of Morte kept a robust garrison. At the hamlet of Ellton, Will saw a tiny fairy palace, gorgeous in all details, yet no taller than his shoulder and fit for folks no more than a foot in height. But it was lived in now only by hens.

When he showed his amazement at it, Gort said, 'Oh, but these are the Marches of Cambray. There were once little people hereabouts, though that was long ago and none of their works now remain. Perhaps this small house was built as an encouragement to them, in hopes of a return.'

Finally they came to Ludford Gate and Will saw it was a lively enough place, with town walls that were thick and well-kept, and a welcoming gatehouse. Here the gatemen were red-cheeked and stout and jolly. 'Not like Caster used to be in olden times,' Gort told him. 'In that city the great gate had a secret false beggar, ha ha!'

Will raised a wry smile. 'How can a beggar beg in secret, Wortmaster? And who would bother to impersonate a beggar anyway?'

'Ah, well! You see, it was like this – this beggar used to call out lustily to those who would come in, "Alms!" he would shout. "Alms for the needy!" But he had been set there by the Lord of Caster himself to see which of the wealthy merchants showed charity, for reports were made on all who came in and then they were treated accordingly!'

But it was news of the coming of Ludford's own lord that had brought the townsfolk here out into the streets. There were horns calling and bells pealing and a cheering procession that came along with them. Will saw how the duke had been missed from this place like an absent father. He passed among his people now, at first on horseback but now on foot, enjoying their adoration until he came to his own high walls.

The town was neatly planned, with straight streets, many of them finely cobbled, though Will was dismayed to see a large chapter house and cloister dominating the market square with its tall stone spire and monument. As at the chapter house close to Eiton the spire carried the device of a white heart and a weather vane bearing the letters A, A, E and F.

'What does that mean on the vane?' he asked the Wortmaster.

'If you asked them they'd claim it was the names of the four winds in the mystical language of Tibor. That's where the Slavers came from.' Gort looked about, then spoke from behind his hand. 'They named the winds after their four cardinal points – North they call oliuqA, East is suruE, South retsuA, and West suinovaF. But that's no simple wind-cock. Oh, no! Watch it long enough and you'll see it stir, though there came not a breath of wind to move it. The letters really stand for "satinretarF dA tE bA". It means "From and To the Fellowship." Those ugly iron masts atop their spires – that's how the chapter houses and cloisters talk with one another across the land.'

Will shuddered. He imagined the vanes moving in magical sympathy with one another, spelling out in some secret cipher dark messages, telling all that the spies of the Fellowship could gather, and passing it on swiftly across the Realm. The face of the stone monument that stood outside the chapter house was incised with unreadable words and lit up now with votive candles. A hooded Fellow stood guard at the entrance. Will's skin prickled as he smelled the greasy stink and heard the solemn dirge that issued from inside. It seemed to him an organization of the most tremendous and malevolent power.

The throng followed as far as the castle and gathered at the gate. Edward's marcher stronghold stood at the top of the town, and Will thought it a testament to the duke's reputation that he should be so well received by his people. But seeing the gleeful faces all around he knew there was as yet no understanding of the real reason their lord had come. Nor did they have any inkling of the terrible calamity that was foregathering.

What's wrong with me? he wondered, unable to lift his spirits another notch. Why am I seeing things through dead eyes? Is it me, or is it that the world is truly darkening? I don't know, for I've never seen war gather before. The knights won't say much about that for fear of spies, and I cannot get an uncluttered answer about the stones from the Wortmaster.

As they passed beneath the gatehouse Will chanced to look up at the battlements and fancied he saw the figure of Death, waiting there in his black robes. A sudden terror swarmed through him and he gasped at the reek that came sharply up into his nostrils as if from a great chasm. He shied back as a man would from a sudden precipice.

A soldier at his elbow bumped him and cursed. But then Willow was beside him and asking him what was the matter, and he shook his head and said he was just a little dizzy and not to fuss.

But it had seemed to him as he looked up at the teeth of the portcullis that he had had that same feeling of dread before. And he had done the same thing before, even down to imagining the men hauling hand-over-hand on the bars of the windlasses above him. When first arriving at Foderingham he had feared the gatehouse men would make a mistake and allow the great barrier to fall down on him, and he wondered at why such a feeling might have over-whelmed him a second time.

'Come along,' Gort said, slapping his back. 'Don't block the entrance, hey?'

The castle of Ludford, having been forewarned by messengers, was now ready to receive them. Here too there were outer and inner baileys, except that here the guards called them 'wards'. A wall of grey limestone enclosed the outer ward – two of its corners were rounded and one square, while built into the fourth corner was the moated inner ward with its tall, square keep and high walls. Ravens circled the highest tower, and the duke's standard flew there.

When they entered the inner ward Will saw there was a great hall, a 'solar' which was the lord's private quarters, and Gort pointed out the magnificent Round House, the place from which the duke administered his affairs. Various other lodgings were built inside the castle walls and here, as at Foderingham, a great iron engine of time clanged out the hours from inside its special high tower.

'They all come from the Castle of Sundials,' Gort told him. 'That's a great house in the north belonging to the duke. Braye, the Lord Keeper there, is a loremaster and a watcher of the skies. These machines are of his making, though I wish he'd stuck with sundials!'

'Then there is an Old Father Time, after all,' Will said, taking it all in. It was easy to see why a castle had been built here, for this place was a high point from which the land fell away steeply to the north and west, on which sides it was also guarded by the River Theam and its tributary, the Ludd. But, once inside, the castle was far from the forbidding fortress that it appeared from outside. There were servants everywhere to welcome them and the many chimneys of a large kitchen and bakehouse were issuing smoke and delicious smells. Will had spent many an hour studying fortifications, and he passed an expert eye over the keep, judging that its foundations had been laid ten or more generations before, and that almost every generation had strengthened it or added some new part, as was only right.

Gort ushered them into the quarters that had been prepared. Will thought the rooms were cramped but adequate, and after a brief look around he sat down with Willow on a bench and tore off some warm bread for her. They munched as darkness fell and Gort unpacked his precious bundles on the table or wandered in and out of the rooms with armfuls of mystery. After a while, Edward came into the inner ward and lingered some distance away, and it seemed to Will that he was waiting for someone. Willow's eyes followed him. She interested herself in him as he stood, hands on hips, staring up at the strength of the walls his father had given him. Will knew it was a fool's question, but he could not stop himself from asking it.

'Is he handsome?'

'Sir Edward? Yes,' she said straight away. Her eyes followed Edward again. 'But he's got a high opinion of himself.'

Will felt some of the hollowness leave him, pleased despite himself to hear that Willow disliked some aspect of Edward. 'I suppose he has every right to have a high opinion.'

'What do you mean?'

'Well, this is his castle. It's his by title, and he'll be the Duke of Ebor one day. A great man.'

'Most people are impressed by belongings and rank,' Willow said with a private smile. 'Some girls would walk a long way to marry a miller's son.'

'Huh! Edward's no miller's son.'

She laughed at him. 'You don't have much idea what girls like in boys, do you?'

'You mean you're not impressed by him?' he asked. He watched the way Edward moved. He had learned to copy much of his father's manner. Something made Will say: 'You know, noblemen don't often make friends among churls.'

'They have trusted servants, men they trust with their lives.'

'But they're not friends. Not real friends. Edward finds it hard to be close with anyone.'

Willow looked at Edward with undisguised interest. 'Why do you say that?'

'You've seen how he looks up to his father. He secretly thinks the duke's shoes are going to be too hard for him to fill. He isn't confident he can do it. That's why he doesn't let people get close to him. In case they get to find out about the real Edward.'

Willow folded her arms. 'That's nonsense.'

'It's true.'

'Sir Edward's confident to a fault!'

'That's just what he wants people to think. He's trying to make something special of himself, but it's all just show.'

'That's how you get to be special, isn't it? By trying?' She tilted her head as she looked at him. 'I don't know why you're talking this way. You're not jealous, are you?'

He could not stop himself. 'I saw him give you his ring. Why did you take it?'

She looked at him for a while, then her anger showed. 'That was his signet, Will. He told me to take it to the scribe, because he needed to seal a letter. He couldn't be bothered to walk through the mud himself! Anyway, what's it got to do with you what he gives me?'

'Now, then! What's this? Hard words? Raised voices?

Squabbles, hey?' Gort came in and asked Willow if she would take a fresh charm to hang in the wine store. It was a harvest sigil, a token twisted out of ears of wheat and made up in the form of a vine leaf to stop the wine from spoiling. She took it, but Will followed her out into the innermost ward.

A terrible feeling, one that he had never felt before, gnawed at him. It was as persistent as hunger, only a thousand times worse. He looked up at the well-head and brewhouse and the high walls of the keep that seemed to lean in on him. He trailed Willow through a small door and down to the keep cellars where the wine was stored. A stout, barred entrance led off to the left and he knew at once it was a solitary cell in which a prisoner could be held in darkness. He heard a cry. An infant. Then a smothering feeling came over him, and he almost choked.

'This place . . .' he said. 'There's a baby in there!'

Straight away she went to look. But there was nothing living in the dank gloom except perhaps a rat.

'What did you say that for, Willand? There's no child in here.'

'But . . . I heard it crying.'

'I don't know what's ailing you, but I think you ought to see the Wortmaster about it. And soon.'

She finished placing the charm over the wine and stood back, hooking a wisp of hair over her ear. Then she made her way up the steps, annoyed that he was shadowing her. Eventually he let her go.

He watched moodily as she crossed the dark innermost ward. He was feeling even more unhappy now she had gone than he had before. He made a fist and hammered the wall until the side of his hand hurt. The movement attracted Edward and he came over.

'What goes?' he asked. 'Do you want to come to the armoury? I'll show you what we have here.'

'Go away!'

Edward stiffened, mystified by Will's sudden unprovoked rage. No one was permitted to speak to the duke's heir that way, least of all in his own castle. It required an immediate apology, but none was offered and their eyes met in a wordless challenge. Even so, Edward saw what was the better part of valour. He merely looked Will up and down, said, 'As you wish,' then nodded curtly and withdrew.

'What's happening to me?' Will asked the night air when Edward had gone. He put his hands to his temples and stared into the sky, shivering. 'The duke's brought it with us,' he whispered, shocked by his sudden revelation. 'By the moon and stars, I know what he's done! He's brought the Dragon Stone here!'

'Now then, Master Miseryguts!' Wortmaster Gort was down on hands and knees, busying himself like a great badger rooting through his disordered belongings in the pale light of dawn. He set down an armful of gear, looked up and said pleasantly. 'So how are you this fine morning?'

'I didn't sleep much last night,' Will said wearily. 'Do you have a draught for me? One that settles a person down?'

'Oh, yes, yes, yes. Plenty of draughts for anger.' Gort broke off the unpacking of a large mortar and pestle to examine his pouches. 'Draughts for lots of other things too. Melancholy, sloth and falling out of bed and – ah, and what's this?' He sniffed at it. 'Jealousy, or maybe envy. Hard to say. Both probably! Very popular at this time of year among the boys and girls.' He began to crawl under a table. 'Have you seen Osric? Hmmm?'

'No, but yesterday I saw Death again.'

The Wortmaster got up too quickly and bumped his head. 'Death? You mean . . .' He made a meaningless gesture. 'The . . . apparition? He's followed you here?'

Will nodded, unable to meet Gort's eye. 'It was standing

on the gatehouse. And I've been having nightmares again. I need something from your leech garden to calm me down. Please, Wortmaster.'

'Last night you were jumping around, frisky as a Cuckootide hare. Crossed words with Willow too, did you not? What was all that about?'

'Please, Wortmaster, no more questions.'

'You just go and soak your head in a pail of water then, and perhaps that will dampen your spirits, hey?'

'But I need a draught! I feel terrible.' He considered telling Gort his conclusions concerning the Dragon Stone. Instead, he said, 'Maybe it's the winter solstice approaching – I can feel something gnawing at my bones.'

'Well, I don't have a draught for gnawed bones or even for solstices.' When Gort looked at him his little piggy eyes were unsmiling. 'And, you know what? If I did have one I wouldn't give it to you. Grumpiness is most often its own cause and its own reward. Now you keep away from other folk in case what you've got is catching!'

'Stubborn old man!'

Will turned on his heel and slammed the door as he left, but he heeded Gort's advice. He spent the morning pilfering from the kitchens or up on the walls and towers, skulking around the jacks who wished he'd go away so they could get on with their crafty games of dice.

In the afternoon a dreary procession of Fellows led the marking of Ewletide's Eve. It was no jollier than the Ewle that Will had suffered at Foderingham. Three Sightless Ones came to the castle and walked about with lit tapers. There was a vigil and solemn rites, and good wishes expressed for the health of Grand High Warden Isnar, but it was a mirthless and numbing occasion. There was no laughing and no dancing, and all the songs were droning, melancholy chants. Afterwards there was a meagre breaking of dry bread, and then the ladies began to talk together across the table, and some moved away to plot the marriages of their daughters, while the lords began to gather at the other end of the Great Hall to sit about the fire with flagons of wine and slices of meat on their dagger points.

Will was sent to sit several places away from Edward, who was excluded from none of the lords' councils. He did as he was told, but knew he must guard his feelings with care. His brittleness went unnoticed as the lords debated their great matters above his head. But as he sat among the duke's blood relatives Will began to fear for himself. The madness that had blossomed inside his head like a hideous grey flower was growing beyond his power to control. It was a terrible urge to endure and nothing short of a dagger plunged into his own heart, it seemed, would save him.

He sweated, not daring to move. He did not know why, but the idea of stabbing himself had become as attractive as it usually was repugnant. He tried to fight back against the strange manner of thinking that was turning his thoughts against themselves. Was it something to do with the solstice? Or something to do with a solstice happening at new moon? Had the duke really brought the battlestone secretly out of bondage? Had he been fool enough to fetch it from Foderingham like some possession, like some prize?

Of course he has . . .

The duke thinks it can be his weapon. He thinks he can use it against his enemies. He doesn't understand that the holding and binding-spells that keep the harm from rushing out are geomantic and will only work properly in one place. Without those spells the stone will turn the mind of anyone and everyone.

Will felt his defences slipping. Opening wide. Being opened forcibly it seemed . . .

He warned himself that he was, even now, being chosen by the battlestone. He was to be its spokesman, its agent, its *weapon*. His special sensitivity had caused it to choose him. A plague on the wizard for having taken him away, for ever having turned on such a talent in his head!

But no! This is an honour . . .

He felt a sudden tremendous clarity of mind. The feeling was overpowering, exciting. He felt certainty bathe him like brilliance, and it seemed that he could see truths with crystal sharpness, vivid truths, bright and bold. His new sharpness enabled him to see the evidence that truths carried inside them. For the first time he could determine what was real and what was not. All his previous thoughts were shown to be mere confusion and doubt. They no longer made sense, for now he had seen the real truth. And he knew what he must do.

His eyes flickered to left and right. These lords and knights around him, drinking and laughing, they disputed over the smallest trifles, their minds were consumed by petty rivalries and the plotting of fruitless alliances. Things here were just as they had been at Clarendon. Here was Duke Richard, owner of six strong castles, and all the lands of the Dukedom of Ebor. Over there sat the Earl of Sarum, another man of vast wealth, whom thirty thousand men called lord. And there – his son, the Earl Warrewyk, still in his twenties yet richer even than his father if servants' gossip was to be believed, the richest man in the Realm, Warrewyk, Captain of the port of Callas across the Narrow Seas, and possessor of fabulous wealth that had come to him through marriage. Together these great magnates and their allies accounted for fully half the land that made up the Realm and five-ninths of its riches, yet here they were arguing over who should have the last leg of roast Ewletide swan, and questioning the quality of the wine. Was it not obvious what must be done?

Will reached forward and pulled the long knife from a haunch of mutton on the table before him. The blade seemed to glitter with deadly encouragement as he turned

it over in his hand. Light ran along its edge like the moonlight frosting a dead deserter's skull. Sweat seethed in Will's
scalp. He watched the noble sons listening avidly as their
fathers and uncles fell to debating the parts of the Realm
that might be added to their estates, how the lands confis-
cated from Duke Edgar and sundry other allies of the queen
would be divided up among themselves once the power
was theirs. They seemed to Will to be no better than a pack
of dogs, snatching bones back and forth. It seemed that
their lives had been swallowed up into a monstrous game
in which the fortunes of lordly families were all that
mattered, and in which fellow feeling and the common good
had no place at all.

Which of them can live in more than one castle at a
time? he asked himself, feeling anger boil over inside him.
Which of these earls can even stand straight under the
weight of all the furs and fine velvets he possesses? They
are all as bad as each another – except this duke who is
their foremost! He will not rest until he is pronounced king!
Such greed as his deserves to be repaid in steel!

Duke Richard turned to the windows as the great castle
clock began to strike the hour of midnight. The long carving-
knife with the plain wooden handle invited Will's hand. He
saw his fingers close on the handle. 'You will die!' he shouted,
rising. 'Die!'

'Die he must in time, but not at your hand, Willand.'

And Will felt his wrist caught in an invisible grip as a
familiar voice resounded in his head. The chimes of the
castle clock had ceased at the sixth strike. It was as if time
itself had stopped, for all was frozen.

Then Gwydion danced elegantly into the hall, his
gestures and words of magic crystallizing the air except
that which spun and twisted in colours about him. His
robes flowed and flew, blurring like flame, then all Will
could see was the wizard's unutterably mysterious smile.

349

The knife dropped slowly from his palm. The wizard laid a steadying hand on his shoulder, then everything came alive at once.

CHAPTER SEVENTEEN

IN THE HALL OF KING LUDD

The moment the duke saw Gwydion he rose to his feet and drew back like one who has seen a ghost. The other lords stared and muttered oaths, offended that their privacy had been so rudely invaded. Gasps and gestures of surprise came from the ladies at the far end of the hall, then a threatening quiet fell.

'Master Gwydion,' Duke Richard said, cutting the silence at last. He glanced from face to face before returning his gaze to the wizard. 'You gave no warning that you would come among us. May I ask how long you have been skulking here? And why you have seen fit to enter this place by magic when a simple knock at the door would have won you your usual welcome?'

Gwydion's expression was uncompromising. 'I did not come here seeking a welcome, Friend Richard. And you will forgive me if I have disturbed your conversation.'

'Tell us how long have you been sitting among us unannounced!' the Lord Warrewyk demanded angrily.

'Long enough to hear what you mean to do.' Gwydion raised his arms but then let them fall like one who is much wearied. 'After all the warnings I have given you, Richard, I find you here preparing for war.'

The duke's fists balled and the golden signet ring on his little finger glittered. 'War is our business! I was appointed Lord Protector of this Realm, not you! How dare you tell me what I may and may not do?'

The wizard drew a blazing forefinger through the air and left behind a hanging hoop of fire. Then he spoke to Edward, 'Lad, tell me: what is the best way to fight fire?'

'With fire,' Edward said straight away, though there was mistrust and perhaps even a little fear in his voice.

Gwydion spread his hands. 'Do you see? Do you see how this favourite firstborn son betrays his father's style?'

Now the wizard's arm made the motion of a serpent reaching forward to strike. Tongues of orange flame spewed from his palm. Fire engulfed the burning circle, which drew strength from the new flame and burned up all the brighter. The lords flinched back as the fire billowed out towards them. The fiery circle gave off a crackling noise now, a palpable heat, and thin black smoke that curled up into the dark timbers of the roof. These were not the paltry sorcerer's powder fireworks that Will remembered the conjurer Jarred producing in the hall at Clarendon. These were great, coloured tongues of flame, fires that seemed to make the shapes of living things, vital flames that writhed and fed upon themselves with a roaring intensity.

Gwydion held the hall spellbound with his flamecraft. Mighty as these lords were, they had no answer to his accusing finger as it wavered fire over them, nor to his compelling voice. 'I ask again: what is the best way to fight fire?'

The eyes of the lords were fast upon the flaming circle, and none dared to give an answer.

'Then you had better tell them, Willand!'

Will found himself standing up and saying, 'With a pail of water, Master Gwydion.'

'Indeed, lad!' All at once a pail appeared in Gwydion's

hands, and as the water was dashed from it the circle of fire was quenched. 'Indeed so! With a pail of water!'

The circle turned to vapour as water and pail both vanished away. The rich carpets that were laid over the flagged floor had not been wetted at all. Gwydion moved to stand beside Will and put a hand on his shoulder.

'You see, my friends? This lad knows.' He turned to the duke. 'Tread softly and go lightly upon the earth, Friend Richard. Be honest in your dealings. Conduct yourself nobly and champion justice. Do not lose sight of your chivalric promises, for if you do all your loyalty to one another, all your prowess in battle, all your indomitable courage will avail you nothing.' He turned. 'Come with me, Willand. We must take our leave, we have something important to attend to. And *Shail fadah hugat* to you all!'

The guards opened the doors as if falling back from a terrible curse, though Gwydion had merely wished a long life on those in the hall. Then they were out in the cold darkness and Will was exhilarated. He could feel Edward staring at him as if he had been betrayed by Will's leaving with the wizard. But it did not matter. It seemed as if a great weight had been lifted, for the madness had gone from him and his mind was clear again.

'Now tell me what has been ailing you,' Gwydion said as they crossed the inner ward.

'It's the Dragon Stone, Master Gwydion. It's been freed. I knew nothing about their plans to move it here, I swear! And I couldn't have stopped them even if I had.'

Gwydion turned on his heel. 'You are talking nonsense, lad. The Dragon Stone is safe in its coffin at Foderingham. I have just come from there.'

'But I felt its power last night. And again just now. That's what made me want to . . .' he looked around and lowered his voice '. . . want to kill the duke.'

'It was not the Dragon Stone that made you want to do that.'

Will stopped stock still. 'Then what?'

'A part of you wants it.'

'But I like the duke. And I respect him. And—'

'Do you? Do you really?' Gwydion turned a dark eye on him, then he placed a hand on each shoulder. 'Plainly, Willand, there must be another battlestone buried near here. One that is working on your unrealized weaknesses.'

Will felt the blood drain from him. 'Another battlestone . . .'

'I can see no other explanation. Can you?'

'But . . .' Will's eyes danced wildly from tower to tower and across the battlements. 'What about the journey? All the way here I felt something gnawing at me. If it wasn't the Dragon Stone hidden in one of the carts, where did that feeling come from?'

Gwydion smiled a secret smile. 'A most important rede of magic is this: "First, know thyself."'

What the wizard said seemed to make little sense. Will pushed the conundrum away impatiently. 'I do know myself.'

'Hah! You have been doing a lot of changing since last we met, Willand. For two shakes of a lamb's tail you have inhabited a man's body and already you are an expert on how it is with men, is that it?'

The wizard waited but Will made no argument. He could think of nothing to say. And what would be the point? It was a hopeless task arguing with wizards at the best of times – and this was far from being the best of times.

When Gwydion spoke again, he was more kindly, and in the subtle way he often showed he crept upon Will's concerns almost as if he had read his mind. 'You are stronger than you think. Let me tell you so for the sake of all our futures. Far stronger. You must begin to believe that.'

He forced a smile. 'Do you think so?'

'Oh, Willand. Ewle may be the darkest night, but it is also the most promising of times. Come! We should make merry! We have seen six months of the dying of the light, but tonight the light begins to return! Can you feel the sleeping spring? It is waiting green and furious inside every seed and root that lies cold in the earth? From this night the sun begins his journey back! Now isn't he worth a small celebration?'

A celebration! Sudden joy leapt up inside Will. It was good to be back in the wizard's company once more, so strange and powerful was he.

He stretched like a cat. 'Master Gwydion, I feel as if a great pain has been taken away.'

'Of course you do. The moment of solstice is past and the power subsides. The sun and the moon have now begun to move away from one another. Ewle is come!'

'But how can we celebrate? They don't know what Ewle is among the duke's household. Last year, at Foderingham, for all their wealth there was no dancing and no feasting. It was as dead as a door nail.'

'The lives these lords lead are killing them from the inside, and they are too blinkered to see it. They strive and connive, they rend and contend, but have you ever seen one of them dance? Agh! They cannot dance to save their lives!'

Will shuddered, thinking of Edward's narrowness of spirit. He reflected that a lord's wealth and power were all that he possessed. In their way they were as crippled as the Sightless Ones, and as impoverished as the poorest peasant. How foolish he felt now for having envied Edward his lot.

'You haven't changed a bit, Master Gwydion.'

The wizard gave him a penetrating look. 'But you have.'

He blushed at that, though he did not know why. 'I . . . I thought you'd put me among them so I could learn their ways,' he stammered. 'I thought you wanted me to become like them.'

The wizard snorted. 'You? When does any of them feel the good earth between his toes? They ride often and walk seldom. And when they do walk it is on stone-laid paths with their feet cased in great spurred boots. They look for the harm in others before they look for kindnesses. They enslave with chains of silver and gold just as binding as the manacles of iron that the Slavers of old used. And they try to chop time into pieces with their foolish machines. You cannot measure all there is in the world against gold when the veriest fool knows in his heart that anything worth the having cannot be so measured. I hoped you would learn a lesson or two of this kind at the lordly hearth, Willand. Perhaps you have.'

Will's head was in a whirl now. 'But doesn't a lord have to behave that way? Someone has to impose order.'

Gwydion spread his hands. 'Does order come from men imposing their wills upon others? Every time a man surrenders his true self, Will, there is born a new problem into the world. I would that the hearts of our great men may one day be renewed with a saner sort of courage than they possess at present, but until that time comes I fear that talking to lords is like talking to tree stumps.'

As they reached Will's quarters a shrouded figure moved in the shadows, shocking him as it emerged. He started, and a gasp escaped him.

Gwydion gripped his arm. 'What is it you fear, lad?'

'Evil.'

'Evil? But this is your best friend.'

Gwydion mustered a magical light on his fingertip and raised it. It burned with a pale and vivid glow that picked out a tress of pale hair and cast a bluish luminance onto a face that was as pretty as a March marigold but one that was full of concern.

'Will? Are you all right?'

Relief flooded through him as he heard the kindness in the question. 'Master Gwydion,' he said, 'this is . . . Willow.'

'It seems you startled my young friend. Well met! I have heard Willand speak nobly of you.'

Willow was beautiful in the elfin light.

'Well met, Master Gwydion,' she murmured. 'If you are truly a wizard, and if you love your apprentice, then I ask you to heal his mind, for he's been unwell of late, and I fear he may do himself a mischief if he's not helped soon.'

Gwydion turned to Will. 'I see you still have one friend left to you despite your efforts to upset all those around you. I have already spoken with Gort, and he has told me much about you that I had not noticed. I am happy to say there is no need for healing, but a warning or two may well be heeded with profit. In the meantime I see two spirits in need of winter sunshine, and since this should be a time of renewal and there are too many Fellows infesting this place for my liking, I shall show you how the Ewle ought to be celebrated! But first—' He strode briskly to the door and struck it wide with his staff. 'We must leave this bleak fortress if we would see a real Ewletide, for only the churlish folk are still so much themselves in this land that they can fully feel what is there to be felt and clearly see what is there to be seen. It's a blessed truth that while the people's spirit remains hale and untrammelled there can be no final victory for those who would take away all freedom!'

They went out of the castle and down into the town. Will wanted to tell Gwydion much and to ask him countless questions, but the wizard strode on out of the castle. They passed a cage of lions at the gate. Four real, live lions pacing like sentinels, caged near the town well, so that all in Ludford who came to draw water might see them. Will stared at them, wondering how he had missed seeing them when he had first arrived.

'They were a gift to the duke,' Gwydion said. 'They came from an eastern merchant who traded across the Narrow Seas at Callas. Friend Richard meant to give these beasts to the king to put in his menagerie at Trinovant, but somehow the gesture was never made.'

'You mean because lions are a royal symbol?' Will asked. 'Because such a gift would be taken by some as an acceptance of King Hal's kingship, and a sign that Duke Richard was denying his own claim?'

'That is very perceptive of you, Willand. You have come on nicely since last we met.'

'I've been attentive to my lessons, Master Gwydion.'

Willow sighed. 'Don't those cats look unhappy? Poor creatures, locked up in a cage in this cold weather.'

Gwydion put his mouth close to Will's ear. 'You have often asked what evil is. Look at your friend, Willow, and see what it is not.'

'I know she's a gentle person, and kind,' he whispered back. 'Though she's also strong, if you see my meaning.'

'The closest description of evil I have ever found is that it is a lack of fellow feeling. No more, no less.'

'Fellow feeling?' Will asked. 'What's that?'

'The ability of one spirit to sing with another, be it man's or beast's.' The wizard looked at his perplexity and laughed. 'Fear not, lad, for though you say you do not know the words for it, your spirit sings as well as any I have heard. Come, we shall let it sing out loud tonight!'

They hurried on, down past the monument of the Sightless Ones. It was dusted with new-fallen snow and seemed somehow less immoveable than it had been before. The night air was very cold and the ground iron-hard underfoot. Candles burned in niches just inside the entrance of the chapter house. The smell that came from it was greasy and thick. A hooded, sandaled Fellow guarded the door. He seemed neither to feel the cold nor to heed their passing, though breath steamed from his cowl.

'He is the spider ready to welcome flies into the web,' Gwydion said. 'The bereaved, the needy, those of troubled mind – all such he seeks, for when the spirits of folk burn low and they are overcome by the three weaknesses, it is then that they are most easily persuaded to surrender themselves to the mind-slavery of the Great Lie. But tonight, I think, this spider will not gather a single fly from Ludford town.'

They crossed the dark and icy square. Snow swirled as it fell and when Will turned to look again he saw the lights that had earlier burned around the monument of the chapter house had all blown out.

'Ewle, when the sun begins her return! Ewle, the day of Alban Artain! See the snow on yonder holly wreaths! The green, the red and the white! Those are the true colours of Ewle. Once the folk hereabouts roasted a pig in memory of Arduinna's boar, and the warriors sang,

> *'Sacrifice the Ewle boar!*
> *Pour his blood to east and west!*
> *Roast him by the fire of the Ewle log!*
> *Serve him whole with an apple in his mouth!'*

'That doesn't rhyme,' Willow said, grinning. 'It doesn't sound right at all.'

Gwydion looked askance. 'Of course, it's a translation. And it was written by warriors.'

'So, what if it was?'

Gwydion raised an eyebrow. 'Well! Have you ever seen how poets *fight*?'

Tonight, all the houses were deep in darkness, but in the burgesses' hall there shone a golden light. As they approached they heard the sound of merriment – drums and the bleating of pipes. There were long benches and plenty of good things to eat and drink and hundreds of people of all ages and sizes dancing about in a frenzy. The whole gathering was bathed in a glorious firelight of rich, buttery yellow. But when they stepped inside the music stopped and the dancers turned to see who was letting in the cold night air.

'Call forth the ushers!' went the cry.

Men came forward to enquire who had entered uninvited, and to see if they expected a welcome.

'Friend or foe?' they called.

'We three come to share your feast!' cried Gwydion. 'Will you let us in, though we be empty-handed?'

'Take them to Mother Brig!' came the cry. 'Let Mother Brig decide!'

Folk gathered round to stare at the newcomers, then without another word an aisle opened for them to walk down. Nothing moved except the flames of the great rejoicing fire at the end of the hall and, running in a wheel-shaped cage, a dog, its tongue lolling, driving round a shaft on which a pig was spitted. A boy wearing a tall hat and a ladle stood ready to baste the pig in its own juices.

The ushermen marched Gwydion and his companions to an ancient crone who was sitting in a corner away from the bagpipers. A large black raven stood on the left of her chair back. Beside the crone were two young girls in festive dress sitting by a spinning-wheel. Will rubbed his eyes in wonder for they were identical in every way. He watched how they looked Willow up and down with interest. The centres of the crone's eyes were as pale as milk, and Will thought that maybe tonight the girls were the crone's eyes.

'The boar, the tree, the wheel and the raven!' Gwydion said. 'Ah, all is well here!'

'Twrch Trywth!' said the raven.

'Ah, Twrch Trywth,' repeated the crone, 'who some called Torc Triath, the king who was turned into a boar! He who was chased by Great Arthur and plunged into the sea rather than be taken. How good it is to hear your voice again, Master Gwydion!'

'Friend or foe? Friend or foe?' the ushers shouted out.

'He's as true a friend as ever I've had need of,' the crone scolded them.

'Then he's welcome!' said the ushermen, leaving them.

'Come sit by me in the place of honour,' the crone said. 'Rufus! Bring wine and bread!'

The chief of the ushers, a hunch-back dressed in black, clapped his hands three times. A beardless lad brought out horn cups for them and knives that they might have what they wished at the board. Stools were brought, then drums and brisk pipes struck up and wild dancing began again. The crone reached out faltering hands to touch the face of the wizard, and to grasp the charms she found on a cord about his throat. She began reading the design embossed there with her fingertips.

'The tall ailm is hard to find these days, Master Phantarch.'

'That is so, good lady, but his fire is true. And you are as beautiful as ever you were.'

'To some, Master Phantarch!' She smiled a coy, tooth-less smile. 'Only to some. Answer me this before you eat: would you rather have half a loaf with my blessing, or the whole of it with my curse?'

'Dear Brighid,' said Gwydion, laughing. 'Why do you ask? You know I would not have your curse if all the world came with it.'

'Then eat what you will at Ludd's board with a thou-sand blessings of my own upon you! And perhaps later you will favour me with the presence of the one who must hear his fate.'

'Ah, Brighid, seer you were, and seer you remain! But we must interfere only with care. I know little of the part he is to play in coming events, except that pitiful portion which was revealed by the Book. Take care therefore that the words you utter do not influence his choices unduly.'

'You should know, Master Phantarch, that the words of a seer are only ever offered whole. Others do the taking and the choosing. Advice is your business.'

'What are they talking about?' Willow whispered, awed by the strangeness of it all.

'I don't know,' Will said. 'But whatever it is, you can be sure there're more meanings than one in it. That's always the way when Gwydion speaks.'

'Wortmaster Gort told me that "ailm" is the old, secret name for the silver fir,' Willow whispered. 'He said it's the tree that traps winter sunshine. That's why it's best to make into a Ewle log because it yields the truest Ewle flame.'

Will pointed to the corner. 'See how the top of the Ewle tree has been lopped off. It stands there like a little tree of its own.'

Will hoped that, as at home, chippings of the Ewle log would be kept by the village girls. In the Vale the girls guarded them the year round, so that next year's Ewle log could be lit from them. It was the task of the village boys to scatter the ashes of the Ewlefire around the houses as charms against their burning down. Tonight, everyone would try not to look at the shadows cast on the walls by the Ewle log, for it was well known that if the light of it threw up a headless shadow that person was doomed to die in the coming year.

Thinking of the Vale made Will remember Eldmar and Breona and the good times they had always enjoyed at Ewletide. But then he thought of what they would be doing now, and he knew they would be thinking of him. That linked all three with a bond as strong as any magic that Gwydion could make, as strong as that linking any other family. He took out the leaping salmon talisman that had always hung about his neck. The red eye seemed to look at him approvingly, and he squeezed the little fish in his hand and felt himself flood with good feeling.

Tonight all the folk of Ludford who still followed the Old Ways had come together to eat and drink and be wrapped in music and happiness. It felt like a great privilege to have been welcomed among them.

'Who is this?' the crone said, her fingers reaching out to Will. Her eyes, milky as pearls, still sparkled, and for a moment he saw her as once she must have been, a rare beauty, for she looked much like the two sisters who stood with her. So strong a resemblance did they bear that he knew they must be her great-grandkin.

'But you are not the one who must hear his fate tonight,' she said, sitting back.

'What's that you say?' Gwydion stroked his beard, thinking her oddly in error. 'This time your second sight has failed, for this one is surely the maker of fate.'

'Ha!' The crone threw her hands wide as if basking in the radiance of a warm fire. The twin girls who stood to each side gazed at him. 'Let him approach, then.'

'My name is Willand, my lady,' he said, bowing.

'Ah, a respectful lad! And respect to you likewise, Willand!' She cackled, then swayed and said, 'I like his manners, but he wrestles with the viper of jealousy. That is the way of young men when young women are worthy.

> 'Will the dark,
> Will the light,
> Will his brother left and right?

> 'Will take cover,
> Will take fright,
> Will his brother stand and fight?'

Will listened politely and wanted to ask if the ditty might be an omen, but he decided not to, for some omens were better not looked into. Instead the moment passed, and though he looked for Gwydion he could not for the time being find any sign of him. Then he and Willow were invited to join the dance, and that they did with gusto, laughing and whirling around the hall with all the others.

When the midnight hour came it was unmarked by any strike of the curfew bell. On the people danced, faster and faster, until Will was fit to drop. But then the crone gave a sign to her barker, a big man with a musical voice who called for silence and sang out:

'Enter now, lord of the dark year!'

And in came the Holly King, an old man decked about with prickly leaves and a great ball of mistletoe tied before him. He carried with him in one hand a rusty sickle and in the other a small birdcage, in which a tiny bird was kept.

> *'A wren, a wren!*
> *The King of all birds!*
> *On King Strefon's day flying,*
> *Was caught in the furze!'*

The crone gave her sign and the barker shouted: 'Enter now, the lord of the year of light!'

And now the Oak King, a beardless youth, came forth, girt in dark green with a wreath of twigs and dried oak leaves. He carried a golden sickle, which Will saw was no more than a thatcher's hook painted yellow. The twin girls accompanied him, throwing acorns all about and sang:

> *'By rush and reed,*
> *By lead and by tar!*
> *I'll break the knuckles*
> *Of the Kelog Var!'*

Two sickles clashed, clang, clang, and two kings danced face to face then back to back around and around. Will understood it all, for the 'tussle of the years' was much the same in Nether Norton, though the words were different and the dances not at all the same.

At last the Holly King called out: 'Oh! Oh! Oh! Now I am done to death!'

And hunch-backed Rufus, to whom the greatest honour fell, cut off the mistletoe. It was caught in a white cloth by the two young girls who now stood to either side. They carried it carefully, making sure that no part of it touched the ground. And after that there was the splendid entry of King Ludd into the hall. And what a king he was, dressed as a great warrior of olden times with a golden torc and a bronze helm with a fearsome mask, a round shield and a coat of many rings. He lifted a sword shaped like a long leaf that looked like the one that had lain beside the figure of Leir.

'See, Willand!' the crone whispered. 'He has come from the city, down from the Great Gate of Trinovant, where still he watches over all who dwell in that city. He has come from the place where he lies all year round to be among those who are yet true to his memory.'

'Is it really him?' Will marvelled.

'Do you doubt it?'

And it seemed to Will for a moment that this was no townsman done up to look like a king of old, but the king himself. But when Will looked to Gwydion to see how seriously he should take the kingly figure, the wizard was nowhere to be seen. Then the door burst open and there was a commotion. A cry of astonishment went up and the townsfolk fell back. Those around Will got to their feet, staring in disbelief, for Gwydion had entered the hall anew. Nor was he alone, for he came forward, leading another, and Will saw with equal amazement that it was Duke

Richard. The lord was barefoot and dressed only in a plain nightgown, his hands tied before him with rope and a halter loose about his neck. The duke stared around him like a man lost in a trance, and the gathering fell silent as he was led before them. 'Good Mother Brig,' Gwydion said, his long face stern. 'Here is the one of which I spoke. He is come from his bed to be among us. Will you give him entry?'

'Twrch Trywth!' said the raven.

'So here is the one who must hear his fate!'

Everyone caught their breath. Such a thing was unheard of, and many thought it an intrusion and a great error to have brought any lord here, especially this one. They all looked to King Ludd, but the great figure made no royal pronouncement. He merely stood with his huge arms folded across his chest and so the crone proceeded.

She waited for the whisperings to die down, and for Gwydion to cause the duke to kneel before her. Then the twin girls spoke eerily. 'Are ye of good faith, Richard of Ebor?' they asked in unison.

The duke's eyes rolled unseeingly in his skull, and he murmured to the rafters, 'I am as honest a man as I may be.'

'Then tell me what you see before you?'

His eyes opened. 'I see three young sisters, speaking as one.'

Then the twins said, 'Three sisters says he. And what of the middle sister? Is she beautiful to your eye?'

'She is the fairest of them all.'

There was a gasp of approval among those who watched, and a rumour went round as if great consequence was to be expected of this answer.

'That is enough!' the crone said, raising her hand. 'Now mark my words, Richard of Ebor, for I do declare that I am Sovereignty. Regarding the matter of the enchanted

366

chair: you will die in the first fight that follows should ever you dare to lay your hand upon it. Do you take what I have told you as a truth?'

'I have heard you.'

'If you would know the future then look to your shadow upon the wall. But be warned! Not all prophecies comfort those who seek after them.'

The duke's eyes rolled in dream again, but this time he seemed to see the several shadows dancing across the white plaster. 'Mine,' he said haltingly, 'is . . . the . . . right!'

'Then go from here with all your strength and a thousand blessings upon you.' Mother Brig's voice echoed from the girls' mouths. 'But you had better hope with all your might and main that understanding comes to you before death does.'

Will sat quietly with Willow as Gwydion, grim-faced now, led the duke out of the hall. Will wished he had understood even a seventh part of what had happened tonight, for it seemed greatly important. But then the doors banged shut, and Gwydion and Duke Richard were gone. Slowly the people fell to talking and then the music struck up again and soon there was dancing and laughing again as if the duke's visit had never been.

Will looked at Willow and he saw how fair she was of face, and the more he looked the fairer she seemed to him. She looked long at him likewise, and though a glow burned in her cheeks she would not turn away from his gaze. At last he took her hands, then drew her to him. He put his arms around her and kissed her on the lips, and her taste was far sweeter than any wine.

After that the dancing took them again and they danced all night for it seemed that a spell was upon them and they could not sit down while it held sway over them.

Will awoke the next day with a heavy head but a light heart. The terrible mood that had been affecting him had vanished away with the Ewletide. The day dawned cold, and sunrise blazed in the sky as the world came reluctantly alive again. When he looked outside he saw that everything lay under a thick blanket of snow. In the outer ward the horses that usually watched the comings and goings with interest had retired inside their stalls and the poultry looked around, amazed at the deep whiteness that had appeared.

Will trod a path through the virgin whiteness. The snow was knee-deep and dangerous on the battlements, but he climbed up to see what wonderful view would be revealed. And wonderful it was – the fields were quilted in white, stitched together by black lines of hedgerows. All the lanes were filled and drifts had piled up, burying fences and ditches and gates and making the whole land seem as if it had been wrapped in white fur. He pitied any army that tried to march in the next few days, and he wondered if Gwydion might not have gone out upon a peak somewhere in the small hours and tampered with the night airs to make time for the duke to think again.

Out there like an ominous shoulder loomed the dark Forest of Morte rising to the south-west. A broad, flat vista spread away to the south-east. Fields made another patchwork to the north, and a solitary high peak called the Giant's Chair dominated the east. In the opposite direction, sunk in the western darkness where many rivers rose, there stretched a land of frosty hills, a wild, unconquerable land that could swallow up whole armies in its mists. The castle of Ludford had been raised here by the heirs of the Conqueror to guard against the ancient magics that even now prowled the princedoms of Cambray. That was why Ludford's lords had always been called 'marcher lords' for they protected the Marches, or borders, of what was a still-dangerous land.

Will took a moment to breathe deeply and take in the beauty that had come into the world, but then hunger got the better of him and he went down and breakfasted on fried leftovers before Gwydion found him. Together they went to the Round House, a free-standing tower in the inner ward that served as the duke's place of work, and where visitors were received.

Guards flanked the entrance, which was a beautifully carved and pillared arch. Inside, the chamber was richly decorated and bedraped. The heads of the Twelve Austere Queens looked down as if in judgment on the business transacted here. The duke was sitting at his offices, courteous and cool of manner, but looking like a man who lacked sleep. He dismissed his secretary and scribes with a gesture, and when the door was closed he said, 'I've told you, Master Gwydion, that I'm happy to leave matters of magic to you. But you must leave matters of state to me. Your gift to the queen, and what it may signify, remains at the root of my displeasure with you.'

'That is not what you imagine.'

'It was a bribe! Offered without my sanction! Intended to win for me the Protectorship of the Realm! You may have meant well by it, but it was unwarranted interference.'

Gwydion faced the duke's anger calmly. 'Friend Richard, see how the eyes of the Twelve Austere Queens look down upon you. Have you forgotten why your father, Richard de Coneyburgh, set these dozen effigies here in his Round House? It was to remind those who make important choices to consider twelve times, as a woman does. Do you not have the courage to change your mind even once?'

The duke sighed, tense, curbing his annoyance. He began to toy with an ivory rod that Will recognized. 'I thank you for your counsel, but I regret that my decision has been made and cannot now be unmade.'

'How then if I tell you that there is already a prophecy on the head of Duke Edgar?'

The duke's eyes came alive, and his grip on the ivory rod tightened. 'Edgar of Mells? What prophecy?'

'I told him that he must "beware castles on pain of death".'

Duke Richard stared hard at the wizard. He put down the rod and instead began twisting his signet ring on his finger. 'And what is the meaning of it?'

'Folk must make of prophecies what they will.'

The duke's shortness of temper showed again, though this time it seemed more prompted by worry. 'I tell you, I care not for prophecies. So many of them are falsehoods, deliberately invented to confound good decisions. Neither do I set store by rumours or prophetic dreams.'

'Dreams?' Gwydion leaned close in on the duke. 'Did you, by any chance, dream last night?'

Will recalled Mother Brig's curious words about Duke Richard dying if he touched an enchanted chair – had the old woman sworn a destiny upon him? He looked at the way the duke's hands gripped the carved lions' heads of his seat, and wondered again about the ivory rod. It was undoubtedly the unicorn horn that Edward had once purloined.

The duke broke away from Gwydion's stare, and made an attempt to sound reasonable. 'Master Gwydion, I do not want you to tell the meaning of my dreams. I called you here to try to make you understand that my decision is made fast, that you must not interfere any more, or our friendship will reach an unsatisfactory conclusion.'

'How like your great grandfather you can be,' Gwydion said softly, but he continued to look hard at the duke, and then he nodded slowly. 'If your decision is made, then so be it. But regarding my quest, a grant of men and silver and a ship to carry a stone from the Blessed Isle. Men and silver to help in the guarding of the other battlestones that must be found and lifted – will you afford me such help as I may need?'

A pale smile passed over the duke's face. 'It was a pretty trick of fire you played before us all last night. With such magic at your command what need have you of ships and companies of men? And it is strange to hear you speak of purses of silver.'

Gwydion gestured the remark away testily. 'It is a rede of magic that "Magic helpeth those who have already sought to help themselves." Others will speak of the importance of free will, the impulse of charity, the origination and offering of ideas, that which may be offered in openness and honesty. But it is in the nature of magic that *giving is receiving*. Do you see?'

The duke rolled his eyes. 'All this is high and arcane science – your concern and not mine. I am a practical man. Now, you see my reluctance to tread in your domain, Crowmaster, so why not do as I do, and leave statecraft to me?'

'Richard, there are some tasks for which my own skills may not easily serve. I do not ask favours lightly – I cannot sail stones across the Grey Sea without help. A small gift from you would aid me in secret work that may yet avert disaster.'

'Oh, this is nought but beggary, and tiresome beggary at that!'

'I have told you I must root up the stones before it is too late.'

'You are reported to be a wise man, Master Gwydion,' the duke said distantly. 'Perhaps that's why your requests seem so strange to ordinary men. But I sometimes wonder if, in memory of the friendship you had with my father, I don't indulge you rather too much. You warn that war is coming, but in that event I too will be hard pressed for men and silver.' His fingers drummed on the arm of his chair. 'However, if you were to offer some compensating protection to me—'

'Richard, do not try to bargain with magic.'

'Surely one favour deserveth another, does it not?'

'And do not quote the redes wryly at me! Magic is never for sale, and never for negotiation – you know that. You cannot buy advantage with it. Magic must always be requested never summoned, always respected and never treated with disdain. Ask openly, ask honestly – for honest men alone have the right to speak words of power.'

The duke's face froze. 'Now you are being unreasonable.'

'Am I? Because I see so easily through your wiles?'

'But "battlestones", Master Gwydion?' The duke shook his head. 'How can I tell a common soldier that he must follow me unto death because the comrades who should have been protecting our flank were, by my order, sent off to grub up magic stones in some far distant part of the Realm?'

'Your soldiers will follow you anywhere. Of that I am quite sure.'

The duke accepted the compliment graciously. 'But if there were to be a general spell of protection set upon the arms of Ebor—'

'Richard! Think what you are saying! You are asking for sorcery. And woe shall betide those, even in the greatest distress, who look to a sorcerer's embrace for advantage. They shall find only misery there!'

Will saw the difference between wizard and duke widen. Gwydion came forward and seized the other's hand, but the duke stubbornly took his hand away. 'Master Gwydion, you have received my answer thrice already. Do not press me!'

Gwydion rose, stepped back, gathered himself with formal dignity. His face betrayed no wrath at the foolish ways of men. 'Richard, my old friend, I must take my leave of you. The tide has today begun to turn against your cause.

As for the Dragon Stone, I will arrange to have it removed from Foderingham as soon as may be. Meanwhile examine every motive that invites you to battle, for such invitations will not be all they may seem. *Shail fadah hugat* to you.'

Will followed as Gwydion turned to leave. When they emerged from the Round House the whiteness of the snow brought a sudden hurt to Will's eyes. Mention of the Dragon Stone had set old fears a-jangling, and he wondered if he should try to tell Gwydion about what had happened on the night that Edmund's hand had been burned, but now did not seem to be exactly the right moment.

'"I was appointed Lord Protector of this Realm, not you . . ."' Gwydion said, wearily repeating the words Duke Richard had used. 'And now he resents having been put into the Protectorship by me. What's to be done with him?'

'Did you see what the duke had in his hand?' Will asked. 'What?'

'The duke – he had a piece of unicorn's horn.'

Gwydion turned, reluctant to be jogged from his thoughts by Will's unconnected concerns. 'Not so. I would have felt it if there had been a piece of unicorn horn present.'

'But the duke had it in his hand. It was—' He broke off, seeing the trap he was setting for himself. This was not the best time to begin making admissions. He decided to leave Gwydion's ill humour to settle. Instead he asked, 'Did you really give King Leir's diamond to the queen?'

'Leir's diamond?' The wizard turned, suddenly interested, suddenly intense. 'Oh, that was never Leir's. It was only buried with him. Did I not tell you about it, that diamond of Great Arthur's?'

'Yes, you did,' Will said, unable for the moment to untangle quite what he knew from what he thought he might have imagined. 'You said . . . you said it was long ago brought out by Great Arthur from the Realm Below. You said the Star came from a chamber that lies deep under the earth. A place called Annuin where all the Hallows lay until Arthur stormed the fortress of Caer Rigor. He and Taliesin and his heroes sailed there aboard the ship, *Prydwen*, and fetched the Hallows away, though only seven returned alive . . .'

A curious half-smile was on the wizard's mouth. 'Did I tell you all that?'

'You must have,' Will said, his shoulders falling. 'Or how else could I have known it?'

'How indeed.' The wizard stirred. 'Perhaps you learned it from one of those twisted tales they tell down at the Green Man.'

'Yes,' he muttered. 'That must be it.'

'But to answer your question about the Star of Annuin: I gave it to the queen, for I know very well that she covets large and pretty jewels for their own sake. She knows not what it truly signifies, nor why I have made a gift of it to her.'

'But why did you give it to such a calculating vixen? That's what Duke Richard can't understand, and neither can I.'

'Oh, spoken like a true son of the tribe of Ebor! Be careful, Willand. Be careful what you're turning into.'

'Don't say that, Master Gwydion. I'm not one of them, really I'm not. And while we're about it you still haven't answered my question.'

The wizard sniffed at Will's insistence. 'You are growing up quicker than I thought. I gave the diamond for a reason that cannot yet be spoken about – and most weakening to me it was to give, I might tell you!'

'And how do you expect Duke Richard to understand your schemes, if you won't speak of them?'

'I dare not speak of some matters. A little faith is all I ask of Friend Richard. Long and patient has been my diplomacy on his behalf, but because he does not understand the whole of my purpose – nor the reasons behind what I do for him – he takes easy umbrage.'

'Maybe there's more to Duke Richard's troubles than you allow,' Will said, going after the wizard.

Gwydion's cloak swirled as he turned. 'Indeed?'

'It's just that I saw the figure of Death walking in the Garden of the White Rose on two occasions while you were away, Master Gwydion. And I've seen it again here. What do you think it portends?'

'Gort told me you had been seeing apparitions.' The wizard's eyes showed concern as he examined Will carefully. 'Gort puts what you saw at Foderingham down to leakage from the Dragon Stone, and whatever you may see here down to that which lies in the ground hereabouts. I am not so sure he is wholly right. I might say that matters concerning you have begun to make a deal more sense to me of late.'

The old fear seized him. 'Matters, Master Gwydion?'

The wizard's breath steamed in the cold air. His face was frozen as he looked into Will's eyes. 'Gort tells me many things. Do you know what premonitions are, hmm?'

'Yes. They're portents of the future.'

'Indeed they are. Warnings. Do you know why it is that you fear a portcullis will fall on you and kill you?'

The unexpected question floored him. 'No . . .'

'Did you never think that perhaps one day such a thing would actually happen to you? That your fear of portcullises comes of a special kind of knowledge of happenings received by you ahead of time?'

'You mean . . . foreknowledge?'

'Something of the sort. It is thought that this is the main cause of premonitions – your future self is speaking a warning to you back across the barriers of time.'

'Is that how I'm to die?' Will asked, horrified. 'Chopped in two by a portcullis?'

'Chopped in two?' Gwydion raised his eyebrows then said lightly, 'What more would you have me say to you about it? It is your premonition.'

The knowledge made Will stare at the slushy ground. 'But I can't believe that . . . oh, no!'

'Why can't you believe it? Have you perhaps planned a more glorious end for yourself?' Gwydion seized his shoulder. 'You may think Gort is an old fool, Willand, but he is not. Quite the opposite. I came here because he told me you had to be taken away. There is something here at Ludford that you cannot abide and you must go from here.'

'Do you mean the battlestone that's buried nearby?'

'That perhaps . . . but more. You saw my diplomacy with Richard fail. All my strategies for peace are collapsing. Ludford is not fruitful ground for us. Something is weakening my influence here, something I do not yet fully understand, but I do know that it involves you mightily.'

'And what if I don't want it to involve me!'

The wizard's eyes were suddenly glowing coals. 'It hardly matters what you want. Here your sanity has been fluttering like silk in a gale. All your failings are magnified as by a glass. You have been carried along by the dread currents that are blowing through the house of Ebor, and it is now too dangerous for you to remain among them. Mother Brig can read little enough of your future, but she says that one day you will return here, and the knowledge you have gained of the powers that collide in this place will change the way the past is chosen and fixed from all the manifold futures.'

He swallowed, unnerved now. 'Master Gwydion, who is Mother Brig? What did she say about me?'

'Brighid the High Queen of Imbletide! Called by the Slavers, "Brigantia". She is a seer.'

That did not satisfy. 'But she's surely more than just a seer.'

Gwydion looked at him suddenly as a man regards a dog that had learned a clever new trick. 'More than just a seer, he says. You heard her speak it out plainly what she is.'

'If I did, then I don't remember.'

'Then you should have attended more closely, for she declared herself in an important way. She is Sovereignty. She is seen by one and all as an aged crone, except by the man who would be king – and he sees her as a fair young maiden. But as for you, Willand, she says that one day history will turn on your actions here in this place, but that for the moment you should leave Ludford and leave it right away.'

They had reached the gates that led to the outer ward and Will halted as they opened. 'Leave? What? Right now? But . . . I can't just leave,' he said numbly.

Gwydion's expression was dark and haunted. 'War is a terrible business, Willand. Every battlestone unearthed and dealt with will be a calamity averted. Many thousands of lives can still be saved. Come with me and we shall look for them together.'

Will swallowed dryly. His head swam. 'But I can't come with you just like that. What about . . . Willow?'

Gwydion's eyes flickered. 'You must make your choice.'

'But don't you see? Willow's part of the true path, the destiny you're always talking about. It couldn't have been a coincidence that she just turned up at Foderingham. She must be part of the greater pattern. We're meant to be together. Don't you see that?'

The wizard shook his head. 'You speak of destiny as if you understand it, but you do not. One day you will grasp its coils and they will grasp you, but not for a while yet.'

He stiffened. 'Master Gwydion, I'm not coming with you this time.'

'Are you certain about that?' The wizard directed his glance upward.

Will followed his glance, saw the iron-shod teeth of the portcullis hanging above him, and as he stepped smartly out from under them he felt his resolve waver. 'But I can't leave Willow . . .'

The wizard's words resumed their understanding tone. 'With Edward showing such an interest in her?'

Will bowed his head, feeling nothing but agony now. Duty warred with desire inside him. He had not promised himself to any wild goose chase this time. The desire he felt for Willow was real, and thwarting it was painful. 'I'm sorry, Master Gwydion . . . I can't come with you.'

'So be it.'

The wizard turned and walked away, looking to Will like nothing so much as a stubborn old man trudging through the winter white and bent on a fool's mission.

What am I supposed to do? he asked Gwydion silently. Wander around barefoot in the tracks of a madman?

'May the frozen ground break asunder and swallow you up, Master Gwydion,' he whispered bitterly. But it was no good. The more he watched the wizard's back the more his decision rang hollow. By choosing selfishness he would allow fear and desire to shape his destiny instead of taking command of himself in the way he knew he ought.

'If you truly believe it'll save one life!' he shouted.

Gwydion stopped. He turned and let his staff fall and held out his hand so that he could clasp Will when he ran to him. There was nothing but gratitude now in the wizard's face. 'I knew I was right about you. We may triumph yet in our perilous quest, you and I, Willand!'

But though he cried with the wizard's joy, he also felt

the pain of his own sacrifice. 'You must give me a moment to be alone with Willow,' he said, tearing off his shoes in readiness to go barefoot once more. 'She deserves to know.'

PART FOUR

WILL'S TEST

CHAPTER EIGHTEEN

□ □ □

THE PLAGUESTONE

Winter slowly released the Realm from its icy claw as Will and Gwydion went in search of the battlestones. The crocuses came, opening saffron yellow, then the buds of the trees, swollen to bursting, began to unfold delicate green leaves, and it seemed to Will that the world lay before him like a land of dreams. In the afternoons the sun and rain together made sky-bows of brilliant iridescence that overspread their wanderings. The yelping of vixens made the nights eerie and the smell of fox laced the moist woods, but the rainy days lengthened and grew warmer, and soon the night frosts stopped altogether.

Will put two braids in his hair once more, made himself a wayfarer's staff out of an oak sapling and tried to feel pleased to be free of the world of heavy crowns and high castles. Here he was again, walking the land in the company of a wizard, and that was something very few folk ever got to do. Yet for all his enthusiasm, he had to admit that he had come to enjoy many of the comforts of the Duke of Ebor's household, and one overriding regret continued to gnaw at him.

Willow had accepted his decision with an understanding that made him want to hug her and never let her go. Instead they had exchanged a promise, he had clutched her to him in one last forlorn embrace, then she had watched him leave with tears in her eyes.

He had turned back many times, had seen her waving from the walls until they passed out of sight. And there had been little to compare with how that had made his heart feel. Even the memory of it had the power to plunge him into a sighing mood.

Now, after many sleepless nights setting his body against the cold, he had begun to learn how to mend his ragged feelings and to understand the power of wild ways. Gwydion showed him how to send a comforting warmth coursing through his flesh, so that even when a gale of sleet was blowing his body could roar with a dry heat within the tent of his cloak like an owl inside its jacket of feathers. Thawing the ice in his heart had been a harder matter though, and only passing time and training up his powers of forgetting were able to lessen the ache.

One evening, when the light was dying, Will looked away from the fire and said, 'I sometimes think about what happened at Preston Mantles. I feel bad about it, like it's my fault.'

There was no comfort in the wizard's reply. 'If Maskull could find you he would do the same to you. Or worse.'

'Is there a worse?' Fear turned his stomach over. 'What does he want with me?'

'Quite simply, you are blocking his progress.'

'But how? What is he trying to do? I could understand if you told me he wanted to gain the overlordship of the world or something.'

'In a way, he does.'

'I think it's about time you told me what would happen if Maskull won.'

'You have been a long time in asking that question,' Gwydion said, his eyes in complete darkness now. 'And now that you have asked, I must answer you.'

He shifted closer and propped himself on one arm against the crane bag. The fire kindled, spat and crackled and red sparks flew up. Will had the sense of a lull before a storm.

'If Maskull triumphed, then all that is fine in the world would start to fade from it. The spirits of men and women would yearn for peace, but they would know only war, even unto the thirteenth generation. The inner spirits of men would be dimmed. In such a world no satisfactions could endure long. Neither love nor delight would be felt. There would be only impoverishment and fear.'

It seemed too immense to comprehend. 'But how could such things come about through the actions of one man, Master Gwydion? Even a sorcerer like Maskull who was once of the Ogdoad? How could he change everything like that? And why would anyone want to?'

Gwydion's form shifted, and for the first time Will thought the wizard appeared tired beyond endurance. 'Once there were nine of us – eight guardians and one betrayer. Now the Ogdoad is no more, and I am all that is left. The end of another Age is coming. The times are soon to change again. And who can say what will follow in the after times? Remember, Willand: it is never beyond the power of a single convinced man, sorcerer or not, to degrade the lives of everyone in the world, if he is allowed to rise and do what he will and remain unopposed by those who have it in their power to stop him.'

'Convinced man? Convinced about what?' he asked, alarmed. 'Convinced about what, Master Gwydion?'

But the wizard had decided that he should say no more.

The next day they dined in a manner fit for kings – fresh mutton given to them in the last village and truffles that Gwydion had found in a beechwood. Will took out the two succulent chops, and set them over the fire that Gwydion whispered up. It was not long before they were ready to eat.

'But I feel guilty having both chops,' he said when Gwydion refused his portion.

'Guilty? Then eat only one. Or none at all.'

'But that would be a waste, and wizards don't like waste. Besides, I'm hungry.'

'Then eat them both.'

He deliberated for a moment, then tucked in. 'Do you never eat meat, Master Gwydion?'

'I have no need of flesh, fish or fowl.'

Will chewed the meat from the bone. 'It's very good.'

'So I see.'

Will frowned and rubbed the grease from his chin onto his sleeve. 'Is it that a wizard may not eat meat?'

Gwydion sighed and sat back, his fingers motionless on his knee. 'I do not eat meat because I have no need of it. And because I have no need of it, it is not to my taste. Do eagles pluck up grass stalks, or doves dine upon leg of lamb?'

Gwydion told him then about ages past and the days he had spent in the wilderness that were long and cold and lonely. He spoke of rigours and toughness of mind. How sometimes a man's body deceived him, desiring sleep when sleep would only kill him. 'Such are the journeys in the Far North and over the high mountains where snow-ghosts swirl and a man may easily be caught by a sudden change in the weather. Many have been taken and lie frozen still in those high passes, their bodies trapped in ice that never melts.'

Will shifted uneasily. 'Why are you telling me about this? You, who chooses what he speaks about with great care.'

'Because wisdom is often underlain by a tissue of small unregarded things. Perhaps in coming time it may be useful to you to know what lies in the Far North. And it may be that you can develop habits of mind that will help you.'

'Habits of mind?'

'Mental disciplines, let us call them, like *opening* your mind.'

'How do you do that?'

'In time I believe I can teach you how to do it.'

Will wiped the last of the grease from his hands. 'If you have no need of meat, then I shall have no need of it either.'

Gwydion smiled. 'Brave heart. Now it remains only for you to conquer your taste for it.'

Will thought about that, then he scratched a hole and buried the bones, saying a short formula of thanks over them. It had been Gwydion's habit to sing the Brean histories. He committed a part of each day to it – usually just after Will had eaten, when his scrying talent had waned into slothfulness. But no sooner had he begun today than Will interrupted him.

'You've already told me about Hely and Ludd. Don't you remember? It was just after you brought me away from Lord Strange's tower.'

'You wanted then to know about how the Slavers first came into the Isles. Shall I tell you now how they left?'

Will brightened. 'I was taught by Tutor Aspall that Caswalan was succeeded by his brother, Tervan, and Tervan by his son, Cunobelin, who was eighty-first king of Brea's line – which being nine times nine was a fortunate number, and—'

'You were given much sound history,' Gwydion cut him short. 'But I am about to tell you much that Tutor Aspall could not teach about the Slavers, for I was there and he was not . . .'

Will marvelled at the casualness of that remark. It set him wondering again why one of the names Gwydion had been known by was 'Master Merlyn'. Merlyn was the wizard who had appeared in all the stories about Great Arthur, and not for the first time Will was inclined to ask himself if Master Merlyn and Master Gwydion might not have been one and the same person.

But Gwydion was now telling of other histories, of a tumultuous time when the Slavers' deadly grip on the Isles began to falter. Will tuned his mind to the flow of wisdom and bathed in it willingly.

'. . . For many years the Brean kings became the Slavers' willing puppets, ruling always in subservience to them until a great calamity befell Tibor and the Slaver armies were at last withdrawn. Nor could the Realm return to its former glory when the Slavers left, because by now the lorc had been broken. And so, in the years that followed the Slavers' going, invasion followed invasion. Semias's time as Phantarch was not an easy one, for though the Slavers had gone, they left behind them something far more destructive.'

'The thing that broke them,' Will ventured. 'The Great Lie.'

Gwydion nodded. 'The Great Lie. In the latter days of the Slavers, blank-eyed men came from the East with but a single song on their lips. One of them was called Swythen, the first of the Sightless Ones to recruit in these isles. He, and those who came after, were a part of that vile fellowship of sorcery that had eaten the Slaver empire from within. It interposed itself between the people and their rulers and so gained power over the one and influence over the other. And it grew ever richer by driving folk toward insanity.'

'How?' Will breathed.

'By telling them the Great Lie. Did I not already tell you that whereas Slaver soldiers enslaved the body with shackles and chains, these teachers of untruth imprisoned minds? The Fellowship built in mournful stone many desolate palaces, temples with roofs like skulls, wherein echoed a hatred of the Old Ways. They sought ever to dupe and delude folk away from true knowledge, and to rule them by the lashes of fear and falsehood.

'When the empire of the Slavers devoured itself, new invaders came as a fresh torment to the now defenceless land. Northlings they were, fierce men, land-hungry hewers of trees and stealers of cattle, men who lived in a land where there grows a giant, brooding tree. Across the darkling seas they came in ships, each year a different tribe of them, every spring a new invasion. With swords and axes they came, and because each battlestone brooded now in solitary malice and could no longer do its work in concert with its brothers, these warlike invaders were victorious and satisfied their lust for blood without disturbance from the lorc. For many years, the rivers ran red. Famine and pestilence stole over the land, and in every place where once the writ of the Slaver empire had run, there now reigned the lawless Northling.

'Thus was the blood of these isles mixed for half a thousand years. The hundredth king reigned at the start of those times, and his name was Uther. Do you recall that name?'

Will was uncertain. 'I don't think I know it.'

'Did not Tutor Aspall ever speak to you of Uther Pendragon? Or of his magical union with Ygerna? Or the one who was born of that union?'

'No. Or if he did, he didn't dwell overlong on it.'

'The child was called Arthur,' Gwydion said, looking hard at him.

'Great Arthur . . .' Will repeated enthralled.

'None knew it at first, but this was his second coming, and one that had been long awaited, for Arthur had lived another life ages ago, in the days of the First Men when he sailed upon the ship *Prydwen* and brought out the spoils from Annuin. This latter coming, however, was his second incarnation, and I was ready to receive him.'

'Then you *are* Master Merlyn,' Will said, hardly daring to breathe it.

'I was your advisor then, as I am your advisor now.'

'*My* advisor?' Will felt as if all the blood had been drained from him. He took a deep breath to fill the hollowness that had grown inside. 'You still might be wrong about me, Master Gwydion.'

'I might, for in many ways I am fallible. But the prophecies of the Black Book have never been known to fail, and you fit them like a glove. You are the third incarnation that was prophesied, of that there is no doubt.'

'But I'm no king! Look at me!'

Gwydion looked and laughed. 'Do you know, that is exactly what the Wart said to me.'

'Who's the Wart?'

'Just a nickname. It was what I used to call Arthur when he was a child.'

As the bracing winds of the month of March finally blew themselves out in refreshing April rains, they wandered into the south-west to survey the high moorlands, but found the lands there too clean and too sweet to help them in their task. Will was unable to find the least sign of a lign beyond a kick he felt in the village of Norton Fitzwarren. And even that, Gwydion said, might have come from the bones of a great dragon that were buried under the gardens there. At any rate, well before they came to the borders of the Dukedom of Corinow they turned their backs on the sunset and went away east and north instead into the Levels.

Before they left the wetlands Gwydion pointed out the sacred Tor at Galastonburgh and it made Will shiver, for there brooding hard upon the top was the dark mass of a chapter house, and so terrible a thing as that he had not ever thought to see in so sacred a place.

'Why does it pain me so to see that sight?' he asked solemnly.

'Because you are well used to seeing it how it was. You see what the Sightless Ones have done, how their promises to you were all of them broken.'

After that, they went north along by the Vale of Malmesburgh, and rested two wet days in a barn in Hooke Lydiard while Gwydion sang more of the histories and then interpreted them until Will's understanding of the context of his life was made good. On the third day the sun came out and they went on again. By midday a west wind had dried the ground considerably. Gwydion whispered up a fire and made them a warm meal, and Will ate gratefully.

As he finished he stirred and stretched and said, 'But you haven't spoken of the times that lie between the leaving of the Slavers and the coming of Gillan the Conqueror. What happened in those days?'

Gwydion let his his eyes settle again on Will's own. 'Half a thousand years and more lie between Great Arthur's days and the Conquest, but little of that concerns us now. Suffice to say that in the bloody wars that followed the withdrawal of the Slavers, the lorc continued in its ruptured state and gave no protection to the land. The Realm was fractured into many small territories. More shipborne invaders came from across the sea, until they struggled one with another, and so more blood flowed. I had seen the Realm broken into parts before. It happened after the reigns of Ferrex and Porrex, the quarrelling sons of Gorboduc. Back then, the Realm was reunited under one strong king, King Pinner by name, but in the Northlings' time the Six Kingdoms emerged from the fighting.'

'Wesset, Marset, Umberland, Essalby, Kennet and Lindisay,' Will recited, remembering well the lessons given by Tutor Aspall.

'Indeed so! And it was my friend Semias's greatest

achievement to manage the diplomacy whereby the six were made one again. And later, when Gillan the Conqueror came here twelve generations of men ago, Semias made what compact he could with him, which was little enough, for Semias's strength was by that time already failing, and his grip on affairs loosening. The Conqueror's allies attacked in the North. There was a great fight at Stennford, and another at Senlack Ridge, when King Hardy was shot in the eye and fell under the hooves of Gillan's horsemen. Still, much bloodshed was averted by Semias's interventions, and the wilder excesses of Gillan's harriers were discouraged. An agreement was made that if Gillan would be king and his nine score barons would deign to become tenants-in-chief of the Realm, then they should regard themselves not as owners, but as stewards whose duty was to care for what was a venerable land. And this was the pact that was solemnly sworn to.

'But Gillan was ambitious and overweening and his knowledge of occult powers was great. He had brought a great army here, promising riches to all who would fight alongside him. And now, in victory, he was true to his word. He built, first in wood, but later in stone. This was a land of many parts, all of which Gillan accounted carefully in his "Great Book of the Realm", which every king since has kept.

'Gillan made a crown for himself, dispossessed the thanes and eorls of the Northling folk, and gave the Realm piece by piece into the keeping of his friends. Those who had ruled formerly were made Gillan's slaves in one way or another. The eorls and thanes were made into overseers and the churlish folk put to the hard labour of heaping up the earth to make mounds and moats for Gillan's lieutenants to raise their towers upon. Thus, in harshness and in cruelty did these new barons seize a grip on the land which they had lately won. In time, they fashioned all the great castles and bastions that stand today, and the sons of their sons dwell in them even now.'

'At least there's been a sort of peace for the last few hundred years,' Will said.

'Peace?' Gwydion said sharply. 'I would not call it that. The power of the lorc has been warped too much. There has been bloodshed of some kind in every generation. Always a new war has come – sometimes in the North, sometimes in the West – and between times there have been sundry risings of the common folk against the tyranny of their masters. But there has been no true peace such as once reigned in these Isles.'

'And all this without the battlestones.'

'Quite so. The battlestones are still in the ground. And each one remains a hub of darkness from which misfortune leaches. And that is why the coming war will be nastier than all the fights that have been before. Matters are now worse than in the days of the Slaver legions, for the heirs of the Conqueror have built no new stone roads to keep the now-corrupted flows of the lorc in check. They have let the Slaver wall decay in the North so that the poison is spread even into Albanay, and they have allowed the Great Dyke of King Offa in the West to be filled and flattened, so tainting Cambray. The highways of the Slaver empire are now falling fast into their final decay, though they have outlasted the great boast of their makers, which was: "A thousand years!" Now there are gaps here and holes there, for never in all that time has any real repair been made to them. The looking-glasses are cracking, Willand. The dams are holed. You saw the Akemain, the road that cuts through Wychwoode. Lengths have sunk under mud or been swept away by flood, torn up by the roots of trees or undermined on purpose and taken away in carts to make the fillings for castle walls.'

'Now I see what you were talking about,' Will said, feeling that his understanding had been suddenly broadened.

Gwydion smiled and poked a twig among the ashes of the fire. 'Rest assured that you have a lot more yet to learn.'

Will said, 'I have one last question. If Maskull was an Ogdoad wizard like you, then how has he remained ignorant of the lorc all this time?'

'He is not ignorant of it, and we must hope that he knows no more about it than I do. The wizards of the Ogdoad learned much about the world, but we did not come to know everything, nor in the latter Ages did we necessarily share what we knew with one another. There was a good reason for this.'

Will rubbed his nose. 'You mean, the betrayer who was among you?'

'We did not know who he was – not even, it seems, the traitor himself. We knew only that he never left us as the ages declined, and therefore as we diminished in number his share of influence grew ever the greater. When I discovered Gruech's treacheries, which I did after finding fragments of the Black Book in his possession, I told Semias about it, but not Maskull.'

'Why?'

'Because by that time it had become clear to me that Maskull must be the betrayer – for Semias was Phantarch, and therefore fated to go into the Far North in time. That left only Maskull.'

'But didn't Semias try to help you against Maskull?'

Gwydion sighed. 'How could he? How could he choose between us?'

'Hmmm.' Will watched the lights of the grove shifting for a while, but then he got up and helped Gwydion prepare to move on. 'Master Gwydion, why did we not scry for the stone that you said lies near Ludford?'

'Because it is far more urgent that we find another stone, the one to which the Dragon Stone points.'

'What do you mean by "points"?'

And Gwydion said, 'While you were at Foderingham I travelled far, and consulted with many knowledgeable folk, but I heard little concerning the lorc, and what I did glean was usually far-fetched. Even so, some tales had, I think, seeds of truth in them. In the same way there are verses tying each sister-stone to its brother, so also are the battle-stones tied one to the next by their inscriptions. That is why they carry two distinct readings. It may be a relic of some magical mechanism. A safeguard perhaps. A way to dismantle the array. I do not know. But each stone we find will lead us to others so long as we have the wit to understand what the clues mean. Furthermore, I believe there is a set sequence in which the stones are meant to awaken.'

'Do you know which is meant to be the first?'

Gwydion stroked his beard ruefully. 'It would seem to be the one called the Doomstone. But even that is not wholly certain.'

'Do you know how many there are?'

'There may be nine, or there may be nineteen.' The wizard sighed, and decided to say it plainly. 'If I were given to gambling I would stake my wager on thirty-nine.'

'*Thirty-nine?*' Will shut his eyes and opened them again.

'Thrice thirteen. It is as likely a number as any, and far more likely than some.'

Will blew out a heavy breath. 'One for each of the earldoms of the Realm? That many, do you think?'

'Let us not burden ourselves with numbers. But I was right to think there are two kinds of battlestone, the greater and the lesser, and that only the greater stones call battle down. What then, you may ask, do the lesser ones do? Nothing in themselves, it seems. They are merely guide-stones, but it is my surmise that these lesser stones must be present for the lorc to draw earth power and effectively direct the harm.'

'That'll make our task all the harder,' Will said. 'Because

we might discover lesser stones when we're looking for the greater kind.'

'More than likely. But do not gallop too far ahead. To discover just one more battlestone would be a fine thing. Our task appears daunting. First we must go where the Dragon Stone points, then find the next stone, then the next after that, and so on until we arrive at the Doomstone.'

'But if there are as many battlestones as you said, then the search could take years!'

'I do not see any other way. At least, by then you will be properly grown up and will have come fully into your powers.'

'By then, the war will be over and done with!'

'Come here then, and let me try to instruct you again in how to open your mind.'

As the spring days continued to lengthen and the noonday sun rose ever higher, Gwydion tried to teach Will the knack of opening his mind. 'Our senses are limited. No man sees, hears or feels the world in all its glory. You must learn to let fall the barriers you have built up against knowing the world as it truly is.'

'But how, Master Gwydion?'

'First consider the difference between seeing and watching, or that between hearing and listening, and you will begin to grasp what your mind must do. You have been through enough lessons to know what it means to concentrate. The first step in opening your mind is almost the opposite of that.'

But Will found it harder in practice than Gwydion had made it seem. Though they scried the land to north and south and to east and west, it was all to no avail, until one afternoon they came by the hamlet of Aston Oddingley.

For most of a wet, spring morning Gwydion had been steering them away from the farms and manors they saw, and now he drew Will off the road and into hiding while they took their lunch.

'As you know, some places welcome my arrival,' the wizard explained as they made themselves scarce. 'Others do not. The landowner here is Baron Clifton, whom you may remember from Clarendon. He wore his colours of six gold rings upon red and his badge was the red wyvern.'

Will nodded. 'A clipped black beard and a sly scowl?'

'Then you do remember him.'

'I guess we're unwelcome here, then.'

'You guess well. He has warned his people against me, so it would be unsafe for us to pass undisguised among them, or even to show ourselves to any of the local folk. The only succour we would receive now would be hard words and harder steel.'

They rested under a hedge that Gwydion had covered with his cloak, sitting by a small, smokeless fire of twigs, warming themselves as a fine rain fell. Minute drops misted the surface of Will's woollen coat like tiny diamonds. The rain showed no sign of letting up as the sky shredded itself in slants of grey. Will made an effort to 'feel the moment' just as Gwydion had taught him, and when he did he found there was an unspeakable beauty to what his usual mind had dismissed as no more than grey and miserable.

'So,' Gwydion said, a twinkle in his eye. 'You still have not told me how you enjoyed life at Foderingham.'

Will laughed. 'It was no hardship compared to living in hedges.'

'I had hoped that castle life would teach you some harder lessons.'

'I learned how to hunt wild boar and how to stalk a hemule – which I later found out to my disappointment is nothing more than a roe deer in its third year. They showed me the different sorts of hounds that verderers keep, and the way to use hawks to catch fat pigeons, what vervels and jesses are, how to tell different hawks apart, and that the first point of hawking is to hold fast . . . oh, and plenty more besides.'

'Was there no fighting?'

'When I'd been living at Foderingham for a few months, they began to teach me how to use a sword and buckler, and then a long sword called a hand-and-a-half. How to swing the blade in attack and to parry in defence. I told them I preferred the quarterstaff, but Edward always laughed at me for that. He used to call me Willy Wag-staff, so I gave it up.'

'Then he is a fool and so are you. The well-wielded stave is the most effective of all weapons,' Gwydion said, patting his own staff. 'Though few noblemen know its secrets.'

'I told Sir John you never carried metal about you, except a little blade of star-iron. He called that wilful stupidity. He made me recite the names of all the different pieces of armour so I knew them by heart, and then he had me learn how to put them all on in the right order. I had to wear mail and steel until they felt as easy upon me as a silk shirt. Then he taught me how to ride to arms and how to tilt at a quintain, which is not a poem of five lines as once I thought, but a brutish wooden thing that turns about as you pass and tries to knock you off your horse.'

When Will fell silent Gwydion asked, 'And did you enjoy those lessons?'

'It was exciting, but—' he shrugged again '—it was always about killing. Killing animals, or killing birds or killing people, or trying not to get killed yourself. I know that so much of a lord's life has to be about death, even about killing – but it seems to me they hardly think about anything else. They're so proud, Master Gwydion, and yet so frightened inside. I've seen a kestrel fall upon a mouse and tear it to pieces often enough, but somehow what a kestrel does is different for it's done out of hunger or for its young's sake. When men kill they kill out of hatred . . . or . . . or . . .'

Gwydion's eyes rested, smiling, on the western horizon. 'The seven failings arise out of the three weaknesses. Hatred is one of those weaknesses. And that gets into men mostly through lies. Lies told to the young and supped with mother's milk, or later when weak men have learned how to believe whatever they want. That is how they fall for the Great Lie that the Fellowship peddles. With few exceptions it is only jealousy, hatred or fear that makes folk hurt or kill one another. These three, magic tells us, are to be avoided by the wise man at all costs.'

'Jealousy, hatred and fear – like those stirred up by the lies that seep out of the battlestones.'

Gwydion nodded. 'Quite so. I am pleased that you seem to have sloughed off most of the dead layers of hide that grew over you while you were at Foderingham.'

Yet Will saw in that another opportunity to unburden himself. 'So you see, Master Gwydion, why you must be wrong about me. I can't be the third incarnation of Arthur because I don't have the makings of a warrior-king.'

'That is by the bye. In Arthur's first incarnation he was an adventurer, in his second a warrior-king. Who knows how he will return in his third and final form? Perhaps it is as a stubborn young ass.'

'My point exactly!' he said revelling in the idea. 'There'd be no point in him coming back as a nobody. Especially one like me. He wouldn't do that, would he? Because how would that help him in saving the Realm?' He laughed and lay back, closing his eyes. Then he let himself slide into that state of mind he had been trying to cultivate for days.

Almost at once he sat bolt upright. 'By the moon and stars, Master Gwydion!'

'What is it, lad?'

'There's . . . there's a stone near here.'

Gwydion looked at him closely. 'Are you sure?'

'I felt something. Just then, when I tried to open my mind. It felt as if I was sleepwalking in a mist and the ground beneath me was rocky and sharp, then down came the mist . . .'

'Show me the quarter in which the stone lies.'

'I . . . I can't rightly say.' Will closed his eyes, put out his arms and began to spin slowly back and forth like a scarecrow in the wind. When he opened his eyes again he said, 'Master Gwydion, what happens if the place where a battlestone is buried has been built upon? How would we be able to raise it if the owner didn't allow us entry?'

'Why do you ask that?'

'Because I fear that this battlestone lies down there, under the manor of Lord Clifton.'

Gwydion seized him. 'Do you know that for sure?'

'It's . . . just a feeling.'

Gwydion stood behind him and asked, 'Is this stone greater or lesser in power than the Dragon Stone?'

Will answered straight away. 'Lesser. Lesser than the Dragon Stone, but only a little less. Perhaps one eighth part less.'

The wizard's eyes narrowed and he shook his head, marvelling. 'Can you be that exact?'

Will closed his eyes for a moment and felt for the stone. 'It's as exact as seeing who's the taller of two men. I can tell it's quite a small stone – small in weight and size, I mean. As tall as a child of four years and as far around as a man might just about clasp his arms. As for weight, I could, I think, just about lift it up by myself, though I couldn't raise it far.'

The wizard began to pace back and forth excitedly. 'How can you know this, when the stone is buried and two furlongs away?'

'I don't know, but the lign is showing up very strongly.

Maybe it's the sun and moon. I've never felt anything so clearly. Maybe it's to do with where I happened to choose to rest. We're on a lign here.'

'Remarkable.' Gwydion began prodding the ground, shaking his head. After a while he called Will along after him, but not in the direction that led towards the manor. 'Come, Willand, we must be on our way.'

'Where are you going?'

'I think that, after all, we should not approach this stone, even though it may be one of the greater sort.'

Will was amazed at the wizard's decision. 'Not approach it? After all these weeks we've spent trying to find one?'

'We must return here at a later season, of course,' Gwydion said, beckoning Will onward again. 'But from what you have already told me this cannot be the particular stone for which we seek.'

'How do you know that for certain?'

'I do not. Certainties are hard to find where battlestones are concerned. But the Doomstone must be greater in power than the Dragon Stone, and the Black Book says of it that "the last which was planted shall foremost be in slaughter". I have taken this to mean that the first great battle will rage in the place where the Doomstone now dwells. We must seek for it elsewhere.'

'But this one's powerful enough, and probably no guide-stone,' Will protested. 'A battle will be fought here eventually.'

'This stone may not grow troublesome for years yet, and much may pass in half a year that might make the eventual solution easier. I would rather use the time while the lign remains strong to try to follow it.'

Will glanced back towards the manor and a sharp pain made him clutch his arm and call out.

'What is it?'

'Nothing, Master Gwydion. Just a cramp.' But it was not

cramp and he knew it. He rubbed at his arm and the agony seemed to run to earth and leave him. When it did he shuddered. As he caught up with the wizard he said, 'I know one thing: if I was Duke Edgar I'd rather fetch an army here to fight than take it to many another place.'

'Why do you say that?'

'Because there's no castle here, and you yourself once told him to beware castles on pain of death.'

Gwydion nodded, then smiled. 'So I did, Willand. So I did. And you're right – that is another clue for us to think on.'

They found that the lign upon which the battlestone of Aston Oddingley stood ran broadly west to east. For the next few days it swelled strongly, and they were able to follow it westward. Then they lost it and wandered aimlessly northward for ten leagues, but as they crossed a great river called the Trennet and so entered the Earldom of Staffe, the moon rose and Will began to feel something stirring again.

He knew at once what it was, and that this lign was different to the one they had been following previously. That was hard to explain. 'They're not as different as the tastes of cider and ale, but still quite different – sort of like the scents of two different flowers, if you see what I mean.'

'If I could see what you meant,' Gwydion said, 'I would be a far wiser man.'

'Well,' he said, grinning, 'just as you wanted Duke Richard to have faith in you, so you'll have to have faith in me.'

And Gwydion laughed at that. 'Well said!'

At last, with the help of the full moon they came upon what Will said was sure to be another battlestone. It was half buried in the ground near a bend in the River Churnet.

The folk of the earldoms of Staffe and Warrewyk were,

so Gwydion said, among the wisest people in the Realm. The local people of Cheddle would not go near the place where the stone stood, which was on the far side of a leek field. They called it the 'Plaguestone', and said there was a story that whomsoever touched it would fall ill and die before the next full moon.

'I have been to this spot many times, and I have known of this stone for many generations,' Gwydion said. 'But there are tens of thousands of sarsens scattered throughout the Realm, and a large proportion of them are either of ill repute or actually show a malign nature. So this one was a battle-stone, eh? How fortunate you are here this time to show me.'

Something about the wizard's words sounded sarcastic, even sinister. The scent of wild garlic was on the air. Will's skin crawled at the sight of the stone. When Gwydion set him to scrying the land about he found four paths of influence, two flowing inwards and two out. Again, he could sense differences between them.

'Ah,' Gwydion said, bending to examine the small wild-flowers that grew nearby. 'It must be because two ligns cross here.'

'The one that passes north-west to south-east is the stronger,' Will said as the hazel wand twitched suddenly.

'There! That must be the lign that was called in the Black Book "Mulart", after the elder tree. The other will be "Bethe", named for the birch.'

'The ligns have names?' Will muttered. 'You didn't tell me. You keep too much from me.'

Gwydion's chin jutted. 'Do I, indeed? Then let me tell you now. The lorc consists of nine great ligns. They were called of old: Eburos, Caorthan, Indonen, Tanne, Collen, Celin, Mulart, Heligan and Bethe. Is that enough for your ill temper to bite on for the time being?'

'If you know so much, why can't you find them yourself?'

'I have told you before, the knowledge of where each

lign runs has long been lost. Pay attention! We must approach the stone.'

'I don't want to go near it,' Will said. A sudden obstinate loathing filled his mind. 'I think you've secretly found the Black Book and don't want to tell me about it!'

When the wizard turned to him he was smiling and pointing like a mischievous demon. 'You're betrayed!' he said, crooking a sorcerer's finger. 'One shall be made two! You're going to die!'

A vivid picture leapt into Will's mind of a portcullis running down and cutting him in two. His fragile courage snapped and he bolted.

When Gwydion caught up with him he was sitting on the grass with his head in his hands. 'Willand, Willand . . .'

He was shaking. 'Go away!'

'Speak to me.'

'Why did you do that?'

'What did I do?'

'Say that I was betrayed! That one would be made two and I would die!'

'I never said you were betrayed, or that you would die. You must have imagined it.'

Will looked up, angry. 'I thought you were Maskull!'

'Maskull?'

'He's a sorcerer, isn't he? He might have taken your place last night while you slept. It's all right for you, you're a wizard. Your spirit is in an egg in the Far North. Nothing can harm you!'

'If you think I am immune from harm, then think again. I have told you more than once that the power within a battlestone is easily sufficient to destroy me. I do not approach these stones lightly, and neither should—' Gwydion stopped suddenly and threw up his hands. 'Oh, listen to the pair of us! We are at each other's throats like Nag and Blaggard. Now, why do you think that is?'

Will made a tremendous effort to clear his mind. 'It's . . . it's the stone.'

'Shall we start again, from the beginning?'

Will dragged himself to his feet, forced his mind to open a crack. A tiny sliver of dread entered and sparkled inside his skull, but he ruthlessly snuffed it out and forced his feet onward. As they neared the brooding stone the sun went behind a cloud and the ache in his belly deepened.

The stone was not very big – two strong men might just be able to lift it once it was dug out. But it was lying at a sickening angle to the ground, like a broken leg, like a ship sinking in the sea, like the tower of a slighted castle. Perhaps someone had tried to pull it up before, but had been beaten back. Will gritted his teeth and forced another forward pace out of his unwilling legs.

'Do not touch it!'

Then, against his own advice, the wizard advanced upon the stone and laid a palm flat against the side. The words he muttered were in the true tongue: *'Acil na dorcais an gealach agish greane . . .'*

Gwydion was demanding an answer and listening for the reply, then he said, 'Willand, what do you make of it?'

Will stared at the warty surface. As he opened his mind a little more his nostrils filled with the stench of infection, and his belly writhed as if it was full of worms. The horror of the exposure made him retch. Near the stone the taste of the two ligns was powerfully combined into a cloying bitterness that filled his mouth and made him spit.

'It's not a stone of the kind we seek,' he said, wiping his mouth. 'This is one of the lesser sort.'

'Are you sure?'

'Yes.'

'And there's no verse.' Will gasped as another sick wave rose inside him. 'Only a letter carved into its end.'

'Which letter?' Gwydion said, then he looked for himself. '*Duirre* – oak.'

'So. No verse. No clue.'

'While filled with malice these stones give only such clues as please them! Perhaps a draining is needed to force more out!'

Will's eyes began to sting. He blinked and bloody tears came. Gwydion seized him and led him away. He limped for a hundred and one crippled paces, then fell down.

'It's over,' the wizard said. 'You've done all that was asked. Rest now.'

Slowly, the revulsion ebbed and Will began to recover his senses. He sat on the damp grass feeling his heart beating out a stumbling rhythm. After a while it slipped back into its usual regularity.

'This Plaguestone appears to be one that is spoken of in the Black Book as the second most powerful of the lesser-ranking stones. Important but not, alas, what I had hoped to find.'

Will lay propped on his elbow. He did not want to consider the Doomstone. This lesser stone seemed vile enough. He said with foreboding, 'The question is, now we've found it, what do you want to do with it?'

'This time we must raise it.'

Will groaned. 'It's been here as long as any of them. Why raise this one and not the other? Surely another year or two—'

'I think we should not leave this stone here.'

'You can't mean you want to try draining it?'

'Oh, that would be far too dangerous. And unnecessary. But we should move it. If the lorc is becoming active, the good folk of Cheddle and all the other towns and villages nearby might be drawn here and hurt.'

'Now tell me the real reason.'

Gwydion threw down his staff. 'I have reason to believe

that taking a guide-stone out of the lorc might delay the awakening of the rest.'

'And where will you take it? Where would it be safe? You bound the Dragon Stone with spells, but it has seeped a lot of harm.'

The wizard looked sharply to him, then bit a knuckle. 'There may be a place. Stay here while I go to spellbind the stone.'

After Gwydion had danced out his magic, they went to borrow a cart and ropes and other tools of work. They lifted the Plaguestone just as they had the Dragon Stone, and set about driving it northwards. Will spat again, unable to rid his mouth of a foul taste, unable either to shake from his mind the image of the blemished, toad-like skin of the stone. 'Would it really have killed me if I'd touched it?'

'Perhaps not right away,' Gwydion said with a wry smile. 'But you can always try it and see.'

He asked what kind of castle they were going to this time, and what guardian might have the strength to resist the stone's whisperings. But Gwydion would not say. Instead, he distracted Will with tales about what life was like at Trinovant. He spoke of the Great Spire and the White Hall, and the White Tower where the kings of the Realm kept a menagerie and how there was a huge ice-bear kept on a long chain that walked out every summer day into the River Iesis to catch trout and salmon fish for its dinner.

At length they came into a wild and unkempt land, and Will knew they must be nearing their destination. They had come many leagues and he felt far away and under threat again. He supposed that was the stone's defences eating at him, but still he could not avoid looking round at the wasteland and suppressing a shudder.

'Where are we?'

'Be cheerful,' Gwydion said encouragingly. 'You are quite safe in this place. No one dares to come here.'

Will looked around all the more. 'Why not?'

'Because a leper lives here.'

'A leper?'

'Don't look so ill at ease. He is a leper no more. He is a man well known to me, for it was I who halted the serpigo that ruined his flesh. Once he was a most accomplished mason.'

'What did he build?'

'All his life he worked on raising new towers and soaring spires for the Sightless Ones. But in his fortieth year he began to lose the feeling in his fingers. One day he dropped his hammer and it narrowly missed hitting one of the chapter house Elders. After that, the Fellowship found him out and expelled him from their works. He was too proud to beg for charity through the bars of a lazar house. Instead, he was brought to a quiet place to dwell alone, a place close to the village of his birth.'

'Here?'

Gwydion indicated the rocky cliff they were nearing. 'Anstin the Leper lives alone in yonder cave. I halted his ailment, but no spell of mine could restore the damage that had already destroyed much of his hands and face. I could do nothing about that, for it had come to him during the days of his service to the Sightless Ones and had arisen out of Anstin's own troubled heart.'

Will stared around at the bleakness of the heath with its wide tracts of heather and scrub, and, here and there, rocky outcrops. 'How does he live out here?'

'This is a disused quarry. Anstin's trade-tools are fitted to leathers which are bound to his stumps. He ekes out a living sculpting figures from the stone that lies around him. A Sister leaves food and drink close by this spot every week and takes away what finished work he leaves for her, but she never looks upon him.'

'That's sad.'

'I think there is no better place for the Plaguestone to rest than in Anstin's cave, for he will not touch it himself, and no one else dares to come here. The remedy is not perfect, but it will have to serve until I can find its sister-stone and bring it here.'

'But you haven't even brought the Dragon Stone's sister yet,' Will said, looking sidelong. 'I thought that was one of the things you were supposed to do when you went away from Foderingham.'

'There were many matters more urgent than the Dragon Stone, which is, despite your fears, far safer in its bindings than it was while at liberty.'

Will cast another glance at the Plaguestone, wondering if the wizard's unwillingness to entertain obvious measures was any of its malicious doing. 'What would happen if you tried to pair the wrong stones?'

'I fear that would be my final mistake.'

The creaking cart came to a halt and Will began to hear the slow clinking of a mason's chisel. A faint smell of corrupted flesh lay on the air. It caused Will to turn suddenly and look at the Plaguestone again.

Gwydion said, 'It would be better if you climbed down and waited here.'

He stood by the entrance to the quarry as Gwydion took the cart inside. The clinking that came from the wounded earth stopped. He sat down on a rock, brooding over what the wizard had said, standing guard over his thoughts as they turned to Anstin. It was a sad life that Gwydion had revealed, and Will wondered how many other private sadnesses were being silently suffered throughout the Realm, sadnesses that need never have been. If I was king, he thought, I'd proclaim a Day of Sadness when all such wounded folk would be able to walk together and let their hearts sing as one. That would be real kingship and better than all the greed and quarrelling.

He steeled himself to look into the quarry and catch a glimpse of the form that no one dared look upon, but as he rounded the corner he was stopped by a sight so unexpected that his hands fell loosely to his sides, for flanking a cave mouth were two perfect naked human forms, both life-sized and carved with such grace and beauty that the breath caught in Will's throat and tears came to his eyes.

'A leper did that?' he said. Then he remembered the rede that said, 'True beauty most often has a spotted rind, yet is delicious fruit.'

He replaited his braids as he waited, thinking about Willow and missing her more than ever. Then Gwydion came out and led the cart into the quarry to unload the stone. Seven flashes of blue light lit the rocks, lightning intense but soundless, then a more mellow feeling began to settle through the air and the sound of sobbing. When Gwydion reappeared they got back on the cart and they started out on the long journey back to Cheddle. The wizard said nothing about what had passed in Anstin's cave, nor did Will have the courage to ask about it.

□ □ □

CHAPTER NINETEEN

AT THE NAVEL OF THE WORLD

After returning the cart to Cheddle, Gwydion urged Will to pick up either the Bethe or Mulart ligns once more, but that was easier said than done. 'Our lifting of the Plaguestone seems to have lessened the flows,' Will told the wizard.

'I may have forestalled the lorc,' Gwydion said. 'But I may also have made a rod for our backs.'

'It surely feels as if we've sent the power deeper underground.'

Will found that the strength of a given lign was never constant. It varied with the weather and with the quality and aspect of the ground. It also broadly rose and fell according to a daily rhythm and also a monthly one, and when all had been taken into consideration the hardest task remained to disentangle it from Will's own varying moods. But whatever his mood, he searched endlessly, going sometimes northward and at other times to the south, and though he did notice a faint tingling in his arms or legs once or twice, following the feeling for more than a few dozen paces was always too difficult.

One day as they reached the northern village of Stoneyfold, Gwydion's patience ran thin. His staff went *toc-toc-toc* as he strode the woodland path. A pair of magpies sported in the branches ahead of them, showing great curiosity as to who might be passing through their wood. Spring was here and the days were growing lighter and warmer – and longer. The weather would soon be pleasant enough to let men fight a war. The wizard's manner had been losing its cool disguise for some days, and after a difficult morning with Will showing more than his usual indecision, Gwydion tried to hurry him along with too sharp a remark.

'Master Gwydion, I'm doing my best!' Will said, stopping. 'With all that tapping of your staff I can't concentrate. And I can't get that maddening verse out of my head.'

'What verse? Not a poetic word has passed my lips today!'

'The verse on the Dragon Stone, I mean. It has a long-striding rhythm, sixteen beats, just as you walk, and it's plaguing me.'

'You have an ear for song. That is good, but I would rather you attended to the matter in hand.'

'I can't attend to anything. That rhythm just goes on and on, round and round inside my head until I'm dizzy from it!'

'The music of the true tongue is powerful, I grant you. It sticks ideas inside the head better than the debased tongues of latter days. Though in translation the battlestone verses keep barely a shred of their original power . . .' And then he sang,

> *'Northern King's bewitched son,*
> *Queen of the Moon in her father's field.*
> *Dragon of Darkness, awaken and slay!*
> *Lonely Stone take war away!'*

'What can it mean?' Will asked again, wearied and frustrated. He spoke aloud the cross-reading.

'King and Queen with Dragon Stone.
Bewitched by the moon, in darkness alone.
In northern field shall wake no more.
Son and father, killed by war.'

'That reading would seem to foretell the deaths in battle of King Hal and his son, Master Gwydion. But that surely cannot be for some years yet for the child is only just grown from being a suckling infant.'

'On the other hand,' the wizard said, 'it could refer to another king.'

'What other king?'

'Not the one who was crowned, but the one who by the strict laws of blood should have been.'

Will gasped, for he had not anticipated the possibility. 'You mean, Richard of Ebor . . . and Edward.'

They left the larger woodland path for a smaller, deeper way, passing through a scene that was dappled many shades of green by the sun. When they came out it was onto a lane that was hedged with hawthorn. A wild cherry tree blazed in pink, shedding its blossom in the breeze. It was so beautiful to see the petals falling in the wind that Will was amazed he had never noticed such delicate magnificence in quite the same way before. In that place of good aspect he opened his mind wider than ever he had dared.

'We must go south,' he said, hardly knowing why he said it.

'The Dragon Stone verse mentions a northern king and a northern field,' Gwydion reminded him.

'Still, I . . . I feel we must go south.'

The wizard nodded slowly, his face betraying the message that, this time, Will had better be right.

They celebrated Beltane in Aston Gravel, one of the pretty little villages along the River Rea. Gwydion said nothing to the villagers about Will turning fifteen that day, wanting no doubt to spare his blushes. On Will's whim they headed five leagues to the north-west, and at Gwydion's suggestion they visited Atherstone then went on to Bilstone and lingered at Congerstone. Then they moved up to Shackerstone and wandered away over to Snarestone and even up to Swepstone before coming down again by Nailstone and Barlestone to Odstone.

'There is not a place in this Realm so confoundedly afflicted by places named after stones!' the wizard said. 'Are you sure you can feel the lorc here?'

'Yes. Well . . . no. I mean, I'm not sure. But there's something. It's like a background hum. Or a smell, if you take my meaning. It could be coming this way – or it could be drifting over that way.'

'But that is exactly the opposite direction! Oh, confound you, Willand! This is maddening!'

'Not half as maddening as it is to me!'

'Don't shout at me!'

'Well, don't shout at me, then!' Will's finger stabbed out. 'Master Gwydion, you just don't understand what it's like. I feel as if I'm somebody who's been blind from birth who suddenly gets the power to see. He wouldn't know what he was looking at any more than I know what I'm feeling! Oh, why don't you just leave me alone?'

He stumped off in a rage and went to sit by himself and to attack a spot that had come up on his chin. It felt good to burst it and make it bleed. Nobody understood. Nobody could. Nobody!

When he had sulked himself out, they tracked westward to a place called No Man's Heath and there he declared that he had had just about enough of scrying and wanted to eat. They made camp and broke bread, but Will sat sullenly throughout and infuriatingly, just as he lay down to sleep, he felt the lign.

This time, despite all the confusions in his head, it was strong enough to identify – it was definitely Mulart.

The next day he tried to pick up the lign again. Gwydion gave him a freshly-cut hazel switch and asked him to do whatever he had done last night.

'Last night, more than anything else I was wishing that Willow could be here with us,' he said, opening out the hazel wand ready to scry.

'I realize you are very fond of her.'

Will came to a halt and smiled. 'You know, I liked her from the first moment I saw her. I suppose she's my best friend.'

'Not . . . Edward?'

'Edward? No!' He gave Gwydion a sideways look. 'Willow and I, we sort of think alike because we're so different – if you see what I mean.' He searched fruitlessly for what he was trying to say, knowing he was not saying anything particularly well. 'Edward, though, he's . . . he's . . .'

'Perhaps what you mean is that Edward is too much like you.'

Will shook his head, feeling uncomfortable now and out of his depth. 'Edward's not like me at all. He wants to be a great man and a worthy heir to his father. He's impetuous and full of brash show. I don't think we're alike at all. Do you think we are?'

'Underneath perhaps you and he are more similar than either of you would care to admit.' Gwydion shifted his weight from one foot to the other. 'Let me tell you, Willand, the Rede of Magical Converses says simply: "Opposites attract." It is often so with people. Perhaps that is why you like Willow, and perhaps also why you and Edward do not get along as easily as you might.'

Will scratched his head. 'I do hope that no harm comes to her, Master Gwydion.' And a moment later he said,

'Master Gwydion, are you sure you didn't do anything to bring Willow to Foderingham? Anything . . . magical?'

'I did nothing. You may rely on that.'

He felt glad to hear that, but it opened up a greater question, one that he could not ask Gwydion about. If no one had magically steered Willow towards Foderingham, then how had such an unlikely thing happened? Had the Dragon Stone brought them together so that it could inflict a greater suffering upon them later? Or maybe Willow was right: maybe it had been his own magic after all. Could he have worked his desire without even knowing it? Did he have that kind of power? Old Gort had seemed to think so. Maybe that was what Gwydion had meant by calling him a Child of Destiny. And maybe, if he *was* the third incarnation of Arthur, and if Gwydion was right that Arthur need not necessarily turn out to be a king this time, then maybe he was destined to become some kind of magician . . .

That thought was even more unsettling than thinking that one day he might have to win the throne of the Realm, because as a magician he would surely have to go up against Maskull.

As they wandered on, Will decided it was high time he concentrated more closely on his task. He noticed the soil changing again – heavy clays alternated with crumbly brown loam, and the plants growing all around had changed too. The Wortmaster had said that it took hundreds of years for a wild meadow to settle down properly to itself after crops had been grown on it, and so they avoided tilled fields so that Will could let his feet feel the texture of the natural carpet that lay under his toes. His eyes delighted in the tiny multicoloured flowers that clothed the verges of the chalky brown fields. He let the land guide him until their path became not at all the path that would have been chosen by a traveller, or even by a wizard. Though Gwydion's feet knew the best way forward and were able to find perfect paths of least resistance, they could not locate a lign. But, then, neither could Will's today.

The Middle Shires through which they now passed became rich farmland, green and fertile, with well-fed folk, but increasingly they found a shadow hanging over the towns and villages. Wherever they went they heard news that the Earl Marshal and the king's commissioners of array had visited and had taken men from their homes. In the towns, numerous levies had already been raised, and on the estates of the great landowners camps had sprung up in which men were being trained in the arts of war.

When they came to Wootton Wyvern in the district of Arden, Will looked around anxiously, remembering Lord Strange's book of animals and the 'man-eating beasts of the air' that had been described against the picture of a wyvern. But Gwydion only called in at the sign of the Bull's Head and there he learned from the innkeeper a piece of news that was far more dangerous than any ravening beast. King Hal had suddenly shaken off his illness, and the queen and Duke Edgar had used Hal's surprise recovery as the pretext to oust Duke Richard and his followers from every office they held. For now the king's sanity was restored there was no longer any place for a Lord Protector, though the king's capacity seemed not to go far beyond the work of stripping the Ebor faction from their livings and replacing them with all the queen's cronies. Already the Earl Sarum had lost his chancellor's chain, and Lord Warrewyk had been deprived of his Captaincy of Callas. There could now be only one outcome.

'Rumour has it that two great armies are forming ready to clash,' the innkeeper told them. 'Can't be long before events are brought to a reckoning.'

Gwydion's grip tightened on his staff as he spoke softly

but fiercely to Will in a private aside. 'Maskull has bided his time well, and now he has released his spell from the king's head, so that all I have worked for has been brought to ruin!'

'Is that bad?'

'It dashes your hope that war might come later rather than sooner. But it does not surprise me, for every measure I put in place to restore the fortunes of the Realm has been used by Friend Richard to enrich the House of Ebor and its allies. I warned that such greed would in the end bring him low!'

'There's one benefit to us,' Will said, anxious to rescue a little hope.

The wizard cast him a withering look. 'What benefit could possibly come of this news?'

'Well, it's just that as war comes closer I expect it'll be easier for me to feel the emanations.'

And Gwydion stared at him, then threw back his head and laughed fit to burst, before clapping him on the back and saying, 'Oh, you are a diamond among men, Willand! Truly – truly, you are!'

The next day they crossed the River Arfyn and then the Stoore, and on the night of the new moon Will cut himself a fresh hazel wand and began to feel something moving in the earth.

'Might this not be the Caorthan lign?' Gwydion asked anxiously as they bent down to examine the ground. 'We are no more than a dozen leagues from Aston Oddingley.'

'I can feel something,' Will said, still unsure. 'But it's confused. All I know is that my feet want to go this way.'

'You wish to head south still?' Gwydion asked doubtfully. 'Surely, the lign runs more or less west to east.'

'But I feel something drawing me the other way,' Will said. He sensed the wizard's frustration. 'Does it seem wrong to you?'

'It is you who must be certain. Open your mind. Are you reading the land as you should? Or are you listening to the desires of your heart?'

'They're one and the same, Master Gwydion.'

'But perhaps they are not.'

Will felt the wizard's words cut like an accusation. 'Don't you trust me? Don't you believe I'm trying to lead you the right way?'

'Do not take it amiss. Perhaps there is a battlestone nearby.'

'No. No, I don't think so. This time I'm just angry with you.'

'Face it, Willand. There is something else in your mind that is interfering with our task.'

'Well, I don't see it that way, Master Gwydion.'

'For three days now you have been homing like a dove on a dovecot.'

'A *dove*?'

Gwydion put his hands together and said with a despairing smile, 'You have been heading straight towards the Vale!'

'Oh . . .' Will's shoulders sagged. 'I see . . .'

He looked inside himself. Of course it was true that he wanted to return home. And nothing would have been nicer than to have seen his mother and father again. His hand went to the leaping fish talisman that hung around his neck, the one that Breona had given him with her love. Despite all he had learned, the words on it remained stubbornly beyond his skill to read. He showed it to Gwydion again.

'Breona said this token was with me when you found me. Can't you read it?'

'It is written in no script that I recognize. Nor can I guess at what the sigil means.' Gwydion gave it back.

'Three triangles nested inside one another – it's a riddle, wrapped in a mystery, inside a . . . a . . .'

'An enigma?'

'Yes. An enigma.' He stretched and yawned. 'I could certainly eat a piece of apple pie tonight, but I really don't think I'm forgetting about our task.'

The wizard nodded, satisfied. 'I believe you. But what I would like to know now is what else might have been drawing you this way.'

'I don't know . . .' Will fell silent, but then he sat up and cried. 'Master Gwydion!'

'What is it?'

'I've been thinking a lot about the Dragon Stone. Three times now in dreams I've thought myself its master only to find the key to it had slipped away on waking. But now I think I know what the second reading means. I wondered where I'd heard the like of it before, and now I think I know.

> *Northern King's bewitched son,*
> *Queen of the Moon in her father's field.*
> *Dragon of Darkness, awaken and slay!*
> *Lonely Stone take war away!*

'Do you remember you once said you brought me into the Vale because of its nearness to the Tops and to the Giant's Ring?'

The wizard's eyes were as unwavering as an eagle's. 'That is so, I did.'

'You also said you thought the Ring might be near a lign, and that a form of protection flowed from it.'

Gwydion nodded. 'The true name of the Giant's Ring is *Bethen feilli Imbliungh*, or the Navel of the World.'

'This is where one of your history lessons pays back your efforts, Master Gwydion, for when we were in Dimmet's snug you told me the story of the Giant's Ring back in the time of the First Men. You told me about the tomb of Orba that stands nearby. You said she was the wife of Finglas, and called Queen of the Summer Moon!'

Gwydion became thoughtful. 'By all that lives and breathes, so I did!'

'You also said that Finglas came from the north country. So we have: "Northern king's bewitched son" – that could be Finglas – and "Queen of the Moon in her father's field". Finglas came south to take her as his wife, so this must have been the land of her people, and not his!'

'That is so. She was later buried in the heart of her father's domain, which later still was ravaged by the black dragon, Fumi.'

'So: "Dragon of Darkness, awaken and slay!" And then the Dragon Stone itself: "Lonely Stone take war away!"'

Gwydion walked in a circle, but for once his thoughts flew straight as an arrow. 'It all fits, snug as a bud! And here is the clinch: Finglas quarrelled with those druida who came twice a year to *Bethen feilli Imbliungh* to acknowledge the power of the lorc. He feared that it would involve him in war, and so he had a magical stone of his own fashioned and erected close to the Ring. It was called after him: Liarix Finglas – or as folk now say, the King's Stone. If I had to make a guess where the next battlestone is to be found, I would say it lies close by the King's Stone. Most likely it lies within the shadow made at the moment of Midsummer sunrise, for that is said to be the time of year when all the ancient stone rings of the Realm are most flooded with power.'

'Then maybe we have a helper!' Will cried. 'Maybe the Liarix has been doing part of our work for us – what better place for a battlestone than under the shadow of a guardian stone all these years?'

'But consider this: it could be that the failing of the Liarix is one of the reasons the lorc has sprung so suddenly back to life. The Giant's Ring was always a place of great power.

I suspect that it is the navel through which influence is fed into the lorc. That is what is understood by all land-feeling folk who have ever passed it by. In our age, shepherds are rarely men of great book learning, yet few mortal men appreciate the land as they do. And it is the shepherds who have always said that a piece of the Liarix gives them good luck as they drive their flocks to market over the Tops. In all these centuries they have chipped away many small pieces, so that now much of the Liarix is missing, and with it no doubt a portion of its blissful strength. Come, Will! We must visit the Giant's Ring, for there I think we shall find our next clue.'

They pressed on southward until sunset, and Will began to feel by the mood of the ground that they were coming very close to the Vale. Homesickness seized him as he remembered the day he had left. Cuckootide at home had always been a happy time – old Valesmen sitting on the benches in the sun outside the Green Man, lifting their cider flagons and telling tales of the olden days. Then the raising up of the May Pole, and the racing round the Tarry Stone. He thought of Eldmar and Breona then, and the stinging that came at the corners of his eyes told him he was about to weep. And when Gwydion called a halt, he was caught by surprise. He tried to laugh off his tears, and protested that there was no need to stop and that he could easily walk another league or two. But the wizard said softly, 'Little enough remains of our day's journey, and perhaps it would be better if we reached the Giant's Ring tomorrow, in morning light and fully refreshed. So let us rest here and prepare for supper.'

Will did not argue. He was grateful for the chance to stretch out on the grass and to breathe the balmy air of a late spring evening. All day the ground underfoot had been changing colour to a more familiar brown, and now the very air tasted like it did at home. He realized they were closer to the Vale than he had at first supposed, for they were now on the Tops.

While Gwydion went to find woodland food for their supper, Will stared into the flames that licked from under their simmering water pot. He felt greatly pleased to have solved the verse at last and guided Gwydion towards another battlestone, but he knew that finding it would only lead to another and then another, and all that would take him further from home.

A powerful longing seized him. He imagined what Eldmar and Breona would be doing now in the cottage that he had not visited for two years. They would be preparing for bed, most likely. Breona saying goodnight to the neighbours, or going inside to lean over and kiss Eldmar on the forehead as she so often did. Or perhaps his father was coming in from the horse or finishing off an hour or two of tall tales and jolly songs down at the Green Man.

Will could see nothing of the green cleft in which Nether Norton nestled, yet surely he could not be more than a league from the place he had always called home. If only he could steal back there for a moment and take a look at it . . .

But how? The Vale was under a cloak of concealing magic, and even if it had been spread below him as plain as a pike-staff he would not have thought it right to go there until his duty was done.

Yet he was filled with a powerful desire to speak with the folk he thought of as his mother and father, to hug them and to be with them just for a little while, and so be a wandering orphan no longer.

He took the little green fish out of his shirt and rubbed it between finger and thumb. He felt the comfort it usually brought him, but then an eerie feeling came over him and he got to his feet and moved away from the fire. The night was clear and the moon a thin crescent, no more than a fingernail paring that was falling into the afterglow of the west. He thought of that strange Cuckootide when everything had changed, and of the fateful wish he had made to go up onto the Tops. So much had passed since then. So much had changed. But home never changed. The Vale would always be the same.

He looked at his hands and forearms held up against the dusk sky. They were broader, a man's hands and arms – arms that had often scried the land, hands that, if Gort were to be believed, had more than once projected great magic. Will recalled the curious book of spells he had once played with, and that memory sapped away some of his lightness of spirit. Then he remembered the terrible moment he had seen the yew tree of Preston Mantles split open, and the skeleton of young Wale flashed before his eyes, sending a thrill of horror through him.

'Why am I thinking all this?' he asked, suddenly wary. 'It's the battlestone. It must be closer than I thought.'

He tried to get control of himself. Even so, a cold dread continued to creep over his mind, and he shivered. It feels as if somebody just stepped on my grave, he thought. That's what Gwydion says when someone shivers for no good reason.

The moon had not yet come to first quarter and there was something unusual about the way the earth stream was rising in the hollows of his bones. Its strength surprised him. He looked around for Gwydion to tell him that something seemed to be going amiss, but the wizard had gone in search of water herbs and had wandered down into a fold in the land where the Sware Brook ran.

A faint feeling of despair floated upon the air, a mustiness, unmistakable like a characteristic but half-forgotten reek . . .

What was it?

He had noticed it at Clarendon, faintly at Preston Mantles, then again at the dead pond. Now he knew what he had smelled at Foderingham in the middle of the night, and once more as they entered Ludford . . .

It was not Death he had smelled – it was Maskull.

He jumped up, looking round, alert and on his guard. But there was nothing to see. He pulled his cloak tighter about him, then directed his thoughts inwardly and tried to open his mind to see if he could detect the reek. But it was gone.

Slowly he relaxed. He had imagined it. It was another phantom inspired by the nearness of the battlestone. But the impact of the revelation remained and the idea continued to tingle bleakly through him like shock. Does Gwydion have any idea how close his enemy came to finding me? And how often?

The feeling that overcame me in the Great Hall at Ludford was enormously powerful – so powerful that I wanted to kill, or to die! Could that have been Maskull's doing too? Could there be a clever game being played by him? One that Gwydion knows nothing about?

He looked up at the sky. It was at least an hour after sunset now, and there was a lingering light in the west, but an undue darkness lay upon the moon's yellow crescent. He took a few steps towards it, then halted. The land still did not feel good under his feet. He went back to the small fire and sat down to warm himself, but as the slender moon sank ever towards the skyline he began to feel the insistence of the lign. It ran close by, there under the dark mass of a wood to the south, visible now to his eyes as a faint greenish glow. He turned his back on the fire, allowing his sight to adjust to the faintness.

There was no wind. Instead, a deep silence lay over the land like a blanket, and Louvan, the milky-pale tether of the sky, blazed overhead, echoing the faintness of the lign.

Will could smell stinkhorns in the nearby wood, strange fungi that burst out of witch's eggs. They filled the woods wherever they were found with the smell of rotten meat, drawing flies to them in the day and black beetles by night. It must have been their cold scent that he had mistaken for the presence of the sorcerer.

On the far side of the copse he could see the lign emerging. According to Gwydion, the lign they might expect to find here was Eburos, the lign of the yew tree, the greatest of the nine green lanes to have been flung across the Isles. He walked a few paces towards it, groping over uneven ground, then he saw against the skyline what looked like a group of people, and a little way from them stood a tall, angular stone.

He wanted to shout out 'Master Gwydion!' but his words strangled away in a whisper. He stumbled towards the tall stone, seeing how the pale-glowing lign passed very near to it. When he looked back neither Gwydion nor the little fire that he had lit were to be seen. This was the very crest of the Tops, the highest land for many leagues in any direction. He saw now that what he had taken for figures was a collection of standing stones.

So this, after all, was the Giant's Ring. But it was not as he had imagined it. Instead of a circle of huge, oblong slabs many times the height of a man, these stones were small, hunched and shapeless, like a group of beggars standing at the round table of their beggar-king. But there was no table, just a circle of grass forty or fifty paces across. By starlight and the eerie glow of the lign, he could just make out the chief stone, the largest of them, standing to the north. He approached boldly and, as if he had been invited, laid both hands upon its gnarled and pock-marked surface.

He did not know why he had done so, it just felt like the respectful thing to do. He felt no fear or sickness as he had while approaching the battlestones. Strangely, the lign did not pass through the circle as he had supposed it would, but ran instead some way to the north, nearer to where the King's Stone brooded. The touch of the stone was cold on his palms. Its surface was rough, covered with dry, scaly growths and deeply pitted as if eaten into by stone-devouring worms. It seemed to him vastly ancient and connected to some enormous mystical structure that brooded under the ground.

Had Gwydion been close by he would have called out to tell him what he had found, to say that although the feeling was strong it was unlike the horrible feelings he had felt before. The Giant's Ring felt sweet and warm and caring, as if it truly was the navel of the world!

But Gwydion was not in sight and Will did not break his silence. Instead he walked into the middle of the Ring and put out his arms, turning about so that the sky and all the stars whirled about above his head. Then he noticed the flickering in the earth. He steadied himself, a little dizzy now, planting his feet more firmly for balance in the turf. The ground was pulsing with an almost imperceptible lilac-coloured light. He saw sparkles here and there in the stones. Bands of purple were revealed in the earth under his feet, making a great spiral pattern, and there were faint tremors shaking the ground. Then a great spike of blue light flashed from the top of the Liarix, reaching like a blade upward into the sky.

'Whoaah!' Will cried as the tremors grew and almost threw him off his feet. He lifted his eyes and saw overhead what looked like a purple shooting star, only this was coming down straight on top of him, faster and faster and—

There was a whooshing that grew quickly into a deaf-ening roar. Then the purple light from above struck and he felt himself blown into dust.

The next thing he knew he had been raised high in the air above the Giant's Ring and was looking down on a carpet of spreading light. Colours and patterns blasted out from the ground. A repetitive humming, a four-fold thumping music, seemed to come from all around. He saw the blue glow on the Liarix and the green lign stretching far to east and west and running by the dark hollow he knew must be the Vale. But all this was gone in an instant from his mind, for the pain hit him and he heard himself screaming out. He began writhing and turning helplessly in the air like a hanged man, his flesh burning in a mass of purple flame.

He screamed, but his agony rose higher. It seemed to last forever as he hung there, twisting, roasting in a demonic flame. His braids crackled, thrashed against his cheek like burning serpents. He flailed his arms and screamed again, but then he was hurled violently from the flame and slammed down into the ground with bone-snapping force. He rolled over and over in the damp turf, just grateful that the fire had stopped and that he was still alive.

He could smell wet earth and the pork-stench of singed hair. He was outside the Giant's Ring now, lying in the dark where he had fallen. The immense, head-filling music had gone, and only his own gasps resounded in his ears. But still the flickering purple played all around, eerie and grotesque and indomitable.

And Gwydion was there. He stood tall, glowing within a faint blue aura, sparks sputtering from the silver-white brilliance at the end of his staff. He had brought Will down alive, and bones unbroken, but now he was himself being tested.

A figure stepped out from behind the King's Stone and faced the wizard. He gleamed and spangled in brilliant purple light. He was a sorcerer, young and handsome, elegant and self-assured. He wore no mantle, but weeds of midnight black set about with silver signs. His hands were gloved and his iron-shod feet bespurred like a knight's. He also held a staff, except his seemed to Will to be a rod of iron, for when he struck it against the Liarix it rang, and the ray that swept from it burned an eye-searing violet line across the night.

He swept his cloak from where it lay on the ground to reveal the fallen battlestone. It was half buried and glowed dull red as the sorcerer stepped up onto it.

'Is this what you seek, my brother?'

His face, when he spoke, shimmered, turned momentarily to a death's-head. Gwydion made no reply. Will watched from the darkness, utterly unable to turn away. Even in his pain and confusion he felt the intense power that resided within the one who wielded the cruel, purple light.

A violet ray leapt out from the sorcerer's staff, but before it could reach Gwydion it burst as if against a wall, spreading out like dragon's breath into a sheet of orange flame.

Will dived down in terror and hid his face as a great gust of scorching air passed over him. It sucked all the breath from his lungs, then roared on. He expected the ray to lance out and finish him. He wanted to rise up like a hare and bolt into the darkness. But an immoveable instinct kept him pressed hard to the earth. He had to call up all his courage just to open his eyes.

The sorcerer walked along the rise of a weathered barrow. 'Much have I travelled, since last we met, Gwydion,' he called out. His voice was deep and affecting. 'Much have I tried, and much have I tested the powers of this world. You should have walked with me, or walked with Semias when your time came.'

Two blue thunderbolts hurtled from Gwydion's hands, but were dashed to pieces before they could cross half the distance. Then the violet fire blazed up like anger, roaring all around the sorcerer, enfolding him harmlessly in cold flame.

'Do you hear me, Gwydion? Semias was wrong. In the end he was no more than a dreamer who thought the world could remain as it always had been. His meddling brought us to this.'

'You were always the meddler, not he!'

'I was interested to learn. That is why I grew more powerful than Semias. All the power of the Ogdoad resides in me now. Look at the flame, Gwydion! It does not hurt me. It cannot, for I have bathed in the Spring of Celamon!'

Gwydion's blue aura was burning less brightly now. 'You were always the more foolhardy, Maskull. You are greatly skilled, of that there is no question. But to what use have you put your skills? There is in you, and ever was, the fatal defect.'

Will marvelled at the wizard's courage, yet here was one who had lived through all the ages, and who was now facing his most formidable foe.

The flame that engulfed the sorcerer stopped and he raised his arms. 'You may say what you will, for you are mine now.'

'Vainglory, Maskull! The worst of the failings is stamped right through you! I see that now. Selfishness always writhed in your heart like a maggot, but even that could have been cut out had it not been for your overweening pride!'

The sorcerer laughed. 'Listen to yourself! You dare speak of failings! What is this but envy? You can know nothing of what passes in a mind greater than your own. How could you?'

'Great thinker you may be, but what good is a thinker who knows nothing of compassion?'

'Again you presume to judge me! Measure your own arrogance before you lay blame upon others!'

'Oh, it is plain enough where the arrogance lies, Maskull! You think the world can be as you want it to be, that it should be so, that it must become so for its own good.'

The purple light flared again. 'You were ever a coward, Gwydion. You and Gortamnibrax together! What a pretty pair of cravens you make! You are scared to change. You have never tried to understand the true nature of what must be. And you have not the faintest idea what the true path means!'

Gwydion raised his staff in accusation. 'If only you had once been able to see yourself as Semias eventually came to see you. That is all it would have taken. We knew how your pride drove you to hide your faults from the rest of us. But instead of asking for our help as you were sworn to do, you secretly went your own way. Semias, in his profound wisdom, understood your hidden heart.'

'But he did nothing to stop me. You are as weak as Semias was, and just as ignorant. There is a whole new world out there, one greater than ours, and I have found it. Long ago I anchored our two destinies together, set us on a collision path, and we have been drawing steadily closer through all the ages of this world. This was ever my plan, Gwydion, ever my ambition, to bring two worlds together . . .'

Pain pulsed in Will's face and hands. He could not properly focus his mind on what Maskull was saying, but neither could he turn away, for the sorcerer's voice rose now, sharp and ice clear.

'There will be war, just as I have planned it! War! And with it there will come change! There must be change, Gwydion, for the two worlds to collide. Only afterwards can there be peace. But then there will dawn a true peace, an endless peace, a peace such as neither this world nor the other has known.'

'It will be the peace of the grave! You are deceived by your own insane dreams, Maskull. You must listen to me, while there is still time.'

The sorcerer spat back. 'It's over, Gwydion! Soon we shall stand at the crossroads. And when we do we must take the right track. We must, or else our world will circle endlessly forever in the same rut.'

The great violet flame roared out again, to be stopped again just a few paces short of the place where the wizard stood.

'Maskull, when the loremakers become lorebreakers, then there is no lore!'

Will crouched lower, shocked to his very core by the hideous exchange. Maskull's every thought seemed turned to the furtherance of a vast and unknowable plan. 'Don't let him win, Master Gwydion,' he whispered. 'Don't let him kill you . . .'

'You are a tiresome fellow, Gwydion. The Ogdoad is no more, and you yourself are failing. You should have taken the Long Walk north with Semias when you could. You have clung on too long to the Old Ways, but a new world is coming, and that is why the power is deserting you.'

A new purple flame blasted out, this time with much greater vigour than before. It dissolved just short of Gwydion, and set fire to a small hawthorn bush from which flames licked and crackled. Maskull's voice rang out again, 'As the blade is forged in fire, so must the future be reborn in the pain of war! It is time for the Old Ways to die! Prepare yourself, for your last moment in earthly form is upon you!'

And with that there lashed forth a storm of purple flame that enveloped the wizard. It wrapped his stark figure in a blast of white heat. A roaring fire raged around him. Smoke rose up. Grass burned. Gwydion had resisted as well and as long as he could, but Maskull had triumphed.

Fear gripped Will by the heart and by the guts and he believed there was nothing he could do. He saw the wizard sink down to his knees at last in the centre of the patch of smoking grass. He was burning. Flames flared then died all around him. Then Maskull prepared himself for a final blow. He raised a semblance of Gwydion out of the black, smoking skeleton, up from the ground and cast it into the gnarled grasp of an elder tree.

The wizard's form was impressed upon the tree, trunk upon trunk, arms against branches, limbs caught, melting and melding now so that skin became bark and the figure of the wizard faded from mortal view.

Will could not tear his eyes away from the ghastly sight as the tree consumed the flesh of his friend. Thoughts of the yew tree at Preston Mantles assailed him. Tears coursed down his face as he tried to hold back the horror that was bursting inside him.

Maskull staggered, dizzied it seemed by the tremendous effort he had made. A visible weakness overcame him, though he mastered it, and finally he stumbled wearily down from the barrow until he stood before the tree. In a voice slurred with exhaustion, he said, 'In the end it was the simplest of traps that caught you. I knew you would never be able to resist the urge to save your apprentice. What a fool you were to take a boy into your service at such a time, for the last thing you needed was a hostage to fortune. The Ogdoad is finished. Loremasters are done with. The new world is almost here and we will have no need of any of you. I must leave now, for I have a war to watch over, so fare thee well, Gwydion Elder-tree! Stand sentinel, and keep vigil over my victory stone. And when the armies come as they must to this place may they cut you down with their war-axes and feed you piece by piece into their camp fires . . .'

Will was lost to terror. He could do no more than push his face into the earth in an effort to stifle his sobs. Any moment now, he knew, a gust of violet-white heat would come to sear the flesh from his bones, but he hardly cared, for Gwydion was gone, and the fight was over, and nothing mattered any more.

CHAPTER TWENTY

THE NIGHT RIDE TO HOOE

At last the moon set and the pale light that showed the track of the lign began to fade. For some time purple flames danced like King Elmond's fire above the tips of the stones, but then all guttered low and the night returned to its customary darkness.

Will lay in the dew-damp grass, shivering, feeling nothing but the hollowness that echoed inside him. His clothes stank of smoke, and the burning in his face and hands sank bone deep. Strange, he thought, how fate had delivered him back home in the end. There was not far to go now. If he could only find the Vale, then Breona would fuss over him and cover his burns with a cool compress and soothe his hands with goose grease, and inside a week the skin would start to heal and all his cares would fade away. He would be an ordinary lad again, living an ordinary life, in an ordinary place, and everything would be as it should have been – as it would have been had not this desperate duty come upon him.

Well, now it was over . . .

But as he watched the uncaring stars wheeling in their courses overhead, he knew that he was dreaming a hopeless dream. Things could never be again as they once had been. Maskull had won, and the world would turn sour.

In utter wretchedness he lifted himself up. His body trembled so much he could hardly stand. His hair was singed, scorched away all down one side where his braids had burned like candle wicks. He limped across the swathe of charred grass until he reached the elder tree. How he wished now that he had had the courage to rush forward and fling himself at the sorcerer in a last act of brave defiance. But he had been far too afraid.

But what was worse than everything was knowing that he had been the lure that had drawn Gwydion to his doom. 'You shouldn't have chosen me,' he accused the tree. 'You said I was a Child of Destiny, but I knew I wasn't. You ought to have left me at home and living my happy little life, but you didn't! And now look where all your wisdom's got you!'

He half expected the tree to answer him, but it did not. Instead a cool breeze sprang up and the smell of green came in from the west, taking away some of the stink of charred grass, and the old tree rustled where its leaves were caught by currents of air.

Will looked miserably up at it, and in a voice cracked by anguish, he began to argue. 'I know I shouldn't just go home, Master Gwydion, but what else can I do? I can't go wandering round the Realm looking for stones while there's a war raging. Not on my own. What would I do with them? Cart them all up to Anstin's cave? How long do you think it would be before Maskull found me and turned me into a pile of ashes too?'

The tree creaked, but otherwise stood in silent judgment on him. In the faint starlight, the grass was singing, and he recalled something that Gort had once said about the fae and the Green Man, that they were always remembered by the trees and by the grass.

He felt a salt tear roll down his cheek.

'I suppose they're all lying abed down there in the Vale

looking up at the Tops and telling one another there's a thunderstorm been blowing up. Poor folk! They don't even know there's a war coming. They don't know anything at all about the world.'

He searched for the glow of his camp fire. He wanted to find the crane bag. There was a shirt inside that he could use to bind up his hands. But when he got there his fingers were too burned to untie the thongs and he had to tear at them instead with his teeth.

Something shiny fell out, and he stared at it. It was the silver horn he had won so long ago. He had forgotten all about it and now it made him cry out in fresh agony because in the crucial battle he had not given it a single thought, and so Gwydion had died.

'It was my fault after all,' he wailed, thinking how things might have been if the Green Man and all his elfin warriors had heard the summons.

He let the horn lie among the ashes and started back towards the tree, but something else caught his eye in the darkness, and he went to where it lay. It was close by the huddle of smoking rags that was all that remained of Gwydion's brave last stand. It was the wizard's staff, lying half hidden in the grass where it had been thrown clear of the burning. He reached down to pick it up, and as he did a movement at his back made him turn.

There was a white shape curling there, vaporous and indistinct. Terror spasmed in him, but then a cat miaowed.

'Pangur Ban . . .' he whispered, too drained to feel anything other than gratitude that a friend had come to him in his hour of need.

He propped Gwydion's staff alongside the gnarled trunk of the elder and sat down, his back against the tree, and took the cat in his arms. When he closed his eyes the burning roared in his hands and face and his head seemed filled with red noise. But the cat rubbed himself against

Will's chest and purred, until the pain thinned and Will wept.

He did not know how long had passed, but by the time the chill of night had entered his bones he knew what he must do.

'Wortmaster Gort,' he murmured through blistered lips. 'He'll know how to help. I must find him, but first—'

With a concentrated effort, he put the cat aside and got to his feet, then he climbed the barrow on which the now-darkened Liarix stood. Waves of pain flashed through him. He groped across the scorched grass, and would not stop until he had come to the disturbed earth where the battle-stone lay in the dirt. Pangur Ban would not go near the exposed stone, but stayed close by the elder tree. In the darkness, Will almost fell into the pit, but he felt his way slowly around the edge with outstretched hands until he came to the ink-dark place where Maskull had lain in wait. When his fingers touched the stone a fresh torrent of pain flowed in him. He took his hand away and screamed, but then slammed his hand back against the stone and tried to feel through the pain for the inscription.

It was like thrusting his hand into molten lead, but even though the pain blotted almost everything from his mind, still it seemed to his tormented fingers that the surface was as smooth as slate. The agony was so great that he could feel the shutters of his mind closing. He knew he must not fall into unconsciousness, and drew back. Instantly the magnified pain lessened. He fell to his knees to draw breath, his eyes streaming. When he had gathered his wits he saw that anything he got from the battlestone would have to be taken by magic. Perhaps it had never borne any mark. Perhaps Maskull had read and erased whatever there had been.

So even this was a dead end. With no ogham to read,

all ways forward were blocked. He got up and came back to where Pangur Ban waited.

'I tried,' he told the cat, holding up his hands. 'I'm just not cut out to be a hero.'

'It is a great rede of magic that only he who seeks can eventually find.'

Will's eyes opened wide and for a moment he thought he must be hearing things because cats do not talk and the voice was unmistakable.

'Gwydion?'

'Maskull may have pillaged the darkness from every hidden corner of the world with the intent to undo all the work of the Ogdoad, but he is still not as great as you and I when we stand together!'

'Gwydion!'

'And what happened to *Master* Gwydion, may I ask? Are you always so quick to lose your manners?'

He stared around but saw no sign of the wizard. 'Where are you?'

'Inside the tree. Trees seem to be Maskull's favourite trick these days.'

Will felt his stomach churn and tears came to his eyes. 'I thought you were dead,' he said. 'Like the lad at Preston Mantles.'

'Wale was not a wizard, alas! But even I will be trapped in here until the tree dies, unless you can find a way to release me.'

Will wiped at his stinging eyes. 'I'll get an axe and chop it down!'

'What? And torture me?' the voice cried. 'I would feel it keenly, for my consciousness is now one with the tree. If this old witch-elder should die I would not soon be able to return to the world.'

'But you told me your spirit was inside a philosopher's stone, buried in a secret place in the Far North!'

'So it is. And I have hidden it well – you would never find it.'

'Then . . . what should I do?'

'The only way I can be restored is by the use of great magic, the kind that only Ogdoad wizards can accomplish.'

'But who shall I bring? There are no other Ogdoad wizards left in the world, except . . .'

'I do not think you can very well ask Maskull.'

'Then who?' Will's heart was thumping. 'I thought I would go and fetch the Wortmaster.'

'There is no time for that. And in any case this work goes far beyond anything my good friend Gort has ever dealt with. Maskull's spells often employ the power of night. It's likely that if I do not find release by dawn I will have to stay here.'

'But what can be done in just a few hours?' Will asked. 'Master Gwydion, tell me what to do and I'll do it!'

'It will require great magic. It will be both delicate and dangerous. Are you ready to try it?'

Every fibre of Will's being recoiled from the idea, but he nodded. 'I'll do it.'

'First you must open your mind as I have taught you. Then you must allow me to borrow your body for a little while.'

Will blinked. 'Borrow my body?'

'I need to – how shall I put this? – I need to use it for a little while.'

'But what about my own spirit? Where shall I go in the meanwhile?'

'Your consciousness will have to come in here.'

'You mean, I'm to go into the tree? And you'll be standing out here – inside me?'

'That is more or less the gist of it. Only when I am free to move will I be able to work the magic needed to release you.' There was a pause. 'I shall not pretend that the procedure is without danger. Let us hope your understanding of the true tongue is by now as deep as it needs to be. For the invocation you must appreciate the shades of meaning in the words that I shall ask you to speak, for intention counts for much in the uttering of spells.'

'Master Gwydion, I'm not sure I can do this.'

What he meant to say was that he was sure he could not.

'Heroes do not know they are heroes until the moment of proof comes.'

Will closed his eyes and looked inside himself. He was trembling. There was only fear there, but what had Gwydion said about the three weaknesses? Hatred, jealousy and fear. In his own way he had triumphed over hatred and conquered jealousy. Now it was time to banish fear. Though he felt almost ready to faint, he drew a deep breath and said in his strongest voice, 'Master Gwydion, I'm ready.'

'Then lie down close to the foot of the tree. Hold the foot of my staff in your left hand. Make sure the head of it touches the trunk. Open your mind and I will do the rest. Now, say after me . . .'

Will did as he was told. He composed himself and closed his eyes. His face and hands raged maddeningly, but he tried to clear his mind of pain then opened it and repeated the ancient words. It was not difficult, because the true tongue was beautiful, and what he had learned of it made it even more so. Gwydion's staff began to tremble and even though his eyes were tightly shut Will saw a blinding light that seemed to come from the head of the staff.

A strange sensation began to pass through him. It felt as if he was floating, but it soon became like falling, endlessly as if into a bottomless void. Yet almost before he had time to grow fearful the feeling was gone and he began to feel a wind caressing his skin, blowing through his hair and across his face. A profound sense of place came to him, as if he had been here for all eternity. The seasons and cycles seemed to wheel overhead endlessly. The stars and the clouds were his friends, the moon was his lover, and the sun both mother and father. He fed on sunlight and drank in the rain and gloried in the spring and slept through the winter and felt the earth streams rising and falling in the ground all around . . .

Yet when he tried to open his eyes he found he could not. He could not move at all. He realized that he was no longer breathing, and that no pulse was stirring his heart. 'I'm trapped!' he thought. He tried to struggle, but there was nothing to struggle against and nothing to struggle with. It was how he had imagined being buried alive must feel. He thought again of the Preston Mantles skeleton and his mind reeled at the lonely, terrifying death Wale must have suffered. It was a death he knew he too would soon suffer, if Gwydion made a mistake.

Why is nothing happening? his mind screamed. Why doesn't Gwydion do something?

But then a cooler, calmer part of him replied that all his struggles were against nothing more than his own fear. He could hear Gwydion's voice now, faint, as if coming from far away. He could not understand what it said, though he strained to hear. Then there came three taps against the tree, and he felt them like touches against his own flesh. He tried to call back but he was mute. He could do nothing. The floating, falling sensation took hold of him once again and this time he recognized it for what it was. The time had come to let go and allow himself to leave the tree, or he would be as stuck as Gwydion had been. All at once he felt the bonds that held him begin to slacken. He opened his mind and trusted to his deliverance.

This time the blind fall stretched out endlessly. What had felt like a terrifying plunge before now seemed more like flying. A pure sense of freedom took him, as if his spirit had been released to go where it would. It seemed to him that he was very high up and looking down over all the sleeping world. But then a terrific jolt hit him, and the sense that he was hurtling down from a great height came back. He gasped, gulped air and the stinging returned with a rush into his face and hands. The next moment he was lying crumpled, his face pressed into the ground and the dewy turf cooling his forehead. It was miraculous – when he tried to turn over, his body did exactly as he told it. When he tried to breathe, a great lungful of fresh air plunged into him.

He opened his eyes. The dark of this now moonless night was brilliant compared to the darkness he had just known. Stars spangled the sky, but there was a dark patch among them.

'Who's there?' he cried.

Gwydion leant heavily on his staff. He was exhausted, barely able to speak, but he murmured. 'Who do you think?'

He tried to jump up and hug the wizard. 'Oh, Master Gwydion!' He staggered. 'I tried to read the stone, Master Gwydion, but it has no verse on it!'

'Steady! You have been out of your mind. Your thoughts were smashed up by the clash. Magic does that sometimes.'

Will gasped, caught hold of Gwydion's staff and clung to it. When its head began to glow with a weird light, the wizard braced his feet and quietly helped him take a long draught of restoring power from the earth. With refreshment came renewed pain. It throbbed in Will's face and hands. He blew softly on the backs of his hands in turn, but found little relief.

Gwydion urged him to approach the battlestone. He saw that despite its great strength, its emanations did not spread far for they were pent up by the Liarix. Even so, Will could feel its power surging eastward along the lign.

'Be careful, Master Gwydion. The lorc is in spate tonight.'

When the wizard reached the pit he bent down to look in. The battlestone was smooth, and in the blue glow of the wizard's staff it looked as if the dirt had been whirled out from around it by a vortex.

'What has the fool done with his magic?' Gwydion said, laying his blackened hands on the stone. He made words, then stood up. 'As I feared. Maskull's skills were ever showy and incomplete. He was always more concerned with appearance than substance, which is a true sign of knavery. Nor has he used much care in his magic this time. Hasty casts have been made, and one has been used to hide the inscription.'

'Can't you take the spell off again?'

'Perhaps, if I knew what it was. But magic is not an endless resource to be raised at need. After the struggles of tonight my strength needs a little while longer to recover.' He looked around as if seeking for something in the darkness. 'And a guard-spell has been mounted that will work at least until sunrise. As I suspected, Maskull has used the powers of the night. No doubt he is gambling that dawn will come and trap me forever in yonder tree. He is a difficult adversary, for he knows me well – but not half so well as he thinks!'

'Why did he not kill me, Master Gwydion?'

'Because he still thinks you are no more than a wizard's bag-carrier, an upstart fledgling crow, for that is how I have represented you all along.'

'But he came to Foderingham and then to Ludford. I saw him, thinking I saw Death.'

'It was not to find you that he went to Foderingham, but to look for the Dragon Stone. And later, he went to Ludford in anticipation of my arrival there, for it was ever the habit of the Ogdoad to draw nigh to the meeting places of temporal power, and it has lately been his way to watch for what I might have left unguarded so that he may lay down traps for me.' Gwydion speared his staff into the displaced earth. 'Maskull knows me of old, but equally well do I know him. He is a beetle who will fly over many a sweet flower to land in a cow-shard. Remind me sometime to school you in the Rede of Friendship, which lies close to the heart of magic.'

'What did he mean by all that talk of worlds colliding?'

'Vanity! Vain dreams of supremacy and domination. He thinks there is freedom in that. And he supposes there must be war to bring about this "collision of worlds" that he craves. Whatever it is, he thinks he is bringing it upon us by his own efforts. He does not see just how much he has become a slave to the power of the lorc.'

Will looked down at the baleful slab that was greedily supping strength in the werelight. 'I know one thing,' he said, and made Gwydion look up. 'This must be the Doomstone.'

The wizard's glance was so penetrating that it scared him. 'Do your talents tell you that?'

'I don't feel it, but I think it must be so.'

'Tell me why.'

'Because Maskull said so while he was gloating over his victory. He said something like: "Stand here, Gwydion Elder-tree, and keep watch over my victory stone. When the armies come as they must they'll cut you down and feed you into their fires." I think it must mean the first battle will be fought here.'

Gwydion placed his hands on Will's shoulders. 'Do not think, Willand. *Feel.*'

He opened his mind and new fears overwhelmed him. 'What do you mean to do?'

'I want you to look and listen.' Gwydion straightened, his face grim in the dull blue glow of his staff. He hissed at the stone like an angry cat and then stretched out his left arm. A moment later a silent white shape flashed into the werelight. It was a barn owl and it perched lightly on the wizard's outstretched sleeve.

Will was amazed at the bird, and at the way it looked at Gwydion. It seemed to understand when he spoke.

'*Mar achoinni, cueir foras a-chuen Cormac-t . . .*'

Then the owl departed as quickly and as silently as it had come.

'What did you say to it, Master Gwydion?'

'I was making arrangements. When I have finished my work there will be no difficulty in moving the stone. I will send it safe over the seas into the keeping of my friend Cormac the Strong. He is lord of the Clan MacCarthach, builder and master of the stronghold of An Blarna. Don't look so stricken, lad! If I am successful the husk of this monster will confer on him and his guests for ever afterwards not a plague but a special boon!'

Will's heart was beating like a drum. 'You . . . you're going to drain it, aren't you?'

'I am.'

He half-turned to look over his shoulder towards the Vale. 'But you said that was too dangerous!'

Gwydion turned his face skyward. 'It is our only chance. Two great armies are marching to war. Their first encounter is at hand. I am going to do what I must.'

'You told me that to drain a battlestone would be slow, painstaking work. You said the harm had to be let out a drop at a time, and each drop dealt with piecemeal before the next could be allowed out.' He crowded the wizard. 'You said that if all the harm escaped at once it would—'

'Then give me room to work! The Plaguestone taught me much that I did not know when we raised the Dragon Stone. I shall move with speed, but also with caution, for Maskull's crude binding-spells will surely complicate my task.'

Will's eyes rolled. Gwydion's plan struck horror through

him, but what else was there? He let himself be turned aside as the wizard planted his feet in the earth and drew inside himself a second great draught of power. Then Gwydion began to dance, stepping out the complex bodily movements that gave form and strength to his incantations. At last he addressed the stone. His fingers crept over its surface as he began to interrogate it, searching out as far as he could the magical snares that had been laid for him.

Will calmed his own tumbling thoughts then dared to open his mind. He felt the churning, evasive darkness contained within the stone. After a while he began to fear for the wizard, for Gwydion seemed to fall into a trance, and when he climbed out of the pit and wandered into the Giant's Ring he began to mouth words in a language that Will did not know, speaking in a voice that was not his own.

'. . . *tireauq eroproc ni otcnufed mecov te,*
tinev ni sarbif erenluv enis setnats idigir sinomlup,
salludem ataturcs otel sadileg . . .'

At length he came back to himself and spoke again in simple fashion without opening his eyes. 'I have had words with the Morrigain. She is the hag who portends war. She says she walks now in the East, and looks forward to her feast of flesh.'

'What does that mean?' Will breathed.

'It means that the armies are not heading this way after all.' Gwydion's face looked worn and grey in the werelight. 'It means that we have been deceived – this stone is not the Doomstone.'

Will felt the realization jolt him. 'But it must be! It's far more powerful than the Dragon Stone!'

'It is not the Doomstone. You are confused by its nearness to the Ring and by the spells that Maskull has applied.

We have been wrong-footed by my clever foe. Yet one detail still favours us – Maskull's spells have been made cheaply tonight. I shall draw aside his night veil and reveal the clue beneath, for the verse is now our only hope of finding the real Doomstone in time.'

'Wouldn't it be better to wait until daylight?'

Gwydion smiled a humourless smile. 'The bloodbath is now less than half a night away.'

'That soon?'

'Do you not feel it?'

He nodded grimly. 'The lorc is brim-full.'

'And the Doomstone, wherever it is, has been set a-wailing. It is calling men to their deaths even as we debate. The Morrigain has said that the next sunset will be stained red with blood. Stand back! For I must make a start, and in this you cannot help me.'

Will sat by the elder tree. Thirty paces was not enough for safety, but it allowed Gwydion to gather calm undisturbed. Wanting comfort, Will looked for Pangur Ban, but the cat had wisely gone. Back on the shallow rise, on the far side of the Liarix, the weird light of Gwydion's staff waxed brighter and spread a lustre over that sombre graveside as he laid out his materials. He blew powders from his pouch over the stone, then poured silvery drops from a phial.

'*Aircill u mas brethar,*' he told the stone gently. '*Foscleig te criedhe mo!*'

The first mass of harm drawn from the stone glowed with a fearsome blackness. It sucked the wizard's magelight into itself hungrily as it rose from the stone, then tightened into a spinning ball and hovered above the battlestone making the light of the staff turn drear and brown. Gwydion danced. He played the globe like a bee-charmer plays a swarm, singing out to it in different tongues and voices, his movements and gestures enmeshing it in spells, persuading it, containing it, while all the time he coaxed it ever higher above the stone. He steered the spinning mass with care, veering and backing his steps this way and that in front of the battlestone. Each time he withdrew a pace, the black globe fell, trying, or so it seemed, to re-establish itself upon the stone. But every time Gwydion moved in again to drive it upward. Though it circled and spat back at him, it could not find a way to pull itself down. He worked it further and further into the air and finally, when it was high above the ground and could be seen only by the way it crimped and dulled the starlight, Gwydion sent a burning bolt soaring against it.

Brilliant blue fire shot straight to the heart of the globe, and penetrated it. It bellied out, growing hideously bigger for a moment. Will feared it had absorbed the bolt, but as it bloated it also grew greyer and thinner, so that finally it ruptured and blew itself to pieces.

A shell of exploded substance rained down. As it passed through Will, he felt pains in his teeth and the joints of his bones. Pains gripped his stomach and head, coming to a terrifying peak, but then dying away to leave a profound weariness behind. He understood then that each battlestone has its own quality of harm. That each of them would be different, not like so many arrowheads and billhooks forged alike in Grendon Mill, but every one possessing a particular character.

'So far, so good,' Gwydion said. He examined the stone's stubborn surface for marks. 'Stay back! We have a long way to go yet.'

But the wizard stood still and stared into space. Will called out anxiously, 'What are you waiting for, Master Gwydion?'

'I must replenish myself and find my centre. It is hard to remember humility when the words of great magic are forming in the mouth, for often they make a man feel as if all the world is his own to play with. In this lies the great pitfall for those who try to employ magic that is too powerful for them. Stay with me in spirit, Willand, and try to feel what I feel!'

'I will, Master Gwydion!'

He watched, patiently trying to maintain hope. Each release of harmful spirit from the stone must be wholly dispersed. But how many times would Gwydion have to repeat the drawing before the stone was forced to show its verse? And if, by some mischance, he underestimated the battlestone's strength, or overrated his own?

Will tried to push these corrosive thoughts away, knowing that through fellow feeling he must add his own strength to the wizard's. He must become his fountain of hope. But still the stone was getting to a part of him, for he could not but wonder at the many hurts that must surely befall the world now that such a mass of malignity had been set loose. Would there now surface a rash of ills and losses, unexpected injuries and setbacks, unlooked-for infidelities and betrayals? According to Gwydion, that was how the world worked.

But already, the wizard was dancing and applying his magic to the stone once more.

'*Nai dearmhaida, lirran, tar an gharbade sa echearitan, arieas aragh e gundabhain!*'

The next gobbet keened like a banshee. It differed from the first, being larger and in shape more irregular. It was also faster moving, like a gigantic flock of starlings gathering to roost. The wizard had used a different, more powerful, spell to extract the harm, and it pulsed and moved in the air, reminding Will of the round jelly creatures he had seen floating in the ocean. He clenched his fists and stood up, wishing he could help, but knowing he must not interfere.

A deadly struggle was developing above the stone. He

saw shapes like fists and human faces forming in the cloud.
Three times it gathered itself and lunged forward in an
attempt to overbear and seize the one who tormented it,
but each time Gwydion's resolve held. And at last it was
the wizard's turn to inflict and to punish. He mouthed a
great spell in the true tongue that found a weakness in his
adversary. As the black motes gathered angrily above him,
his magic squeezed them together and they began burning
up as red as fire sparks. Most were confined by the spell,
but some lunged down in violent bursts or swung out as
if trying to claw the wizard away. But Gwydion had clothed
himself in protections, and any mote that came too close
burned out in a trail of orange fire. He stood fast until the
vigour of the cloud was spent, then the second mass of
harm blew asunder and was cast outward to the four winds.

This time Will was thrown to the ground. He winced in
pain and all the seams of his shirt tore in tatters, but then
he jumped up and cheered at the smuts and cinders that
floated down all around.

'You did it, Master Gwydion!'

'I told you to lie low!' Gwydion snapped. His face had
paled with the effort. He showed irritation that the skin of
the stone had again refused to yield up its message. 'This
is sore and thirsty work,' he called. 'And now I must engage
again!'

Without pause he plunged back into the fight. The third
draught of darkness pulled from the stone took on the indistinct shape of a great winged thing. It rose, terrible and
threatening. It hovered over Gwydion, a beast woven of
shadows, a carrion-feeder that stank of death. Will felt the
gust of its wing beats and smelled the stench of all the fears
that he had ever known. It roared and flapped like a rising
phoenix, burning in dark flame, but despite its efforts it
could not quite take to the air.

Gwydion danced forward boldly and struck it with his

staff. He overcame its menace and it slid apart into the grey smoke of nothingness, and when that smoke passed over Will he felt his stomach clench as if he had fallen into a chasm. He reeled and passed for a moment into unconsciousness.

When he woke up he saw Gwydion staggering and ran to help him. The wizard was trembling. His body felt wiry and insubstantial, like a man who has not eaten for too long, his cheeks were sunken and his eyes rimmed red.

He looked up at Will. 'You should take greater care,' he said wanly. 'Your nose is bleeding.'

'Stop now, Master Gwydion. Stop now, I beg you! At least rest a while.'

'I cannot,' the wizard said, taking his arm. 'But I must tread with greater care. I should not have used my staff so quickly, for the stone is getting wiser to my ways. The last release almost gained earthly form, and woe betide us if that should happen!'

'How many more times must you do it? Rest a while first. And drink.'

Will offered him water. Gwydion looked up at the sky and emptied the flask over his head. It was now only a month short of the solstice, and the first purples of dawn were already beginning to creep along the rim of the sky. Soon long fingers of light would reach out of the east.

'This stone is not yet half drained. Not until the night's work is done, and wholly done, shall I rest!'

'Oh, no!' Will cried, pointing at the battlestone. 'Look! Master Gwydion, what's happening?'

They approached the stone together, warily yet with grim fascination. Its surface was seething and bubbling like a cauldron of boiling blood.

'I know you for false dissembling villainy!' Gwydion cried, stepping quickly up to the stone. He entangled the emanation in a counter-spell. 'At last! Now I can unbind the foul casts that Maskull has put in here. Until that is

451

done we cannot trust the truth of any verse that we may stir out of the stone.'

As he hauled the illusion out, it writhed and roared on the end of the wizard's staff until it was extinguished with a flourish. What was left on the stone was a mass of half-bestial faces that screamed and pleaded for mercy as they too were drawn out. Gwydion paid them no heed as he destroyed them. When they had gone what remained was the stone's true appearance. It was not smooth at all now, but deeply scored with ogham all along its exposed edges.

'*Feh fris!*' Gwydion shouted in delight. A flood of blue brilliance lit the craggy stone. 'Now we'll see what was hidden. Quickly. It must be raised and read.'

Will jumped down, forced his fingers under the stone, heaved and strained, helping to lift it onto its end. Then Gwydion made him stand back and he circled to read out each of the faces in turn:

> *'The Queen of the East shall Spill Blood,*
> *On the Slave Road, by Werlame's Flood.*
> *The King, in his Kingdom, a Martyr shall Lie,*
> *And Never Gain the Victory.'*

'A worthy translation,' the wizard told him, but then he turned, leaning on his staff as if deep in thought or fighting with some unspoken doubt. 'I believe I now know where we shall find the Doomstone.'

Will marvelled. 'You've solved the verse? So soon?'

Gwydion's haggard face brightened in the magelight. 'The meaning is unmistakable. When the Queen of the East rose up against the invaders of the Slaver empire her armies put three cities to the torch. One, and only one, stands upon a river named in honour of Werlame. It is even now called Verlamion by all save the Sightless Ones who have their own name for it.'

'What do they call it?' he asked.

'Swythen. The red hands raised one of the greatest of their chapter houses upon Werlame's hill because the first recruits in the Realm were gathered here. Swythen is the one they call "the Martyr", for he was killed for his trouble by the Slavers and has lain entombed upon the hill for a thousand years.'

'Does what this stone says have to come true at Verlamion? Must King Hal fall a martyr to his kingdom in that place?'

Gwydion ran his fingers over the stone. 'So we have been told by ancient magic. Whatever happens, King Hal is not fated to win the coming battle, it seems.'

'But if King Hal is fated to lose, that means Duke Richard must win.'

'So you might suppose.'

Despite himself the prospect of a victory for the duke gave Will a secret feeling of satisfaction. If Gwydion had not returned to claim him he would more than likely have been riding to war now alongside Edward. He said, 'So, now it's our task to deprive Duke Richard of his victory, I suppose.'

Gwydion met his eye like a mind-reader. 'It is our task to prevent a bloody slaughter.'

Will straightened. 'How far is Verlamion?'

But Gwydion made no answer. Instead, he began circling the stone, staff in hand, calling out the alternate reading:

> *'When a Queen shall Enslave a King,*
> *Travel at Sunrise a Realm to Gain,*
> *Werlame's Martyr shall Lose the Victory,*
> *And Lie where Blood Never Flows.'*

Will tried hard to commit the lines to memory, but even before he could consider their meaning, a great pore opened up on top of the stone and black slime began to vomit forth. Straight away Gwydion reached out with his staff and tried to cauterize the hole with blue fire, but no matter what spell he tried he could not shut the hole. The stench that came from it made Will gag and drove him back. Then a humming sound rose, filling his head until he felt as if he was being hit with a hammer.

'I warned you that too much harm remained within the stone!' Gwydion shouted as they staggered back. 'Maskull's magic must be emptying it! His last spell was not a binding-spell as I thought, but one designed to release the harm in a rush! If you had not made me pause when you did – if I had kept on dancing out my own opening magic – it would have killed us both!'

Will backed away, his eyes fast on the top of the stone. It bubbled and dripped now as if with molten tar, but this was no illusion, no trick of Maskull's as before. This was all the harm left in the stone, fully half of all there had been, pure harm, emerging now uncontrolled.

This time no unformed mass moved up into the air at Gwydion's command, no shapeless thing quite unable to become itself that danced upon a spell: this was a fully-formed nightmare. It struggled forth, wriggling out into the world through a hole that now seemed much too small to give it birth, and a curse was already burning in the air around it:

'*Anaichte ishubaich na't slaughe immer Werlamich,*
Biedh fordhagan argh fehdair fhuill!
Bidthwe imada oig ishan guihnn!
Caine goirfen Badhbi ta' gach peirte!

'*Bidh de tiudbha da lucht na Trinobhaend!*
Budh d'tiudban dau cuchtar nai!
Buedh tiudhbha dorlin abusgh leaia!'

'Run!' Gwydion shouted.

Will needed no second telling. He turned and bolted as the dread words boomed out over the fields. He could hardly follow the meaning, but he knew that the insane laughing voice spoke of blood and of death. At that moment, nothing could have persuaded Will to leave the wizard's side and they fled together. Gwydion raised his arms and shouted spells and threw up a crackling lightning bolt, but that served only to excite pursuit. They made for the ruined tomb of Orba. Four great weathered stones were all that remained of it, huddled together, heaped in the field. By now the harm had grown to a size greater than the Liarix. And as Will watched, it changed its appearance, having the power to fascinate the eye. It did not look the same two blinks together, but grew more terrible each time.

'This way!' Gwydion cried. 'Over here!'

'What are you doing?' Will called out, astounded that the wizard should be bent on attracting the monster.

'We must draw it away! If it takes power from the Ring it will be impossible to stop! You go that way, and I will go this. Willand, do what you can to make it come to you, for I must replenish my strength!'

Then the wizard climbed up onto the stones of Orba's tomb. He planted his feet wide, his eyes rolled back in his head and he fell into a muttering trance as he tried to draw power from the earth. In that desperate pass it seemed to Will that he had been left to face the danger alone. He stared at the harm that writhed and boiled like a dark flame above the red glow of the battlestone.

'Master Gwydion!' he cried, shaking the wizard. 'Master Gwydion! Be quick!'

The harm struggled one more time and kicked itself free, bursting the battlestone into a dozen fragments. It looked about itself and gave voice to a blood-chilling cry, and when it began to head their way, Will felt pure terror. He knew he must try to draw it off. He waved his arms and shouted, and when the beast advanced upon him, he ran.

The harm's roar was deafening, its footfalls shook the earth. Will drew it away from the wizard, heading neither towards the Ring nor back towards the misshapen finger of the Liarix. He stopped again and again to throw clarts of earth at it and make sure that he was enraging it and tempting it onward. He ran until his knees gave way, got up and ran again, but then he burst through a hedge and crashed down hard amid a mess of half-burned branches. The ground was full of ashes here and still warm – it was the remains of his own camp fire, the place where just a few hours ago he had dreamed of home.

Under him was something hard – the crane bag! He remembered the silver-bound horn and what was engraved on it in the true tongue:

> *Ca iaillea nar oine baiguel ran,*
> *Ar seotimne meoir narla an,*
> *Aln ta'beir aron diel gan.*

> *Should you stand in time of need,*
> *Blow me, and you shall have speed.*

He pulled it out, put it to his lips and winded it with all his might.

Nothing! The air went straight through. And now the harm was coming towards him, bellowing and steaming. Will blew again, harder, spluttering and spittling, but still he could raise no sound. He was about to run on when he remembered how the jacks on Foderingham's walls blew up their trumpets to give warning of approach. He pressed his lips together, and this time the note rang out, clear and high and wavering. He blew upon the horn three times, but there appeared no Green Man, no retinue of elfin warriors as he had hoped. Instead the harm roared and bore down, closing on him as surely as the darkness of night closed upon the twilight world.

Then, just as he thought his last chance had gone, there came an answer to his call. A huge, white mare galloped out of the gloom, and Gwydion was on her back.

'Behold Arondiel!' Gwydion said, riding up swiftly from his place below the stones of Orba's Tomb. 'Arondiel, steed of the Lady Epona of old! Fleetest of horses! You have called her out from the hill above Dumhacan Nadir, for though I missed it at first, her name was hidden upon the horn!'

Will mounted up and bent over the horse's mane and they rode for their lives. 'Run swift into the East, my sure-footed friend!' Gwydion shouted. 'Run fleet and run fair! Race the harm to Verlamion! Speed us into the sunrise, for in the East lies our only hope!'

And they went like the wind, and the harm came in pursuit, its roars shaking the leaves from the trees, its shadow overspreading the sleeping world. It came after them as fast as any earthly horse might gallop, but Will lay forward along Arondiel's mane, fistfuls of silver gripped in his fists, his face pressed against the side of the horse's neck, and they sped onward.

Gwydion hung on behind, casting pitfalls into their wake. Will heard the power of the wizard's spells, but nothing availed them and the harm drew ever closer. 'Master Gwydion, why doesn't it heed your magic?' he cried fearfully.

'Because I do not know the name that would give me power over it.'

'Then, are we lost?'

'Not while I breathe!' Blue fire burned and spun in

Gwydion's hands then was let fly. 'Back, fierce one! Or I shall sting you with a blinding fire!'

Though every bolt delivered into the gloom struck their pursuer, nothing could halt it. Each ball of fire exploded in earth-shuddering booms and shocks of livid light. In those flashes Will saw fields and woods burst into being then vanish again. Over shallow brooks and rivers wide they rose. Past hedgerow elms and hillocks green, galloping at last between two aged oaks that Gwydion webbed with fleeting strands of magic. And all the while he whispered up more spells as Arondiel's hooves hammered onward. The brave mare flew over gates and across brooks, by wood and wold, by heath and hedgerow, but always eastward, as if she knew the swiftest road to glory.

But behind them the harm continued undaunted. Each rushing stride that Arondiel took, it made up a little more ground. Up hill and down dale they dashed, through thicket and glade, across open meadow and iris marsh. But no matter which way their path led them, the harm followed, and nothing that Gwydion threw down could make it stumble or turn aside.

Will hung on, sure not to lose his grip, for he saw that to fall from so fleet a steed as Arondiel would mean certain death. They had soon ridden twice as far and twice as fast as any natural horse could have carried them. They travelled the sleeping land, thundering through dark Hundreds, past the villages of Thring, Wing and Ivangham, then they slowed as they leapt the Slaver road called the Ickenold. At last there rose up a great chalky scarp that stood like a bulwark across their path.

Will was sure the beast would catch them now but though it closed, Gwydion cast up a coruscation of fire before it and Arondiel flew headlong away, taking them up and higher up, towards the ridge above. Beyond lay the Plains of Hooe, but Will saw they would never reach them.

'Hide us!' he cried through gritted teeth. 'Vanish us away as once you did before!'

'We cannot hide! I have been unable to prepare a vanishing-spell. Nor would it or any lesser magic deceive this terror. Wherever we go it will follow us, for we have released it and it is set on our destruction.'

'But if we can't outpace it, and we cannot hide from it, then there's no escape! We must turn and fight it now!'

'Then take courage while you may, Willand! For I fear matters will come to that here upon Beacon Hill!'

But Arondiel was not exhausted yet. She raced up the winding path that led up towards the ridge, while the verse the harm had screamed as it had emerged from the stone rang loud in Will's head. In the true tongue the words had the power to drive men to dread, and their meaning was clear:

> *As the armies approach Verulam,*
> *Gore shall redden the spears!*
> *Young men shall slaughter!*
> *The Crow of Death shall be heard in the Isles!*
>
> *Blood fall upon the folk of Trinovant!*
> *Blood fall down upon them all!*
> *Blood upon each and every one!*

'Arondiel must run no more!' Will called back. 'We must turn here and make our stand!'

'If we do, we shall surely perish!'

'We must stand, Master Gwydion, for we've come to this hill and we must go no further!'

The wizard looked at where they stood and shook his head. 'What certainty brings you here?'

Will begged to be heard. 'Better that we two fight and die here, than go to a place where the harm can feast on the blood of two armies.'

Arondiel reared and set them down. And Will blew a second blast on the silver-bound horn and vanished the horse away as if she had never been. 'Farewell, old thunderfoot!' Gwydion cried out as the mare's form dissolved before them.

'Our thanks go with you!' Will called into the night. 'If I do no more in this life I can fairly claim to have ridden the finest horse that ever there was – or ever will be!'

But there was no more time for thanks and farewells.

'We are unarmed and there is little left of my stock of magic,' Gwydion warned. 'But you know there is one yet who would fight the harm on our behalf. He will come wherever and whenever I might request him.'

'Then request him here and now!'

Gwydion turned. He looked down the hill and saw the shadow emerge from the woods below. It slowed and stopped, suspecting treachery. Then, thinking them at bay, it let out another air-shattering roar and came on.

'Stand firm, Willand! It will not take us without a fight!' Gwydion shouted, then the words of emanation came to his lips. The ground began to shake and break, and as large as the shadow was, that which now emerged at the wizard's request was larger still.

'Alba!' Will cried. 'So he was real, after all!'

'Arise, earth giant!' Gwydion commanded. 'Once summoned, Alba will not suffer such harm as this to roam his realm with impunity.'

And it was true, for in the grey fore-dawn light the giant Alba emerged once more from the dewy earth, as huge-shouldered and mighty as he had been on a day long ago. Again his anger was plain. He grew as he rose, throwing off clods, and when he had stood up he turned his warty face to confront the malign power that stalked the land.

The wrestling was fierce, as first one huge form and then the other seized the advantage. Will looked on, astonished as the harm ripped into Alba's flesh, yet each time he sent his tormentor reeling. Full-fisted blows rained down as the harm coiled, serpent-like, around one of Alba's great limbs and spat venom into his eyes. Alba throttled the harm and threw it down heavily, then the giant took his adversary in a grip of steel. Sinews strained to squeeze the strength from it. Alba gave his all, but just as it seemed he had won the shadow of war dissolved away.

Now a mirage of back smoke was wreathed all around him. It moved, taunting the giant, showing how easy it was to escape his hold. Alba tried time and again to seize the harm once more, but he lost himself at last in the grey mists. Then the air around him began to spark with hurts each more painful than a knife slash. Alba was by now blind with rage. He roared and staggered and cast about again for his enemy, but no enemy could he find. The harm had vanished from sight, yet he was racked by so many maddening pains that he cried out. At last he twirled and flung up his arms, calling out to his enemy to do battle with him. Roaring and stamping furiously upon the ground, he sought in vain that vile serpent head to smite, and had it not been such a fearsome sight Will might have thought it tragic to see Alba's great guardian strength so easily deceived by malice.

But there was more, for now, having thrown the giant into a bewildered passion, the harm drew itself together again and grew up at Alba's back. Once more it assumed solid substance, a clawed limb that ripped at the giant's shoulders and tore his neck. In this way the harm bore Alba down.

Will saw at once that the giant was sorely hurt, for when Alba threw the harm off he groaned like one who knew his fate was sealed, and when the harm came at him again it was clear that Alba's huge strength was spent.

'He's broken!' Will cried.

'The stand was brave, but against such a foe neat bravery could never be enough.'

'Then we are lost!'

Will watched Alba's brown blood flow. He heard the woeful sound as the power left him and he sank to his knees. He fell and began to melt back into the cold clay from which he had arisen. A last groan escaped him and then Alba was gone forever, leaving behind only a hump in the earth like the tomb of an ancient king to show his final resting place.

With Alba's downfall came the vanquishing of their last hopes. Gwydion said, 'It will take one greater even than an earth giant to save us now.'

'Who?' Will asked.

'Who but Great Arthur could face down such a foe?'

He stared at the harm that gathered itself among the shadows below. It melted and merged with itself again, becoming huge and hideous, and taking on something of the shape of the adversary it had defeated. Swirling mists crossed and recrossed and drew themselves up into giant form for the onslaught.

Gwydion raised his fire-blackened hands imploringly. His voice roared out, 'Did I not tell you there would come a day when you were no longer afraid of giants?'

Will smiled grimly. 'I wish I had a worthy weapon in my hand.'

'That wish at least may be granted, for see what place Arondiel has brought us to! Now they call it Beacon Hill, yet this was a great battlefield of old.'

And something in Will stirred and he said, 'Is its name not . . . Badon Hill?'

'The very same! Now ask for your sword and it shall be granted to you!'

And Will went to a knoll below the road and stared down it, enthralled now, and lifting up his arms, he called out, '*Anh farh bouaidan! An ger bouaidhane!*'

And this time as the words came to his lips, he knew that he had once exhorted a great army to victory with the same formula. But now it was Gwydion's turn to make subtle words. He stooped down, for there, shimmering before Will in the grass, there had appeared a sword hilt.

As Will took it in his right hand, a great power seemed to flow in him. He drew the blade from the earth as easily as if he had been sliding it from a scabbard. It was not unlike the sword that had lain at Leir's side, a blade forged long ago. He raised it and saw that it was bright, nimble to the hand and well-balanced. It shone with a high, golden polish that reflected the pale sky and the last of the stars of night. It pleased him very much to take it in his hand.

'Its name is "Branstock",' Gwydion said, his eyes as live as coals now.

'The Sword of Might?' Will whispered, recalling the histories.

'It is the hallowed blade and none other!'

'But how did it come here?'

'How? Because your fate follows you as closely as shadows follow other men. Wield that sword with all your skill, and prepare to die like a hero of old!'

Will turned to face his doom. Down below the victorious harm shrieked until all the hillside echoed. Arm in arm, wizard and warrior backed the last few paces to the summit of the scarp and there stood ready to receive their foe. This is where they would make their stand, here upon the beacon, facing into the darkened west, Gwydion with his staff, Will with his sword, and defiance in both their hearts. Gwydion planted his feet and prepared what spells he could for the last moments. It was now his plan to bleed as great a quantity of harm as he could, to diminish as far as possible the plague he had unleashed upon the world.

Below them, the harm showed its rage. It uttered a laugh rich in menace and triumph, yet as it climbed the scarp towards them, Will raised his sword against it defiantly. He stood shoulder to shoulder with the wizard. No longer did he feel any impulse to run. If he was going to die it seemed fitting that he should die here, beside his friend and teacher, protecting the last Phantarch for as long as his strength might last.

He opened his mind wide, then, and drew in a deep breath of cold air. At last, the oppression of fear began to lift from his spirit. Little by little he took good heart and resolved to fall upon the harm and not to hang back as he had hung back from Maskull. He took two paces forward and held the sword before him, unmoving as the foe came for him.

It tried to swipe him down, and pain flashed through him as the semblance of an arm lashed out at his head. It nearly threw him down, but with a cry he swung the sword and leapt aside, driving the blade upward as Gwydion's blue thunderbolts burst in the air all around.

The harm coalesced into a vile parody of its vanquished enemy. A great, craggy head appeared above Will. A mighty limb tried to crush him, stamp him down, but he danced out of reach, and the giant beast, blinded by fury and malice, tore open air and shivered empty ground impotently.

Then, suddenly, Will's brave blade tore into solid matter and stopped dead. He stumbled forward as agony ran down through his arm. One! – two! – three! – thunderbolts crashed against the beast, forcing it to let go of the blade. Will saw how the wizard's efforts weakened each time. Down Will went. Yet Gwydion stood astride his body, flinging out feeble dregs of magic until the beast turned and tore him aside.

A torrent of dirt swirled up, pelted him with stones, and he was blinded and another pain reared up to fog his mind. But he dashed the dust from his streaming eyes and saw the harm change its shape into that of a fierce and fearsome beast.

Gwydion lay on the ground, exhausted and defenceless before it, and as Will's sight cleared he found his feet and advanced, raising the blade one last time over the body of his fallen friend.

'*Ar Gwydionh!*' he cried in the true tongue. 'This is for your sake!'

And though the harm loomed close over them, something made it halt. Will could not see what it was, but when he raised his sword again, lifting it high above his head, the blade flashed crimson and the grotesque form snarled and turned from side to side as if it was in pain. It roared in rage and threw up a great spurt of dark fire as if to ward off unseen blows. Then, like a wounded bear, it flailed and faltered and began to stumble backward.

'Master Gwydion! Get up!' Will said, waving Branstock aloft. 'Look! It's turned away!'

And on the dark side of the slope the shadow of war was indeed falling back, groaning, crouching low against the hummocky ground. As its marrow failed, so it crawled, cringing lower, as if seeking now only some kind of escape. Will stared in wonder, then looked behind to see what could have worked such a miracle. And there, across the stretch of open land of the Plains of Hooe, pulling itself clear of the eastern horizon, was the magnificent crimson disc of the sun.

The shadow roared again, but this time it was a roar of impotence and despair, the cry of a beast that knew its fate. It struggled, thrashed, sought to dig itself into the ground to avoid the rays that would destroy it.

'We've won!' Will shouted, shaking with joy. He laughed and danced and kicked his legs until he fell down again. 'Look! We're still alive and we've won!'

'*Maithei thuir!*' Gwydion cried as he sank to his knees. He opened his hands to the sky and spoke now the tongue of the Isle, calling upon the memory of Danu, Mother of

Lugh, a lady revered so long ago that no one had offered words to her name in over a thousand years. But Gwydion Truthseeker, the last Phantarch, made mention of her three times over, for this was the closest any wizard had ever come to death.

CHAPTER TWENTY-ONE

SKIES OF FIRE

And so they came down at last onto the Plains of Hooe, and saw the land stretching away eastward in the blue mists of dawn.

Gwydion rejoiced. 'The harm was given entry into this world by the hasty, night-woven spells of a sorcerer, therefore it did not have the power to outlast the darkness!'

Will marvelled. 'So Maskull has unwittingly saved our skins. And he is the one who has brought us within sight of Werlame's Flood.'

'Now you see something of the circles that make up our world. As the rede says, "What goeth, goeth about again."'

'We have a saying much like that in the Vale.'

'Quite so, for I set it there. Though Valesmen have no doubt changed it in the telling. Come! We must still hurry!'

Their chosen way took them to the north of Verlamion, but then Gwydion stopped. He whispered down a calm, then went to stand alone in a meadow for a moment to ask strength from the earth. Will tried to copy him, and followed him through his motions. Once the wizard had replenished himself with a rich draught of earth power, they went on, and Will too felt in some way that was hard to explain that he had been refreshed.

They crossed two immensely strong ligns that Will needed no hazel wand to scry. Then they saw in the fields to the east the banners and tents of a great host. In the far distance Will's keen eyes noticed the rays of the sun glinting upon bright metal, and he knew at once that this must be the army of the Duke of Ebor. Thousands had marched south with their lord, more men than Will had ever seen gathered together in one place before. The sight astonished him and made him pause, but Gwydion led him urgently onward.

They trod fields that were alive with knapweed and plantain and saxifrage. The smell of bruised herbs rose all around them as the sun climbed towards the south, and Will took his bearings once more on the powerfully flowing green lane that ran beneath his feet. By the time they had come close to the camp, the army had already quit their halt and was beginning to marshal in readiness to march on the town.

What a place Verlamion was to look upon! The tower of the great chapter house dominated everything. Lesser buildings lay like a sleeping dog around its feet. The town was built on the tail of a long hill that ran away to the north. The whole of it was enclosed to eastward by an ancient ditch that Gwydion said was called the Tonne. It had been strengthened with sections of wall and hurdle. Will could see how tall beeches had been felled and their grey trunks dragged across the roads to bar the town to man and horse. No traffic moved, and all the way along the ditch Will could see men with mattocks digging the Tonne deeper and raising the bank behind it as high as they could before the attackers made their assault.

'Trinovant lies a long day's journey from here south along the Great North Road,' Gwydion told him. 'Once an ancient city of the Slaver empire stood in the valley where an old slave road still runs. But of the city there is now little trace, except here and there, where Slaver brick and dressed stone have been robbed from the ruins and set into the houses and cloisters of the Sightless Ones.'

Ensconced on the favoured southern side of the hill, their powerful, square tower of stone and brick rose high above a long, buttressed hall. Around it stood a maze of private outbuildings, yards and enclosed precincts. Black-mantled figures could be seen hurrying through the grounds.

'At least we know that no attack will be sent against this side of the town,' Will said.

'True.' Gwydion gestured dismissively towards the hill. 'Yet those walls are not made for defence. They are there to mark the separation of town and cloister.'

Will thought about what Gwydion had said about the Fellows never being allowed to leave their order, and shuddered. He could not take his eyes away from the giant chapter house which loured over the smaller curfew tower and thatched roofs of the town. It was an awesome building, as big as anything he had ever seen. The stolen wealth that it represented was vast, and every penny of it had been robbed from the labours of others.

In the neat lands around Verlamion the dew was lifting. Bumble bees and corn-blue butterflies had come out to forage for nectar and larks were warbling in the sky above. It was going to be a beautiful day. Or it could have been beautiful, Will thought, had it not been for the two armies that had come here bent on slaughter.

'The Doomstone has called them,' Will said, sensing a vile, sweet odour that was drifting on the air. 'I can hear its voice whispering into men's minds. If we hurry, maybe we can still scry out the ligns and find where it lies!'

Gwydion shook his head. 'Too late. The stone cannot be drained now. Our one slender hope is counter-persuasion. I must bend all my arts to bringing the two dukes together to talk. Perhaps, in that way, I may buy a little time, though it seems to me that a battle of some kind is inevitable. With Maskull present, the best that can be hoped for is that the outcome might be turned somewhat to our advantage.'

Fear surged in him. 'Maskull? Here?'

'Did you doubt that he would come? He will be with the King's retinue even as we speak.'

Will grasped the wizard's sleeve. 'But how will you bring the two dukes together? Richard of Ebor and Edgar of Mells? They hate one another with a rare fierceness. With the stone making its madness they'll not listen to persuasions.'

'They will listen to mine.' Gwydion faced him grimly. 'And if they do not I shall apply a contrary enchantment to their minds that forces compliance.'

Will's mouth fell open. 'But to oppose the Doomstone's will with magic inside a living man's skull – that must be dangerous!'

'It is lethal. At the least an irreparable madness will befall them both.'

'Then you cannot do it!' Will took hold of the wizard's robe again and Branstock flashed in his hand. 'Master Gwydion, that would be murder! And it still wouldn't bring an end to the battle.'

'I have done this kind of work before, and would do so again, for many innocent men's lives may be bought for the price of two or three of the stubbornest fools!'

'But the Doomstone whispers to all men! The armies would fight on, even without their leaders. I must find the stone if I can! At least let me try!'

'And then what?'

'You'll find a way. You always do!'

'Willand!' Gwydion seized him, and his eyes blazed. 'Do not forget: the Doomstone is affecting you too.'

'And you, Master Gwydion!'

'You will be obedient to me in this!'

'No!' Will struggled and took possession of himself long enough to curb his tongue. 'Yes, Master Gwydion! If you say so!'

Only when he had stepped away from the lign and fought the influence fully out of his mind did he see the truth: Gwydion would never allow him to go up against the Doomstone – he would have to do what he must alone.

The wizard made Will take off his cloak and wrap it around the fabulous sword. He said the sight of a naked blade in the hand of one who wore no friendly colour of livery might easily be misunderstood. 'As you have said, the minds of these soldiers are already inflamed by the prospect of battle. They will see all strangers as enemies, and foreseeable trouble is best avoided.'

When they stopped to take a look at the defences of the town Will asked, 'What do you think is in Duke Richard's mind?'

Gwydion shaded his eyes and peered at the long, lazily curling pennons that flew near the town's curfew tower. 'I think it would have been Friend Richard's wish to march here and win Verlamion before the royal army did. But he has been beaten to the mark.'

'The streets are already full of men, and I can see many who were at Clarendon with the king.'

'The colours of Duke Edgar are flying beside the royal standard.'

'I don't know what Duke Richard will try, but if I were him I would fall on the town at its weakest point.'

'He will try to fight his way in,' Gwydion said. 'His men will not be deterred by dry ditches or felled trees, not with the Lord Warrewyk's people beside them. His knights are fierce men, born of an overproud caste. They would rather die than back down. That pride is ever the source of our misfortunes. I believe there will be many deaths today, for the gaining of a town is a most hazardous enterprise.'

Will felt his stomach clench, knowing what course his heart was resolved upon. He looked again at the town sitting on its ridge, and uneasy forebodings began to assail him. 'I must do what I can, Master Gwydion.'

'Take care to stay by me, lad! For you have never seen a great battle unfold and I have seen it too often. There are many ways to die.'

Will suddenly feared to open his mind in such a dangerous place. He heard drums beating up, warning of the arrival of large bodies of footsoldiers. The men wore coloured livery and bright steel helmets, and moved together in ranks, their lords' banners flying above them. Some wore riveted kettle-hats and shouldered pole-arms and gavelocks and marched to the orders of appointed men, while their captains rode up and down the lines on horses splendidly accoutred for war.

Here was a body of Ludford men, with more behind who had come down from the Ridings of the North. Yonder stood a company drawn from the garrison of the Castle of Sundials. There came a body of the Earl Warrewyk's Kennet billmen as Will knew from the red colour of their surcoats. And by the road were many men bringing forward in their midst a great engine of wood and iron they called 'ye Warrewyk Boare', that by some art of fire made holes in stone walls.

Will followed Gwydion through a trampled meadow, and soon they were moving among a sea of the duke's own troops as they assembled to the east of the town. The first company they came upon wore white and blue, proud men, clear-eyed and laughing. But they were commanded by a young and uncertain captain. He was bad tempered and harassed by his duties. His skittish horse stamped and snorted when Gwydion approached.

'I seek the Duke Richard,' the wizard called to him. 'Where is he?'

But the captain turned his horse away and would pay Gwydion no heed, until one of his men spoke up.

'Sir, I know that lad as a page of the duke's household, though he is now much changed.'

'Jackhald!' Will cried.

'Fall in a camp fire, did you, Willand?'

The captain turned his horse again. 'What say you?'

Another man said, 'Sir, this lad was once page to the Earl of the Marches before he ran away!'

'Is this true?' the captain asked severely. Then looking to Jackhald he said, 'The duke has other matters on his mind today than runaways. If the lad has come to fight with us then bid him join our company. And drive off that beggar with the flat of your sword!'

'Nay, sir!' Another man said, stepping up boldly. 'Begging your pardon, sir. But you mustn't talk like that, for that's his grace the duke's own wizard!'

The captain's face was red with exasperation now. 'Wizard?' he snapped. 'What wizard? The duke keeps no mage except the old gardener.'

'Oh, but it be true, sir! I saw him do conjurations with my own eyes!'

'Aye! Cleared all of Ludford Castle's inner ward of snow one time he did. All by himself and in the twinkling of an eye, sir. Saved us all a right heavy morning's work.'

The cords stood out in the captain's neck, and he bellowed, 'Enough! Get back in line!' He stared hard once more at Gwydion, but then suddenly his eyes rolled up and he fell forward against his horse's neck just as if he had been shot through by a crossbow bolt.

'The captain!' one of the jacks shouted. Instantly the soldiers crowded around and slid their chief to the ground to tend him, while others looked around for the cause.

'Darts!' came the cry. 'Have a care!'

Then, 'Not so! He's gone and fainted out cold!'

'Then it's sorcery!' another voice quavered. 'Look! The wizard's cut him across the face!'

'Ah, that's just a nosebleed!'

More men came forward to see, but their captain was already sitting up and blinking. Gwydion took Jackhald aside firmly and made a sign over his forehead. 'Now tell me: what rumours have you heard?'

A vacant look came over Jackhald's face, and he said, 'I heard that old King Hal got to know of how our host was coming down to visit him in Trinovant, so he quits his great city and sets out north. That would've been the day afore yesterday. They're saying that Trinovant was still too webbed about with the Crowmaster's spells. Too hard for King Hal's own sorcerer to work him any advantage there . . .'

Gwydion shook Jackhald by the shoulders. 'What else?'

The soldier looked back dreamily. ''Tis said our own liege lord is better liked by the common folk in Ludd's city than the king himself.'

'Jackhald, listen to me. Where did King Hal wish to go?'

'Why, into the North. To Leycaster, mayhap, where the Duke Edgar and the queen surely have more friends than they can muster in Trinovant. The Duke of Rockingham is with them, and his son, the Earl Stratford also.'

'And the Earl of Umber,' another soldier who was watching with big eyes said. 'Aye, don't forget the Black Knight.'

'And two lords of the Middle Shires too,' said a third trooper, adding the total on his fingers. 'And there's the Baron Clifton, who men say is mad.'

'What's that?'

'He's maaaad, sir! Our spies say he is come here with his son, John, and three hundred spearmen.'

Will recalled to mind the stone he had scried on the

estate of Aston Oddingley. That was the home of Baron Clifton. That must have been what warped his mind, he thought, recalling the way the Dragon Stone, even though mightily spellbound, had still lured the strong-willed Edward to visit it.

'Have heralds come from the king yet?' Gwydion asked the soldiers.

They looked from one to another and some shook their heads. 'We don't know.'

'Where is the Duke Richard presently?'

'Over by the wood.' The jack pointed to where more men were massing.

Gwydion made for the duke's company and Will hurried after. First they found Sir Hugh Morte, fully armoured and on his warhorse, which was a great sturdy beast of eighteen hands. When they asked him if the king's heralds had come to propose a parley, Sir Hugh laughed him down.

'That's already done with! In answer to our letter of grievances false messages came to command my lord to keep the peace of the Realm. But it is not my lord of Ebor who disturbs the peace!'

'False messages, you say?'

Sir Hugh gave a knowing look. 'I'll warrant that the only time his grace the king has authored a letter in his life was to command more milk for his cup. It is the queen who speaks in his name. She works him like a puppet, and everyone in the Realm knows it!'

Gwydion pointed at the knight angrily. 'You would do well, Friend Hugh, to remember that your liege lord has sworn allegiance on bended knee to him whom you mock so easily.'

Sir Hugh's thin patience burned away. 'Away with your arguments, wizard. This is old ground and we're already determined to ride against treachery.'

'It will be bloody ground soon, and that I will freely fore-tell to you!'

The warhorse snorted, and Sir Hugh reined her tight. 'Then get you to the queen and enthrall her to your will if you can! And mind this: while you parley at the front gate of Verlamion, my Lord Warrewyk will be breaking down the back door! Aye! And I beside him with my best steel!'

'Where is the Wortmaster?'

'Gort? Gone back to his stinking weeds at Foderingham, for all that I care!'

'He is a healer. He should be here.'

'Aye, and we are slayers! And with no more time for foolish talk!'

With that, Sir Hugh tested the visor of his sallet and the charger stamped away, though Will had wanted the answer to one more question. A terrible suspicion had begun to haunt him – *where was Willow?*

He allowed his mind to open a little. It was just a habit he had developed, something he did as a necessary prelude to using his intuition. But this time it was seized upon.

He staggered, and a sudden faintness overcame him.

'What is it?' Gwydion said.

He put up a hand, his sight blurring. 'I can feel move-ments in the ground. They're upsetting my eyes. The grass looks like the waters of the ocean . . . or clouds seen in a still pond. And the earth is heaving. It's what I felt at Ludford. I shouldn't have let my guard down.'

'Could it be *another* lign? Here? Have a care, Willand, this is the full-charged power of the Doomstone! Shut it out!'

'It's . . . it's talking to me, Master Gwydion!'

'Shut it out, I say! This is how unsuspecting men are taken by weird influence. It fills the air when a stone comes to life, so that all good judgment is warped.' The wizard cast about him. 'So . . . not two ligns meet here, but three! And that is what gives the Doomstone its great potency!'

476

Gwydion dragged him away from the lign and they pressed on together until they reached the duke's body-guard. A flowing mass was gathered – flags and horses draped in white and blue and every point showing the devices of the white rose and the falcon-and-fetterlock. All was flurry and activity around the duke. The air was filled with shouted orders and the stamp of hooves. Will saw two score knights wearing their finest armour and carrying long fluted maces. Every plate of the duke's harness shone with a high polish, so that he appeared to Will as if clad in pieces of a looking-glass.

The air was filled now with the sound of the jangling and clashing of mail and harness. Will's trained mind repeated the names that Sir John Morte had drilled hard into his memory – head and body, then arms, then legs – going over them again now like a singing charm to keep the voice of the stone at bay:

> *Sallet . . . bevor . . . pauldron . . . back and breast.*
> *Rerebrace . . . couter . . . vambrace . . . gauntlet.*
> *Tasset . . . cuisse . . . poleyn . . . greave . . . sabaton.*

The visor of Duke Richard's sallet was up, but his bevor was strapped up around his throat and chin, which seemed to give him an uncomfortably upright posture. Sir John had always stressed how important it was never to slacken the throat-guard once it was in place, for therein lay a fatal weakness: once loosened, a gauntleted hand could not easily do up the strap again, and certainly not in the heat of battle. Archers always sought the nobleman's throat, for there were few other ways that a churl, by a single act, could do so well by his family.

Around the duke rode the men of his household, his closest knights and retainers. The other lords, his kin and allies, had already broken left and right to their own commands. Heading the column to the left was the Lord Warrewyk, to the right that fierce lord's father, the Earl Sarum.

Despite his haughty bearing, the duke called down as they approached. 'Welcome to you, Master Gwydion! See how our cause prospers! See how we've raised this fine host and ridden here to relieve the king once and for all of his burdensome companions. I am well glad that you've ceased your wanderings and come to lend us your support this day!'

Gwydion strode out alongside the warhorse. 'And I have told you many times, Richard, that magic is not to be traded. You cannot buy personal advantage with it, nor should you try, for that which goeth—'

'Goeth about again,' the Duke finished. 'I know that lesson well enough.'

'Then why do you defy all wisdom?'

All eyes were on the wizard now for his words sounded like a challenge, and everyone who heard them looked to the duke to see what he would say. He seemed to Will hard pressed to keep his humour light, though he attempted it.

'I was not proposing to make a purchase of your powers, Master Gwydion. But since you have come here to us at this most crucial moment, should I not assume it is to aid those who are come to fight for the triumph of good over evil?'

'Do not speak to me of good and evil, Richard, for you know naught of either – unless you have had traffic with sorcerers!'

'Confound you, Crowmaster! I know what is right as well as any man does!' The duke turned away, unwilling to conduct further debate, but Gwydion raised his arms, forcing him to turn back.

'My enemy is the sorcerer, Maskull. Take care how you sport with the Realm in his presence, for a dead tree gives no shelter!'

The duke's eyes blazed with anger. 'Dead tree? What are these riddles? Say now! Are you with us, or against us?'

'If you have had commerce with Maskull, then you must tell me, or you will soon know what misery such dealings bring. As for me, I must divine Maskull's intent and oppose it as I may. If he seeks to destroy you, then I shall help you. But if it is his strategy to raise you up in victory then I shall steal that triumph from you, Richard! So be thou warned!'

The duke's bodyguard bristled at what they took to be a magical threat.

'Save your curses! I know what is mine by right, Crowmaster!'

'Ah, Richard! Dwell rather upon what is right by thine.' Gwydion lifted his staff on high. 'Think of your firstborn son and choose the patient path as I now counsel you!'

But the duke made no move to halt the column or take the wizard aside and speak privately with him. Instead, he lifted up his powerful voice. 'If you are come to aid us, Master Gwydion, then I bid you welcome to this company. But if you are here to preach, then you are welcome only to quit us.' He lifted his broadsword, Fregorach, aloft. 'For with you or without you, wizard, I am resolved this day to cure the main ill that afflicts this Realm! We are here to break the bonds that have been strangling us!'

Fierce shouts of assent burst from the duke's kinsmen. Lesser swords were thrust skyward. Then the army began slowly to move forward.

'Will!'

Just then, amid the noise, his own name rang clear. He looked up towards the second squadron and saw a fine, tall figure in full armour astride a charger that was armoured and caparisoned in wine-red and blue – Edward, riding in splendour as the Earl of the Marches.

'You've been playing with fire, I see! But you've come

479

back to us in the nick of time. I knew my father's wizard would not fail us!'

'Well met, Edward,' Will said gruffly. 'But we're not here to fight. Nor is Gwydion your father's wizard.'

Edward glanced back, perplexed. 'Not here to fight? What else is there to do in a battle? It's a man's chance to prove himself in arms. Join me, Willand, we'll be like brothers together again!'

'You have brothers enough. Where's Edmund?'

A cloud passed over Edward's face at the memory of his brother, still crippled in body and mind from his encounter with the Dragon Stone, but all he said was, 'He's too young. But you're not. Someone give this man a mount!'

Will, walking alongside, felt another undulation pass through the ground, and with it a powerful impulse to unwrap the sword he still held under his arm. Whatever had seized him when he dropped his guard was asserting itself.

Why not take it out? he asked himself. It's yours by right, a gift you received in your hour of need. Unsheath the sword, for its light has saved you once already.

He steadied himself.

But still, Branstock was beautiful to the eye and he would have loved to draw it out.

Again, something in Will kicked against the idea, and he told Edward, 'I have no need to prove myself in arms. And as for the battle, Master Gwydion has come here to build peace, and that is a far greater thing.'

'It's too late for peace!' Edward, as brilliantly armoured as his father, now drew a shining broadsword. 'See! This is "Dalgur", symbol of my knighthood. At last I'm honoured to ride in my father's bodyguard.'

'I'll show you my own sword, Edward, for mine is no buckle-pin. Mine is the hallowed blade!'

He had shouted it back before he could stop himself, and now found that he had already taken the bundle from under his arm. He tried to stop, but then Edward said sneeringly, 'Brave words, Willy Wag-staff!'

'I'll show you!'

It took all Will's powers to master the urge. He could see what the Doomstone was doing, seeking out his weaknesses and exploiting them. He forced an icy calm to settle over him, then he set his face stubbornly and began to wrap up the bundle once more.

But Edward, laughing, reached down with Dalgur and flicked the bundle up into the air, and when Will looked down, there on the grass was his wayfarer's cloak, torn now, and beside it a sword. It was not Branstock now, only a crude wooden sword made from a blackthorn stick, the sort that a child might wave in play.

The young earl threw back his head and brayed, and all the knights around him brayed too. 'You'll have to do better than that if you're to ride with us,' he said. 'Behold! Willy Wag-staff and his wooden sword!'

Will was stung. He stared angrily after Gwydion, believing some trick had been played on him. But the wizard was still pleading with the duke, wrangling fruitlessly with him even at this eleventh hour. The hooves of Edward's mount trod Will's cloak into the ground as the squadron walked on.

The idea came suddenly into Will's head to ask Edward what he had done with Willow. A surge of rage coursed through him, but seeing Gwydion's dauntless efforts to keep the peace, he found the strength to throw off his anger, and as soon as he did he began to see with far greater clarity.

The road of the peacemaker is the hardest road of all, he told himself, and made all the harder for me because I already know how this battle will end. The battlestone foretold a defeat for King Hal. I dare not tell Edward, for certain knowledge of victory would only spur him on . . .

But then he remembered the Dragon Stone, and Edward's hunger to look upon it. Once he came abreast of the charger again he said, 'Edward! Listen to me!

> *"King and Queen with Dragon Stone.*
> *Bewitched by the moon, in darkness alone.*
> *In northern field shall wake no more.*
> *Son and father, killed by war."'*

'Do not read him pretty poems,' one of Edward's body-guards shouted. 'He is a warrior! Do not interfere with his day of glory!'

'Wait!' Edward looked down, his posture stiff and haughty. 'What was that?'

'It's the verse you first saw on the Dragon Stone. The one you called a prophecy!' Will wrestled to clear his mind. The pain rose inside his skull and he beat at his head, staggered and almost lost his footing. He called up. 'Edward, Master Gwydion said the verse predicts the death of the true king and his heir!'

At that there was bridling and one of the guard raised his sword ready to cut down the daring upstart. Will knew very well the penalty for the crime of 'imagining the death of a king'.

But Edward did not give the order to kill. He passed glances around his men. 'The beggar's as soft in the head as old Gort. We'll fight this day and we'll win! We fear nothing!'

When Edward raised his own sword a great roar came from the mounted men who moved off along with him. Their pennons streamed, their suits of steel clattered. The column was picking up pace now. Groups of men were shouting and moving forward, forming themselves into the dense battle lines that would soon assault the Tonne.

Will ran faster alongside Edward's horse. 'But there's good cause for you to fear. A great sorcerer is moving among the king's army!'

'We know about him.'

Will's eyes widened. 'You do?'

'Yes. He's the queen's great boast. He can make coloured fire appear in his hands just as the Crowmaster does. But Father says he's just a juggler, a catchpenny from a country fair who puts on mystical airs and graces and uses sorcerer's powder to amaze fools! My Lord Warrewyk's arquebus men can surpass such tricks. Their weapons use sorcerer's powder to make flame and noise, and also to cast stones and iron nails towards the enemy. They will shoot Jarred through for his insolence!'

'I don't mean Jarred! The one of which I speak is called Maskull. Master Gwydion fought with him last night. He is a deadly sorcerer.'

'I know of no such magician.'

'Gwydion has come here to protect you from him, for if he should turn his thunderbolts upon your army, your men would burn like heather before a heathland fire.'

'Let them all come! Sorcerers! Wizards! Whomsoever! If they betide us well or ill, it is no matter. Verlamion shall fall this day whatever they say or do!'

How like his father Edward sounded now, for he had studied well and modelled himself closely on the duke. Will shouted. 'Come to a parley! Master Gwydion says that once war begins it'll devour a whole generation!'

'I'm not like you, Will. I'm of royal blood. I was born to ride and to wield a lordly blade like my forefathers. This is my birthright!'

'True chivalry doesn't glory in blood!' Will shouted, taking hold of Edward's stirrup. 'True chivalry always regrets the unsheathing of the sword.'

'Get out of my way, Will!' Dalgur swept down and the

flat of it shimmered against Will's temple, making him let go. 'Today shall see my blooding! Aye, and my sword's too, so get out of my way!'

Edward kicked his warhorse on and Will was left to save himself from being ridden down by the young earl's bodyguard. He came to a breathless halt.

They're all beyond reason now, he thought, filled with dismay. All of them.

But as the horsemen galloped away, his eyes fixed on a body of archers, men who had come out of Cambray. They were dressed in green and white and proudly wore the badge of the Red Dragon of Rannor. Each was already laden with two packed quivers, but their bows were not yet unbagged. They waited by carts, or came forward each to take a wooden stake that could be used as a defence against mounted men. He saw a figure jump down from the nearest cart, and there was something about the way it moved that made Will's heart shiver. When the figure came out from behind the cart he seized her arm.

'Willow!'

'Will?'

He felt the shock jolt her.

'You're . . . *burned*.'

He knew how he must look. Maybe she had good cause to be distant, but he had not expected repugnance. He tried to tell her what had happened, but she would not listen and began to work all the faster to unload the cart.

'You must get out of here,' he said, seizing her arm. 'Master Gwydion says—'

'Master Gwydion!' she snapped back at him. 'Do you always do what Master Gwydion tells you?'

'Willow, dressed like that you'll be mistaken for a soldier! When the battle starts, who knows what—'

'I am a soldier!' she said. She pulled her arm free and caught up a stray wisp of hair behind her ear. 'We're here to fight. My father's a fine bowman. The men from Leigh are all here with us and we've sworn an oath to the duke. We're with the company of Westerners who were raised at Presteigne in Cambray – good men all of them.'

'But you can't fight!'

'Why not? It's the duty of all those provided for by their lord to come to arms when he desires it. Don't you know that?'

'But you can't!'

Her anger flared. 'I can shoot a bow as well as any man – not as far maybe, but I'm often closer to the mark.'

'You have no bow!'

'I'll have one soon enough. And meanwhile I'll be a runner for the company.'

He groaned knowing that the runner was the one who gathered arrows that had missed their mark so they could be shot back at their owners with thanks. 'But that's the most dangerous work on the field!'

'What of it? I'm nimble.' She paused and looked hard at him, and he saw that it was a strange and unnatural look. 'And I'm not afraid to do my duty!'

Will did not doubt it. She was full of loyalty and conscientiousness, and it pained him to see how those virtues had been warped by the Doomstone.

He fought through the haze that filled his head, took hold of her and shook her. 'Master Gwydion says that hundreds will die today because two dozen overproud men have refused to share a tent for an hour!'

She threw him off. 'Does Master Gwydion say that? Well, my father says the Realm must be cleansed of a great evil!'

'Don't speak of evil!'

'I will speak of it! It's called greed, and it kills more folk than war ever did. We've been talking all morning about what death five dozen arrows per man might deal to such an enemy!'

'Enemy? What enemy, Willow? We are not being invaded. The men in Verlamion are not evil goblins to be hated and slaughtered. They're poor country folk like us! This is madness!' He winced at the pain that suddenly burst in his head and put a hand up as if to ward it away, but he still fell down, doubled to his knees.

Willow looked at him pitilessly. 'Wounded already, are you?'

He clenched his jaw until the spasm had passed, then he got up. 'A hateful voice is talking in all our heads. I'm fighting it. You must too, for it uses everything we know against us.'

'I don't hear any voice. Are you drunk?'

'Willow, it's a rede of magic that every change contains the germ of its opposite! If the voice is speaking to us and has knowledge of our minds, then we must be able to gain knowledge from it also. Listen to me:

> "*When a Queen shall enslave a King,*
> *Travel at Sunrise a Realm to gain,*
> *Werlame's Martyr shall lose the Victory,*
> *And lie where Blood never Flows.*"

She turned away scornfully, bending once more to her task. 'Get away from me with your poems!'

'But it's a battlestone's prophecy! It concerns what's taking place here. It's a riddle, a clue to a greater stone that I must find. Can't you help me?'

She tossed her head. 'I thought you were supposed to be the great magician's golden boy. Aren't you clever enough to see that the queen is Queen Mag, and it's our army that's been travelling since before sunrise to claim the victory?'

'But where does blood never flow?'

When he looked into her eyes he saw they were bright with anger.

'Leave me alone, Willand. I have work to do.'

He grabbed her. 'Where does blood never flow? Tell me! Where? I must find the Doomstone!'

'Get off me! You're mad!'

She put a hand to his chest and pushed him away. He staggered back and fell down. When he tried to get up he rolled over, wrestling now with the Doomstone, fighting to shut it out. At last he dared to slam his mind closed, and fell momentarily into unconsciousness.

When he came to, he was wiping the spittle from his mouth. He watched in a dream as Willow, compassionless and cold, climbed up onto the cart to continue her unloading. His glance slid to the great chapter house, where the three ligns seemed to converge. He tried to focus his thoughts. 'The red hands . . . they raised a great chapter house upon the hill of Werlame . . . because the Fellow who first recruited here . . . the one they call "the Martyr" . . . was killed here . . . he's lain entombed upon the hill for a thousand years . . .'

When he forced himself to his feet, Willow looked right through him. It seemed as if the love she had had for him was locked away, that the Doomstone was keeping her bound to her work and blotting all natural thoughts from her mind.

He roused himself, went to the head of the cart and began to unharness the dray-horse. Unnoticed, he led the beast forward from between the shafts, then he climbed up onto her back. As soon as his feet were clear of the ground his mind lit up like a ray of sun playing suddenly across a hillside. The horse's great, calm spirit gave him succour. The beast was no Arondiel, but she lumbered forward will-ingly enough when he asked her, and suddenly he too knew what he must do. He sent her towards the open fields that lay between Duke Richard's army and the town. Three blocks of men were now drawn up in readiness, and as he broke away from them he wondered what he would meet at the barricades.

He had begun to expect a rude reception, perhaps a hail of arrows as he came upon the Tonne, but the soldiers there watched him riding alone towards their lines with shouts of glee. Cheers and whoops rang out and he was beckoned in, the king's soldiers making much of a lad who was deserting from the enemy and showing the way for others.

When they let him past the breastworks he snatched a piece of folded parchment from his pouch and called out to them, 'See! I bring with me an important paper for the king! It may yet save all our lives!'

They laughed at first, but seeing him unarmed and without livery and holding up the written word, they thought again. And having once let him inside their barricade they were now at a loss what else to do but keep him among them.

'Hold him!' said one of the defenders.

'You hold him,' said another. 'We've no man here to spare as his keeper.'

'Let him go up into the town if he will!'

'He's a chancer! What if he means the king harm?'

'Then let him try himself against the king's guards!'

'If he's to fight, let him stay here and fight with us! We're soon to bear the brunt, and we'll have need of spare hands once the enemy sets upon us!'

'Aye! Aye!'

But then a big man among them pushed his companions aside, saying, 'And what if he really does have a message for his grace the king? What then?'

'If he does, then let him show it!'

'See here!' Will opened out the folded page over them. It was one of the Wortmaster's recipes and spoke of peas and oats and thyme. He opened it up and showed them the black ink marks and they looked up at it in awe. None of them had ever seen a proper written page before, though all believed in the power of words. They jostled, marvelling at the magic marks, knowing that the king's laws and tithe bills and property titles and most other items of high importance were always done out in writing.

'Quickly!' Will said with all the authority he could muster. 'Where am I to find his grace the king?'

'His standard flies up by the sign of the Castle Inn,' one of the soldiers said, pointing up the hill towards an alehouse.

Will turned to the road that led up to the market square. He thanked the soldiers and kicked the horse on until he arrived among the buildings of the town and at the foot of a great, square curfew tower. It was tall, and he saw the eight-sided stair-house that was built up from one corner of its top. Eight stone gargoyles projected from it. Around the tower stood many neat timber-framed houses and tradesmen's shops, all of one or two storeys. Paving stones had been laid at the place where, on a market day, a dozen money-changers and Verlamion's far-famed hazelnut sellers would ply for trade, but all that remained of the market now were a dozen tattered traders' awnings, for thousands of soldiers were packed into the street, and Will could now see that there were just as many men inside the town as there were outside it.

Three or four alehouses stood facing the market square. Above the door of the nearest was a painted board showing a castle, and nearby Will saw the royal standard. It was more than just a flag of quartered red and blue set with golden leopards and lilies and fringed in gold – this was the sign of present kingship. Under it stood a mass of lords in full armour gathered about the person of the king. Around these noblemen many royal soldiers stood guard with glaives and bill-hooks in their hands. They were watchful now and anxious, for all in the market square was brittle since the fear and thrill of war had settled fully upon the army.

Will could ride no further. He jumped down and pushed his way towards the curfew tower. When he looked back down a side street, the sound of drums from the approaching army assailed his ears. He heard a spattering of loud bangs from distant arquebus men, as they burned their sorcerer's powder and cast lead and stones towards their fellow countrymen. Then there came the deeper, louder noises of a great wall-smashing engine as it roared forth flame, and he knew that Lord Warrewyk must have unleashed his attack on the Tonne.

A horse whinnied at the sound, and began to rear dangerously, and when Will turned he saw men in the red-and-silver livery of Lord Strange, then the Hogshead himself, looking more pig-like than ever, lips foaming and yellow tusks gleaming, his wedding ring still hanging moistly in his nose. Doubtless he had brought men to fight in the king's name, no doubt seeing his opportunity to regain the queen's favour after the loss of the armoury waggons.

Will had no wish to be recognized. He turned away, hiding his face until Lord Strange had pushed his way past, then he found he had come to a barrier manned by royal guards. Will craned his neck and recognized in their midst a pale-faced man with long nose and sad eyes. A face less likely to be looking out from a suit of armour could hardly be imagined. Among the crowd of lords that surrounded him were two small, frightened boys who were acting as his pages. Both carried cushions, one supporting a sheathed war-sword, the other a helm set with the crown.

Will marvelled at the king. At Clarendon he had appeared fallow-minded and stupid. Now he seemed alert and fully aware, though horrified by all that was happening around him. Nearby stood Queen Mag, who was so concerned with the arrangements that she had overlooked her own departure to safety. She was wrapped in a blood-red cape trimmed with black fur made from the tail-tips of a hundred ermine. Her gloves were red, and her face so white that it seemed almost waxen, yet set with coal-black eyes and perfect lips of crimson. The burly figure of Duke Edgar was at her side, bellowing orders and doing whatever she told him.

Will's eyes narrowed as he looked upon the man who had once tried to cut him in two. Then suddenly he sensed a familiar reek, and he turned his head in fear.

Maskull!

Where was he?

Will shrank against a wall, looking to left and right, not daring to open his mind again for fear of giving himself away. Fear froze him, and he felt the Doomstone's malice take a firmer grip on his heart. A press of men were suddenly all around him, their faces red and angry. They looked on him cruelly, for the emanations were stirring them into a blood frenzy. An uncontrollable shiver passed through him, and his thoughts began to dissolve.

Why not go to Lord Maskull? he asked himself. Why not seek him out while I yet may?

'No!' he shouted, staggering now under the pain in his head.

The soldiers nearby cast monstrous glances at him.

But what if Lord Maskull is the rightful Phantarch, and Gwydion the impostor? he thought. What if it was Gwydion who refused to take the long journey to the Far North with Semias? Perhaps a new Age is coming into the world, an Age of War and Wonders that will endure five hundred years. It must be that Lord Maskull is its appointed herald, and Gwydion the broken reed. He could not even draw himself from the elder tree without help.

'Help me!' Will wailed and sank down to his knees.

'Courage, lad!'

He felt the pulsing inside his head slacken. Then an arm was under him and lifting him up. Gwydion was there, and as Will was raised to his feet his whole body flooded with relief. He stared round, not knowing how the wizard had come here, or for what reason, unless it was to foil his plans. He began to struggle, but Gwydion steadied him with a single touch on the forehead, then he produced a scroll from a fold in his robe.

This was no crumpled parchment but a real instrument of peace. 'See here! I have a sealed letter from Duke Richard, got by no art of mine. Richard has, by an effort of his own free will, given us one last chance, a promise in writing that he means no ill to King Hal, but that he has assembled here in arms only to redress certain grievances. Now let us see how the king receives the news!'

'But the fighting has begun.'

'It has reached the barricades, but the madness can still be stopped before Richard's men reach the town.'

'I . . . I'm going to find the Doomstone,' Will said doggedly. 'And you mustn't try to stop me!'

The wizard's eyes filled with admiration. 'You are terrified, and yet still resolved on your course?'

'Don't try to stop me, Master Gwydion. It's not the Doomstone that's telling me what to do. I know it in my own heart.'

'Go then, and tread softly. But before you do, see out my diplomacy, for it may yet suffice.'

Gwydion drew back, and Will watched him thread his way along the cordon. The sergeants tried to bar his approach to the king, but signs made over their foreheads caused them to forget their duty and turn away. When the wizard slipped into the very centre of the royal army, even the watchful chamberlain did not see him. Will saw Duke Edgar, attended by his son, Henry. They were dressed in glittering steel and arrayed in blue and white, and seemed to be very much in charge, but they were too busy issuing orders to notice an old man garbed in mouse brown.

But then Maskull's reek came again, and Will turned his head aside and pressed himself closer into the wall. At first he could not see the sorcerer, but then his eyes rolled upward. Maskull was leaning out from the top of the curfew tower ready to survey the butchery that would soon begin below. The darkly shrouded figure peered out across the thatches of the town. He was cowled and mantled, his black-gloved hands were ringed in bands of gold and there, about his neck, flashing glints of blue-white light and hanging upon a golden chain was the great diamond that had for so long graced the death cloak of King Leir. Maskull must have taken it from the queen! he thought, alarmed that so precious a thing as the Star of Annuin was now in the sorcerer's possession.

Will looked desperately to Gwydion. Maskull might have seen his enemy had he chosen to look directly beneath him, but his thoughts were wholly given over to relishing a victory that he had worked most patiently to gain. Duke Richard's troops were closing on the Tonne, and the day's first blood was about to be spilled. Will felt another dreadful rippling in the power that streamed beneath his feet. But even as his stomach rolled over and blood welled in the sockets of his eyes, he tried to fathom the direction in which the power was flowing. Here the ligns were narrow, concentrated. He could see their effect. The mood of the soldiers packed into the market square began to grow ugly as a wave of violence passed through them. A mutinous turmoil broke out that Lord Strange's sergeants had to move swiftly to put down.

Then he saw Duke Edgar moving away from the king, and Gwydion seizing his opportunity. The wizard made a rapid sign over the queen's forehead astounding her to blankness. Then the king was suddenly receiving the letter, taking the wizard's hand in his own. His eyes were as innocent as a doe's . . . and then the surge that was travelling along the lign passed directly beneath them and threw everything into the air.

'Filthy meddler!'

Will saw how the king flinched at the enraged cry. The bloody lips of the queen twisted, her eyes grew fierce as she came upon them.

'Treachery! Guards! Take the old man!'

Will saw the scroll of peace dashed from the king's hand by Duke Edgar's gauntlet.

Gwydion blazed at him, staff outstretched. 'Fool, Edgar de Bowforde! By this act you have sealed your own death warrant!'

'Wrong! I shall not die today, for I've taken care to remember your own prophecy! I've brought the king's army to do battle here by the Shrine of the Martyr for there is no castle in Verlamion!'

High above, atop the curfew tower, the sorcerer was jogged from his great thoughts. But he had already been slow to act. So close was his enemy to the nobles upon whom he relied that he could not profitably loose off a death-dealing thunderbolt among them. His adversary sprang away from the royal guards with astonishing agility. Then Will's heart missed a beat as, with a twirl of his mouse brown cloak, he seemed to melt away, and the men who had been about to take hold of him collided empty-handed.

All eyes searched in vain for the vanished wizard, and Will realized that he too must make his escape when Henry de Bowforde's eyes fell on him. There was a flash of recognition and the young nobleman started forward, his dagger drawn.

'Enemies!' he cried. 'There! Over there!'

Will struggled back into the crowd, but suddenly all was confusion as a great plume of violet fire spewed out over their heads. It gushed high over the thatch of the houses and down into the fields beyond.

'The rebels are attacking!' Maskull shrieked. 'Smash them! Destroy them!'

As if in confirmation of the warning, a shower of black motes appeared in the sky. They arced purposefully in the middle airs, and a moment later howls burst out all around Will amid the clattering of shafts as a thousand war-arrows struck home.

It was a deadly rain and no sooner had it ended than another volley whistled in. This time a spout of unnatural flame roared forth from the curfew tower to scorch the goose quill flights from the arrows, but still the shafts dropped down to deal death among the king's soldiery.

And now up to meet the purple flame there came a fire of brilliant blue. Where the two tongues met, a burning ball exploded. Fire drakes snapped and snarled at one another, great sparks flew from the centre of the firestorm, and for a moment the town roofs were threatened by a scorching breath. But when the fireball died there was left only a single stream of fire, half violet, half blue, contesting, wavering, spilling sometimes down towards the ground, and at others back up into the sky. Once or twice the purple flame drove the blue out of sight. But then the blue flame blazed back and licked the grey stones of the curfew tower, turning them black before being driven back again.

Down below, Will found that he was trapped amid a great press of bodies. Two thousand of the king's troops surged fearfully beneath the raging sky. They were drawn up and ready to fight, but there was as yet no enemy to engage. Crushed tight inside the market square, they made sitting ducks for the unseen archers on the far side of the houses. The soldiers near to Will cowered down. Some tried to make for the cover of the houses or threw up arms to protect their iron-bound heads as best they could from the lethal shafts that appeared among them.

But nothing afforded protection from so deadly a hail. The burning arrows dropped steeply to the ground, transfixing men through head, shoulder and back. Barbed tips plunged deep into flesh, and among the darts there fell many bodkins – arrows with long heads made to force open links in mail – and others with chisel tips that could pierce steel. Will saw the men who had fallen. Some were screaming, others vomited blood. Whatever their plight, they were soon crushed underfoot.

Panic infected those who stood in the open. As men fell and arrows clattered down all around, Lord Strange squealed and grunted in fear and began to cut his way towards cover. He was followed by Henry de Bowforde, and then Duke Edgar, who grabbed King Hal and pulled him to the side of the street. 'Hide him!' he growled thrusting his charge towards the queen whose guards had already kicked in the door of a tanner's house. She hurried her husband inside while the duke and his company made a dash to the far side of the street where overhanging eaves gave better protection.

The men around Will groaned and cursed as yet another volley of arrows arrived. Dozens more died in the street, their screams pitiful. Soldiers called upon their commander to have mercy on them and send them against their enemy without delay, but Duke Edgar gave no such order.

Will lifted himself up to try to see over the sea of leather hoods and steel helmets. Down the side street, at the barricade, men in the colours of Baron Clifton were fighting furiously with Duke Richard's men. Sunlight glinted and flashed where the struggle was hardest. The duke himself was in the thick of the fighting, on foot, amid a well-armed bodyguard and leading his men on. And there was Edward too, wielding his sword as the attack broke upon the barriers.

Now a flood of men in red jerkins charged in upon the barriers to deal death upon hapless defenders. There was a moment of doubt, then suddenly the attack broke through and hundreds of men were surging over the Tonne, trampling through the vegetable gardens that lay between ditch and town. It was not long before the attackers had reached the backs of the houses, and Will saw their badge was the white bear, device of the war-loving Earl Warrewyk.

Another hail of arrows found their mark, worse this time, for the men of Cambray had now advanced and they shot higher into the air. The darts that now rained down would have split a chapter house door. Will saw how fear turned to struggle. And there was worse, for the Earl Warrewyk's falchion-men began to hack out the wattle-and-daub walls of the houses that fronted the market square. Warrewyk men-at-arms burst through only a few paces from where Will stood, and carried death into the street before them.

Here the fighting became hand to hand, with great stones being thrown down from upper windows and bills and pole-axes doing bloody murder among the crowd. Will found himself carried helplessly along in the press outside the alehouse when a hundred or more of Earl Warrewyk's troops broke through. The wall of the house next door to the inn gave way, and he saw Duke Edgar and some other nobles retreat swiftly inside. They were hoping to save their lives, for the royal army was now in rout here, having been cut off by the movement. But the alehouse was a death trap. Seeing his dilemma, Duke Edgar rallied his men too late. He gathered them with an adamant will, roaring, shouting that they must not stay to be killed one by one. Then he led a dozen of them bursting out from the doorway, rushing and slashing in a mad bid for freedom.

But it was a fight against overwhelming odds. There was escape for only two men, one an excellent red-haired swordsman who cut his way through Earl Warrewyk's men, and another man in blue and white who followed close behind him. That was Henry de Bowforde. But Henry's father was not so lucky. Duke Edgar of Mells was chopped down then cut to pieces by men wielding axes and bills.

The last Will saw of him was a body lying careless in death beneath the signboard of the Castle alehouse.

By now, Will could hardly move, so tightly was he locked among the hundreds of heaving, wrestling men. Overhead, further gouts of contending flame roared in purple and blue. The fire drakes had grappled then become locked in stalemate. He pictured Gwydion standing rooted in the earth, gathering all his power to hold immobile the malevolence that Maskull was trying to hurl from the tower. Thus were wizard and sorcerer both cancelled from the fight, and it was plain that unless the power of the Doomstone was broken the battle would go on until thousands lay dead.

Will knew what he must do. He dared to open his mind, and found the strength to fight his way out of the crush until he was free.

CHAPTER TWENTY-TWO

THE SARCOPHAGUS
OF VERLAMION

By the time Will broke away he had been carried close to the chapter house walls. They were twice the height of a man and unclimbable, so he ran to the great gates and found them shut tight.

All around the stone arch was carved the mysterious motto of the Fellowship:

And in the middle of the door there hung down a great handle – it was cast in brass, life-size and formed into the shape of a man's arm. Will banged on the gates, pushed uselessly at the cover of a small, barred hole set within the gate.

Nothing happened.

'Sanctuary!' he shouted, his voice breaking on the word. 'I claim the sanctuary of the Fellowship!'

It was the dread formula that Gort had once told him, the one that the Fellowship could never ignore.

'You must admit me! You must!' he cried.

For a moment Will thought his efforts would fail. But then, horrifyingly, the handle reached out and grabbed him by the wrist. Then the gate cracked open, first a finger's width, then wider, pulling him in with it.

He tore at the brazen grip, fearing that he would be delivered into the hands of those posted to guard the gate. But this was no ordinary day and the two garbed Fellows he saw there were in no state to do their duty. They were rolling on the ground, twisted up in their own robes, their red hands clutching like claws, screams strangling in their throats.

The brazen arm flung him towards them as the gate slammed itself shut. Will stared at them. The ghastly, eyeless faces of the two Fellows struck horror through him, and he scrambled to his feet, heading now towards the soaring building.

He saw that he had been thrust into the main yard of the chapter house. Here the sound of battle was muted, but in its place was a terrible whine.

Close to, the great chapter house of Verlamion was a staggering sight. It was made of stone and ancient Slaver bricks, its walls set with pinnacles and towers and pierced by tall casements glazed in a maze of black glass. He looked up at those blind windows and it seemed that a brown glow came from inside – a brown glow and a terrible discord of sound.

The whine grew louder as he tried to feel where the three ligns crossed. He dared not open his mind further, for here the power of the lorc was like a fiery furnace. As he ran towards a widely spreading tree the ground shook and a shower of needles and seed-cones fell to the ground all around. He stumbled over roots and broken pavement, knowing now that the place he sought must be inside the chapter house itself.

He ran up to the huge doors, and burst in through the entrance, but once inside an awesome sight halted him. Before him, in the vast space of the lower house, the entire assembly of Fellows was gathered together. Hundreds of them knelt in rows on the stone floor, their black hoods thrown back, their disfigured hands pressed over their eyes, and their mouths held open. All were howling just as those at the gate had howled. If Will had not been halted by what he had seen previously, now came a sight to stop his heart, for in the candle-blackened roof were dozens of carved figures, winged creatures, half-man perhaps, yet bat-winged, needle-toothed and gruesome.

But how could they be carved, when their hideous faces snarled at him and their eyes followed him so hungrily?

They made no move towards him, rather they clung closer to one another at the sight of him as if in fear. The high walls were thick with greasy soot, and as he forced himself to venture further into the chapter house the stench of burning animal fat made him gag and retch. Incense burners filled the air with an acrid perfume. Thick candles flared in their tens of thousands, their light vainly illuminating the filthy interior. Pillars, walls, screens – all were ornately carved and richly painted, but what they showed were scenes of unimaginable torture and suffering.

Everywhere there were images of pain: marble statues of starving men, golden paintings of pierced and bleeding flesh, skulls and skeletons broken and scattered, even the aisles were paved with gravestones, so that the bare feet of the Fellows would be reminded of death as they passed to and fro upon the ground.

This is how they spend the tithe, Will thought, angered

by the sight. They take food from children's mouths and turn our wealth into candles. Candles that burn only to light up these ghastly treasures! Treasures they can't even see! Can this truly be all that happens to the tribute gathered according to the Iron Rule? No wonder there's black glass in all their windows. No wonder, for who would tolerate the Fellowship in town or country if the truth was known?

The ground trembled again, moved sickeningly beneath his feet, as if the building itself had noticed the intrusion. But not so the Fellows. They paid him no heed at all as he ran among them. Their hands and arms were red and scaly, waving in the air as their open-mouthed dirge rose up in a tower of ugly sound. It filled the tall, dark space above. The singers were enthralled by their own song, or perhaps they needed to block from their minds the competing whine that came out of the eastern end of their vast house.

The way forward seemed clear, but as Will went deeper among the blind faces some of them twitched and others turned towards him as if sensing an offence had been committed. He easily evaded their weak grasps, but more and more of them began to rise up from their dark devotions to grope towards him. Soon he found his intended way blocked. He clambered out from among the lines of Fellows into an open aisle, fearing that if just one of them was to lay a firm grip upon him he could soon be overwhelmed.

He dashed down the aisle, darted past golden tombs and stone memorials to death, as the Fellows felt their way towards him with grasping, outstretched claws. Their mouths slavered, their voices gibbered in unison. Dozens had joined the pursuit. They came towards him and the horror of their wasted faces and raw hands was fully revealed. Will groaned as he saw the staring eyes that had been painted on their sunken eyelids – horrible parodies of what once had been. He backed up another half dozen paces. His pursuers were neither strong nor swift, but they were growing in number, and they were surely relentless. When he hunted about for a way to go, he saw there was no alternative. Every way led him deeper into this most sacred heart of the chapter house – and here lay only death.

He turned, ran, turned again. The last path led him into a hidden dead-end, for here was the Martyr's shrine. It stood bathed in candlelight and glowed in a fog of crimson incense, set about with even more candles than those which lit the torture pictures of the lower house. The shrine was a huge monolith of intricately carved stone, rising up in flutes and pillars and set about with swags of cloth of gold. But it was also fenced with iron spikes, for inside lay the alabaster statue of the Martyr himself.

Grim-faced and impressive, this was Swythen, lying upon his deathbed. Will looked about despairingly. The deadly emanations were coming from the shrine itself! There were holes in the base, and an intense light blasting out. Gwydion had said the Fellows maintained a secret place here into which deformed and diseased limbs were thrust for healing. Will now saw the power that lay behind such hopeless cures – the numbing persuasion of the battlestone. And he saw too why the Fellowship maintained such practices – doubtless the report of miracles drove many who were in pain to surrender themselves and all their worldly wealth.

This flashed through Will's mind as he stared about like a cornered fox. Now there was no escape. Above him the tall windows soared, obsidian, black glass, decorated with scenes of vile mutilation. Their dismal brown light threw cruel patterns across all that it touched. The windows themselves were impassable. There were iron bars in them that made the spaces too small to get through.

Shafts of brown light played upon the crowd of moaning

monstrosities as they crept forward to take their revenge. They had already formed a wide semicircle around him, a groping mob that stretched back along the aisle. Weaponless, he could not plunge into them with any hope of cutting a way through. Ahead of him, hands were thrown out ready to seize him. Behind him, there lay only a great stone plaque and behind that a wall.

Dizziness shook him and he fought back the pain that was now flooding up into his head. But his thoughts stayed sharp and he saw his chance. He edged as close to the approaching hands as he dared, then ran straight at the wall.

At the last moment he jumped, jammed his foot into the lip of the stone plaque and sprang up and off the wall just far enough out to make a grab for the big wheel that hung on chains above the south-eastern aisle. The great candle-holder shook as he thrust his arm through it. He swung precariously, then began to lever himself up. A great shower of hot fat spilled out of ten dozen thick candles, making the Fellows below flinch away.

Will hauled himself up onto the swinging wheel and stood on its rim, balancing himself by one of the three chains that disappeared far up in the darkness above. As the wheel swung, Will bent his knees and bore down with his weight. Soon he had worked the arc of the swing up enough to worry him that the chains might not hold. The swing carried him up almost as far as the windows, then swiftly down across the heads of the enraged Fellows, then up again towards the bars of a tall, iron screen. He was the bob of an enormous pendulum that cut back and forth through the air.

All around the Martyr's shrine there stood an open-topped cage that formed an exclusive enclosure, and inside it the powerful Elders knelt in a parody of piety. They were distinguished from the lesser Fellows of the lower house by their great age and costly garb, but they too knelt with their palms pressed over their empty eye-sockets and their mouths agape. The most repulsive of them all Will took to be Grand High Warden Isnar, who grovelled on his knees before an empty throne.

There was no other way to save himself. At the top of the next swing, Will leapt up and launched himself at the screen that enclosed the shrine. He clung on and scaled it like a tumbler, climbing until he was three or four times the height of a man above the ground. As he hung precariously close to the top, his fingers grasping oily, black wrought iron, he felt his scryer's hazel wand slip from his waistband. It fell and a Fellow's blotched hand found it, but though he dropped it again quickly as if it burned, others fell upon it and fought one another to tear it to pieces.

There were hundreds of sightless faces turned towards him now, hundreds of red fingers outstretched. The voices rose to deafen him. He was choking on tallow smoke, shielding his eyes against the red glare coming up from below. The light shafted through incense-laden air, half blinding him. But as he looked down, he could see tell-tale sparkles in the fabric of the shrine. Light glittered inside the stonework like powdered gems, like snail-trails glistening in the morning sun. Six tracks radiated from the sarcophagus. He had found the place where the three ligns met, the place where the Doomstone lay. But what now? The battlestone was encased in the sarcophagus of the Martyr.

He felt the iron strap-work below him give. The screen began moving back and forth as some of the Fellows tried to climb up after him. He swung round the top and clung to the inner side of the cage, and when the crimson claws started to come through the bars, questing for his legs, he drew them up as far as he could. There was no more time to think what to do. In a moment the Fellows would lay their red claws upon him, he would be dragged down into torment and yellow fingernails would tear out his eyes.

He began to wish that he had not leapt off the candle wheel. But as he looked down he saw, set into the floor beside the Martyr's last resting place, a square hole. Surely that was big enough to let a man through, but it was covered with an iron grille. The bars stood enrayed now, as beams of red light shafted upwards from somewhere below.

That was it!

From his high perch he could see that, beneath the grille, a stone stair descended. It seemed there was a croft under the shrine.

New-kindled hope blazed inside him, but then fear gripped him afresh as he looked down into the hole, for what if he dropped down and found the grille was fixed in place? But there was nothing else for it. He knew he would have to jump. The northern windows of the chapter house flared again with brown light, and he knew that at least Gwydion's duel had not yet come to an end. He took hope from that, and committed himself to the drop.

By now, the ache in his head had become almost unbearable, the noise a constant pain to his ears. He breathed deep and shook himself against the dizziness that was creeping over him, then he tried to wipe the sweat and grease from his face and hands in preparation. When he looked again his courage almost failed, for it was a long way down, but a dozen hands were groping up for his ankles, so he muttered a charm of protection and let go.

The next thing he knew, pain jolted his knees and ankles. He was down and rolling over and over among the Elders. They writhed ecstatically in the shrine chamber as he fell among them, but before the nearest of them could stir from his raptures, Will had thrust his fingers into the iron grille and was pulling at it. It was heavy, but his second effort wrenched it up. He jumped down, and let it slam back down behind him.

In the cramped passage below, the crimson brilliance was doubled and the whine became so immense that it tore at the roots of his sanity. As he approached the chamber he had to hold his hands before his face like a man battling through driving sleet. To advance against so loathsome a power as this seemed impossible. It was not just any battle-stone; this was the Doomstone, a power that, even now, was consuming human lives by the hundred. Thousands were trapped within its compass. Thousands would have to die to quench its thirst for blood.

But Will had not fought his way here to consider the Doomstone's appetites. Though it probed him and tore at him he stood his ground, tight-lipped, and forced himself to look directly upon it. It rested upon a tomb, a great black slab, leopard-spotted, its blemishes shot through now with crimson radiance. It was the very lid of the Martyr's grave.

Abhorrent power streamed from the stone. It would have made the strongest man flee, but what saved Will as he inched closer was the stone-lore that he had already gained. He knew very well the vile feelings that were awakened in him. He recognized the horrors that crawled into his mind. Great magic would have to be invoked if he was going to destroy this stone.

He heard laughing as the stone's emanations flooded out. Madness streamed through him, a force trying to lever the lid off his mind.

He halted and snarled at the roaring stone, and it seemed that he was surrounded by his enemy, that axes swept down upon him, that suddenly he was on his knees, his ribs ripping apart and his heart's blood spreading out in a dark pool before him like Duke Edgar. Yet through all that ghastly vision, a tiny unassailable part of him held on, knowing the

Doomstone's ways, seeing it use his own fears and turn them into a weapon against him.

When he forced one foot in front of the other, another panic swept suddenly over him. A vivid belief broke upon his mind that he could not stand up. But then he grasped the reason was that he was already standing up, and once he saw that, he was able to throw off the deadly fear.

He struggled to approach another step, all the while his mind scrambling and shredding, but whatever fell away his resolve remained undimmed despite all that came at him. And as his screams echoed away he remembered how magic was dirtied by wrath and cowardice and all the other failings that men were prey to.

And then the raging din stopped. Suddenly, there was silence. The madness was gone. It was as if he had struggled through into the eye of a storm, a place of calm and cold sanity in the midst of terrible carnage.

He took another step forward and an avalanche of pain exploded inside him. A broadsword sliced him in two, the marish hag's sucker fingers caged his face, he struggled against bursting lungs, his skeleton dissolved into maggots in the heart of a cursed yew, a mother and father he had never known called facelessly out of the shadows . . .

He gritted his teeth against them all, knowing the time had come to plant his feet hard and begin to recall the words that Gwydion had spoken at the draining.

'*Aircill ur maesa bretharbhi,*' he began, adjusting the words of the true tongue to present circumstances. '*Foscleiga ter criedhen mo!*'

At the sound of the true tongue the Doomstone began to shudder. Light leapt out of it like the bright burning flash of a predator's eye. But Will was ready for the strange perceptions that the use of great magic brought. Gwydion's words came to him, 'Magic cannot be rehearsed. Like the firstborn child, magic just comes and is perfect.'

The surge of empowerment lifted him and he gave a great shout. The power seemed like a hand passing into his flesh, gripping him by the spine, feeding limitless strength into him. He felt he could summon infinite power, and the arrival of that power as it rushed to his fingertips was all commanding.

'*Nai dearmhaida, lir-dah, teaor an gharbade saon echear-itan . . .*'

The spell that formed in his mouth made him feel as if he could tear down the whole chapter house, rip it apart with his bare hands, grind it to grit. A flick of his wrist seemed enough to send flames high into the air. Nothing was beyond his power now. And no weapon, no matter how fearsome, could lay a mark upon him.

But then a flash of insight came to him just in time. That's the trap, he told himself. The pit that catches and consumes the unwary. That's the snare that waits for those who venture to use magic dirtily. How many times has Master Gwydion said it? 'Magic must always be requested, never summoned, always respected, never treated with disdain. Ask openly and honestly, for the honest man alone can speak words of power!'

He took a step closer, fearless now, empowered, sure. He bared his forearms, leaned in against the stone. Then deliberately placed his hands on the slab, and gave the challenge that here was one who would wrestle with that which misused the power of the earth – whatever the cost to himself.

The stone glowed in answer, but it was a dull cherry-red glow, a feeble echo of the crimson brilliance that had once radiated from it. And when he lifted his hands, a pale, golden fire sprang from them. Flames licked across the surface of the slab, then died.

Back came the red glow, and he tried again. This time he braced himself against the stone and pushed down with both hands. For an enduring moment his body rocked and the lightning of his eyes was able to probe deep inside the Doomstone.

He saw all the horrors that were made there, how it drew in what the lorc supplied, how it misused the power of the earth, infecting men's minds, putting fear and hatred into them. And he saw too what was happening outside and all across Verlamion – murderous soldiers pouring up into the town, the royal army making their stand around the curfew tower, and above it all a great fire-duel spilling flame and fury across the sky . . .

Will sought the world again, and as he opened his eyes he saw the stone pulse like a blown cinder. The sarcophagus chamber was filled with heat and stench and a thin, white, choking haze. Two red patches glowed on the slab where his palms had touched it. Both his hands were black and numb.

But just as he thought he had found the key, a voice spoke to him, and what it said was so exquisitely aimed it hit him like an axe between the eyes.

'I know where you come from . . .'

Sweat began to pour from his face. Where it dripped onto the stone it danced madly and fried up into steam. The demon that had troubled his mind ever since Gwydion came into the Vale reared up before him, and with it a howling gale of fears.

'I know who you really are . . .'

'Liar!'

'Leave me be, and you will learn the truth too . . .'

He staggered back. Doubt cut the ground from under him. All his suspicions came alive and the stone fed greedily on them. The crimson glow surged, forcing him another step back, and then his mind wavered, distracted by the wailing of the Fellows above, by the sound of an iron grille being opened.

'You're a liar!' he shouted again. But he knew well enough that the wound the Doomstone had found in him was deep. It was what had driven the dreams of many a dark night, the helpless nightmares in which he imagined Death to be his father. He thought he had cut that terror out of his flesh long ago. 'Fearmonger! I command you to silence!'

Angrily, he leaned forward and placed hands and forehead hard against the fiercely-glowing slab. This was the crucial test, the thing he had suffered everything for. Yet it felt wrong. In the end the Doomstone had knocked him off balance, undermined his confidence, sullied his sacrifice.

Then something rattled onto the surface of the stone. It was the leaping fish, the talisman Breona had given him at his leaving. She was not his mother, he knew that, but she had cared for him and loved him as well as any mother could, and he had taken the token of that love in the same spirit. He kissed it now, broke the cord and laid it flat upon the Doomstone.

The spinning whine rose up, raved, raged at him. The stone strove to reply. A bloody light blasted from it, more sullen and deadly now than it had been before, but he would not let it move him. He would not. He. Would. Not!

And when the vivid shock came to him of a portcullis running down and cutting him in two, he was ready to turn the malice back upon itself.

'You're the one that's broken,' he told the stone steadily. 'For I bring with me a riddle wrapped in a mystery inside an enigma. I have come to fulfil the prophecy of the Child of Destiny, and now one shall be made two! *So be it!*'

And as he spoke the last words a great shock passed through his arms and chest and his world collapsed down to a pinpoint. There was a tremendous bang and he felt his body being hurled through the air and his mind dissolving. And then – nothingness.

CHAPTER TWENTY-THREE

ALL IS WON,
YET ALL IS LOST

When he came to, he was lying on his back, staring up at a drifting pattern of grey that floated above him. At first, he could make no sense of it, but then he remembered the masses of harm that Gwydion had drawn from the battlestone at the Giant's Ring and it seemed to him that he must now be at the Doomstone's mercy.

He could do nothing to save himself. Everything seemed to exist at the end of a very long tunnel. All his strength had left him, and he felt as helpless as a baby. Surely this swirling, menacing shape must coalesce into demonic form and destroy him. But, if so, why was it waiting so long?

This is going to hurt, he thought. But no harm came to him, and so he opened his eyes again. As his vision cleared and he returned a little more to his senses, he saw that the swirling, twisting grey mass was nothing more than smoke lacing the air.

He tried to sit up, to waft it away, but it was more than he could do, for all his limbs were leaden and refused his commands. The smoke was thick. It caught at the back of his throat, made him cough. That made him realize how much his ribs hurt, and to understand just how weak he had become. His hands felt as if they had been burned to charcoal . . .

Sleep beckoned. He lay back and was beginning to drift away when his mind fastened on a strange sound coming from above. My ears, he thought. They're ringing like a blacksmith's anvil, and I've only just noticed it. He wished the noise would go away and leave him in peace. But it would not. Nor would the idea that he was still in danger. He shook his head and slowly the sound above began to resolve itself into screaming voices.

The Sightless Ones!

Suddenly, he remembered where he was. Those screaming voices were in the chapter house above him. His eyes were closing, but he knew that if he fell asleep now the Fellows would find him and make soap and candles out of him. This dreary, smoke-filled cellar would be the last thing his eyes would ever see . . . and that could not be right.

He watched the smoke rising up through the leper-holes in the shrine for a moment, before trying for the second time to sit up. Then he forced himself to approach the glaring world of pain that waited for him.

The cellar was utterly changed. He had been flung halfway across it to the furthest corner near the steps. Where a brilliant crimson glow had been before, now there were faint bars of light shafting down through the smoke, sculpting the walls into improbable shapes. And there was the culprit – the great slab of the Doomstone, cracked clean in two.

Its blemished grey surface was dark and inert now, and Will knew for the first time that he was the one who had broken it. Hope lifted him up. It was time to get out of this place. To leave the tomb! To find life again!

He drew a deep breath and forced himself to rise, first to his knees and then to his feet. Then he began to climb the stone stair. When he reached the top he pushed up the iron grating and emerged into the shrine chamber amid a cloud of acrid smoke. Brilliant sunshine now cleansed the space where tall black windows had once blocked out the light. The cold, dead-white effigy of Swythen seemed almost transparent now that it was flooded with warm rays. The Elders were wandering around it in confusion, casting up their red hands against the painful sunbeams and crying out.

Suddenly Will could breathe again. Escaping the tomb seemed to let the strength flood back into him. But the Fellows beyond the shrine had not fared so well. The cracking of the Doomstone had left them bereft and without order to their thoughts. They twisted and turned about as if in agony. They sought shadows like maggots caught in the sun's glare. Some ran shrieking in circles. Many lay on the ground, clustering together with their hands pressed over each other's eyes and mouths. Will found his way out of the shrine cage and struggled through the madness towards the great oaken doors. He fell out into the yard below the shattered windows, and when he looked back he saw great plumes of smoke pouring out, forming into a gigantic mushroom that rose high above his head, a column twisting and thinning now in the breeze.

The big cedar in the yard was wholly bare now. He ran under it, across a pavement scattered with countless needles and glittering black shards that had been blasted from the windows. Then he climbed onto the roof of an out-house and vaulted the wall into some adjoining gardens. An ancient black cat sat near a fountain. It regarded him warily, but stood its ground. The May sun was shining down, radiant and warm. He could hear no birdsong, but neither were there any streams of fire spoiling the clear blue of the sky. Despite everything, his thoughts ran first to Willow and the dangerous part she had elected to play in the battle. He was glad he had freed her from the stone's embrace, and hoped he had not left things too late.

When he jumped the fence into a side alley and ran on,

the fresh air in his lungs felt like cool water on a parched throat. But when he came out into the main street, he was hit by the dreadful hush that had fallen over everything. It was as if thousands of sleepwalkers had suddenly awakened at the same moment and found themselves to be murderers. All fighting had ceased. Weapons had fallen from hands, and faces were slackened in bewilderment, pallid, unshaven, thirsty. Many men were staring up at the great many-legged cloud that curled and twisted above the town. It seemed for a moment to billow into a threatening thunderhead, but it was only the smoke from the chapter house caught in an updraught and it was now melting away.

As the cold shadow it cast over Verlamion lifted, Will ran back up into the town. He was making for the place where the king's standard flew. There he found all was in confusion. Above him the top of the curfew tower was fire-blackened and the door at the bottom had been broken down.

'Master Gwydion!' he shouted, knowing that one battle at least might not yet be wholly done.

He leapt over the shattered door, raced up the hundred narrow steps that spiralled to the tower top. All the while he feared he might be met on the stair by Maskull's fiery wrath. But when he reached the first landing unharmed he took heart and dashed onward again.

At the second landing the innards of a great engine of time loomed out of the darkness, a thing made of black iron with a huge bell attached – it had stopped dead on the point of noon.

Will's caution stopped him again, but still Maskull's purple fire failed to come flooding down upon him, and he ignored his inner warnings. He glimpsed daylight and pressed on, remembering what Gwydion had said about Maskull's strength being great, but not great enough to beat them when they stood together.

When he came bursting out onto the roof, everything

was warm and fire-blackened and sooty. And there stood the menacing figure of Maskull.

'Master Gwyd—' he began.

But Gwydion was not here.

The sorcerer turned. 'You!' he snarled. 'The apprentice boy! I should have known!'

'By the sun and moon! What have you done with Master Gwydion?' Will launched himself at the sorcerer, but his body froze in mid-leap, caught, enmeshed helplessly in a magical snare.

The sorcerer spun, gestured disdainfully. 'I made you, I can just as easily unmake you.'

'Nooooo!'

Will saw the sorcerer's hands splay in readiness to stab fire through him. But then the great blue-white diamond at his breast flashed a fire of its own. A beam of paler blue seemed to explode upon it in a halo of brilliance.

Suddenly Will was in motion again, and colliding hard against the parapet. He twisted around, leapt to his feet ready to attack the sorcerer again.

But Maskull had vanished.

Will gasped, went to each of the four walls in turn and looked over. The heat of battle lingered in the stone and in the iron railings. When he checked the eight-sided stair-house set into the corner of the tower, he saw that it too had been blackened and much of the lead melted from its pointed roof. But what could have happened to the sorcerer? Where the corners of tower and roof met there had been eight stone gargoyles. Now there were only four. Could it be that the others had been brought to life so that Maskull could make good his escape?

What did it matter if Maskull was gone?

Will staggered, grateful now to be alive. His only thoughts were to find Willow and Gwydion. He shielded his eyes from the sun and looked out over the town. Thousands of soldiers from both sides filled the marketplace. It would be impossible to find anyone in such a crush. Even so, he hurried down the stair and leapt into the road. His feet led him to a street where many of the wounded had been brought to be tended. Willow was not among them. In another place, outside the biggest of the alehouses, many more dead lay where they had fallen.

It seemed there was a mist rising from the bodies, a strange miasma that hung in the air for a while and then wafted into nothingness. He backed away, wanting more than ever now to find Willow – only not here.

There was a pitiful squealing. He turned to see Lord Strange kneeling abjectly under guard, protesting his innocence and begging to be taken before Duke Richard to make his excuses. When Will turned away he saw the house into which the queen had hurried with King Hal. An immense idea came to him. Inside were piles of cured hides and animal pelts. It was a tanner's shop, though the tanner had long ago made himself scarce.

As Will entered he sensed a confirming presence, then he saw the shop was scattered with pieces of armour that had been cast aside like shells after a crayfish supper. And there lay on the floor a bright sallet onto which a golden circlet crown was fixed.

He turned, looked about, but the queen and all the rest of the courtly party had fled to save their lives once the battle had turned against them. In their haste they had abandoned the king.

Will pulled back a pile of sheepskins and a figure cowered away from him. King Hal crept further under the table. His eyes were wide and there was blood where an arrow had grazed one of his cheeks.

'Fear not, your grace,' Will said, beckoning him to come out. 'The battle is over. It is time to show yourself to your people.'

'We are wounded . . .' the king said, blinking.

The wound was little more than a scratch. Will picked up the king's helmet, lifted the crown from it and tried to place it on his brow, but it was a battle crown made large enough to adorn a helmet, and it fell down about the king's neck.

'You must come out,' Will said firmly. 'For I have need of a king. There is someone I must find, and though my voice is by no means as soft as yours, your grace, mine won't carry nearly so far.'

Though King Hal had not yet seen thirty-five summers, nevertheless he moved like an old man. Perhaps it was gruelling lifelong fear that made him bent-backed and uncertain, perhaps only the strangeness of having been left alone for the first time. At any rate, Will saw how the crown dismayed him, and he reached forward to take it from around his neck. But crown or no crown, when Will led the king outside, all who saw him knew him immediately and were amazed. The rumour of his presence spread like fire in a haystack. Soldiers began to fall to their knees across the whole market square. Then Gwydion was revealed among them, and he came to the fore, seeming taller and stronger than Will had remembered him. His beard was singed and his hands sooty, but he was unharmed and striding through those who knelt before King Hal.

Will ran to him and hugged him. 'We did it, Master Gwydion! We did it!'

The wizard seized him by the shoulders and looked into his eyes. 'You did it, Willand. You, and you alone.'

'I've fulfilled the prophecy of the Child of Destiny at last! I have made one into two right well and cracked that Doomstone clear across the middle!'

At that the wizard looked at him quizzically, then said, 'Willand, I am prouder of you at this moment than you will ever know.'

But Will was not listening. 'Master Gwydion, please – I

have to find Willow. She's here somewhere! I thought that if I could find the king then he could put out word for her—'

The wizard took his arm. 'And I will help you, but as we go you must tell me what happened, for the power of the lorc seemed to fall dead on the stroke of noon. It was as if someone had stilled its heart.'

Will told all that he could, but at last his glance strayed up to the curfew tower and he said, 'What I still don't understand is what happened to Maskull.'

'He is gone.'

'Do you mean he's dead?'

'Merely gone away. I have sent him far from here upon a vanishing-spell.'

'But you said you hadn't prepared a vanishing-spell. Last night, when we were being chased by the harm, you said—'

'I said I had been unable to prepare a vanishing-spell to ensure our safety. I also told you some time ago that only one vanishing-spell may be prepared at one time. The reason I could not prepare one to rescue us was because I already had one woven and ready to trigger.'

'And the trigger was carried by Maskull? You mean he was foolish enough to take something from you?' he said, recalling the bird's skull that Gwydion had once worn about his neck, and the cliffs to which it had vanished them.

'Indirectly.' Gwydion smiled a broad smile. 'He was wearing it as he stood upon the tower. Do you remember the diamond that came from Leir's swan cloak?'

'The Star of Annuin? Then it was important after all!'

The wizard's arch smile changed to one of satisfaction. 'You see, my aim with the diamond was not so much to bribe the queen, nor even to gain a protectorship for Richard, as to bring the queen into ostentatious possession of it. I know Maskull of old. And I reckoned on his desire to have that stone for himself. He did not disappoint me.

He coveted it, yet he never guessed what it was, nor, more importantly, where it had come from.'

'So . . . is Maskull now trapped in Leir's tomb?'

'Do not worry on that account, Willand, for Maskull is not anywhere as insecure as a barrow.'

'Then – where is he?'

'You saw me take the Star of Annuin from Leir's tomb, surely. But I told you once before that it belonged to a king even greater than Leir, for it was fetched from the Realm Below by Great Arthur in the days of the First Men. From the beginning of time it lay with the other Hallows in a chamber far under the earth. That was where the hand of man first touched the Star, and that is where Maskull has been sent down to now. It required only that I caught him unawares to land the trigger-spell upon the gem. He is wily and most solicitous of his own skin – a hard enemy to distract, but when you appeared at his back and he turned on you, then my chance came, and thus was he, in the truest manner of speaking, defeated by us both.'

By now they had come almost to the king, and Will's impatience was setting him on fire. 'Master Gwydion, I must learn what has become of Willow. Though all is won, all will be lost for me if I can't find her!'

'Tread softly, Willand . . .'

Will endured a wait while the wizard gave King Hal into the keeping of Duke Richard's captains, bidding the king work such healing touch as he might among those who had fallen. Then the king's heralds were discovered and sent out to ask if there was one called Willow among those who yet lived, for she was eagerly sought by the king.

'Do her proud,' Gwydion told him. 'And wait for her usefully. Take this salve and look to the wounded, for there is much bloody work to be undone while we still may.'

And though Will's heart was breaking he took the salve and went dutifully to those who had fallen. He passed among them with his healing, and as his own hurts melted away he saw the truth of the rede that said 'a healer's hands heal in the healing'. And all the while he looked urgently for Willow and foreboded the reason why she had not yet come at the king's command.

At last he could stand it no longer. He broke away from the dying and went out in search of her himself. But how could he find her among the many thousands of soldiers who were crowded into the town? He called her name, and looked in vain for the green and white of the Cambray archers in whose company she had served. Once again he came to that place of horror which he knew already, under the sign of the castle where Duke Edgar of Mells lay dead.

Beside his body was that of the Earl of Umber, his neck shot through with an arrow. Humphrey, Earl of Stratford, son of the Duke of Rockingham also lay dead, and 'Mad John', Baron Clifton of Aston Oddingley, along with many more victims of lesser name. All of them had been hideously butchered and stripped.

Suddenly he felt a gauntleted hand upon his shoulder. He turned to see Duke Richard himself, come as his warrior's code demanded, to look at his fallen adversary and make peace with the dead. His helmet was under his arm and his eyes were sad. 'I have heard that Duke Edgar was warned by Master Gwydion to beware castles. See how he has made the wizard's words famous by his death.'

'Your grace's personal enemy is slain,' Will said heavily. 'Perhaps the dead will forgive, but what of Duke Edgar's son, Henry? I know I would find it hard to pardon you if this were my father's corpse lying so in the street.'

'Aye, and I too, if it were mine,' Edward said, arriving. He had not properly understood Will's words, yet he said, 'Willand's right, Father. Beware the sons of all these whom you now look upon, for they will not easily forget this day!'

As the duke stood in contemplation of the dead, he laid

his hands upon both their shoulders as if he had been laying hands upon Edward and Edmund, his sons. Will thought of the limping, bewildered son who now would no longer grow up to be any sort of warrior. For a little while Will truly felt part of the family in which he had grown to manhood, but the moment passed away, and in parting Will asked the duke if he would send men to search out his company of green-clad Cambray archers and so make enquiry for Willow.

Will recrossed the market square and came to the top of the lane where more bodies were laid out on the ground. They were arranged in rows and someone had covered them with white linen brought out from the wealthier houses. It looked as if fifty men had made their beds in the street, and that the dead were only sleeping. But they did not move and their faces were pale and the illusion outlasted itself to become something terrible. Will knelt down when he saw Willow there among the dead.

She was kneeling also, and her grief was the greater for she was tending the body of her father.

'I was too late,' she told him desolately. 'The slash of a blade has swept him away from me. Oh, Will!'

He let her cling to him, and he hugged her close, and there they stayed for a long while as she poured out her heart in falling tears.

It seemed an age before Gwydion found them again. Already, beyond the Tonne, two large grave pits had been started, and there was much for the wizard to supervise. Willow was washing her father's face and combing his hair. She was in the care of one of the Wise Women who had come into the town to do what they could now the fighting had ended. The Sister exchanged soft words with Gwydion and then he brought Will away so that father and daughter could spend one last quiet moment together.

Gwydion took him before the king once more, for there

were certain matters that could wait no longer, chiefly explanations concerning the Doomstone of Verlamion and what had happened at the moment of noon when the windows of the Martyr's great chapter house had burst out and a cloud had issued into the sky. But when all had been said on the subject, Gwydion brought together the king and the duke and made sigils above their foreheads while they faced one another.

'Behold!' he said, turning and lifting his staff on high. 'For now we are to witness the sealing of the peace!'

Duke Richard, using all leniency, mercy and bounteousness, knelt formally before the king. He would not look upon him then, but bowed his head most humbly, saying, 'By your leave, sire, I shall ride in procession to Trinovant, going as escort. And once in your royal palace you shall decide what is to be done for the best.'

The king looked back, his face moon-pale, his dark eyes mournful and infinitely deep as he made formal reply. 'Richard of Ebor, you have shown yourself to be our true and well-sworn servant. We will not go into our royal palace at Trinovant, but instead shall enter into the White Hall, and there, within the ambit of the Stone of Scions, shall be summoned a parliament of lords to debate the good governance of the Realm. There we shall make plain our recommendation before the gathered estates, which is that the Duke of Ebor should be once again Lord Protector of the Realm, and the Earl Sarum shall have the Great Seal delivered unto him as Chancellor, and the Earl Warrewyk should be once again made Captain of the port of Callas.'

And when all was said, and all those who were present pronounced themselves satisfied, Gwydion brought Will before Duke Richard again, saying quietly, 'I would know how this most crucial man is to be rewarded. Though you know it not, he has served this Realm more than any today.'

'Crucial, you say? He does not seem so, but I will believe you, Master Gwydion, for your knack is truly uncanny.'

Duke Richard was now almost childlike in the wizard's presence, for his ardour was quelled and he no longer presumed upon Gwydion's meanings but stood in awe, for all had come out as Gwydion had told him it would, and the battle had ended mysteriously and a victory of a stranger sort than any he had thought possible had been won.

'Yes,' the duke said, humbly. 'All shall be done as you wish, for you are wiser than I have been able to see.' Then he summoned his standard-bearer to him, and soon a servant came with rich gear, and he asked Will to choose among whatever was there and decide what he would take for his own gift of gratitude. It was a generous offer, made honestly, for there were coin purses and weapons whose blades were chased in fine gold and gems of great worth among what was displayed.

Will came forward and bowed and kissed the duke's signet ring to show him respect, though his heart was still hollow with Willow's grief and he would rather have been with her than choosing among all the gold of Fumi's lair. 'I thank your grace for your kindness,' he said, 'but I would prefer now only to return to my home, and nothing of this kind will be of use to me there.'

'Then you shall have my own destrier to carry you home.'

The horse was brought and when Will saw it he said, 'I accept gladly, for this fine white horse reminds me of another that I once rode.'

Gwydion said, approving of the gift, 'His name is Avon. He is the finest of his blood. They say a strong horse, a stout staff and a good wife are the three boons that will make a man's smile broad.'

After that, the wizard took Will before the king once more, and after Gwydion had set a mark on the king's brow he spoke privately with him. Then King Hal called to his scribe and set his seal to a paper which he offered to Will.

'What is it?' he asked as he was called forward to receive it.

'We hear from Master Gwydion that you love your home above all things,' the king whispered.

'Above all things but one, your grace. I thank you.'

Gwydion spoke softly in his ear. 'Friend Hal's gift to you is but one among many that he will make today in healing the Realm. Yours is a secret charter which you must deliver safe home with you. Henceforth, the Vale and each of the villages and hamlets that lie within it shall be relieved of the tithe. The cost of it shall be borne instead, upon this secret order, by the royal exchequer.'

'Your grace is too generous,' Will said, overwhelmed by the honours done him. Yet he was still anxious. 'I must go to Willow now. Master Gwydion, I must—'

Gwydion stayed him. 'Wait one more moment, for we may not see one another again for a while and I would like to have a proper parting from you.'

'Parting?' Will felt a cloud pass across the face of the westering sun.

'Bid me farewell, Willand, for a horse is being saddled for me. I shall leave Verlamion before nightfall.'

'So soon? Where will you go, Master Gwydion?'

'First, to Trinovant. I must see that this hard-won peace holds. Then I will go alone into the North, for there is much for me to debate and study upon and many wise men I must consult. I must decide what is to be done with the Dragon Stone, and all the other battlestones that lie scattered across the Realm. These are large questions, and their settling will be no easy undertaking.' He fixed Will with a searching look. 'But all that is now none of your concern, for as you yourself say you have fulfilled the prophecy of the Child of Destiny . . .'

But there was something in the way the wizard's words trailed off that made Will question if the cracking of the Doomstone might not have been due to the final fulfilment of prophecy.

'But one has been made two,' he said. 'It was the power of that prophecy that broke the stone. Wasn't it, Master Gwydion?'

The wizard's expression was impenetrable. 'Still you do not know your own strength. And as the Wortmaster would say, "when it comes to prophecy, who knows?" I will say only this: the lorc may have fallen silent, but it is not dead. Therefore, I expect we shall hear Gort's "trumpet of ancestral voices" again in future time.' He glanced about. 'Meanwhile, you should return home – live well and be at your ease and remember to be kind to yourself. And against such a day as may yet come, you must leave me to stand guard.' He reached inside his sleeve. 'Now, see here! I have decided upon this as my parting gift to you.'

Will took the slim volume. It was old and bound in scuffed brown leather. It had no iron clasp as most other books did, but on the cover were tooled the words,

Ane radhas a'leguim oicheamna; ainsagimn deo teuiccimn.

Will smiled for he knew their meaning pretty well in the true tongue: 'Speak these words to . . . read the secrets within . . . learn and so . . . come to a field of brightly-coloured mushrooms? Eh?'

'—and so come to a true understanding.' Gwydion corrected him.

'Hmmm. Well, a pretty little book of my own at last. What fun!' he said, turning it over. 'But it doesn't seem to have any place on it to put a chain.'

Gwydion grunted. 'Pity the man who tried to put a chain on that book. The words on the cover are clasp enough.'

'Can such a small book have more than a little wisdom in it?' he said impishly.

'Ha! More than enough for the likes of you, I think. The more you read that book the bigger it will grow. You will see!'

'Then I'll treasure it, Master Gwydion. And I hope it becomes so large that in time a dozen men won't be able to turn a page of it! Would it make me wise if I was to read all of it?'

The wizard chuckled. 'No book could do that. But I fancy it will make you more learned, and stronger. And you cannot be strong until you are a little wise, and you cannot be wise until you have stocked at least a little learning inside that unruly head of yours – so says one of the redes of true manhood, at least.'

Will grinned at that, very pleased with his gift, but sad that it had to have been given to him in parting. When he tried to open the book the covers would not budge until he had spoken the golden words. Even then, the pages appeared blank, though as he looked at them words began to show mistily, and when he looked away again everything faded.

'That is the usual precaution,' Gwydion said, then lowering his voice he added. 'In matters of reading, make habit your friend. Read from it every day. If you do that faithfully, you will find that by the time you reach the Vale your eyes will know enough to see your way in. And – mark this very well – should you find yourself in dire need, you must find the page where flies the swiftest bird. Call it by name and that will be enough.'

They embraced, and Gwydion whispered words in the true tongue, and then they swiftly parted. Will watched the wizard go, and as he passed out of sight he went to look for Willow. When she came to him he hugged her close and enfolded her in his cloak.

'Do you wish to remain in service with the duke's household?' he asked.

She hesitated. 'I don't know what else I can do.'

'He will agree, for Lady Cicely says you are a hard worker and good tempered and much liked by everyone.'

She said nothing, but looked away, and he saw how her tears had washed some of the dirt of battle from her cheeks.

'It's funny,' he said, hardly knowing how to put it, 'but

in my real home there's a mother who always longed for a girlchild of her own. What I mean to say is, I'd like it if you decided to return with me to the Vale. I mean, if you wanted to.'

'Oh, Will! I want that more than anything!'

And she wept then, for she feared to be left alone and the truth was that she had wished for many a long year that she could be some mother's daughter.

By now, the long shadows of the day were falling across the market square and a cool breeze had sprung up to add poignancy to their leavetaking. They stayed only to see brave Stenn committed to the earth. Will stood in sadness at the graveside while Willow wrapped him in his shroud and then they both laid him down among the heroes. And Willow watched over him through tear-filled eyes until evening began to fall and flaring torches were lit. And there was a great gathering that came past in a long and silent line, each man casting down a handful of earth upon the dead of both armies. And so the slain were given as one the solemn dignity of a soldier's burial, and every man who looked upon the scene was in his heart glad that he too was not himself down in the cold clay.

Afterwards, Will lifted Willow up onto Avon's back and turned the horse's head towards the last of the western glow. And so they left the fateful town of Verlamion before the day was fully done and looked for solace in one another's company.

□ □ □

CHAPTER TWENTY-FOUR

THE GREEN MAN

The caress of approaching summer was now soft upon the land, for when day came the whitethorn was all in bloom and fragrant, and there was the sound of crickets and the buzzing of bees and the sweet song of larks. Willow spoke much about her father as they went along, and Will listened, knowing that the pain of loss would be lessened only by letting her share happy memories.

And so, for two days and two nights they wended westward together, while the summer of the Realm deepened all around them. Willow would ride while he led Avon by the bridle, and when she had ridden long enough they would change places, or walk together side by side. The hurts on Will's face and hands healed with surprising readiness, and he began to enjoy a new peace of mind – a state he had not known before and one he suspected might have had more than a little to do with Gwydion's farewell whisperings.

At noon on the second day he and Willow blew the fluff from a dandelion, and he asked her to make a wish and to keep it a secret. Then he showed her the leaping salmon talisman that once more hung about his neck. He told her it carried another wish, one made with a mother's love more than two years before.

'*Gunhe robh arh chlachsan ammet adhorn,*' he said as he squeezed the token. '*Gesh an ruigha ma mer cheanat uidhe.*'

'Is that what it says on your fish?' Willow asked.

'No. It's just a wish – spoken in the language of stones. It means something like: "May this ornament remain in my keeping until I return home".'

It was a far longer journey back over much the same ground that Will and Gwydion had covered so swiftly on Arondiel's back. Avon clip-clopped along the dusty roads, and many were the country folk they met who admired the great white horse and enquired after the terrible battle that had lately been fought upon Werlame's hill.

Will would not speak of it, except to shake his head and call it 'a very bad business'. And it seemed to him when he thought of it that some of the vividness of what had happened had already begun to fade from memory. Still, on that slow road home, Will thought much about the tragic king and what might be the true fate of his realm. He thought too about the lorc, a thing that had been intended as a boon for men, but which had ended up putting hatred into men's hearts. But the more he thought about high matters the less he seemed to understand. All that had been agreed upon at Verlamion was that King Hal would continue to reign in name and dignity, but in deed and in authority Duke Richard would be sovereign. It seemed to Will, after all, to be a deal that could have been struck quietly by two Valesmen over a mug of ale without any need to raise voices much less entail the maiming and killing of men.

When he looked upon Willow's grief, he saw that the harm of war came to many more than those who took hurts upon the field, for as Gwydion had once said in his wisdom, the acts that men do, be they kind or otherwise, spread out like rings across the flat of a pond until all the folk in the world are touched by an echo of delight or despair.

Every day on the journey home Will did as Gwydion had bidden him. He read from his little book, though it never seemed to grow any bigger as he had expected it would. Each time after he had read it he found himself thinking about the battlestones that yet lay undiscovered, and what Gwydion had said about the lorc not being dead despite its rottenest tooth having been pulled. Will thought of the great pond of fate too, and saw just how close Maskull had come to casting a great stone into the waters of the world and making it impossible for them ever to find their proper level again.

What had truly happened to Maskull? For the sorcerer could not be dead, and it seemed from what Gwydion had said that he had been banished rather than beaten. When Will thought about the sorcerer, his last words came like hornets to plague him.

'"I made you, I can just as easily unmake you." What did he mean by that?' he asked the sky.

But the sky would give no answer.

On the morning of the third day they rode up over the Tops and came to a place from which Will could see the Giant's Ring. His jaw set as he came upon the crooked thumb of the King's Stone and saw below it the ruin of the battlestone, still lying where it had been shattered – one large piece and a dozen smaller. He rode a little way down the slope towards the huddle of pock-marked stones that were all that remained of the tomb of Queen Orba. Avon would not go near the scorched earth around it, and so Will led him away again, and when they reached the sheep track he took out his little book and opened it with due ceremony.

As he began to read the words that appeared, they lifted

a corner of the cloaking-spell and the woods at the top of the Vale came mistily into plain sight. He jumped up on Avon's back, and pulled Willow up behind, then they galloped away a little way eastward again. It was not long before he saw Nether Norton laid out prettily below. Swallows called to them from their looping flights overhead, and Will felt a wonderful tingle in his bones. Then they dipped down into the Vale and Willow marvelled at how the briars and brambles parted to let them pass.

The path led them down through Foxberry Woods and by the beechwoods of Overmast and past Gundal's cottage. It seemed to be a different world here, warmer and greener underfoot, and shining with a mellow light. And there was a special joy in Will's heart, a lightness, so that everywhere he looked he was reminded of happy times that he had half forgotten. The way wound down between soaring beech trees, grey and smooth of bark and shady, and as they approached the solitary dwelling many tame white doves came to meet them, and one landed on Will's shoulder.

A dog barked as they approached the house.

'Who's there?' Ysenleda, widow of Gundal, called.

'Friends,' Will said, though she looked at them as if they were not. 'Do you not know me, Ysenleda? For, by the sun and the moon, I know you very well!'

She peered closer, then burst into laughter. 'Why, Willand! It's you . . . but look how you've changed! Where're your braids? And who's this pretty girl with you upon such a great big horse? Come down, both of you, and share a cup of milk with me, if you will!'

And they did, for they were parched and the Widow Ysenleda liked to speak of old times to any who would listen. For his part, Will wanted to know much that had passed in the two years he had been away, but at length he stood up from the widow's table and told her they must take their leave, and in truth his excitement to be truly home had grown unendurable.

They came into the village by a dusty way, Willow sitting on Avon now and Will leading him. Nothing had changed. Nether Norton was as it had always been.

Will was recognized only with difficulty by the boys playing outside the Green Man. Their fathers and elder brothers stopped their chewing and stared at him. The sign above them was the same old weatherbeaten sign, but now the Green Man was smiling in a way he had never smiled before.

'I'd like to go straight home,' he whispered to Willow, 'but I suppose we'll get no further than this for the time being.'

'Well, well, well! And if it ain't Willand the Wanderer!' said Baldgood, pointing up at him as if at a ghost. 'Hey, Breg! Look who's here! And with his hair cut short and the sproutings of a beard on his chin!'

Bregowina put her head round the door. 'Now there's a sight I never thought to see!'

Half a dozen Valesmen came out. They pulled Will into the Green Man and pressed a welcome cup of ale on him.

'I'd hardly know you!' said Baldulf, who was fatter and rosier-cheeked than ever.

'Wybda told us all you was dead!' said the landlord of the Green Man. 'Says you come to a sticky end and was et by hobgoblins.'

'If he was et by goblins,' Baldgood said, 'then they soon spat him out again.'

'Oh, I never did say no such thing!' Wybda called from the back room. She was still embroidering. 'What I said was: it wouldn't surprise me if he had got himself done to death going off like he did.'

'Ah, never mind old Wybda!' said Baldulf, looking now at Willow. 'But where's your manners, Will?'

He turned a little shyly. 'This is a friend of mine. She goes by the name of Willow.'

She smiled at them and they all nodded to her and confessed themselves very pleased to have met her. Then Baldgood fetched out mugs of foaming ale that were passed around, so the entire room could drink Will's good health and give a welcome to his friend. But it was amazing to Willow that although the Valesmen were kind to her, and all seemed genuinely pleased to have Will back among them, nobody asked where he had been or what he had been doing, or even where Willow had come from.

'It's the cloaking-spell,' he told her quietly. 'I guess that if Gwydion hadn't made Valesmen a little incurious about the outside world, they might all have wandered out of the Vale by now and never have been able to find their way back in again.'

Word of his arrival spread quickly, for as he supped his ale, Will began to see familiar faces appearing at the door in ever greater numbers.

'Now, then!' he said, standing up when it seemed that half the village had arrived. 'Everybody look at this! We've brought back a gift for you from the king himself!'

Willow handed him the king's charter and Will read the words off the paper with such expert smoothness that everyone ooh-ed and ahh-ed in wonder. Then they started to ask what it was that Will had actually told them.

'It means that the king has promised that no more tithes are to be gathered from the Vale.'

'No more tithes? For a whole year?'

'This year. Next year. And forever.'

There was surprise and delight and then cheering at that, and when Will turned, there at the back of the crowd were Eldmar and Breona. He rushed to them and they clasped one another wordlessly, their eyes filling with tears of joy.

'Mother, Father,' he said, taking Willow's hand and bringing her forward. 'There's someone I'd like you to meet.'

AUTHOR'S NOTE

Nowhere in *The Language of Stones* is mention made of Britain or Ireland or any other familiar country, for these are places in our world. But the world in which Willand grew up is not wholly imagined; it bears a complex relationship to our own world in both space and time. There is correspondence between episodes in the book and events that took place in our own fifteenth century, between the various settings of the novel and locations scattered about Britain.

Readers wishing to explore these settings might start in Oxfordshire, in that part which lies midway between Oxford and Stratford-upon-Avon. Nether Norton, and the rest of the Vale, seem to have their origins here. Dedicated beer drinkers will doubtless know the name 'Hook Norton', but there are several other Nortons here.

Not far away, the most easterly, and most delightful, of Britain's neolithic stone rings is to be found near a road that runs between Little and Great Rollright. It might be said to be on 'the Tops' because it is locally the highest point of land. Associated with the ring is a crooked stone called the King's Stone, though the king may not have been called Finglas, and also a ruined tomb, which may or may not have belonged to a queen called Orba.

South of the putative Vale, run our rivers Windrush and Evenlode, passing the lordly estates of Cornbury and Blenheim. All near here was once dominated by the great royal forest of Wychwood, almost two hundred square miles of it. It was at Woodstock that King Henry I kept a menagerie of exotic animals, though there were never any unicorns in his collection. Memories of the forest still persist in the names of several of the villages that lie to the west. Through our Wychwood once ran the Roman road known as Akeman Street, part of which is still trod by walkers enjoying the Oxfordshire Way. Although there was a Lord Strange in fifteenth-century England, he did not live in Wychwood. Nothing now remains in our world of the place where Will's Lord Strange kept his tower – nothing, that is, except a moat. Sadly, no sacred oak grove has been replanted near here, on the other hand all trace of arms production has ceased. A modern visitor who wants to see a tower like Lord Strange's could do no better than to visit Castell Coch in the nation we call Wales or Cymru, and whose equivalent was known to Will as Cambray.

The journey which brought Will and Gwydion to Clarendon would have taken them, in our world, across the River Thames at Radcot Bridge (where a fourteenth-century battle was once fought) and through Uffington, famous for its White Horse. There really is a Dragon Hill below the scarp, and the Wormhill Bottom mentioned in passing lies on the Downs just up from Lambourn – which of course is still famous for its horses.

Climbing up onto the Ridgeway near Wayland's Smithy and turning first west and then south, a modern traveller might arrive eventually at Savernake Wood, near Marlborough. And from there it would be an easy matter to pick up the headwaters of the River Bourne, which runs more or less along the Wiltshire-Hampshire border and down towards Salisbury.

The ruins of Celuai na Sencassimnh, also stand in our world, though 'the meadows of the storytellers' is today walked around by far more visitors than ever assembled on the quarter days among the stones of the Great Henge to listen to epic tales being told in the true tongue.

The ruins of Old Sarum and Figsbury Ring still exist too, near modern Salisbury, as do traces of Clarendon Palace. This was the place where in our summer of 1453, King Henry VI of England went insane, and so precipitated events which would eventually culminate in the Wars of the Roses.

Visitors to Ireland will find extraordinary neolithic treasures in abundance. It is tempting to believe the cliffs to which Will and Gwydion clung were the Cliffs of Moher in County Clare, sheer faces of rock which fall six hundred feet into the Atlantic, the brows of which afford the most astonishing sunsets on earth. However, it must be said that the barrow containing the Dragon Stone's sister could just as easily be situated along the rugged coast of an alternative County Kerry, down by Cnoc Breanainn.

A small boat sailing from a port on the south coast of Ireland – let us say Cobh – would probably try to catch the prevailing westerlies that whip up the grey waters of the Irish Sea. People dwelling on an island in that sea might just recognize the name of Gwydion's birthplace, 'Druidale'. But let us suppose that our small boat runs well south of the isle of 'Ellan Vannin' and sails eventually past the isle of Lundy and along the coast of South Wales into the estuary of the Severn. After passing Bristol and going under the two magnificent suspension bridges that now link England and Wales, if the tide was just so, our boat might be caught up by the Severn Bore and carried along for a while towards the city of Gloucester. However, a landfall on the eastern shore and a walk south into the hills could easily bring our traveller to near Uley and the famous long barrow known as Hetty Pegler's Tump.

Wandering north through our Cotswolds might put modern travellers on a line that coincided with Will's and Gwydion's journey. If so, it would parallel the Roman road known as the Fosse Way. They might pass across it eventually, and let their feet take them into Warwickshire, then westward across the northern extremities of Oxfordshire and into a region of Northamptonshire where the River Cherwell rises. Keen-eyed readers might even be able to discover the spot where the Dragon Stone once lay, though the names of the villages have become, in our world, a little worn down.

Taking a path along an increasingly north-eastward track, following the River Nene as it flows towards the Wash, would bring the modern explorer first into what remains of the great Forest of Rockingham. To the east of Geddington, most famous for its Eleanor Cross, lies the village of Wadenhoe on the Nene. Five miles to the north of that lies Oundle and five miles north again, Fotheringhay. Today there is a pleasant village there, and an extraordinary church which seems far too grand for so modest a place. Nothing much guards the river crossing today, but those who trouble to look behind the farm buildings near the bridge are apt to discover the mound that is all that remains of a once magnificent castle.

In our world, Fotheringhay Castle became famous as the fifteenth-century stronghold of Richard, Duke of York, and the birthplace of his son Richard, Duke of Gloucester, who later became King Richard III of England. In a later century Fotheringhay became sunk in infamy as a scene of judicial murder, for it was in the Great Hall there that brave Mary, Queen of Scots, had her head struck off. When her son, James VI of Scotland gained the English throne in the century that followed, he ordered the Great Hall and the fine octagonal keep next to it pulled down, and the rest of the castle utterly erased, so that now hardly a stone is left. There are few stones to see, but the mound survives and it is said that spearplume thistles may be found growing on the mound every summer and a ghostly form may be seen wandering the ruins when autumn fogs drift in from the Fens.

Shropshire, on the Welsh borders, boasts another of Richard of York's castles, that of Ludlow. It is a fine historic town, and substantial portions of its castle still stand. If you visit, you might like to look down the well, for it is one of the deepest castle wells in England. Will's leaving of his Ludford, and subsequent journeyings with Gwydion, took him far and wide across 'the Middle Shires' and to many places that would appear to correspond to locations in our world. The Plaguestone's 'leek field' gives a clue to the whereabouts of Anstin's Cave, as does the name Cheddle.

The 'pretty villages along the River Rea', where Will spent his fifteenth birthday, have now vanished under our Birmingham, but the nine hamlets whose names end in 'stone' still exist in various forms in our world and, all except Atherstone, cluster to the north of Market Bosworth in a small area just four miles by four.

Young Shakespeare began his career as a dramatist by recounting 'the Contention Betwixt the Two Famous Houses of York and Lancaster', or as we would say, the Wars of the Roses. A look through Shakespeare's *King Henry VI* – especially the third part – will probably reward readers with clues to the dramatis personae of the present book, and the keenest readers will spot other connections.

Those familiar with the Bard may also nod at mention of the 'district of Arden'. Our Wootton Wawen has a Black Bull, but it is debatable if 'man-eating beasts of the air' were ever bred there. England has no Aston Oddingley, nor any estate belonging to a Lord Clifton, but there is an

Oddingley near Worcester, and there were two Lords Clifford, father and son, who made themselves infamous enough to be recorded by fifteenth-century chroniclers.

When it comes to other lordly titles, there has never been a Duke of Mells in England, but there is a village called Mells – another of those places that seems to have a church far too grand for it. It is in Somerset, and in the church-yard there lies one of England's greatest war poets. By the bye, Jack Horner of nursery rhyme fame is also connected with Mells.

Arondiel's gallop might have taken Will and Gwydion across Oxfordshire and Buckinghamshire to the beacon that marks the beginning (or end) of the Ridgeway. They pass 'Thring, Wing and Ivangham' which echo the names of three manors which were said in an ancient rhyme to have been forfeited by a certain lord who once quarrelled with the Black Prince. Sir Walter Scott used the latter name, in the form Ivanhoe. Today we can find three towns – Wingrave, Tring and Ivinghoe – in the vicinity of that chalk scarp.

And so our present day traveller comes at last to Hertfordshire, and to the cathedral city of St Albans. The Romans called their own nearby city Verulamium, and it was at St Albans in May of 1455 that an army gathered around the person of King Henry VI, and another, commanded by the Duke of York and the Earl of Warwick, came to seek redress for perceived wrongs. If our traveller visits St Albans in the summer he may be fortu-nate enough to find the town's old bell-tower open. It is sometimes possible to go up and stand on the roof as perhaps Maskull did upon a similar tower while battle raged below him. A visitor to the cathedral might try to find there a dark slab, 'cracked clean in two' that can be found raised up on a plinth in the south presbytery aisle, close to the shrine. Visitors to a greater cathedral in the north, where the archbishop is styled 'Ebor', will also find an interesting stone. This one is imprisoned down in the crypt and is called 'the Doomstone'.

It is interesting to reflect that a fifteenth-century king of England, say Henry VI, would have had a wholly different concept of his country's history and geography to that which we know. We have accurate maps that illustrate the land we live in and show how its parts relate one to another. We can travel easily to all parts of our Realm. And we are the beneficiaries of over three hundred years of scholarly enquiry and scientific investigation into our past. No mediaeval monarch was ever enriched with such a treasure. Spread before Henry would have been a curious mixture of religion, garbled chronicle and sovereign-serving myths such as the 'Historia Regum Britanniae' composed by Geoffrey of Monmouth in the mid twelfth century. Geoffrey's mythic history sought to construct a proud heritage for England, and in doing so to offer an exalted pedigree to its monarchs. The perhaps puzzling name 'Trinovant' is mentioned many times in *The Language of Stones*. It refers to a great, walled city on the banks of the River Iesis, apparently the seat of government. In Geoffrey's 'Historia' it is related how a certain Brutus, fleeing the fall of Troy, set up a new capital in the island he had conquered and named, after himself, Britain. That capital was called 'Troy Novant', or New Troy, and so – almost – is Will's.

Finally, it is worth remembering that in those long-vanished days of the high mediaeval, it was quite usual to believe in magic and giants and dragons. Twin spectres of fear and wonder stalked England's leafy byways, and who can say at this remove whether the one was worth the other? Will's world has been deliberately imagined as the one in which the outlandish fancies of the mediaeval mind were not only deemed to be likely, but were actually true.

APPENDIX I

ON THE AGES OF THE WORLD

The Affirmation of the Druida

> *'The world is as we behold it.' Thus says the rede.*
> *Before there were eyes to see the world, and minds*
> *to comprehend, there was no world to speak of. And*
> *later, much took place in the time of the fae when*
> *there was only the Ice. About this we have no*
> *certain knowledge, therefore those who seek to*
> *chronicle the world begin by saying, 'First, came*
> *the Ice . . .'*

From the Book of Ages

And when the power of the Sun waxed stronger and the Ice withdrew, it was seen that the Drowned Lands had become ocean and the land of Albion was made an island. And after this came the Age of Trees, and here, among their towers of glass, dwelt the noble fae in a time out of memory, and these are the same who planted the trees when the Ice departed.

And soon after this time there came men into the land,

and these First Men were unlike the men who came afterwards, for they were tall and strong and spoke softly and laughed much. They lived long and wanted for nothing, for their lives were counted out in a time of magic when the world was kinder.

But as magic declined in the world so, after a time, harm grew and the first Age of the world ended. The fae chose to leave the land of Albion, and went down into the Realm Below, bequeathing the realm of light and air to the First Men, who were made sad, as a child is made sad at the departure of kind parents.

But thereafter, the men of Albion lived in peace with the land and knew much that was wise that the fae had vouchsafed to them. Even so, after many generations, there came a great calamity and these First Men declined in their turn, and there came a time of desolation in the Isles. And in this Age the years went uncounted, for the land was stalked by wyrm and wyvern, dragon and drake. Hideous giants lived in the mountains then, ogres and half-men, and dread wights infested the doom-rings of the mountainous North, and all was darkness.

And these Isles were put under a pall of fear, for no man of the eastern lands dared set sail for the Wight Cliffs, lest he be snatched from the deck of his ship and eaten by the monsters that then lived in these Isles, and this was called the Age of Giants.

But then came a hero, a man named Brea, who, having made himself an exile in his own land, was then searching for a new place in which to dwell. He came into the Isles from the East, some said from the kingdom called Amor, and with his band of brothers and their brave families, he came into Albion and defeated the giants and took possession of the Isles for men once again and this was called the Age of Iron.

The line of Brea ruled for more than a thousand years,

until the Age of Iron ended and that of Slavery and War began . . . It continued a thousand years, but ended when Gillan came as conqueror. Thus began the fifth Age of the World, the present Age, which is uncertain and called therefore the Age of Dispute.

Age of Trees
Age of Giants
Age of Iron
Age of Slavery and War
Age of Dispute

APPENDIX II

THE BREAN KINGS

The First Thirteen Sceptred Monarchs

1	*Brea*	Triumphed over the giants Magog and Gogmagog
2	*Loegrin*	Brea's son
3	*Queen Gwendolin*	Loegrin's scorned wife
4	*Maddan*	Son of Loegrin and Gwendolin
5	*Memprax*	Son of Maddan, a tyrant
6	*Ibrax*	Son of Memprax
7	*Ibron*	Called 'Brea Scathgiree', son of Ibrax
8	*Liele*	Son of Brea Scathgiree
9	*Hudibrax*	Son of Liele
10	*Bladud*	Called 'Bladud the Leper'
11	*Leir*	Only son of Bladud, called 'the Great'
12	*Queen Cordelin*	Third daughter of Leir
13	*Queen Goneril and Queen Regan*	First and second daughters of Leir, who ruled jointly

Brean Kings at the time of the coming of the Slavers

77	*Hely*	Son of Dagwen
78	*Ludd*	First son of Hely, a famous king
79	*Caswalan*	Second son of Hely, repulsed the Slavers
80	*Tervan*	Third son of Hely
81	*Cunobelin*	Son of Tervan
82	*Carutax*	Eldest son of Cunobelin, beaten by the Slavers
83	*Avirax*	Youngest son of Cunobelin
84	*Maric*	Son of Avirax, called 'Avirax the Traitor'

Brean Kings around the time of Arthur

99	*Orelin*	Called 'the Old', succeeded his brother
100	*Uther*	Great-nephew of Orelin
101	*Arthur*	Son of Uther, Great Arthur

THE STORY CONTINUES IN

THE GIANTS' DANCE

due for publication in May 2005

■ ■ ■

CHAPTER ONE

THE BLAZING

Flames leapt up from the fire, throwing long shadows across the green and dappling the cottages of Nether Norton with a mellow light. This year's Blazing was a fine one. Tonight was what the wizard, Gwydion, called in the true tongue 'Lughnasad', the feast of Lugh, Lord of Light, the first day of autumn, when the first-cut sheaves of wheat were gathered in to the village and threshed with great ceremony. On Loaf Day, grain was ground, and loaves of Lammas bread toasted on long forks and eaten with fresh butter. On Loaf Day, Valesfolk thought of the good earth and what it gave them.

Today the weather had almost been as good as Lammas two years ago when Will had taken Willow's hand and they had circled the fire together three times sunwise, and so given notice that henceforth they were to be regarded as husband and wife.

He put his arm around Willow's shoulders as she cradled their sleeping daughter in her arms. It was a delight to see Bethe's small head nestled in the crook of her mother's elbow, her small hand resting on the blanket that covered her, and despite the dullness in the pit of his stomach, it felt good to be a husband and a father tonight. Life's good here, he thought, so good it's hard to see how it could be much better. If only that dull feeling would go away, tonight would be just about perfect.

But it would not go away – he knew that something was going to happen, that it was going to happen soon, and that it was not going to be anything pleasant. The foreboding had echoed in the marrow of his bones all day but, unlike a real echo, it had refused to die away. Which meant that it was a warning.

He brushed back the two thick braids of hair that hung at his left cheek and stared into the depths of the bonfire. Slowly he let his thoughts drift away from Nether Norton and slip into the fire-pictures that the flames made for him. He opened his mind and a dozen memories rushed upon him, memories of great days, terrible days, and worse nights. But the most insistent image was still of the moment when the sorcerer, Maskull, had raised him up in a blaze of fire above the stone circle called the Giant's Ring. That night he had seen Gwydion blasted by Maskull's magic, and afterwards, as Gwydion had tried to drain the harm from a battlestone, the future of the Realm had balanced on the edge of a knife . . .

It had been more than four years ago, but the dread he had felt on that night and the redeeming day that had followed remained alive in him. It always would.

'Will?' Willow asked, searching his face. 'What are you thinking?'

He broached a smile. 'Maybe I've taken a little too much to drink,' he said and touched his wife's hair. It was gold in the firelight and about as long as his own. He looked at her, then down at the child whose small hand had first clasped his finger just over a year ago. How she had begun to look like her mother.

'Ah, but she's a beautiful child!' said old Baldgood the Brewster, his red face glowing from the day's sunshine. He had begun to clear up and was carrying one end of a table back into the parlour of the Green Man. The other end of the table was carried by Baldram, one of Baldgood's grown sons.

'Seems like Bethe was born only yesterday,' Will told the older man.

'She'll be a year and a quarter old tomorrow, won't you, my lovely?' Willow said dreamily.

'Aye, and she'll be grown up before you can say "Jack o' Lantern". Look at this big lumpkin of mine! Get a move on, Baldram my son, or we'll be out here all night!'

'My, but he's a bossy old dad, ain't he?' Baldram said, grinning.

Will smiled back at the alehouse-keeper's son as they disappeared into the Green Man. It was hard to imagine Baldram as a babe-in-arms – nowadays he could carry a barrel of ale under each arm all the way down to Pannage and still not break into a sweat.

'Hey-ho, Will,' one of the lads from Overmast said as he went by.

'Hathra. How goes it?'

'Very well. The hay's in from Suckener's Field and all's ready for the morrow. Did you settle with Gunwold for them weaners?'

'He offered me a dozen chickens each, but I beat him down to ten in the end. Seemed fairer.'

Hathra laughed. 'Quite right, too!'

'Show us a magic trick, Willand!' one of the youngsters cried. It was Leomar, Leoftan the Smith's boy, with three of his friends. He had eyes of piercing blue like his father and just as direct a manner.

Will asked for the ring from Leomar's finger, but when the boy looked for it, it was not there. Then Will took a plum from the pouch at his own belt and offered it.

'Go on. Bite into it. But be careful of the stone.'

The boy did as he was told and found his ring tight

around the plumstone. He gasped. His friends wrinkled their noses and then laughed uncertainly.

'How'd ya do that?' they asked.

'It's magic.'

'No t'ain't. It's just conjuring!'

'Away with you, now, and enjoy the Blazing!' he said, ruffling the lad's hair. 'And you're right – that was only conjuring. Real magic is not to be trifled with!'

Two more passers-by nodded their heads at Will, and he nodded back. The Vale was a place where everybody knew everybody else, and all were glad of that. Nobody from the outside ever came in, and nobody from the inside ever went out. Months and years passed by without anything out the ordinary happening, and that was how everybody liked it. Everybody except Will.

Though the Valesmen did not know it, it was Gwydion who had made their lives run so quietly. Long ago he had cast a spell of concealment so that those passing by the Vale could not find it – and those living inside would never want to leave. The wizard had made it so that any man who wandered the path down from Nether Norton towards Great Norton would only get as far as Middle Norton before he found himself walking back into Nether Norton again. Only Tilwin the Tinker, knife-grinder and seller of necessaries, had ever come into the Vale from outside, but now even his visits had stopped. Apart from Tilwin, only the Sightless Ones, the 'red hands', with their withered eyes and love of gold, had ever had the knack of seeing through the cloak. But the Fellows were only interested in payment, and so long as the tithe carts were sent down to Middle Norton for collection they had always let the Valesmen be. Four years ago, Will's service to King Hal in ending the battle at Verlamion had won him a secret royal warrant that paid Nether Norton's tithe out of the king's own coffers, so now the Vale was truly cut off.

And I'm the reason Gwydion's kept us all hidden, Will

thought uncomfortably as he stared again into the depths of the fire. He must believe the danger's not yet fully passed. But with Maskull sent into exile and the Doomstone broken, is there still a need to hide us away?

Maskull's defeat had given Gwydion the upper hand, but he had shown scant joy at his victory. He and Maskull had once been part of the Ogdoad, the council of nine earth guardians whose job it had been to steer the fate of the world along the true path. But then Maskull had given himself over to selfishness, and though a great betrayal had been prophesied all along, that had not made it any easier for Gwydion to swallow.

Will sighed, roused himself from his thoughts and looked around at the familiar surroundings. It was strange – in all his months of wandering he had thought there was nothing better than home. And now he had a family of his own there was even more reason to love the way life was in the Vale. And yet . . . when a man had extraordinary adventures they changed him . . .

It's easy for a man to go to war, he thought. But having seen it, can he so easily settle down behind a plough once more?

It hardly seemed so. Occasionally, a yearning would steal over Will's heart. At such times he would go alone into the woods and practise with his quarterstaff until his body shone with sweat and his muscles ached. There was wanderlust in him, and at the root of it was a mess of unanswered questions.

He stirred himself and kissed Willow on the cheek. 'Happy Lammas,' he said.

'And a happy Lammas to you too,' she said and kissed him back. 'I guess we're just about finished with the Blazing. Looks like everyone's had a good time.'

'As usual.'

'What about you?'

'Me?' he asked, his eyebrows lifting. 'I enjoyed it.'

'It looks like you did,' she said, a strange little half-smile on her lips.

'And what's that supposed to mean?'

She fingered the manly braid that hung beside his ear. 'I saw you looking into the bonfire just then. What were you thinking?'

'I was thinking that only a fool would want to be anywhere else today.'

She smiled. 'Truly?'

'Truly.'

It *was* good to see everyone so happy. They had watched the lads and lasses circling the fire. They had listened to the vows that had brought the night's celebration to a fitting close. Some had plighted their troths, and others had made final handfasting vows. Now couples were slipping off into the shadows, heading for home.

There was no doubt about it, since the ending of the tithe the Vale had prospered as never before. They had put up three new cottages in the summer. They had filled the new granary too, and all this from the working of less land. Now the surpluses were not being taken away to make others rich, the plenty was such that Valesmen's families had already forgotten what it was to feel the pinch of hunger.

'About time this little one was abed,' Willow said.

'Yes, it's been a long day.'

They walked up the dark path to their cottage, his arm about her in the warm, calm night. In the paddock, Avon, the white war-horse that Duke Richard of Ebor had given him, moved like a ghost in the darkness. Away from the fire the stars glittered brightly – Brigita's Star, sinking now in the west, Arondiel rising in the east; and to the south Iolirn Fireunha, the Golden Eagle.

An owl called. Will remembered the Lammastide he had spent six years ago sitting with a wizard on top of

Dumhacan Nadir, the Dragon's Mound, close by the turf-cut figure of an ancient white horse. Together they had watched a thousand stars and a hundred bonfires dying red across the Plains of Barklea.

He sighed again.

'What's that for?' Willow asked.

He scrubbed fingers through his hair. 'Oh . . . I was just thinking. You know – about old times. About Gwydion.'

It seemed a long time since Will and the wizard had last set eyes on one another. How good it would be to wander the ways as they had once done. To walk abroad again among summer hedgerows, enjoying the sun and the rain, or feeling the bite of an icy wind on their cheeks.

'I wonder what he's doing right now?' Will muttered.

'Unless I miss my guess, he'll be striding the green hills of the Blessed Isle,' Willow said. 'Or sitting in a high tower somewhere out in the wilds of Albanay.'

Will's eyes wandered the dark gulfs between the stars. 'Hmmm. Probably.'

'Wilds?' he could almost hear Gwydion chuckle. 'It is not wild here. See! These trees in a line show where a hedge once grew. And what of those ancient furrow marks? The Realm has been loved and tended for a hundred generations of men. It is almost, you might say, a garden.'

While Willow went indoors to put Bethe into her cradle, Will lingered in the yard at the back of their cottage. He could smell the herbs, all the green leaf he had grown in the good soil – plants ripe and ready to offer the sweetness of the earth's bounty. The scents of the orchard were keen on the still air. He heard Avon whinny again, and tried to recall where he had felt the elusive feeling in his belly before, but when he looked inside himself he was shocked.

'A premonition about a premonition,' he told himself wryly. 'Now that would be something . . .'

Willow came out and said, 'I'm glad we chose to call

her Bethe. There's strong magic in naming, for I can't think now what else we could have called her.'

'Bethe is the birch tree,' he said. '"Beth", first letter of the druid's alphabet, and Bethe our firstborn.'

'I like that.'

'You know, the birch was the first tree to clothe these isles when the ice drew back into the north. Her white bark remembers the White Lady, she who was wise and first taught about births and beginnings, the one who some call the Lady Cerridwen. Our May Pole is always a birch, and Bethe was born on May Day, which is my birthday too. In the old tongue of the west "bith" means "being". And "beitharn" in the true tongue means "the world". Maybe that's the reason I suggested the name and why you agreed – because our daughter means the world to us.'

Willow squeezed him close and laid her head against his breast. 'There's such a power of learning in that book of yours.'

She meant the magic book that Gwydion had given him that sad day at Verlamion. He said, 'There's much to read and more to know. It's said that a country swain comes of age at thirteen years, that the son of a fighting lord may carry arms in battle at fifteen, and that a king must reach eighteen years to rule by his word alone – but one who would learn magic may not be properly called wise until he has come to full manhood.'

Willow looked at him. 'And how old's that?'

He shook his head. 'I don't know. But as the saying has it: "The willow wand is slow to become an oaken staff." And so it must be, for if I know anything at all it's that there's much more to be understood in the world than can ever be learned in one man's lifetime.'

Now it was Willow's turn to sigh. 'Then tell me true: do you read that book every day in the hope that one day you'll become a wizard too? Like Gwydion?'

He laughed. 'No. That I can never be.'

'Then why?'

'Because Gwydion gave it to me and bade me read it. And I gave him my word that I would.'

She squeezed him again, but this time it was to stress her words. 'Well, now, you're going to promise me something, Willand Bookreader, that you won't be burning any candle stubs over hard words tonight!'

He grinned. 'Now *that* I'll gladly promise!'

They held one another in the starlight for a moment. A shooting star flared brilliantly and briefly in the west, and then a coolness stirred among the leaves of the nearest apple trees. She looked up, and he felt her stiffen.

'What is it?'

But there was no need for an answer, for there, high up over the Tops, an eerie purple glow had begun to bruise the sky.

'Don't look at it,' she told him, turning away suddenly.

He felt his foreboding intensify. 'It's . . . it's only the northern lights.'

'I don't care what it is . . .' Her voice faded.

He stared at the flickering as it grew. 'Gwydion once told me about the northern lights,' he whispered. 'But I've never seen them.'

As he looked into the darkness he felt the earth power crackling in his toes. The apple trees felt it too. His eyes narrowed as he realized that this flaring glow was not – could not be – the northern lights. This was brighter, more focused, and it spoke to him.

'Will, come inside!' she said, pulling at his arm.

'I . . .' The light pulsed irregularly like distant lightning, though there was not a cloud in the sky. It was livid. It seemed to reach out from a source that was hidden by the dark hills surrounding the Vale. When he recalled what he knew of sky lore, his unease grew, for this was no natural light.

His thoughts went immediately to the lorc, that web of lines in the earth that fed the battlestones. They had glowed with an eerie light. At certain phases of the moon they had stood out in the darkness, clothed with a pale and other-worldly sheen.

'Look!' he said, pointing. 'That halo. It seems to be coming from near the Giant's Ring.'

The ancient stone circle could not be seen from the Vale. It was in Gwydion's words *Bethen feilli Imbliungh*, the Navel of the World, a place of tremendous influence, and the fount through which earth power erupted into the lorc. That, Will had always supposed, was the reason the fae had set up one of their terrible battlestones there, the one that had fought Gwydion's magic and won.

'It can't be the battlestone, can it?' Willow asked as she peered into the inconstant light. 'You said Gwydion had drawn all the harm out of it.'

'So he did. But tonight is Lammas when the power of the earth waxes highest.'

'We didn't see lights there last year. Nor any year before.'

Willow's words ceased as a low rumbling passed through the ground. It was so low that it could not be heard, only felt in the bones. Will heard Avon whinny, then came the sound of ripe apples dropping in the orchard. The ground itself was trembling. As he stared into the night he was aware of Willow's frightened eyes upon him. Then two flower pots fell from the window ledge at the back of the cottage. He heard them crack one after the other on the stone kerb below. Willow jumped.

'What's happening?'

'I don't know.'

'I'm going to see if Bethe's all right.' She vanished into the cottage.

Will let her go, listening only to the night as the rumble passed away beneath his feet and stillness returned to the

Vale. Gwydion had once spoken of mountains of fire that rose up in remote parts of the world, mountains that spewed forth flames and hot cinders. But there were none of those in the Realm. He had spoken too of tremblings that shook the land from time to time. They came sometimes as workings that had been delved deep under the earth long ago shifted or fell in on themselves.

Could that have caused the rumblings?

And if so, what about the light?

There was something about that light that caused a shiver to run up Will's spine. This rippling, eye-deceiving glow was the same colour as the flames that had once trapped and burned him within the compass of the Giant's Ring. It was purple fire that had lifted him up high over the stones and had begun to consume his flesh. Purple fire that would have killed him in dreadful agony had not Gwydion's magic saved him. And such a flame as that came only from Maskull's hands.

'By the moon and stars, he's found me . . .'

A great terror seized him. He recalled the time when he had sat beside Gwydion in a cart and the wizard had told him what could happen if someone tried to tamper magically with a battlestone. *'If all the harm were to be released in a single hand clap . . . it would be enough to torment the land beyond endurance.'*

And who else but Maskull would dare to tamper with a battlestone?

Fears stirred, wormlike, in Will's guts as he looked up at the Tops now. There was no doubt what he must do. He went inside and lit a fresh candle. The damp wick crackled as it caught from a flame that already glowed in its niche. Dust still sifted down from the rafters in the gloom. Willow stood by the cradle, her daughter in her arms. Bethe had been woken up by the quake and was mewling.

'Where're you going?' Willow asked, seeing him climb the ladder into the loft.

'To call on an old friend.'

He went to his oak chest and brought out the book that grew bigger the more it was read. He brought it down the ladder, took a soft cloth and wiped clean the great covers of tooled brown leather. There was not much time. Soon the other Valesmen would notice the glow and they would come for his advice.

He placed the treasured book on the wooden lectern by the fire, a piece of furniture he had made himself specially for it. Then he composed himself for the ritual that should always attend the opening of any book of magic.

He placed his left hand flat on the book's front cover and repeated the words of the true tongue that were written there:

> *'Ane radhas a'leguim oicheamna;*
> *ainsagimn deo teuiccimn.'*

And then he voiced the spell again in plain speech.

> *'Speak these words to read the secrets within;*
> *learn and so come to a true understanding.'*

There were no iron clasps on this book as there were on most others, for this book was locked by magic. As he muttered the charm the bindings were released and he was able to open it. Inside were words for his eyes alone. He turned to a special page with Gwydion's parting words in mind.

> ' . . . *should you find yourself in dire need, you must*
> *find the page where flies the swiftest bird. Call*
> *it by name and that will be enough.'*

His fingers trembled as the page before him began to fill with the picture of a bird, black and white with a russet throat and long tail streamers. He hesitated. Is this truly a moment of 'dire need'? he asked himself. Am I doing the right thing?

He looked inside himself, then across to where Willow nursed their daughter, and suddenly he feared to invoke the spell. But then he saw the livid light flare and heard Bethe begin to cry, and he knew he must pronounce the trigger-word without delay.

'*Fannala!*'

He spoke the true name of the swallow. Immediately, his thoughts were knocked sideways as if by a great blow to his head. A bird flew up out of the book and into the candle-light. There was a flash of white breast feathers and it was gone, so that when Will's bedazzled eyes tried to follow it he lost it in the shadows. When he looked again not knowing what to expect, a grey shape had appeared in the corner.

'Who's there?' Willow shouted, clutching Bethe close to her and snatching up a fire iron.

Will was overwhelmed. It seemed that a great bear or tiger cat had appeared in the room and was making ready to attack. Yet the shape gave off a pale blue light that faded, and then the figure of an old man walked out of the darkness.

The wizard was tall and grave, swathed in his long wayfarer's cloak of mouse-brown. His head was closely clad in a dark skullcap, and his hand clasped an oak staff. Bare toes peeped out from under the long skirts of his belted robe, and he wore a long beard that was divided now into two forks.

'A swift, I told you! Not a *swallow*! Fool!'

Will stared as the wizard stroked the two stiff prongs of his beard together and made them into one.

'Master Gwydion . . .'

The wizard looked around the homely room with heavy-lidded eyes, his brow creased. He footed his staff with a bang against the fireplace. 'I hope you have good reason to summon me thus!'

Will felt the wizard's displeasure like a knife. Their parting had been more than four years ago, and Will expected warmer words.

'Good reason?' Willow said, putting down the fire iron but still unwilling to have her husband roughly spoken to beside his own hearth. 'I should say there's good reason. And less of the "fool", if you please, Master Gwydion. Those who don't mind their manners in this house gets shown off these premises right quick, and that's whoever they may be.'

Gwydion turned to her sharply, but then seeming to bethink himself swept a low bow. 'I have offended you. Please, accept my apologies. If I was rude, it was because I was upon an important errand and I did not expect to be disturbed from it.'

Will stepped towards the door without hesitation. 'I can't be sure, Gwydion, but I think this is something you ought to see.'

Once they were outside Gwydion shielded his eyes from the purple glare, then took Will's arm. 'You were right to summon me. Of course you were.'

Will's heart sank. 'What is it?'

'Something I have feared daily these four years.'

'Hey!' Will called, but Gwydion had already taken himself halfway down the path. 'Hey, where are you going?'

'To the Giant's Ring, of course!'

'Alone?'

'That,' the wizard called over his shoulder, 'is entirely up to you.'

Will watched the wizard stride away into the darkness. He looked helplessly towards the cottage door. 'But . . . what about Willow? What about Bethe?'

'Oh, they must not come! There is likely to be great danger on the Tops.'

Will ran to the doorway and put his head inside. 'Gwydion needs my help,' he said. 'I have to go with him.'

Willow dandled their daughter. 'Go? Go where?'

'Up onto the Tops.'

Her pretty eyes quizzed him, then she sighed. 'Oh, Will . . .'

'Don't worry. I won't be long. I promise.' He held her for a moment, then kissed her hurriedly, unhooked his cloak and left.

'What do you think it is?' he asked as he caught up with the wizard.

Gwydion tasted the air. He made hissing noises and held out his arm, but no barn owl came to his call. 'Do you see how the night creatures hereabouts have all gone to ground? No bird can fly in this glare.'

They climbed up the stony path that no one but Gwydion could ever find. It led up through the woods of Nethershaw, yet it wound past trees and the phantasms of trees and passed through impenetrable thickets of brambles that parted to let Gwydion through but then closed behind Will. He scrambled smartly up a mossy bank after the wizard and felt the earth crumbling away under his toes. But then the trees gave out and a dark land opened before them, stark under the purple glow.

They walked onward across tussocky grass, over pools of shadow and a maze of spirals that Will sensed patterning the earth. Soon five great standing stones loomed out of the night, huddled closely one upon another like a group of conspirators. They were, Will knew, vastly ancient, all that remained of the tomb of Orba, Queen of the Summer Moon, who had lived in the Age of the First Men.

She it was who had ruled the land here long ago, and

close by was the dragon-ravaged tomb of her husband, Finglas. Now no more than a bump in the flow-tattooed earth. The wizard swung his staff before him, his eyes penetrating the dark like lamps. Will's heart was hammering as the wizard paused and shaded his eyes against the sky's sickly violet sheen. 'It's not coming from the Giant's Ring after all,' he said. 'It's coming from somewhere in the west!'

The wizard drew Will to a sudden halt beside him. 'Behold! Liarix Finglas!'

The awesome flickerings rose up in the sky behind the King's Stone like a monstrous lightning storm. Will saw the great, crooked fang cut out in black against the glare. Beside it stood the twisted elder tree where Gwydion had once been trapped by sorcerer's magic. Four years ago he had crossed blackened grass; now it had regrown and was lush and dew-cool underfoot.

A clear view to the west opened up. There the sky was smudged by cloud, and far away a great plume had risen up through the layers, its top blown sideways by high winds, its underside lit amethyst and white.

'Look,' Will cried. 'It's a lightning storm on the Wolds!'

'Did you ever see such lightning as that?' When Gwydion turned a silent play of light smote the distant Wolds, making crags of his face. 'And the rumble that shook down your pretty flower pots? Was that thunder?'

'It seemed to come from far away.'

Gwydion gave a short, humourless laugh. 'You want to think the danger is far away and so none of your concern. But remember that the earth is one. Magic connects all who walk upon it. Faraway trouble is trouble all the same. Do not try to find comfort in what you see now, for the further away it is the bigger it must be.'

Will felt the wizard's words cut him. They accused him of a way of thinking that ran powerfully against the redes and laws of magic.

'I'm sorry,' he said humbly. 'That was selfish.'

'Liarix Finglas,' Gwydion muttered, moving on. He slid fingers over the stone, savouring the name in the true tongue. 'In the lesser words of latter days, "the King's Stone". And nowadays the herding men who come by here call it "the Shepherd's Delight". How quaint! For to them it is no more than a lump from which lucky charms may be chipped. Oh, how the ages have declined! What a sorry inheritance the mighty days of yore have bequeathed! We are living in the old age of the world, Willand. And things are determined to turn against us!'

He heard the bitterness in the wizard's words. 'Surely you don't believe that.'

The wizard's face was difficult to read as he turned to Will again. 'I believe that at this moment, you and your fellow villagers are very lucky to be alive.'

A chill ran through him. 'Why do you say that?'

The wizard offered only a dismissive gesture, and Will took his arm in a firmer grip. 'Gwydion, I asked you a question!'

The wizard scowled and pulled his arm away. 'And, as you see, I am avoiding answering you.'

'But why? This isn't how it was with us.'

'Why?' Gwydion put back his head and stared at the sky. 'Because I am *afraid.*'

A fresh pang of fear swam through Will's belly and surfaced in his mind. This was worse than anything he could have expected. Yet the fear freshened his thinking, awakened him further to the danger. He felt intensely alert as he looked around. Up on the Tops the sky was large. It stretched all the way from east to west, from north to south. He felt suddenly very vulnerable.

With a sinking heart he looked around for the place where they had unearthed the battlestone and found its grave, a shallow depression now partly filled and overgrown, but the burned-out stone was nowhere to be seen.

'You're not as kindly as I remembered you,' he told Gwydion.

'Memories are seldom accurate. And you too have changed. Do not forget that.'

'Even so, you're less amiable. Sharper tongued.'

'If you find me so, that is because you see more these days. You are no longer the trusting innocent.'

'I was never that.'

The wizard gazed up and down an avenue of earthlight that stretched, spear-straight across the land. To Will's eye it was greenish, elfin and fey. But it was a light that he knew well, though very bright for lign-light, brighter than he had ever seen it. It passed close by the circle of standing stones.

'That shimmering path is called Eburos,' Gwydion told him. 'It is the lign of the yew tree. Look upon it Willand, and remember what you see, for according to the Black Book this is the greatest of the nine ligns that make up the lorc. Its brightness surprises you, I see. But perhaps it should not, for tonight is Lughnasad, and very close after the new moon. All crossquarter days are magical but now is the start of Iucer, the time when the edges of this world blur with those of the Realm Below – Lughnasad upon a new moon is a time when even lowland swine rooting in the forest floor may see the lign glowing strongly in the earth. *"Trea lathan iucer sean vailan . . ."* Three days of magic in the earth, as the old saying goes. Even I can see it tonight.'

Will nodded. 'The lorc is once more growing in power.'

Gwydion met his eye. 'I feared you would say that.'

Frustration erupted sourly inside Will. 'But how can that be? I destroyed the Doomstone at Verlamion. The heart of the lorc was broken!'

'But *was* the Doomstone destroyed?'

'Do you doubt that I told you the truth?'

There was silence.

'The battle stopped, didn't it?' Will said.

The wizard inclined his head a fraction. 'The battle did not continue.'

'I only know what I saw, Gwydion. The Doomstone was cracked clean across. It must have been destroyed, for it fell silent and all the Sightless Ones in the chapter house lost their minds.'

To that the wizard made no reply other than to give a doubtful grunt. Then he raised his staff towards the livid glow. They walked the lign together across the crest of the Tops. Earth power tingled in Will's fingers and toes as he walked. They soon came to what looked from a distance like a ring of silent, unmoving figures. He looked at the perfect circle of eighty or so stones, the ring that was forty paces across. The shadows cast by each stone groped out across the uneven land. He felt as if he was intruding and said so.

'You know,' Gwydion said in a distant voice, 'the druids used to come here unfailingly at the spring equinox – and then again in the autumn of each year. Ah, what processions we had when the world was young! They brought their white horses, all marked red upon the forehead like so many unhorned unicorns. Here they made their signs two days before the new moon and sat down to drink milk and mead and witness the waxing of the power of the lorc. They were great days, Willand. Great days . . .'

They entered the Ring respectfully, going in by the proper entrance, bowing to the four directions before approaching the centre and sitting down. The stones of the Ring were small, no taller than children, hunched, misshapen, brooding. The greatest of them stood to the north. When Will had come here four years ago he had made no obeisance, asked no formal permission, but when he had touched the chief stone there had been a welcome all the same. He had been privileged to feel the rich and undiminished power that lay dormant here. Before Maskull's sorcery had ambushed him he had felt an enormous store of power, something as vast as a mountain buried deep in the earth, and its summit was the Ring. That sense was still here, a muted but deeply comfortable emanation, a power that spilled endlessly from the navel of the world. Will understood very well why the stone-wise druids had come here twice a year without fail.

He waited for Gwydion to decide what to do, and meanwhile he watched the distant glow in the west until it guttered low and they were bathed in darkness. Breaths of wind ruffled the lush grass. Overhead high veils of cloud were sweeping in. They were not thick enough to hide the stars, but they made them twinkle violently, and that seemed to Will a sign of ill omen.

He pulled his cloak tighter about him and was about to speak when he felt a presence lurking nearby. As he turned, a wild-haired figure broke from cover. Then a blood-freezing scream split the silence. The figure dashed towards them, and came to within a pace of Gwydion's back. An arm jerked upward, and Will saw a blade flash against the sky.

'Gwydion!' he cried.

But the wizard did not move.

Will was aware only of soft words being uttered as he dived low at the figure and carried it to the ground, pinning it. Will's strength slowly forced the blade from the fist that had wielded it. He was hit, then hit again, in the face, but the blows lacked power and he held his grip long enough to apply an immobilizing spell, which put the attacker's limbs in a struggle against one another.

'Take care not to hurt her, Will. She cannot help herself.'

Will shook the pain from his head and staggered to his feet. The furiously writhing body repulsed him. Strangled gasps came from the assailant as he picked up the blade.

'Who is she?' He wiped his mouth where one of the woman's blows had drawn a little blood. 'It's lucky you heard her coming. I had no idea.'

'I did not hear her so much as feel the approach of her magic.'

'That's a trick I wish you'd teach me.'

Gwydion grunted. 'It was never easy to kill an Ogdoad wizard. And quite hard to take one by surprise.'

Will shook his head again and brushed back his braids. Then he turned the blade over in his fingers. It was broad and double-edged and had a heavy, black handle. 'This knife is an evil weapon,' he said, passing the blade to Gwydion.

The wizard would not take it. 'It is not evil.'

'No?'

'Nor is it a weapon. Or even a knife. Did I teach you to think that way?'

'Well it looks like a dagger to me,' Will muttered. 'And it would've made a mess of you.'

'Look again. It is made of obsidian, the same black glass which the Sightless Ones use in the windows of their chapter houses. It is a sacred object, one used in ritual and not to be lightly profaned with blood.'

'Well, the blood it was intended to spill was yours.'

'It has more in common with this.' Gwydion drew the blade of star-iron from the sheath that always hung on a cord about his neck. He held it up. 'An "iscian", called by some "athame", though strictly speaking athamen may be used only by women. It is not a dagger but a compass used to scribe the circle that becomes the border between two worlds. It is the season of Iucer, and tonight this Sister has travelled here by magic. I do not know why she has chosen to meddle far above her knowledge, but look what it has done to her.'

Will turned to where the woman still kicked and struggled as arm fought arm and leg fought leg.

'Release her, now. But be mindful of the powers that flow here.'

Will rebuckled his belt over his shirt and straightened his pouch. He felt his heart hammering as he danced out the counter-spell. At length the woman's body collapsed into the grass, as if her bones had been turned to blood. Though slender, she was of middle age, with long hair, silvered in streaks now, though once it had been dark. Twenty years ago she would have been a handsome woman.

'Speak to me now!' Gwydion commanded, and made a sign above her head.

The Sister shrieked and writhed, but then her voice became one of malice.

'Slaughter great,
'Slaughter small!
'All slaughter now,
'And no slaughter at all!'

'Peace!' Gwydion said, and made a second sign over her. Instantly she fell quiet, and seemed to sleep comfortably.

'Who is she?' Will asked.

'She comes from one of the hamlets near . . . that.' Gwydion gestured towards the last glimmerings of lilac fire in the west. 'She invoked a spell of great magic to bring herself here. She should not have done that, nor would she unless her life had been threatened. By rights she should not even have known how to use such magic, but curiosity is a powerful urge in some of the Sisters of the Wise. This time it has saved her life, though we shall soon see if it was worth the saving.'

'What do you mean?'

'The spell was ill-wrought. It has touched her mind with madness. That is, I hope, the only reason she tried to fall upon me as she did.'

Will examined the blade critically. 'I didn't know it was the practice of Sisters to go abroad with their athamen upon them.'

'Ordinarily, they do not. Take care to keep that one from her, Will. I recognize it for what it is, and I believe that unless you keep it away from her she will try to kill herself with it when she wakes.'